Planet of the Orange-red Sun

Series Volume 9

Power Struggles

Planet of the Orange-red Sun Series

Volume 9
Power Struggles

by Vic Broquard

http://www.Broquard-ebooks.com
Broquard eBooks
103 Timberlane
East Peoria, IL 61611
author@Broquard-eBooks.com

Artwork by Crooked Willow Studios.

For Morgan and L. Ron Hubbard

Table of Contents

Part III Genetic Warfare

Part I Evolution of Power

Chapter 1 The Beginnings

Doctor Whitney Jones had established quite an impressive list of accomplishments in her long medical career. While she had her share of curing epidemic outbreaks, much as many other top Imperium medical doctors had, her achievements lay more in the handling of individual cures. She'd healed Senator Claxos of one of the most deadly forms of cancer. A former president of the Imperium had contracted a fatal superbug, which had eaten through most of his large intestines, when she'd been called in to assist. A week later, he was totally cured, another medical miracle. After that, Doctor Whitney picked up the nickname of Miracle Worker, a title she flatly refused to accept.

Doctor Whitney had shoulder length, wavy brown hair and pale blue eyes, the color of the latter she had long ago personally created to mask her ugly yellow eyes with their brown speckles. She was one hundred twenty-five years old, but now she looked twenty-one again, thanks to her use of one of the newer models of the Imperium rejuvenation machines. She looked quite trim and fit. More importantly, she was still unmarried, which had caught the attention of Legate Emeryk Donat and hence President Snarry Knoschy.

As her deep space transport slowly began its descent onto Proxima Prime, she again reread the presidential summons. *Well, President Snarry must have contracted some virulent disease. That must be why I am being called away from Dalliard-3 and the viral epidemic there. Why else would he be keeping me from my work? People are dying there, and it's up to me to find a cure. I wonder how sick he is? I haven't heard anything on the Imperium News Channel about his being ill. It's no wonder people get sick living on this metallic world.*

She'd already freshened up a bit thanks to the captain's thirty minute warning. She wore a white silk blouse with a black skirt. For this meeting, she chose also to wear nylons, which she seldom did, and comfortable, black, soft-soled medical shoes, figuring she'd be on her feet quite some time dealing with this latest emergency. She had her old-fashioned medical bag beside her. While most doctors considered their bags to be utterly archaic, she depended upon it for her special diagnostic tools. True, she always used the Imperium medical machines first. More often in the last thirty years now, the cases, which were sent her way, were beyond the machines' abilities to either diagnose or cure. Hence, she needed ancient methods and tools to give her more clues. That such also tended to masked what she really did to cure her special patients was even more to the point. She used her mental abilities for that, and her black bag helped hide that from others, who were always trying to discover her unique secrets of healing.

As Doctor Whitney stepped off the transport onto the tarmac of concrete and steel, the local time was nearly midnight. Great lights illuminated the spaceport, almost as if it were still daytime. Four Security Guards spotted her and rushed towards her. "Doctor Whitney Jones?" one inquired. She replied and found herself being whisked away in the presidential shuttle. Respectfully, she accepted the ride and didn't converse with the men. After all, they wouldn't know what illness the president had contracted. Probably, they wouldn't even know he was ill. Why bother, she thought.

A half hour later, she finally entered the Presidential Office on the hundredth floor. She was taken a bit by surprise. President Snarry sat behind his huge desk and another man, who she didn't recognize, stood just to his right some five feet. He didn't look very ill, she thought. "Doctor Whitney Jones reporting as summoned. How bad is your illness, Mr. President?" she asked, taking a seat across from him and sitting her black bag on the floor beside her.

"Oh. I am perfectly well, Doctor Whitney. I've summoned you here for another reason," President Snarry began.

That he wasn't ill annoyed her. Testily she spoke up, "Mr. President, do you realize how many people have died because you've pulled me away from the viral epidemic on Dalliard-3?"

"Sorry, it couldn't be helped. This matter takes precedence. Now then, your bio here is quite impressive, doctor. You began your career some seventy-five years ago? Is that correct?"

"Yes, of course," she replied, growing more annoyed with him. *Why has he called me here anyway?*

He ignored her attitude and continued. "It says here you do not know your planet of origin? How do you explain that?"

No goddamn way I'm telling him that! Instead, she replied, "Do you remember being born, Mr. President? I certainly do not. I've not found a patient yet who can. As my bio says, I was raised in Felicity Orphanage on Ragnar-4, where I eventually got my medical training." That much was mostly true — the part about her medical training. Back then, she'd carefully removed all traces of her past fifty years, inserting a fake record of her attendance at the orphanage. That had been easy enough to do. She'd cured the Head Mistress of a nasty "social disease." In return, the woman had made the record insertion for her, asking no questions.

Doctor Whitney had vague memories of the planet of her birth so very long ago now. The once pungent memories of her kidnaping and many years as a slave telepath to a wealthy businessman on Ragnar-4 had now been mostly forgotten. She'd managed to escape from his clutches when he died. For many years back then, she'd searched Imperium public records for the planet of her birth, but was never able to find it mentioned anywhere. Hence, she'd long ago concluded the name she remembered was erroneous, and that she'd never be able to return to her home world. She'd given up her search and forgotten all about that nearly a century ago, preferring to live in the present.

"President Snarry twisted his face. "Well, no, I don't. Doesn't matter. It says here that in all these years that you have never once married. Care to explain that detail? You don't like men?"

Doctor Whitney flushed slightly. *What the hell is going on here? Why is he cross-examining me? Bastard. Just another bureaucratic pig!* "Never found a man or woman to

4

love. I am married to my career. I heal people, as your bio should show you quite clearly. I assume you *can* read it," she answered testily, very much annoyed with this entire conversation, to say nothing of being pulled away from working another miracle cure that would save millions of lives. "If you aren't ill, I should get back to Dalliard-3. Thousands are sick there and actually need my attention now," she retorted, having had enough of these silly games of his.

The other man finally spoke up. "Excuse us, Doctor Whitney. I am Legate Emeryk Donat. We've summoned you here in relative secrecy on a vitally important matter that involves Imperium Security, one in which you will play a key role."

"Well, then, get to the point, Legate Donat," she replied, turning her attention to the tall Legate and slightly softening her abrasive attitude.

"Recently, we've reopened our spaceport on Ashford-5, and its absolutely vital fuel refinery on its moon. We've installed a new governor, who has gained the trust and respect of the primitives there. What you may not know about this strange world is there have been an alarmingly large number of local telepaths produced on that planet. Until now, the assumption has always been one is either born with the gift of being a Class V telepath or not. Recent developments have certainly caused us to completely rethink this assumption."

"Why? Telepaths are exceedingly rare throughout the Imperium. In fact, I've never come across one in my whole career, and I've been to quite a lot of worlds," she lied effectively. "Surely, they are born with it." She was a telepath and then some. She had very unique healing gifts that only she knew about. Never in her entire life had she told anyone about her special abilities, which, by now, had earned her the fame and recognition that she had.

"That is the Imperium established assumption. However, Doctor Whitney, what would you say, if I told you that eight of the new crew, who have re-opened the spaceport, have suddenly developed telepathy? Yes, a ninth worker died under mysterious circumstances, and Doctor Becktold Hardt has yet to be able to say definitively what killed him. Five were lowly Rigel-3 workers. We've brought them back to Proxima Prime and have now put them to work as official Imperium Telepaths, the first ever for us."

"Interesting. Rigel-3 workers?" she asked, growing more interested.

"Yes, plus the new governor we sent, Katrina Lutgard, has suddenly become a Class V telepath, as have two of her ministers, Carla Childa, computer technician, and Elfe Heilwig, her mate and archaeologist. As incredible as this sounds, it is true. However, Ashford-5 has become a part of the Ataro Empire, and Emperor Kino Sango flatly refuses to allow us to order all three back here. He insists their positions on Ashford-5 will be for their lifetimes."

"Interesting, but what has this to do with me?" she asked.

"I'm getting to it. You see, telepaths from Ashford-5 all have one unique trait that gives them away. Yellow eyes. It seems when a person there develops their Class V telepathy, their eyes turn yellow. All eight's eyes have become yellow, a bright yellow, though there are some brownish spots in them," Legate Emeryk explained. "We know you are not a telepath nor are you apparently from this world."

"Yellow eyes?" she asked, flushing slightly. "Well, of course I don't. My eyes are blue, unless you have some severe color-blindness," she countered effectively, causing both men to flush slightly. She sensed both men personally had wanted to see the color of her eyes, not trusting official documents, which could be, and often were, forged.

"Yes. Precisely. The reason for your summons is that we suspect, sometime after they arrived on Ashford-5, something happened to these nine individuals, which somehow caused all nine to become Class V telepaths. Something caused them to develop this amazing ability. Doctor Becktold has been unable to discover even a single clue about how this happened."

Doctor Whitney replied, "He is a remarkable doctor. His specialty is curing viral infections hither to fore unknown to the Imperium." She'd recently read his paper on his latest miracle cure.

"Precisely, which is why he is already on Dalliard-3

6

picking up where you left off." She blinked, startled by this sudden news. "We are ordering you to go to Ashford-5 and become Governor Katrina's base doctor. You are to investigate fully just how these nine mysteriously developed telepathy. It will help you immensely, if you can also seduce Governor Katrina. She is a lesbian. Perhaps, you could even get her to marry you. Get her into your intimate confidence. Why? Because we suspect she is withholding vital information about all this from us."

"I've never heard of the planet," she answered truthfully. "Well, if these nine did not have telepathy and somehow developed it, there must be some environmental impact that caused it to occur. As a medical doctor, that intrigues me. For that reason, I'm willing to go there and see what can be discovered. Are you *serious* about me seducing the governor? Marrying her? Really?" she asked, somewhat annoyed with this. Long suppressed memories of many forceful rapes during her many years as a slave telepath came back into her mind. It had been her unique healing gifts, which had allowed her to force her body to expel the many fertilized eggs that her employer was trying to make. He'd wanted to have a telepathically gifted child by her. Whitney refused to allow that. Seducing and marrying a woman would be safe, she thought.

"Yes, I know we're asking a lot of you," President Snarry finally decided to speak up. "You see, Governor Katrina is an avowed lesbian. Doctor Becktold had no chance whatsoever of gaining her confidence, you see. In your case, you are young, attractive, and highly professional. We believe you might stand a chance with Governor Katrina. We've done a more detailed investigation on her social activities while she was at the Academy. You are her type, physically that is. She is attracted to bright, intelligent, attractive, take-charge women and prefers brunettes. We think you may have a reasonable chance of success at getting close to her and discovering what it is that she doesn't want us to know about just how these nine came to have developed into Class V telepaths."

He went on, "As you can well imagine, Doctor Whitney, this is an extremely critical mission we are sending you on. If the Imperium could somehow 'make' new telepaths, so much strife could be avoided. If we had them during the previous war, many thousands of lives could have been saved, as you can well imagine."

"Top spies. Yes, I get it," she retorted. *Nastiest use of telepathy. Bad as the corrupt businessmen!*

"You'll be well paid, Doctor Whitney, whether you are able to discover the cause or not. That's only fair, since we're asking a lot of you. I must admit you might not be able to uncover the cause. After all, if the eminent Doctor Becktold was unable to do it, you might not either. Your salary will be double while you are on Ashford-5. Will that be satisfactory?"

"Yes. One detail, gentlemen. Assuming I am able to seduce and marry Governor Katrina, I reserve the right to remain there with her as befitting her marriage partner. It will look *gross* on my bio to have married someone in such a *high* position only to turn around and divorce her in a month or two. I've my own reputation to think of."

"Certainly. We're all taking a big gamble on this move, Doctor Whitney. If and when you are finished there and want to be extricated from that world, send a message to Legate Emeryk Donat, asking if anyone has discovered a cure for the new virulent virus strain that is decimating Rylan-4. Those will be the key words that will let us know you've finished your work there ,one way or the other. We'll get you off-world pronto, using that as a reason, which will appease all parties. A most reasonable excuse for everyone," President Snarry explained.

Clever boys. They've thought this one through. "Excellent. When do I leave?" she asked. *I don't need the money. Lord, I've amassed my own fortune.* She added, "I ought to make some special purchases before I go — medical supplies I might need."

"Of course. We have a deep space transport standing by to take you there just as soon as you are ready. Your possession back on Dalliard-3 will be forwarded to you on Ashford-5. Can you acquire the things here on Proxima Prima?" President Snarry asked.

"Yes, of course. Give me two days, maybe less." They

discussed a few more details, and she walked out of the office, pleased to have the exclusive use of the Presidential Shuttle for her time on this world. She headed off to take a room at a hotel first, before investigating where she could acquire her supplies. By the next late morning, she had made her purchases: the latest models of medical and rejuvenation machines, along with a hundred stem cell recharges. Doctor Whitney suspected she would have an awful lot of experiments to perform to unravel this one. Then, she visited a tea garden to think this through.

After going over all she'd been told, she decided perhaps she didn't want to find the actual answer. *If I do, then they can turn anyone they desire into a Class V telepath. The Imperium would never be safe again, if they did that! I best be extra careful on this one!* Her own personal sense of ethics was very strong. Thus, before she left Proxima Prime, she already knew she would never reveal the actual cause, assuming that she discovered it. Still, she really did want to know the cause. Such might help her understand her own self.

On the third of May 1292, Doctor Whitney Jones arrived on Ashford-5. She was amazed at the speed of travel, flat out! The fuel consumption was horrific, and they had to refuel on one of the planets in the Ataro System about halfway there. Four days from the hub of the galaxy to its outer rim — an impressive distance and travel time. This alone told her just how vital the president considered her assignment actually to be.

Halfway across the galaxy at this same time, three men met at the Sportsmen's Club on Proxima Prime. Only the ultra-rich had memberships in this exclusive and very private club. Not even President Snarry could gain entrance here. Catering to the galaxy's hundred wealthiest, the club provided a secure and very private place for these men and women to meet, un-bothered by trivialities of the modern world. Founded a millennia ago, membership was by invitation-only, though one's net worth had to be counted in the trillions of credits just to be considered. Retention of one's membership hinged upon not only retaining said net worth, but also increasing it over five year periods.

Calling themselves the Consortium, these three men believed they controlled the vast Imperium — of course, from behind the scenes with their secret organization. The Consortium consisted of Baag Haug of Celtrous-4, owner of Baal Industries, Yinko Urzak of Kun-3, Owner of Urzak Fabrications, and Bindaz Rumani of Zon-2, owner of Mal Dynamics. Baal Industries made computer components. That is, if any object in the Imperium had a computer chip in it, it was manufactured by Baal. Of course, nearly everything had some form of chip in it. Urzak Fabrications produced nearly everything that had steel in its construction, including all spaceships. Mal Dynamics produced engines, whether for use in spaceships, air shuttles, or earth moving equipment. If it had a motor in it, Mal Dynamics probably made the motor. Between them, these three men and their expansive companies built or controlled an enormous amount of the economy of the entire Imperium.

Baal spoke up, "Well, the war we pushed has turned us a very nice profit indeed. Earnings are up fivefold during the last ten years."

Yinko countered, "True, but that's come crashing down now, thanks to Emperor Kino's intervention, damn him anyway. Our lackey Snarry ought to have done something to stop him from ending the highly profitable war."

Baal defended their choice, "Hey, we put Snarry into office just because he was a weak lackey. You can't fault him. Kino pressured him. No way could we have predicted that Ataro would intercede. Uncharacteristic of them."

Bindaz took a sip of his wine and added, "We can just as easily replace Snarry, and we probably should, for that matter. Can we do anything about Kino?"

Yinko answered, "Hardly, he's now been elevated to Imperium Hero status for ending the war. Shame he had to discover the Gamelon-3 mess we secretly financed and supported. Still, the polls are about fifty-fifty on them. Some sympathize with those men and their valiant attempts to save their race from extinction, while just as many are horrified at what they did to their women. Anyway, right at the moment,

Kino's untouchable, but that can change just as easily." All three men chuckled.

Baal pointed out, "We should hold off on replacing Snarry just now. We need to work out our next move and then get the right president elected. Therefore, gentlemen, we need another angle to perk up our profits. This extensive rebuilding from the war's destructions won't last much longer."

Bindaz spoke up, "Mal Dynamics has worked out that we have about three more years before this massive reconstruction push will have run its course. By then, profits are going to drop in a major way. We can't have that, can we?" Again, all three men chuckled. "Seriously, fellows, are we going to go back to the usual ways? Find a new planet, strip it bare of all its mineral resources, and then blow it up to salvage even more, once its magma core has cooled. That's worked historically very well indeed."

Baal rubbed his chin, "No, I think we ought to let that one be a last resort. We've done too much of that. Right now, the Senate is overly sensitive to population movements, what with having to resettle so darn many millions because of the war effort. Our best resource-rich planet, Macheovelli-3, has six billion, if I recall right. While they are loaded with resources, getting the Senate to deal with relocating that many people right now isn't going to happen."

"I suppose you are right, Baal," Yinko replied. "What about creating an artificial fuel shortage — an Imperium-wide shortage? Blame it on the war's consumption of so much fuel. That'll inflame the 'greenies,' who will bombard the airwaves with their talk of going green — solar power and all the other alternatives. That will surely confuse the whole issue a good deal."

Baal answered, "Good idea. It can be well justified in anyone's mind. But how will we create it? That's the one arena we do not control directly."

"Urzak Fabrications has developed massive underground storage facilities. We three could begin covertly purchasing far more fuel than we need, storing it in these new secret facilities. Give it a few years, and I guarantee you the shortage will be most acute. We have our butts covered too.

Everyone is demanding the war damage be repaired yesterday. Our industries can say we are just obeying popular demands," Yinko explained.

Baal grunted, "How long have you been planning this, you old skunk?"

Yinko grinned. "I knew the war would not last forever, so I've been at work. Good plan, eh?"

Baal smiled, "Devious, yes. Clever, yes. But then what?"

Yinko replied, "Once we've sucked up as much fuel as we can, then we announce we've uncovered a new supply of fuel and start doling it out, but at these new higher prices, claiming we need to recoup our development costs. That should be enough to ensure several more good, profitable years."

Bindaz grumbled, "For you, yes. That assumes Bekon Energy doesn't have their own reserves to tap into and defeat our plans."

Yinko countered, "I think they've been stretched thin supporting the massive war effort. I'm willing to take a gamble on this one, fellows. But we'll need to replace Snarry. He is too much of a wimp to take the necessary actions, as the fuel crisis develops."

"Okay, if we accept your plan, then we need a man who is not afraid to take action when the time comes," Baal suggested. "You know, that new Legate Emeryk would not be a bad choice. He's had to make some very tough decisions as Sector ID Minister. He's scheming for power too. If we act properly, we can get him under our control as well as getting him elected president."

Bindaz added his support, "I agree. This Donat fellow has certainly been doing some scheming of his own. I've heard he was involved in some very nefarious dealings with telepaths, but that project failed completely. Now, he seems to have succeeded in getting five Rigel-3 men installed as Imperial Telepaths. Those could be dangerous to us. They might need to have a small accident along the way." Again, they chuckled.

Baal then pointed out, "You know, this plan also will hamstring Emperor Kino a good deal. His Ataro Empire, while semi-autonomous, is still heavily dependent upon fuel. This may well give us some leverage with him as well. Fuel in return for Senate support." The other two nodded agreeing with his analysis. "However, the fatal flaw is that Snarry has seven more years left in his current term. It's going to be tricky removing him and getting our man installed as a temporary replacement. In the event of the loss of the sitting president, the Senate must pick a temporary president from among the current six Legates. We're going to need to carefully maneuver this one towards our desired outcome." Now their discussion focused on ways and means to bring this about.

In his fiftieth floor office suite in the Presidential Office building, Legate Emeryk sat behind his own desk, his feet plopped upon it. *What to do about Snarry? The man's a fool. Still, that makes him quite malleable to my will. He really needs to be replaced, but it's another seven years until his term is up. Can I take another seven years of his buffoonery? At least, there are no impending crises he can muck up. Of course, if he were to meet with an unfortunate accident, the real problem would then be his replacement. The Senate must vote one of us Legates to fill out the remainder of his term. That gives me a one in six chance, not good at all, considering I'm the newest Legate. Could I live with one of the other Legates running the presidency? That's the question I ought to be asking. I need to research these other Legates.*

Each Legate was also an Imperium Minister. Legate Emeryk Donat oversaw the entire Sector ID Ministers. The second replacement was Legate Marhildt Chyldt of Bangor-3 and the Minister of Finance. Emeryk discounted his chances of becoming the temporary president as well, for he'd been appointed a week after Emeryk had. No, the Senate would likely choose one of the other four men. Legate Helyeon H. Hoon, often called H-cubed, was from Broon-5 and was the Minister of State and Planning. All three of these men were officially representing the large collection of galactic hub worlds. Two more Legates represented the far fewer middle spiral arm planets. Legate Jaleck Bestold of Carac-4 was the Minister of Energy, while Legate Zestial Haarms of Etwine-3 was the Minister of Transportation. Legate Dalag Mulack of Hron-3 represented the far fewer rim planets and was the Minister of Resources.

As Emeryk looked over these five men's bios, he knew the ministers of Intelligence, Finance, and State-Planning were the three most powerful positions, controlling the flow of information, money, and interplanetary relations. Of these three, he and Legate Marhildt were out of the running, leaving the remaining Hub Legate H-cubed as the most likely man to be voted to fill the office of the president, should President Snarry have an accident. Certainly, the Senate would not accept a Rim Legate. However, what with the near hero worship of Emperor Kino, who had ended the war, Legate Zestial Haarms stood a reasonable chance, since his world, Etwine-3 was part of the emperor's Ataro Empire. Worse, Zestial would be a very hard man to manipulate, versed as he was in the Ataro Empire's weird methods of rule. Thus, Emeryk's attention focused on Legate H-cubed.

A rotund, jovial man, H-cubed was quite a popular figure around Proxima Prima. Yet, he was quite shrewd and observant. Little escaped his notice. Plus, his opinions on interplanetary relations and on the direction of expansion carried extremely significant weight in the Senate, as well with popular opinion. Of all the Legates, H-cubed somehow managed to get on the evening news at least once a week. The press often sought his opinion. *He'll be a hard one to manipulate, unless I can dig up some extremely nasty dirt from his past. Best get started then.* Legate Emeryk began a very detailed, but totally secret investigation of Legate Helyeon H. Hoon.

Senator Zarita Valen was barely sixteen years old, but she looked more like twenty-one. She'd wisely had her lips repaired, but had retained her Ataro-style toe shoes. She remembered the two choices that she had as Neva and from what Isabella told her. Senators either wore these or they wore the four inch tall platforms with their ten inch spiked heel. Wearing the latter was a recipe for broken ankles and legs, which Zarita aimed to avoid, especially knowing she would have to wear the twelve foot giant hoop skirts so popular on Proxima Prime. As she sat back in the deep space transport, she began plotting her revenge on President Snarry. *Well, first, I have to find out if he was really involved in the assassination of my Neva body. If he wasn't, should I try to ensnare him this time? He is the president, but is he the most powerful man in the Imperium? Really, I ought to find that out. That means I really need to learn to be a computer expert, as Jan is.* She sighed; she had so much to ponder.

Her ship landed on Winno-3 of the Ataro System. Four others joined her, and then the transport resumed its long journey to the hub of the galaxy and Proxima Prime. "Hello Senator Zarita Valen. I am Senator Tabia Zuarta, my husband, Huburt. We're from Etwine-3. I'm your immediate senior senator. It's my job to look after you and our other new senator here. This is Senator Celenia Agahve of Winno-3. She's just replacing Senator Lacy, who wanted to retire from public service. This is her Personal Assistant, Lelane Bughati. She doesn't speak, of course."

"Very pleased to meet you both, and you, Lelane," Senator Zarita replied politely, sizing up the three. Tabia was in her mid-thirties, blonde, curly hair, and blue eyes. Of course, all three women wore pipe corsets and toe shoes similar to hers. She could not help noticing Senator Tabia was dressed properly for a female senator. Her fingernails were twelve inches long, painted a shade of red, matching her lips. She wore the traditional giant hoop skirt, also matching her nails.

Senator Celenia wore a pencil style, form fitting gown, much as her own. But what struck her the most was her empty shoulders. She was just like Queen Amy and Drina, wholly armless. She had very long, wavy black hair, rich and full, much like her own very long hair. While Zarita's hair nearly reached her ankles, Celenia's fell only to her hips. Lelane had wavy brown hair almost the same length and had eyes to match. Both women were twenty-one and rather pretty, especially Celenia. Zarita felt an immediate affection for Celenia.

"Very pleased to meet you, Senator Zarita. You and I

have much to learn, but Senator Tabia is just the best. She'll have us up to speed in no time," Celenia volunteered. "You have such strange colored eyes. I've never seen yellow eyes before."

"I wish they were blue though," Zarita explained, not wishing to get into a discussion of her *mentales* gifts just now.

"Oh that is easily changed, Senator Zarita," Senator Tabia spoke up. "Come. We have time; let's get your eyes the color of your choice. We should also get your nails longer. They need to be twice this long, if you want to be proper and follow Senate rules."

"Of course, that would be really great. I've gotten them this long so I could sort of get used to them," Zarita admitted.

Tabia laughed. "That length is quite manageable, but with claws like these, they are more of a total nuisance than anything else. Don't worry; once we get to Proxima Prime, I'll help you both get properly attired. Senator Zarita, you'll be rooming with Senator Celenia and her assistant. She obviously needs a good deal of help, and, besides, I can then explain things once, not twice. Come on; let's get your eyes and nails fixed up. By the way, stunning jewelry," she added, pleasing Zarita. Later, the two returned to the cabin. Zarita sported twelve inch claws and deep blue eyes, thanks to the dye of her choice having been injected into them.

"Oh Zarita, I do so love your choice. Your eyes look stunning, as do your nails," Celenia replied. Lelane nodded her approval vigorously, a big smile on her face.

Zarita laughed, "Now, I have to get used to these claws all over again. They are awfully long, aren't they?"

"At least you have them. I don't," Celenia replied. Zarita sensed a very deep sadness emanating from her new roommate.

"Well, we have some time to kill. Let's begin your senatorial education now, shall we?" Senator Tabia suggested. We'll be staying in the Senatorial Condo Building. Since you both are the newest senators, you'll be rooming on the lowest condo floor, three. The bottom two floors are filled with every imaginable store. That's where we'll get you properly attired, once we arrive and get unpacked. My husband and I live on the sixtieth floor. Each of you will be assigned an intern from the local Academy. These young teens will arrive early each morning, prepare your breakfast, and get you into your gowns. Heavens, we can't get ourselves dressed in these complex outfits. Then, they leave for school. They'll return around four to prepare your dinner and to help you change into more comfortable clothes."

Your personal shuttle is parked on your balcony. You will use it to go to the Senate Building or anywhere else for that matter. Since Senator Celenia is so handicapped, she'll be unable to operate a shuttle. Hence, for now, Zarita, you and she will be joined at the hips, so to speak. Don't worry, though, Lelane is a computer whiz and a most capable Personal Assistant. She'll be able to handle Celenia's personal needs, so you won't have to deal with such things. Heavens, in gowns like these and with your claws, you couldn't, if you wanted to."

"Of course, Zarita will not have an actual vote in the Senate, though you certainly will, Celenia. Either Zarita or Lelane can help you with the voting controls. Both of you are allowed to speak up on any topic you desire. Zarita, you have all of the rights of any senator, except for a vote. Closed Worlds aren't allowed to have an actual vote, you see. The opening session will be next Monday, so we have some time to get you all settled in and ready. You'll be sitting with all of the other senators from the Ataro Empire. We have a whole block of seats. Normally, Closed World senators are seated in one special section. In your case, Zarita, since Ashford-5 is now part of our system, you're allowed to sit with the rest of us. As I understand Emperor Kino, this is for your own protection as well."

"Speaking of protection, he is having a whole new security system installed in your new condo. He wants to make very sure no harm comes to you, Zarita. I can't imagine how terrible it was for your previous Senator Isabella and her two wives. We've all heard of their kidnaping and mutilations. Just awful. Anyway, Emperor Kino is taking no chances with either of you. You see, there are many in the Senate who are dead set against the Ataro Empire."

"Why is that?" Zarita asked.

"Our empire is the oldest in the Imperium. Two millennia ago, we helped establish the Imperium. Even today, we have the single largest voting block. Which reminds me, Celenia, on some key votes, you'll be required to vote as the rest of us do. We must always present a solid, united front on certain key votes, you see. Some senators are still trying to dismantle our united front. That they've not succeeded in nearly two millennia doesn't seem to discourage them one iota. Ah well. Men."

Her husband cleared his throat rather noisily. "Except you, dear," Tabia hastily added.

He smiled back. "I am along for the ride. I hate these times on Proxima Prima, but it does give me time to devote to my stamp collection," he replied, quite bored already.

"Huburt is an artist, really. He has his own studio in our condo. Honestly, his paintings do sell quite well, but he's rather modest about them. He does portrait work," Tabia added. "Now where was I?" She chatted on until suppertime.

Zarita watched how Tabia managed with her long nails, frustrated at how clumsy she now felt. They were just too darn long. After that, she and her husband retired to their cabin, leaving the three sipping their after dinner tea. An awkward silence followed the departure of the older couple.

Zarita sensed a deep sadness coming from Celenia. She felt a little awkward and tried to make polite conversation, "So it looks like we are going to be roommates."

Evidently, that was the wrong thing to say, Zarita thought, biting her lip. Celenia's eyes watered. "I'm so sorry to be such an awful burden on you, Zarita. It's all my fault. I'm a failure. A complete and utter failure, and now I have to live with my humiliation laid bare for everyone to see." She broke down and began crying, though Lelane slid a comforting arm around her, pulling her close to her.

"I'm sorry to have upset you, Celenia. I don't understand. You are a senator. How is that a failure?" Zarita asked, hoping she'd not make this awkward exchange any worse than she had. She'd rather not probe the young woman's mind to find out.

"I am a failure, really I am Zarita. I failed becoming a

queen, and now everyone can see that. Just look at me, no arms — one look and everyone knows I'm a failure. I'm a walking advertisement of my dismal failure to become a queen of the Ataro Empire," she wailed, continuing to sob onto Lelane's shoulder.

"Oh. Now I see, I think," Zarita replied gently. "You underwent all of their body modifications and then were trained to become one of their queens."

"Yes, I wanted to become a queen really badly. Mom told me over and over that I ought never have such thoughts, but I did it anyway, and I failed, failed miserably, Zarita. I just couldn't pass their tests. I tried, honestly, I tried so very hard," she continued to wail. Lelane nodded her head rather exaggeratedly, trying to let her know she concurred with her charge.

"Bastards, cutting off a person's arms is completely pointless. That's got nothing to do with whether a person turns out bad or not. Really. So I take it Lelane now is being exiled with you too?"

"Yes, I've failed myself and brought poor Lelane down with me. She was so hoping to become the Personal Assistant of a queen of Ataro. Now, she's lost her dreams too, and it's all my fault," Celenia wailed.

"Well, they must have thought enough of you to make you their senator," Zarita attempted to find something positive to say. Her heart went out to Celenia, who had no *mentales* gifts on which to fall back upon.

"They did it to get rid of me. I'm an embarrassment to them all," she sobbed even harder.

Damn, everything I say just makes this worse! Oh hell. Zarita began gently probing Celenia's mind. "Say, didn't you have some young man who wanted to marry you?" she asked, having seen an image of him with her before she'd lost her arms.

"Why yes. Damut. He proposed, but I turned him down. I told him I wanted to become a queen. I'd forgotten all about that," Celenia answered, getting her crying under control at last. "You know I did forget about that. He kept telling me I was not smart enough to be a queen, that my IQ was too low.

He ran me down several times, but I kept on insisting I was going to do it. Hey, he was the one in the test that caused me to fail completely. You don't suppose he was getting even with me for having turned him down, do you?" Celenia had now brightened up considerably. Zarita could see a blur of images aligning in Celenia's mind.

"That bastard! That's why I failed! He set me up to fail the tests. His example had no solution, because he'd made up the whole thing. I'll be damned! Everyone missed it too," she replied rather angrily. "Queen Altha shouldn't have missed that! She's the queen after all," she added antagonistically. "Well, I did fail to discover he was lying and making up the whole conflict I was supposed to solve. I didn't solve it, did I? Oh, I failed the test. I really did fail it. Damn," she added. "I feel so much better now, Zarita, but I am such a basket case."

"Men! Why is it always god damn men who do this to us?" Zarita replied rather antagonistically. Her own memories of brutalities suffered at the hands of men came back to her once again. "Celenia, we women must stick together! The hell with men; that's what I say."

Celenia and Lelane broke into a smile, and Lelane continued wiping her mistress' face with a lace handkerchief. "We must stick together. I agree, Zarita. You are very wise. I'd not figured that one out, until you mentioned him. Amazing. I was duped by him, the bastard. Men! They are disgusting and nothing but trouble."

"I couldn't agree more. Most men, that is. I've known only a few good ones, but they are already taken," Zarita replied, thinking of the Gang of Ten. "Are you able to use your feet in place of your hands?"

"Huh?" Celenia looked up confused.

"Oh back home, three very good friends of mine don't have any arms either. Drina was born without them."

"Oh how awful!"

"And Lena had them cut off by wicked, evil men. Yet, both Drina and Lena now use their feet as their hands, feeding themselves and all manner of things. That's why I asked if you could."

"I've no idea how and certainly not in these outfits. So

they really are able to do some things for themselves?" Celenia asked growing very curious. Even Lelane paid close attention to Zarita's reply. She began describing all of the things that Drina and Lena were able to do.

"I know. Whenever we get a long break, you can come to my world and meet Drina and Lena yourself. I am sure they can really help you, Celenia," Zarita promised.

"Oh thank you," Celenia exclaimed. She leaned over, and gave Zarita a loving, passionate kiss.

Zarita's sexuality long suppressed ignited. She returned Celenia's kiss, and then pulled Lelane into the embrace, touching lightly the two women's minds. Suddenly, she knew Lelane had long wanted to display her love for Celenia, but had been suppressing it. Zarita gently activated her crystals, bringing the three of them into a close rapport and, effectively a Mind Link, so Lelane could finally express how she felt towards Celenia. Emotional and very private thoughts were exchanged between the three women.

The three quickly realized barriers had been shattered. Celenia had held back her expressions of affection for Lelane, because she didn't want to embarrass or upset her assistant, who could not speak her feelings. After her failure to pass, Celenia believed she was holding Lelane back from achieving greatness with another woman, who would become queen. Lelane couldn't easily tell Celenia how she really felt about her. Further, she didn't want to embarrass Celenia or force her into accepting her love just because she desperately needed the assistance of her Personal Assistant. As the three held each other tightly, alternating kissing each other, more and more unspoken barriers slipped away, as each felt the most intimate contact they'd ever experienced with another.

How is this possible? Celenia finally thought.

I am a powerful telepath. I hope you don't mind, Celenia, Lelane. I love you both. We women have to stick together. You both are so beautiful.

I love you too, Zarita! Now, I can finally tell Celenia how much I've longed for her. My heart belongs to you, both of you, Lelane sent. *How can I ever thank you, Zarita?*

Men have power in part because we women are so

ignorant of the complex computer systems. I need to learn all about them, if we women are ever going to be able to level the playing field.

I can teach you, but I can't talk. Zarita sensed another emotional loss swelling in Lelane. She quickly shunted it aside.

When we get together by ourselves, I will unite us together, just like we are now. Anytime either one of you wants to speak to me or each other as we are now, just wink at me. That'll be our very secret signal. It only takes a second for me to join us together like this. It is the most intimate sharing possible, except when we are in bed together, she hinted.

Can we do that too? I'm so helpless to give either of you much pleasure, Celenia sent. Yet again, Zarita sensed another wave of grief creeping its way back into Celenia's mind. Once more she acted, ushering them into a private cabin, which had only a smallish bed. Then, the three experienced the total joy of an intimacy, a joining that came as close to being the other person as possible. This was what Zarita had in mind: each just knew what the other desired without thinking or asking or wondering — perhaps the highest affinity possible.

Physically exhausted, but mentally acute, the three finally lay back beside each other, knowing they were now joined together as one inseparable unit, each bringing their own unique knowledge and skills into the merging. Zarita felt nothing could ever stop her on her march towards ultimate power. Her notions of revenge had somehow drifted into the past. She knew she had so very much to learn, but she now saw the path before her, shining out to sea like a port's beacon. She felt inexorably drawn towards the "light," and she welcomed it with all her heart.

Chapter 2 Settling In

In the Imperial Castle on the southeastern edge of Plateau Grado in the Goza Mountains, nearly eighteen year old Queen Amy Valen Gervasi Bellweather sighed yet again. It was May and spring once more, barely a year after the massive changes around her. Her mother, Queen Isabella, and her father, Hernando, had turned over rulership of the world to her. Both had used the rejuvenation machine of the aliens to become fourteen with their bodies restored to normal. They quietly moved to the far southern coastal city of Arabella, adopted new identities, and settled into new lives, free from the overwhelming burdens they had both carried for so many years. Queen Amy could not fault either for that. Of everyone she knew, these two more than deserved a respite.

Yet, others were growing older too. Inez and Peter Franks had retired from running the worldwide Elegant Fashions Inc. Their older son had joined a tower. Lilly had married Sam Wall. She now ran the chain of stores along with her younger sister, Nita. Sam, a weaver, had expanded the cloth making side of the business, and his company now provided much of the satin, cotton, wool, and leather materials for the giant enterprise, relieving Lilly and Nita from having to also handle this aspect of the business.

Many of the older members of the Underground had also retired. Most had moved into modest homes in Brom. Even the core dozen were approaching their fifties and were gradually beginning to hand over some of their daily operations to their children. Another ten years and they too would be retiring. A new generation was gradually taking over the secret responsibilities of keeping Tierra safe, flourishing, and prospering.

Worse from Amy's point of view, her old Gang of Nine was also taking on more and more responsibilities. Gone were their days of playful antics that had united them for many years. Pranks had diminished considerably, and a more serious mien had settled among them. Ken and Crystal

Blackwater, the leaders of the Underground, were in their mid-forties, grooming two of the Gang of Nine to replace them, Ben and Drina Blackwater, though Drina, a katalyein telepath, was more inclined to deal with *mentales* problems. Daily, she was assisting Rafaela with this. Consequently, Ben's twin sister Lana, who had married Fred Hays, was standing in for Drina, while Drina stood in for Fred, joining Fred's sister Lena in learning to deliver expertly Benjamina's therapy. More and more, it looked as if Ben and Lana would take over for Ken and Crystal in a few more years.

Two others from the Gang of Nine, Henry Franks and Adrianna del Baldo had married. She was Nadja and Diego's daughter. Henry had become the Venerado of the Imperial Tower, while Adrianna had become Capa Adrianna, in charge of the fourth Imperial *mentales* Circle. Indeed, nearly every *Círculo de la Torres* now had four *Círculo de mentes*, though a few had five, as did Brom Tower. The huge expansion in the number of *mentales* gifted allowed the many towers to rebuild their dwindling numbers during the last decade.

With Nita Franks tied up with her co-duties of running Elegant Fashions Inc, the Gang of Nine was down to just the four of them. Queen Amy depended on her wife, Jan Bellweather, though Jan did spend a lot of her time helping the Underground with their electronic equipment. Only her twin brother, Bernardo, and his wife, Lena Squire Gervasi, remained here at the Imperial Castle, her constant companions and assistants. Amy's younger sister, Gabriella, had become quite competent in running all of their new communications equipment, thanks to Jan's lengthy training. She was nearly seventeen and very much interested in boys, though she promised she would always be Amy's Communications Expert.

Lena's body was also going on eighteen now, but she had a long career as a Sector ID Minister and was actually over a hundred-twenty years old at this time. Both she and Amy had lost their arms, but under vastly different circumstances. Amy's had been voluntary so she could be an official Queen of the Ataro Empire. Lena had been the victim of a sadistic plot on Gamelon-3. Lena, like Drina, chose not to follow the dress and ornamentation fashions of the nobles of Tierra. That is, neither wore the pipe corsets, extreme heels, or the monster sized lip plates.

Queen Amy, on the other hand, had no choice but to emulate the many kings, queens, and other nobles of Tierra. While the pipe corset and toe shoes were mandatory for any queen of the Ataro Empire, she also wore the twelve inch in diameter lip plates, further limiting her mobility. Her permanently modified feet allowed her to stand and walk only on her toes, as her exaggerated arch did not permit more than her toes to lie flat on the floor. The tall spiked heel very nearly touched the backside of her toes, giving her the wasp appearance of extremely tiny feet. Thus, her soles had about a fifth of a person's normal area touching the ground, making walking quite challenging indeed, even more so without arms to help keep her balance. Yet, this was the Ataro Empire's way of limiting those who wielded the greatest of powers.

Here on Tierra, her mother, Queen Isabella, had opted for a different way to attempt to limit the immense powers of those who ruled. Checks and balances. The senators, kings, and queens were elected by popular votes and had limited terms of office, with overall maximum term limits as well. She had hoped this would be a better way than to enforce the physical limitations than the Ataro Empire used.

While so far, this checks and balances idea was working well for the senators, it had so far failed with the enforcers of the law, the kings and queens. Many had temporarily modified the agreements so they could rule until they chose to step down. A few had rebelled totally and divided their kingdoms up so they could totally abandon Queen Isabella's reforms, opting to continue their ancient tradition of monarchies. With some like Queen Edda of Turda and Queen Sofia of the Arad, this was what was truly desired by their people. Both queens had been instrumental in rebuilding their kingdoms after the devastating slaughter and pillaging by the barbarian invader, Damiano. King Emilio Bolivar of Brom was a very benevolent monarch, beloved by the people of his kingdom. His people had greatly desired him to stay on indefinitely as their king.

Just now, this was not the huge problem facing Queen

Amy. Rather, it was the giant germanium crystals that had impacted all over Tierra, remnants of the moon, which had been blown up during the great interstellar war. Only the intervention of the god Alleric, who had reformed the disintegrated moon, kept Tierra from being destroyed as well. However, these giant crystals amplified the psi powers of any *mentales* gifted more than a thousandfold.

Indeed, in the hands of a rebel, one of these crystals had been used to very nearly destroy Valen Castle. What the two queens and the Underground feared most was happening again. Via these giant crystals of power, anyone could now wreak incredible destruction on anyone and any place at any time. In their previous lifetimes, Both Amy and Jan had been witness to the Age of Chaos, when similar crystals had very nearly destroyed all of Tierra. Now, it was about to happen all over again, at least Queen Amy so believed. This was the monumental problem facing her reign, and what she strove to solve, futilely thus far.

In the ancient past, there had been a relatively few number of these giant crystals. Now, even the Imperial Circle had several hundred of them, as did most other towers. Queen Amy knew many of the towers had learned from the rebel attack on Valen Castle, and were in the process of developing other weapons of mass destruction, just as the towers had done in the distant past. Yet, there was little she could do thus far, save encourage all of the many venerados and veneradas to use the crystals for the benefit of their kingdoms.

Here at the Imperial Castle, Venerado Henry was doing just that. With the expansion of the number of kingdoms, and thus personnel, who came to the biannual High Council of Lords meetings, along with the addition of three more Circles here at the Imperial Tower, space was at a premium. Venerado Henry had begun a massive construction project, doubling the size of both the Imperial Castle and Tower. He had all four Circles working on the stone work, carving out massive blocks from the nearby mountains and laying them in place, following the fancy designs of Capa Adrianna, whose elegant touches began to be quite noticeable. Her goal was to make the Imperial Castle the premier castle on Tierra.

Queen Amy signed again. Lena picked up on it this time. "What's the matter, Amy? The usual?"

"Well, yes. No matter how I think about it, I keep ramming my head into Adrianna's new stone works. It's just a matter of time now before someone launches a deadly attack, using these giant crystals. Once it starts, it can only escalate, and we are doomed this time. I can't see any way to prevent it," Amy replied.

Bernardo suggested, "We could always start stealing all the crystals from the towers."

Lena laughed. "Now that's a good one dear. Just how long do you think it would be before we got caught and fried ourselves, buster?" He laughed. "Seriously, dear, I've been around a *long* time. I can say for sure either they will use them for the good of Tierra or the unscrupulous will use them for the destruction of the world. It will be one way or the other."

He laughed again, bringing a slight smile to Amy's face, though it wasn't visible because of her enormous lip plates. "That's rather obvious, isn't it? Oh! Good one, Lena. You got me on that one." All four laughed again.

Jan added, "At least, Amy, you are not swamped in judicial matters. We're having very few disputes to handle. I like that bit. Perhaps we'll have some peace for a while. So is it time to have some children? I still like the idea of having kids soon, so in fourteen years or so you can pass the torch onto one of our daughters."

Lena laughed. "This is so weird. If you two use the Imperium medical machines to get each other pregnant, you'll only be able to have baby girls. Nothing like a total control over whether or not you'll have boys or girls."

Jan giggled, "Well, we could use these new ones to change the baby's sex right after birth and so have a boy." Now all four roared again, alleviating Amy's tensions.

"Thanks, gang. I needed to laugh again. I hate it when things get so serious," Amy declared.

"We know, been there, done that," Lena replied. "Honestly, Amy, in many ways, our problems here are vastly simpler than those in the vast Imperium. There, many decisions affect thousands of billions of people, not hundreds

27

of thousands like here. But I prefer here a billion-fold."

Jan changed the topic. "Say, I heard Governor Katrina is getting a new doctor to replace Doctor Becktold, who was called off-world to solve some epidemic virus somewhere. Want to go watch the ship land and check out this new doctor? At least, it's something to do."

"Sure, let's," Amy replied, thankful to be able to get out a while.

"All right, dibs on driving this time," Jan exclaimed rather excited. Governor Katrina had donated one of their electric cars to Queen Amy so she could easily travel back and forth from her Admin building at the spaceport. By now, the guards recognized the four on sight and let them in without checking with Governor Katrina. Lena's black skin was hard to miss.

"But you drove last time," Bernardo protested.

"Don't I get to drive?" Lena asked. She and Amy roared with laughter. Neither had any arms with which to control the vehicle, but her protest caught both Jan and Bernardo by surprise.

"Damn, you got me twice in the same day!" Bernardo exclaimed. "Now you are in for it, Miss Lena! Just you wait, I'll think of something."

"Don't you dare mess with my nut bread, buster or you'll sleep with the dogs tonight," Lena countered playfully. He feigned an innocent look, and the four giggled again. Jan put her steadying arm around Amy, and the four headed out to the courtyard and the electric car. While they didn't really need it, they could just have Bart or one of their Circles teleport them there, this was more fun. Governor Katrina also knew that, which was why she gave it to Queen Amy.

Amy wore a red satin pencil gown of a special design by Nita, who had eliminated the arms and sleeves so that the bodice fit snug over her shoulders. It aesthetically emphasized her unique form, as well as hugging her impressive curves. Her long wavy brown hair fell nearly to her ankles, her pride and joy. Jan, in contrast, wore her warmer leather trail clothes and boots. Bernardo wore one of the camel hair jackets, though not a suit. Lena opted to wear one of her light cotton day dresses, made by Nita especially for her and Drina. Like Amy's gown, her top also fit snug over her shoulders making her appearance as striking as Amy's. She wore flats as usual, since she, like Drina, used her feet in lieu of her missing hands. Even though she had good telekinetic skills like Amy, she continued to rely on her feet, carrying on Drina's teasing of Amy about her "cheating" by using her telekinesis instead of her feet. Her dress was a bright yellow.

"Jan, slow down! This isn't a race," Amy complained, as Jan sped as fast as the car could go across the perfectly flat plateau of the spaceport.

Lena laughed. "I bet they'll give you a ticket for speeding."

Jan slowed down. "They wouldn't dare, would they?" she asked, uncertain whether Lena was teasing her or not. Lena shrugged her shoulders and laughed. They all roared again. Soon, they pulled up to a parking spot close to the Admin building.

The day was warm and rather windy. "Crap! I can't stand up on my own," Amy complained, as she struggled to get out of the car. "Jan, you are going to have to help me, I'm afraid. I can't keep my balance on these toes of mine."

"On it, love. One sec. Okay, got you," Jan replied, coming to her rescue, as Amy wobbled this way and that, trying valiantly to keep on her toes against the wind. All three women moved their heads so the wind blew their long hair behind them. Jan's wavy brown hair fell to her waist, as did Lena's shiny, straight black hair. Together, the four headed inside, as several guards waved to them. They were a familiar sight around the spaceport these days.

Just as they got to the elevators, Governor Katrina stepped out of the open doors. She too wore a red satin pencil style gown, highlighting her curves as well. In fact, all of the women, who had returned to the spaceport, now sported the Tierra melon-sized breasts, whether they wanted them or not. Governor Katrina also wore the large lip plates, pipe corset, and similar toe shoes, emulating the nobles of Tierra. As she had planned when she first arrived, her adopting the local dress and customs had greatly aided her acceptance by the many rulers. Indeed, she had been accepted and was now setting the fashion styles for the noblewomen, just as Inez had predicted. Her gown left one shoulder bare while covering the other. She also wore the huge, long dangling style earrings, quite similar to Amy's.

"So glad that you came to see my new doctor arrive," Governor Katrina welcomed the four. Two other women stepped out behind her. Carla Childa, her computer expert, and Elfe Heilwig, her archaeologist, grinned and said hello as well. These two were married, just as Amy and Jan were. In fact, the four often spent weekends together. All three now had the *mentales* gifts and proudly wore their germanium crystals around their necks. Carla also wore a pipe corset, as did Elfe, who last year went ahead and got her waist done to match her mate's impressive new figure. Both Carla and Elfe wore identical blue satin gowns of the same style as Katrina's. However, they wore the usual six inch oxford stilettos, since neither wanted to have their feet modified like Katrina's. Besides, that would hinder Elfe in her fieldwork. Today, they were dolled up to welcome their new doctor.

"Best have them hold you. It's windy outside, and we can't keep our balance, Katrina," Amy advised. "Carla, Elfe, you both look stunning as always." Both women smiled and moved to support their boss, one on each side.

Bernardo teased, "Golly, this is a man's paradise, surrounded by six elegant women."

Carla replied, "Lena, best keep your dog on a tight leash today or we'll get our new doctor to turn him into a her, which would be better all around, don't you think?" All seven laughed.

"Why is everyone picking on me today?" Bernardo whined, as if he was a victim.

Lena gave him a bump with her hips, "You behave yourself, oh great mastiff." This caused the seven to roar again, as they headed to the doors to watch for the transport ship.

Elfe spoke up, "She's bringing along my new GPMS! It is the very latest in archaeological technology! I'm so excited."

"What's a GPMS?" asked a curious Jan. New electronics always pricked her keen interest.

"It's a Ground Penetrating and Mapping System. It'll allow me to conduct an extensive survey of just what's below the surface of the planet, creating a 3-d image of whatever is there. This way, I can locate buried ancient sites without having to scour the land foot by foot myself. It's quite revolutionary, you see. Of course, it too has limitations. For example, it would not detect that huge man-made cavern complex, where I nearly died up north in the Goza. Still, this is going to be just perfect for me. I can't wait to start surveying everything. I wonder how many ancient sites I'll be able to find? Who knows how much light I can shed on your prehistory." She chatted on about her new machine.

When she finished, Governor Katrina explained, "Our new doctor has excellent credentials. Doctor Whitney Jones has established quite an impressive list of accomplishments in her long medical career. She has cured a number of epidemic outbreaks and has quite a number of miracle cures as well. According to what I've been able to find out, she is sometimes called a Miracle Worker, having done some amazing cures of terminally ill individuals. She must have used the rejuvenation machine, since her apparent age is twenty-one, according to her bio."

"Is she pretty?" asked Bernardo.

"Doctor Whitney has shoulder length, wavy brown hair, and pale blue eyes in her last posted photo. Attractive, you bet," Carla answered him, "trim and fit. She's just what we need around here, more women. There are so few of us on this base. Lena, best keep a tight leash on him, though, Doctor Whitney isn't married."

"Oh no! Do you think I have to worry?" Lena continued playfully.

Bernardo laughed, "No dear. Besides, if she is all that old and hasn't been married, I'd guess she isn't interested in handsome fellows like me, but only in her work."

"You take all the fun away," Lena countered, and they all laughed again.

"Miracle cures? How interesting," Amy changed the topic to what pricked her interest. Governor Katrina chatted a bit, relaying what little data she had on her new doctor, glancing occasionally at her wristwatch. "Ah, there it comes now," she pointed to the sky. Seven heads looked up to see the sleek, silver deep space transport slowly descending.

Chapter 3 A Strange Arrival

Doctor Whitney, dressed in her grey business jacket and skirt with a white silk blouse, black nylons and low heels, watched out her window as Ashford-5 appeared, first as a small dot. The strange orange-red sun looked somehow familiar to her. Soon, the descent began, and the dimly illuminated world began growing larger. She was long used to brightly lit worlds, but this one seemed intriguing to her. *Is this one more like the world on which I was born,* she wondered. Nearly a century ago, she'd all but given up on ever finding the planet of her birth. She felt the warmth of her small crystal she always wore around her neck, concealed within her small cleavage, her only tie to the unknown place of her birth over a century ago.

As the ship descended, she began having the strangest feeling, almost like a deja vu. She saw the rugged mountains and then the flat Plateau Grado growing rapidly larger before her. *This isn't familiar,* she thought. *I've never seen this place, I don't think. There's the Admin building and the barracks. Why is it every spaceport has identical buildings? Uncreative Imperium! Oh, there's a small group near the entrance. Guess I am not the only woman here.*

Shortly, the ship settled down, and the doors opened. Picking up her black bag she was never without, Doctor Whitney rose and made her way to the door and ramp. As she began to step down, she felt the chilly air — chilly compared to what she was used to feeling — and the rich smells of Ashford-5. The aroma of resinous pines filled the air, along with many other smells hardly ever detected on far too many overpopulated worlds on which she'd resided at one time or another.

As she set foot on the tarmac, distant, long forgotten images flooded her mind, triggered by the aromas around her. Now, even the orange-red sun and the chilly air felt strangely familiar to her as well. Vaguely, she saw Governor Katrina waving at her, but her mind was a mass of confusing memories, memories of her childhood over a century ago. She rather staggered over to the welcoming party, fighting to regain control of her mental state. *What's happening to me? Whitney, control yourself! That's the governor ahead. Don't make a fool of yourself upon arrival. My god! This is so familiar. Could this possibly be my home world?*

She's a telepath! Queen Amy sent to the others. *She's mentally confused about something.* Amy focused and sent some calming waves through Doctor Whitney, while she rather stumbled over to the group.

"Pardon me. I'm a little out of sorts. I don't know why. You must be Governor Katrina, at least I think you sort of resemble your photo I saw. I'm your new doctor. Doctor Whitney Jones," she said, fighting off the confusion, but also sensing the calming waves. *They must be coming from one of them. Oh my god! They are all telepaths too!*

"You're right. I'm Governor Katrina Lutgard, my computer technician, Carla Childa, and her mate, Elfe Heilwig, archaeologist. This is Queen Amy Valen Gervasi Bellweather and her wife Jan. This is Lena Squire Gervasi, ex-Sector ID Minister, and her husband, Amy's twin brother Bernardo. Welcome to Tierra, as we locals call Ashford-5."

"Hello everyone. Sorry I'm so out of sorts. I don't know what came over me back there," Doctor Whitney replied, regaining some of her lost composure. She couldn't help noticing all seven were looking her in her eyes. They were a pretty shade of blue, not the yellow eyes with brown speckles that she saw looking back at her. Again, she flushed as more memories appeared unbidden in her mind. The strong wind blew her shoulder length, brunette hair out in front of her face, temporarily annoying her a little.

"Come on; let's go inside out of this wind. Amy and I can barely stand up in it," Katrina took charge, leading them back inside. All of the women kept their heads turned somewhat against the wind, allowing it to blow their hair out of their faces.

Just inside, Carla swiped Doctor Whitney's ID card and entered clearance codes. "There you go. You card is activated now," she explained.

"Let's go up to my office and chat, shall we?" Governor

Katrina suggested, but they all knew that was really an order.

As they walked along, Doctor Whitney commented, "Well, it's exactly the same layout as my last Admin building. Good old Imperium, always make every building exact copies."

Governor Katrina laughed. "Right. You are supposed to feel right at home no matter what planet that you are on." A bit later, they entered her office, and the seven women hastily adjusted their wind-blown hair as best they could and took seats around the room. Doctor Whitney noticed Governor Katrina sat *with* them and not behind her desk.

Now, she got a good look at her new boss. She had these enormous lip plates, golden in color, which dropped to her chest. Etched on them were two people shaking hands. Queen Amy also had the same giant lip plates, but hers contained an image of a castle with tower. She recognized the pipe corsets that Katrina, Amy, Elfe, and Carla wore, but it was the toe shoes that Katrina and Amy wore that got her attention more, that and the armless state of Amy and Lena. Her eyes roamed from person to person, sizing each one up rapidly. They were all telepaths; she could sense their minds. For a moment, panic threatened to swell up in her mind and body.

Almost as if reading her mind, though she knew she had her thoughts blocked, Queen Amy broke the ice. "Well, this is something. Yes, Doctor Whitney, we're all telepaths here. We all have what we call the *mentales* gifts. Perhaps you've heard of this?" She shook her head no, involuntarily. "Well, we have some amazing other mental powers. Our yellow eyes give us *mentales* gifted away. Just a caution, Doctor Whitney, anytime you meet someone with yellow eyes, you can be certain they have the gifts too."

She went on, "We all can sense you have it too, telepathy at least, but obviously your eyes aren't yellow like ours are."

Doctor Whitney made a snap decision. Call it intuition if you please. "Mine were yellow too, but I added some different pigments to hide them long ago."

"Oh! Then, are you originally from here, from Tierra?" Queen Amy asked, rather surprised to hear this.

Doctor Whitney flushed. "I don't know. Maybe. So

confused. So familiar — the smells out there. The air, the red sun, the mountains. So familiar, so confusing." Again her mind was a whirl of long forgotten memories now surfacing. "Sorry, so mixed up. Never happened before," she tried to apologize.

"That's all right, Doctor Whitney. Take your time. Whatever you say to us will be held in the strictest of confidences," Governor Katrina took charge. Her mind was filled with all manner of possibilities, not the least of which was that she found the woman highly attractive to her.

"I think I might have been born here," Doctor Whitney whispered, still unsure of herself.

"Tell us what you remember," Queen Amy asked gently.

"I was just a young girl. We lived on a sheep ranch. I remember roaming through the green grasslands and seeing far distant peaks. I remember the smells, the pine trees. And a tower. Are there towers around here? Circular ones? I remember being taken there and learning things." She saw they all wore a small crystal around their necks too. She added, "They gave me this, my most precious possession." She pulled out her own crystal covered with a finely made silken pouch. She uncovered it, revealing a germanium crystal.

As she watched, Amy's crystal appeared to slip out of its pod-silk pouch, as if my magic. Amy added, "Telekinesis. We've all got them too. They're germanium crystals that greatly amplify our psi powers. And yes, there are lots of towers here on Tierra. When a person becomes of age and has the *mentales* gifts, they're taken to one of the towers to be trained. We have a saying that an untrained telepath is both a danger to himself and to others. After their training, they're given their own crystal. It is attuned to that one person only."

Tears began streaming down Doctor Whitney's face. "I am home! I never thought I would ever find home, not ever. I remember some tall man putting some rag over my face in the middle of the night. Next thing I knew, I was in a dingy spaceship, then sold into slavery to a businessman, but that was over a century ago at least."

"Incredible. Welcome home, Doctor Whitney!" Queen Amy declared happily, but firmly.

"If it is any relief, I've gotten strict new rules that there is to be no more kidnaping of telepaths from Tierra. We are rigidly enforcing that law!" Governor Katrina added.

"I suppose it is. Have there been many of us — kidnaped?" she asked.

"It was always done in secret, so we have no idea how many were taken or when," Amy replied. "So what happened after that?"

"Oh, I was able to keep ejecting fertilized eggs so I never got pregnant from the bastard. Eventually, he lost interest in me, except for my telepathy. Then one day, he died. In the confusion, I slipped away, changed my identity, studied hard, and became a doctor. I've always been able to heal. I think I was born with that, but I don't really know. I've been traveling around the Imperium being a good doctor. Just a few days ago, President Snarry Knoschy summoned me to the Presidential Office on Proxima Prime. He assigned me here," she finished up.

Jan spoke up. "I don't trust that man one tiny bit! What did he want you to do here, if you don't mind my asking?"

Doctor Whitney looked at Governor Katrina. This was a pivotal question. She'd given her word to President Snarry, but then that was before she discovered this was her home. Now that she found it, she didn't want to lose it. "Governor, since this is my home world, can I get Terra citizenship? Then, I can't be forced to leave against my will."

"Of course, you can, dear. If it'll make you feel better, we'll do it right now. Carla was going to have to issue you a new ID card anyway. Carla?"

"On it boss," Carla replied with a grin. She moved over to her boss' computer and typed away. Shortly, the ID card printer shot out a new one. She handed it to Doctor Whitney. Tears streamed down the young woman's face, as she saw clearly marked a second citizenship: Ashford-5. "There, now no one can force you to leave Tierra. Actually, we three love it here." She sat back down beside Katrina and Elfe.

"Okay, please don't think ill of me. President Snarry wanted me to see if I can figure out how those five Rigel-3 men and you all acquired telepathy, this *mentales* thing. He's really desperate to discover the secret. He wants to be able to make many telepaths for himself. Plus, I am supposed to seduce you, Governor Katrina. He thinks you're withholding vital information from him and that I'm your type. He kept citing Imperium security, but he's just another bureaucratic pig, if you ask me. So was that Legate Donat fellow, who was with him. He said he even tried to order you three back from Ashford-5, but that this Emperor Kino fellow wouldn't allow it. Lifetime appointments or something like that. I wasn't paying all that much attention. I was rather shocked by it all."

Governor Katrina laughed. No one else had a clue what was so funny and stared at her. "Okay, okay. At least President Snarry was right about one thing. I hope you won't take offense with this, Doctor Whitney, but he is right. You are my type, very much so. But I won't take advantage of you, not unless you find me appealing too."

Bernardo could not resist himself, "You see, Lena dearest, you don't have to worry about me. With all of these women, I can't possibly stray from our bed!" One by one, his joke registered, and everyone roared with laughter, releasing a whole lot of tensions.

Still grinning, Doctor Whitney said, "You best be careful, Governor Katrina; you're my type too." The laughter continued even longer. Once it died down, she became serious again. "What am I to do? While I would really like to know how everyone got this precious gift, professionally that is, I promise you I will never, ever reveal it to anyone. This is my home, my people — well, they used to be. They are all dead now, even if I could remember more from that long ago."

Queen Amy spoke up, "If we have your sworn word never to reveal this to the Imperium, then you are more than welcome here. For a while, you can send him silly reports if you desire. Meanwhile, I'll let Emperor Kino know about this, and he'll put you on the same lifetime assignment to Tierra that he has done for these three. As long as you're honest with us, you're very welcome to join us, doctor. We do need a good doctor on Tierra."

"I swear I won't ever tell. Oh thank you, Queen Amy, Governor Katrina," she gushed, very much relieved. "Now, I don't have to hide among everyone like I have had to live for over a century! I was always alone, always hiding. I couldn't ever risk any relationship at all, not once. I feel like an entire spaceship has been lifted off me!"

"You are most welcome, doctor," Governor Katrina replied.

"So, can I ask you all a lot of questions?" she asked politely. "This is all so strange to me. I was told Ashf — Tierra was a primitive world, and yet you're so elegantly dressed! Once in a while, I find a few women who wear nice clothes, like I do, but they are usually quite wealthy. I always dressed well and professionally, not those despicable unisex cat suits."

"Yes, of course. But let me explain a few things for you first. I'm shirking my governor's duties. You see, while I'm your direct boss, Queen Amy here, is my immediate boss. Ashford-5 has become the thirty-seventh planet in the Ataro Empire of the Twelve Sacred Planets of the Wasp. Queen Amy is one of their highly trained and official queens. And her mother, Queen Isabella, worked with Emperor Kino Sango to bring this about to keep the Imperium from sacking this world. He is keeping it a Closed World, but part of their empire. So he is Queen Amy's boss."

"Anything the Imperium wants of me or this world must be Okayed by Queen Amy or Emperor Kino. Between us three, we're keeping the Imperium 'mitts' off this world and its wonderful people."

"Incredible. So that explains why she has lost her arms and wears those shoes. I've visited there once," Doctor Whitney replied. "They have such strange ideas."

Amy laughed. Governor Katrina continued, "That's for sure. Anyway, here on Tierra, the rulers, kings, queens, and the many other nobles are rather fashion conscious. When the famous linguist Nadja first came here, she wore these giant lip plates. As Governor Konrad's wife, she became the instant fashion model. Within a short time, most of these men and women adopted them as well. I'm following in his path. That is, when you're new to a world and people, in order to get into meaningful communications and understandings, you first have to create some affinity and reality between you and these others. When I first came here, I adopted their local dress and customs, and it worked very well indeed. I was accepted almost at once. I looked like them, you see. I must admit, it is rather challenging, but my discomfort is nothing compared to what Queen Amy has to endure all the time."

She continued, "Oh, and these knockers of ours — get used to them. After any woman has lived on Tierra for a few months, she develops monster melons as well. No escaping it. That's one thing you could research — just how this happens. As I understand it, there are numerous medical reports on file from the many women who have spent time on Tierra over these many centuries."

"I will look into it," Doctor Whitney agreed, gulping a little. Her bosom had always been rather on the small side. The women sitting around her had gigantic breasts, from her point of view.

"Anyway, we three have a very close relationship now with Queen Amy and her Gang of Ten. They live at the Imperial Castle, which is on this plateau at the extreme southeastern corner, where Exchange City is located. We often spend the weekends together. You're most welcome to join us. Nadja and Diego, her husband, sometimes join us. They are teaching school here; she founded the first school on Tierra."

"I would like that and a chance to see my world," Doctor Whitney replied, very pleased she was being so readily accepted. "But will I need to get different clothing too?"

Elfe, who had been mostly silent, spoke up. "This is my arena, boss. You see, this is technically a Bronze-Iron Age world. No roads and only a few large cities often in the range of twenty to thirty thousand people, just barely classified as at the beginnings of urbanization. Until Queen Isabella's recent reforms, the world was divided up into kingdoms with a three class system. Obviously, there are a lot of farmers. Agriculture and animal husbandry are big on this world, which lacks nearly all heavy metals. Iron is extremely rare, and most now comes from the yearly lease payments for the spaceport here."

"The agriculture is now providing sufficient amounts of food that they can support the second class, townsfolk, who are the crafts men and women. Then, there is the third class, the nobles, who own vast tracks of land or mines or fledgling businesses. Note the businesses consist of home-shop craftsmen and women; there are no large company buildings we are familiar with as yet, save Elegant Fashions Inc, though that is slowly changing, as they are building larger spaces for food storage. Usually, the rulers come from this noble class."

"As with all such cultures, status means everything to the nobles, who are using fashion and ornamentations to display their status to everyone. With so little gold available and so little true art as we know it, they've taken this somewhat unique route to display elite goods, since there are so few elite goods produced here. While there are gems, these are most often used as money, beyond copper and silver. Hence, the boss' description of fashion conscious. It began with the founding of Elegant Fashions Inc a long time ago. Now, nearly every town of five thousand or more people has a branch office. Further, and this may come as a surprise to you, each branch office has their own Imperium medical machine. Don't panic, doctor, most all of them are programmed only to perform the body modifications needed for their fashions, not for curing, though there are some knowledgeable men and women who do use them for that purpose."

"There are no roads as such, but there are well-worn dirt tracks. Travel is by horseback or wagon, though the nobles also use teleportation via their towers and Circles."

"What? Teleportation?" exclaimed Doctor Whitney.

Queen Amy explained, "Yes, the towers have more powerful crystals than we individuals have. Teleportation requires a full Circle of nine members, joining together to do it."

Jan added, "But some of us love to drive around in your electric cars." Several chuckled.

"Anyway," Elfe continued, "around here, you are most likely to be in contact with the nobles and rulers. They meet usually twice a year at Queen Amy's castle. The High Council of the Lords. Most of the women will look much like Katrina, though some opt to wear heels like Carla and I do. Many of the men also wear the pipe corsets and lip plates too. I don't mind the corset, but I can't go any farther. My work takes me out into the field. Amy and Katrina can barely walk in theirs."

"Understood. But will what I'm wearing not look professional here?" Doctor Whitney asked, suspecting the answer that she'd get.

"On any open world in the Imperium, you look a proper doctor, but not here, I'm afraid," Elfe pointed out. "Boss, can't you get her fixed up too, like you did us?"

"Absolutely. Doctor, once you get settled, we'll pay a visit to Elegant Fashions Inc and get you an appropriate new wardrobe of your choice."

"Thanks Governor Katrina. I can pay you for them," she replied, gratefully.

"Just Katrina, when we are alone. No, I get them free from Lilly and Nita, who run the store. It seems I've become the fashion queen for Tierra noblewomen. I've become a walking advertisement." Everyone chuckled. While Doctor Whitney didn't quite grasp it, she did smile.

"Well, we really ought to let you get to your new quarters and settled in a bit. Let's plan on heading over to Elegant Fashions Inc in say a couple of hours?" Governor Katrina suggested.

"Okay, but I've still got tons of questions. They can wait."

"Boss, I'm going to borrow Carla to help me with my new GPMS — my new Ground Penetrating and Mapping System! I can't wait to start using it, but it is heavily computerized so I need me mate," Elfe explained.

"You go with her Carla. I'll make Doctor Whitney here assist me," Governor Katrina suggested. The two rose and left, their heels clicking on the floor nearly in unison. Queen Amy took this as a signal for her party to depart as well.

Finally alone with her new doctor, Katrina said, "Okay, let's get you to your quarters. The servicemen will have gotten your crates there already."

"Okay. Oh, what do I need to do for you?"

"If you will slip your arm around my waist and give me a little balance support, that would be terrific. I've been monopolizing Carla for far too long now, taking her away from her mate, Elfe. I didn't have too much choice though. Thanks. I hope you don't mind."

"Not at all, Katrina. You are my type you know," she teased her.

"And you, mine," Katrina giggled a little.

"What modifications do you think I need to do so I am accepted by the locals?" Doctor Whitney asked, while they moved slowly through the building, heading for her new suite on the ninth floor of the adjacent building.

"Well, probably it wouldn't hurt if you looked like I do, except for these shoes. Since you have to do a lot of walking, I'd recommend that you not have your feet modified. Amy and I have a hard time. I hope you don't mind being my nurse maid some," Katrina suggested. Doctor Whitney chuckled.

Several hours later, the two entered Elegant Fashions Inc. Lilly and Nita were already prepared for their visit. Katrina had notified them earlier, via telepathy. Thus began a lengthy discussion on just what ought to be done to Doctor Whitney. Lilly suggested, "We should enlarge your breasts for you. If we don't, you are going to be over here every few weeks begging for your tops to be altered. Has Katrina told you that all women on Tierra end up with these monsters?"

Doctor Whitney laughed, "Yes, I've been made only too well aware of this phenomenon. I suppose that would be the most practical. I can't be bothering you for constant enlargements. I do need to be accepted by the locals. I know they will not have any clue about how skilled a doctor I really am."

Lilly grinned, "Yes, that's quite true. Since your eyes aren't yellow, they'll be hard pressed to believe you have the healing *mentales* gifts. Thus, the more you look like they do, the easier time you'll have."

"Well, I figured on having the lip things, the earrings and the pipe corset."

"Wise. We probably ought to lengthen your hair some as well," Nita volunteered.

"Why?"

"Women of Tierra prefer very long hair. Indeed, in the Easterlings, it is taboo for men or women to ever cut their hair."

"Wait. I remember that word, Easterlings. What area

are we in?" Doctor Whitney asked, suddenly recalling another fragment from her childhood. "Bound women?"

"Midlands. On the other side of the mountains is the Westerlings," Nita explained.

"Midlands! Yes, I was born in the Midlands," she exclaimed.

"Fabulous. Yes, the Easterlings women used to be bound, but that ancient tradition has changed a lot recently," Lilly launched into a lengthy explanation of the barbarian invasion and destruction.

"Okay, feet," Lilly finally returned to the topic at hand. "Pros and cons. The biggest pro is that you would blend in with the majority of the noblewomen and many of the noblemen for that matter. The biggest con is walking is obviously more difficult. The worst is it cannot wholly be undone."

"Yes, as a doctor I'm well aware of that. I'd have to wear the fancy heels you both are wearing, if I had it undone. I do so want to be accepted here. I was born here, but lord knows if I was born a noble or not. Boss, unless you object, I think I want toe shoes too. After all, you can't keep on using Carla. I'd feel awful keeping her apart from her mate so much of the time. If I have mine done too, then we can help each other and not bother those two. Besides, I might be a noble by birth, and, if so, I should look the part. If it interferes with my work, I can always go back to heels. One good thing about all this is they don't have makeup to have to deal with on this world." Both women laughed, but Katrina sensed Doctor Whitney had some additional considerations, private ones, but she didn't nose.

I could well be nobility. All of the mentales gifted seem to be at the very top of the social classes here. That makes me one too. I sure as hell have at least what some of them have, maybe more. The kids in Amy's Gang are still kids and should not have such modifications for several years yet. Their bodies are still maturing. But me, my birthright definitely has me in Tierra's upper class of people. If they display their social standing in this manner, I simply must do it too. I can't get rid of the blue pigments I put in my eyes to disguise the yellow. If I don't do this, I'll have constantly to have to keep proving to others I'm one of their gifted. That's far too embarrassing. Since only the upper crust has all of these modifications, if I do too, then I'll certainly get fewer challenges. On the other hand, it's got to be just awful to have all of these. Katrina can just barely manage. I surely don't know how Amy can get by at all. Still, I just don't have any real choice, if I want to have my birthrights on Tierra acknowledged by my peers. I've got to do this and somehow make it work. At least most can be undone if I just cannot handle it. Then again, I've carefully avoided all types of personal relationships my whole life. Thank god I did that. Now, I am really **home**. *My people. If I'm ever to give in to love, I'm certainly going to have to look the part of nobility. I don't want always to have to prove it, not here, not where I belong.* After a pause, Doctor Whitney said, "Okay, let's do this."

With the decisions made, Doctor Whitney picked out a dozen outfits. Lilly insisted she also have a few simpler blouse and skirt combinations for working in her lab. Then, Lilly said, "Oh, Katrina, I nearly forgot. It seems our Senator Zarita Valen has set another new fashion trend among the noblewomen. All winter long now, our stores have been bombarded with requests to have fingernails lengthened to match hers. At the spring High Council, most all the women will have them, if not all. I'm still getting a few more requests in."

"I see. What are we talking about?" Katrina asked. Lilly showed her a catalogue image.

"It could be worse. I'm just thankful the noblewomen haven't seen the length of Senator Zarita's nails that she now has as a female senator! They're a foot long, if you can believe that!" Lilly exclaimed, adding, "*Please* don't let other women know that detail." All four women chuckled.

"Okay, do our nails too. We ought to be seen fitting in with this new trend too," Katrina suggested.

"Okay. After growing them out, I add a strong base to them for added strength before they are painted. Red is the most popular choice," Lilly explained.

While Katrina was fixed up with her new nails fairly quickly, all the modifications to Doctor Whitney took a couple of hours. Lilly and Nita were very efficient in getting her dressed in her new outfit before rousing her. She now wore a form-fitting light blue satin gown, her favorite color.

"Oh, I can't breathe!" Doctor Whitney gushed, as she awakened from the procedures. My ears are being pulled off. My lips are too tight."

Lilly and Nita helped her sit up. "Take shallow breaths. Don't fight it. Relax. Doctor Whitney, if you didn't say all that, I'd be shocked. Everyone wakes up saying these very same things." Whitney tried to smile, but realized she could no longer do so; her lips loops were stretched taught. Her design displayed a woman's head with a stethoscope, her constant companion for over three-quarters of a century. "Next, you'll say you can't keep your balance when we get you up on your feet."

A minute later, Doctor Whitney gushed, "How did you know? I can't. I'm wobbling all over!"

"Easy does it. Time to start practicing your walking. We never let anyone go home until they're able to manage well. Here, Katrina is going to help you too," Lilly explained.

A bit later, Doctor Whitney whispered, "I see what you mean, Katrina; this is so hard."

"Yes, no doubt about that, Whitney, but you look ravishing," Katrina replied. "Here, have a look." She paused before a full-length mirror.

"I hardly recognize myself! I do look good don't I? I've never had my hair this long before. It's below my waist. My boobs must weigh a ton. My goodness, how do we ever eat with these plates?"

"Don't worry. I'll show you. It's easy," Katrina promised. After an hour of practice, which also included lessons on how to operate the lip plates and a caution to wear the pipe corset all the time except while bathing, Lilly released them. With their arms around each other, the two women began their slow, careful walk down to where they'd left their electric car. "Oh, these nails are going to cause me problems. More getting used to," she complained, as she had some difficulty pressing the buttons to get it going.

Once back at their Admin building, Katrina took the

doctor to her own suite and ordered their supper brought up to them. "We'll eat in private this time so you can get the hang of it," Katrina explained. "Darn nails. More getting used to for me too."

"Well, that wasn't so bad, except we can't drink anymore. Spooning tea sure is strange, but then, I now know what the noblewomen must deal with, in case I need to treat some of them," Doctor Whitney said.

"Yes, that is another benefit. You have good reality on them and that will certainly help you, but I do hope you don't have to tend to many patients," Katrina hinted. "They've brought all your new things here and left them in your new suite. Just got a message from Carla saying so. She's very efficient. Come, I'll lend you a hand getting them stored away."

Later that evening, having organized all Doctor Whitney's new clothing, Katrina said, "Now let me show you how to prepare for bed." With their lip plates out, both women looked at each other and their strange dangling lip loops. She whispered, "Let me show you something else." She began kissing Whitney, who reciprocated at once. Soon, their passions swept them both into her new bed. Their romance began that night. Each found the other a perfect match. That they both slipped into an intimate rapport with each other solidified their bond with each other.

"Kiss me again! These loops are so sexy!" Whitney whispered, though gasping a little for breath. Morning found them still in bed with each other. Their love began to blossom very rapidly.

Chapter 4 Arrangements

Doctor Whitney struggled to get herself dressed the next morning and needed a bit of assistance from Katrina, who also needed hers, she discovered. "I've never had such long hair before or such long nails. They keep interfering. How do you ever get used to this corset, these lip plates, these shoes?" she moaned.

"Time, gorgeous. Give yourself time. Let me help you with your hair, and then you can do mine," Katrina said lovingly. Memories of the previous evening were still fresh and still greatly excited her. "You are the best, you know. I've never found anyone like you before."

Whitney giggled like a silly schoolgirl. It felt good to just relax, and let it all go. Centuries of tensions evaporated; she felt like a young teen with her mother brushing out her hair for her. It didn't matter she was a century older than Katrina was. She felt loved and wanted for the first time in over a hundred twenty years. She basked in the tender care Katrina was showing her. After both women were finally prepared to face the day, with their arms around each other, they headed down to breakfast.

At first, Doctor Whitney was terribly self-conscious about her new dramatically altered image. She feared everyone would be staring at her, watching her every awkward movement. While a few took notice of her, most quickly smirked and went about their business. They'd seen Governor Katrina often enough by now that the sight of another looking as strange as their boss didn't shock them. Quickly, Doctor Whitney relaxed again, and struggled through her breakfast. I say struggle, because that was what it seemed to her. Having to deal with trying to eat while wearing the enormous lip plates and manipulating the silverware with such long nails gave her fits. Still, she kept a close eye on how Katrina managed and emulated her.

"Sure don't eat as much," she commented, as they finished their coffee, using spoons to drink it.

"I don't want you to lose your scrumptious figure, darling," Katrina teased her. "I can't tell if you are grinning or not."

"I am. Never worried about that before. I do hope my new staff will accept me like this," Doctor Whitney said growing worried once more. Soon, she had to face all these new nurses and assistants.

"Don't worry. I'll take you there and introduce you, doctor." Governor Katrina did just that. A short while later, again with their arms around each other's waists, the two entered the white, sterile medical lab, where three nurses and three lab technicians were already at work.

"May I have your attention," Governor Katrina spoke up. "It is my great pleasure to introduce our new doctor to you. This is the very highly rated, Doctor Whitney Jones. Yes, the famous Miracle Healer of Imperium fame. We are incredibly fortunate to have a doctor of this caliber here with us! However, I do hope we don't really need her incredible magic services." Several nurses chuckled.

"As you can see, Doctor Whitney has kindly volunteered to assist me, so Carla can return to her normal duties instead of assisting me, as much as she had. Let's make her stay here a pleasant one."

After Katrina let go of Whitney and made her slow, careful way out of the medical lab, one of the nurses exclaimed, "Are you really *the* Doctor Jones, who is famous for all of the incredible miracle cures we studied in med school?"

Doctor Whitney smiled, before she realized it would no longer be visible. "Yes, that's me, but honestly, I do hope we don't need me to pull off any miracle cures here." Several laughed, but with her *mentales* gifts, she sensed her six staff were very much impressed with her credentials and fame. "I've got two immediate assignments to tackle. I'm charged with continuing Doctor Becktold's research into just what happened to the six Rigel-3 men, including the one who died from that mysterious illness. So I'll need to see all of his reports first, and then I'll chat with each of you to get your viewpoints on what happened. Second, I'm investigating just how come we women who stay on this world end up with knockers like these," she said, pointing to her massive bosom. Many smiles flashed her way, for all the nurses were eager to know that answer. Their breasts had also become as large as hers. Doctor Whitney now knew Lilly was right in insisting that hers be enlarged to match the other women of Tierra instead of allowing them to grow this large on their own over many weeks. She was accepted at once by her nurses. Doctor Whitney sensed all six were greatly relieved that, at last, someone was going to look into this aspect. Apparently, none of the previous male doctors had even bothered to investigate this phenomenon at all. Men, she thought derogatorily.

Soon Doctor Whitney became absorbed in her work. Doctor Becktold left copious notes and reports; yet, he failed to establish any actual cause, remaining mystified. He even chemically analyzed the *bacal* tea that had apparently had a beneficial effect upon the men. She asked, "Nurse, do we have any blood samples from any of these men long before they became ill? We've got plenty from when they were sick. I need to compare them," she asked.

"Yes, everyone who comes here is required to provide a blood sample. We should draw yours soon," one replied. A bit later, she had a tiny amount of one Rigel man's blood from both before and after on a slide. She adjusted the microscope, which projected its image on her large flat screen. Doctor Whitney sat back and looked from one to the other. "Ah ha. There is some unknown particulate matter in the infected blood. Very tiny. Becktold missed these." She had a lab technician run an extraction process to see if she could get a sample of the particulate matter for further analysis. Meanwhile, she began to think. She reasoned the drastic modification of a human body from non-gifted into a *mentales* gifted had to involve the alteration of DNA genes. The body's blueprint had somehow been altered. But which gene? She made an educated guess and had the lab technicians do a gene deconstruction on the specific genes that controlled the endocrine system. That would keep them busy for days.

Next, she turned her attention to the problem the women faced, the explosive and enormous growth of their breasts. According to all the medical records, the drastic change always was completed after about six months on Ashford-5. It mattered not what planet the women came from originally. The only variable was the length of stay on Ashford-5. Next, she looked at the final results from all the women whose records were available to her. On the average, she noted, the difference between over the bust and under bust measurements were about ten inches give or take only an inch. That yielded their spectacular sized breasts.

Once more, she reasoned something foreign had entered their bodies to cause this remarkable change. Doctor Whitney again resorted to before and after blood samples. Her work proceeded at half her usual pace; she continually found her long nails a serious impediment to her work, but she didn't complain. Finally, she had the before and after samples up on her flat screen. This time, she cranked the magnification up to near maximum, before she spotted the foreign particulate matter in the after blood sample. Once more, she ordered an extraction process, which pleased the six women, who believed soon they'd know the answer and maybe a cure. None appreciated having such enormous breasts, particularly those whose breasts had been relatively small prior to their arrival on Ashford-5. Doctor Whitney also ordered another gene study done on one woman's after growth DNA sample. By now, it was the end of the long day, and they all headed off for supper.

She joined Governor Katrina for supper, very pleased she now had someone with whom she could chat telepathically. For over a century, this had been denied her, and now Doctor Whitney wanted to make up for it. All this being so new to Katrina, she didn't mind Whitney chatting with her this way either, especially since she'd fallen for this lovely brunette doctor. Both were quite slow dining, and found themselves mostly alone when they got to their coffee.

"Boss, I've made some progress. I found foreign particulate matter in the Rigel-3 men's blood, as well as in our women's blood. Different particulate matter, I'm sure of that. It's being extracted now. I should know more tomorrow about the causes, I hope," she reported.

"Excellent. One day on the job and you've made more

progress than Doctor Becktold," Katrina praised her.

"Well, I've had the benefit of all of his reports and studies. That's saved me from having to do all of those exhaustive tests again. A major time saver. Enough of work. I'm so thankful you don't mind me chatting telepathically with you during the day. I've not been able to do that since I was a very young teen," Doctor Whitney explained.

"I can't imagine having this precious gift and not being able to really use it or share such intimacy with another for over a century. It would have driven me half-mad, I know it," Governor Katrina admitted. "Tomorrow night, Friday, Queen Amy has invited us to spend the night and weekend with her and her friends at the Imperial Castle. We can watch the new construction that's going on there too. She wants to introduce you to her Circles as well. They also have a card game that they play. Something like our Three High. They call it poker. Also, she said the rest of their Gang of Nine will be there too and want to meet you."

"Okay. Where you go, I go now. I'm your assistant. But what do we wear?"

"Our nice gowns, I suppose. Come on; let's go to my room for tonight. I've some things we can use to spice up our love making," Katrina teased.

The next day, the results began coming back on the four tests the doctor had ordered. The larger particulate matter in the Rigel-3 men's blood turned out to be raw fuel, germanium dust from which the fuel was manufactured. Doctor Whitney wasn't too surprised by this finding; after all, there had been a refinery on the plateau several centuries ago, at least the records so stated. Just what the connection was with the men acquiring the *mentales* gifts she didn't yet know. The tinier particulate matter in the women's blood turned out to be extremely tiny microbes, so small they could not be filtered out by the base's air filtration system. They were also organic in nature. Doctor Whitney was frustrated; there was a total lack of an extensive biological survey of Ashford-5. Hence, she was unable to ascertain from what plant the microbes came or were related to.

Late in the afternoon, the DNA genetic results came

back from her lab technicians. "Wow. Look at this, gang," she held up the transparent marker overlays. "See, the Rigel men's actual DNA was somehow altered; this gene here. See, it's got a slightly new pattern. It affects the endocrine system. From the autopsy, it most likely resulted in an enormous growth of their pituitary glands. What else it may have altered, I can't tell."

"They were genetically altered?" one nurse asked a little shocked.

"Precisely. That's why the medical machines were unable to diagnose anything or cure them. We still don't know how their genetic makeup was actually altered. Those particulates within their blood stream were raw fuel. However, the Imperium has been refining it for a very long time without any physical side effects on the workers. So we are not much closer to a cure yet," she explained.

"Boss, look at these results on us," another lab technician joined them. She brought the second genetic study results. "We've been genetically altered too! No wonder we have monsters."

Everyone gathered around and looked at these new findings. "Yes, I agree; our DNA has also been altered. I did find microscopic microbes or organisms in our blood streams. They are too fine to be filtered out. There's no biological survey of plants on Ashford-5, so I can't determine their origin. Nor can I say that these things are causing our genetic modifications to occur, but at least, we have some clues now."

"Well done, doc! We know more in two days with you here than all the years before," one nurse praised her. She smiled appreciatively, but quickly realized it wasn't visible.

"Thanks. We've more work to do to get to the root cause," she replied.

"Can the genetic modifications be undone?" another nurse asked, rubbing her giant melons, somewhat annoyed at her new endowment.

"Yes, now that we know precisely what was altered, I can program the medical machine appropriately. However, the bad news is that whatever is causing this is just going to re-modify your genes once they are back to normal. Before we try to undo this, we best get a solid grip on the actual cause and get that handled first."

The nurse sighed, "You are right. They'd be right back here again in six months. Damn it anyway."

Doctor Whitney added comfortingly, "But when you are planning to leave Ashford-5, I can undo it before you go. That would be safe." All six smiled, as they closed up shop for the day.

When she joined Katrina for supper, Carla and Elfe were already there as well. "Look at us, Doctor Whitney. We had our nails done too," Carla announced, flashing her six inch talons painted cherry red. "Bit awkward, but really cool in bed." Elfe flushed crimson, and didn't say anything. Carla added, "We're coming with you tonight."

Around six that night, Carla pulled into the Imperial Castle courtyard, parking their electric car as close to the huge double doors as possible, thinking of her boss and the doctor. Oil lanterns illuminated the cobblestones near this entrance. Behind them, the gate man had already closed the entrance gates. "Wait until you see this place in the daytime," Katrina explained to Whitney. "It's nearly doubled in size this past year. Come on; let's go inside. He's their gate man who'll lead us." All four women struggled a little with their long nails and the door latches, which were not designed with them in mind.

"Whoa, tricky," Whitney exclaimed, as she tried to get her balance on her toes as she got out. Katrina fared little better, she noted, and got to her boss' side. Both put an arm around the other's waist. The gate man said little, but motioned them to follow him. He held a lantern, but this close to the doors it was no longer needed.

Inside, Whitney picked up the odors of local cooking and of some kind of wood polish and soap. Once more, she had flashbacks to her early childhood. All three seemed somehow very familiar to her. Once inside, a servant woman took over. "This way please. Queen Amy awaits you in the study."

Whitney's eyes took in everything, as she and Katrina followed slowly behind the older woman, whose hair was quite long and brown, reaching her upper calves. She wore one of the white cotton day dresses she'd seen in Lilly's catalogue. The stone walls were grey. The floor was also stone, but a thin emerald carpet covered the center three feet of it. Periodically, brass lanterns provided the illumination, attached to the walls just above their heads. Whitney detected the soap odor rather strongly here and guessed the hall had recently been scrubbed.

After passing many side doors, at last, the woman paused beside one door on their left and knocked. "Queen Amy, your guests have arrived." She motioned them to enter, holding the door for the four, shutting it once they were inside. The study was about fifty feet square. Maps, scrolls, and a few books on wooden shelves lined one wall. Great tapestries covered much of the other two walls, and a fireplace with a crackling fire framed the wall opposite the door. Several smaller tables and chairs were scattered around the room, but one very long table occupied the center of the room, with three sofas positioned in a sort of U-shape around the fire. Resinous pine scent filled the room.

With her long brown hair draped across her front and lap, Queen Amy sat at one end of the table. Many others were scattered around the room. As she rose, so did all of the others. Some were dressed in silk gowns much as they were, but some wore leather clothing too. "Welcome Katrina, Carla, Elfe, and, most of all, our new Doctor Whitney Jones. My whole gang is here tonight, as are some others." She looked around to see who was where. Obviously going according to age, she said, "This is Nadja, her husband Diego. This is Ken. His wife Crystal. Rafaela and her husband Andres. Of course, you've already met my wife, Jan, my brother Bernardo and Lena, his wife. Nita. My sister, Gabriella. Here's the rest of my gang. This is Venerado Henry Franks; he runs the entire Imperial Tower here. His wife, Capa Adrianna, who runs our newest complete Circle. This is Ben Blackwater and his wife Drina, who is also a katalyein telepath." For Whitney's benefit, she quickly explained what a katalyein was, as well as the terms venerado and capa.

"There, that's that. Come on in, and find a seat everyone," Amy said, sitting down carefully. Whitney noticed Drina also had no arms as well as Rafaela and Andres, joining Lena and Amy, rather surprising her there were so many of them.

Rafaela spoke up, "So, Doctor Whitney, we've heard a lot about you from Amy. You were born here on Tierra?"

"Yes, I think so; the green lands east of here look somewhat familiar, but not the steep ridges. I wish I could remember more, but it's been well over a hundred years ago when I was kidnaped. Just Whitney, please."

Rafaela smiled, "Whitney it is. Around here, we're all very informal. Katrina sent me a message that you've made some discoveries about how the Rigel men got the *mentales* gifts and about how we women have such monster breasts."

"Well, yes I have. I was just telling her about them over supper. I was able to isolate some particulate matter in the men's blood, as well as in we women's blood. Both are different though. In the men, the particles are really raw fuel dust, I believe it's called germanium. However, the actual cause is somehow their DNA, their genes, well one of them at least, was modified, altered. It's the gene that controls the development of the endocrine system. Oh, I'm sorry. I'm probably using all manner of terms that none of you understand. Sorry."

"No, not at all. We're all familiar, more or less, with genes. I've made quite a study of them; Andres too," Rafaela replied.

"But how? There aren't supposed to be any of our fancy medical laboratories on Tierra, is there?"

"*Mentales* gifts. Some of us can see the genes within cells and their components. You are right; we have none of your fancy medical labs, but we do have some medical machines and even a rejuvenation machine. Please continue," Rafaela explained.

"Wow. Then, you can see inside an ill person like I can," Whitney gushed excitedly. *Have I found someone else who is like me?*

"Nowhere near as good as Diego here is at that. Even Drina has become better at that than I am," Rafaela answered. Whitney glanced at Drina who smiled. Diego merely nodded to her.

"Amazing! I thought I was the only one. Anyway, I've yet to work out just how the raw fuel particles in one's blood stream bring about the genetic modifications. More work to do. As far as we women are concerned, we have a tiny organic microbe in our blood. It is way too small to be trapped by the air filters at the spaceport. This explains why alien women are also affected. Again, we have an altered gene. However, I've discovered a huge gap in our knowledge of Tierra. There has been no complete survey of the plants found here. Hence, I cannot identify from what plant the microbe comes, but I'm certain it comes from a plant. However, it must be a fairly common one that is found all over the world, since all women everywhere are affected. Again, just how this tiny microbe is altering our genes I haven't yet worked out. That's next week's research."

"Excellent Whitney, well done. Yes, we've known for a long time, if a person ingests the right amount of the dust, then their bodies change, and their pituitary glands enlarge. Our special abilities come from that gland. Might I ask what you'll do with this information once you have worked it all out? Publish a paper on it?" Rafaela asked her key question and one that she, Andres, Ken, and Crystal had come just to hear.

"A paper? Let the whole Imperium know about this? Good god! No way! Out there, it's basically a criminal society! They'd just use it to make supermen, who would then control the whole galaxy! I heal people, not make monster killers! Sorry, I *won't* do that. I'll let my boss here know and others on Tierra, who perhaps ought to know, but, other than that, no one. I did promise my lab women I'd find a way to restore their breasts, when they are leaving this planet. I can't imagine why anyone would want to know just how to use these microbes to make monster melons on women, not when medical machines can so easily give women the breast size of their choice. No, it's my own curiosity that's aroused. I do hope you won't take offense with me not wanting to blab this all over the Imperium. It's really not safe to let them know, really it isn't."

Rafaela smiled broadly. "We here all agree with you one hundred percent. I admit we were testing you, Whitney, and you've passed. Some of us know precisely how to make new *mentales* gifted and have done so in the past. Yet, we also know the terrific responsibility we bear while doing this. If we give such powers to the wrong person, as you've said, we've created a psychopathic monster! As a guideline, let no one know about your future discoveries beyond those of us in this room. Just so you know, Andres and I have spent our whole lives working out all the details of this. Oh, we've both used the rejuvenation machine some, so we are much older than we appear. I just had to see this critical work completed for the benefit of the whole world."

"Wow. So you've worked out how these particles actually bring about the genetic mutations?" Whitney asked.

"Not yet. I've got very complete observational records of the process. As yet, this is the missing link in our understanding. I'd love to collaborate with you on this one, if you don't mind having me," Rafaela suggested.

"I'd love to! But my medical lab isn't a safe place to discuss this much further," Whitney replied.

"You can come to my place. Ken, Crystal, I believe this is where you take over," Rafaela handed the discussion off to Ken and Crystal.

Ken spoke up, "Whitney, I must ask you to swear never to divulge any of what I'm about to tell you."

"Of course, Ken. Look, I've been on my own out there in that vicious Imperium empire for a hundred twenty years. I had no one to depend upon except myself. Obviously, I can keep a secret."

"Good. Here on Tierra, some of us are using all manner of means to keep this world safe from harm, to help everyone do well, flourish, and prosper. We do all that we can to keep wars from happening or to defuse them, as best we can. Our organization was founded over a century ago by the then Emperor Amy and Empress Jan. These two here were that Amy and Jan, but they have new physical bodies now. At least, they've kept the names they once had. Long story. We're called the Underground and very, very few people know of our existence. We have quite a lot of Imperium equipment, especially electronics and communication gear, thanks to Jan. We even have our own deep space transport, again thanks to

Jan."

He lowered his voice for emphasis, "All of us here, including your three associates from the spaceport, are part of the Underground, one way or the other. Crystal and I are its leaders, but we plan to retire soon, and our kids will be taking over for us. Yes, Katrina, Carla, and Elfe are now part of us as well. You too are welcome. In addition to all this, some of us have developed a very powerful mental therapy that can remove all traces of emotional and physical trauma that a person has suffered. You probably believe all the operations done with your medical machines are perfectly painless and that there is no trauma associated with such procedures."

Whitney broke in, "Of course, there is no trauma. It's wholly painless. That was the design feature of the Imperium medical machines, in part at least."

Everyone in the room smiled, somewhat annoying her. Ken spoke up, "While that is the apparency of it, in actual fact, all the horrific pain and unconsciousness are there, buried in the person. Worse, it can affect their lives long afterwards. Our therapy fully erases this and any aftereffects. We want you to come and receive what we call Basic Therapy. You've had a number of heavy operations to get your modifications. Fortunately, Lilly is well educated in this and made sure that no one spoke any words around you while you were unconscious. If you don't believe me, ask anyone in this room, including Katrina, Carla, and Elfe."

Drina hastily added, "And most everyone also discovers in the process that they are an immortal spiritual being and have had some past lives here on Tierra too. You won't believe how incredible this is until you experience it for yourself. You just have to get it, Whitney!" She was so enthusiastic that Whitney agreed.

Katrina spoke up, "Unless something comes up, you can head there on Monday, Whitney. I'll make an excuse you are doing some field research on the two problems that you are working on. While you are there, you can meet extensively with Rafaela."

"Thanks, boss."

Diego then spoke up, "Whitney, later this summer,

Nadja and I will be making our usual summer roaming trips. You see, I travel around to all the small hamlets and villages, curing those who are ill or healing the injured, and then I give them a concert. Meanwhile, Nadja here does her language thing. If you tag along, we might be able to flush out some more of your memories and find where you were born, possibly anyway. What do you say? You'll get to see some of the countryside of the Midlands."

"Sure if Katrina can spare me, I'd love too."

"Good. We'll discuss details later on. We'd best be going, and allow you young'ens to have your fun and games," Diego replied.

"One second," Elfe broke in, "as long as everyone is here, I'd like to make another suggestion. This is a little out of my field, but since we don't have a biologist assigned to the governor, I'll act as one. You know there are a great many other domesticated plants found on other worlds, as well as animals. Some of these could well thrive here and give a great boost to your local economy, food-wise and animal-wise. Whitney, they don't have any popcorn plants on this world. How can we ever get by without popcorn with plenty of butter?" Whitney smiled, but quickly realized that it wasn't visible to Elfe. She nodded instead.

"I'd like permission to make a small pilot study and see which ones would do well here and, vitally important, which will also *not* do any harm to the indigenous plants and animals," Elfe suggested. She looked at Katrina.

The governor added, "I know the pacas would likely do well here in the high foothills. If so, their fur is the softest and most luxurious in the Imperium. They can also carry loads of perhaps fifty pounds, as small beasts of burden. They are gentle, kind animals about so high," she demonstrated with her hand. "Of course, all such experiments would have to be very carefully monitored to make darn sure there is no ecological damage to Tierra. What do you say, Queen Amy?" She used her formal title, and Whitney guessed this was because she was making this an official request. She still wasn't used to the fact that her boss really was beneath Queen Amy and not President Snarry.

"Okay, but keep very tight controls. We don't need some new virus spreading around Tierra or some plant growing wildly, killing off the plants on which we depend," Queen Amy replied, using a very official sounding voice.

"Say, as long as we are talking business," Doctor Whitney spoke up, "I'd like to offer a suggestion of my own. I'd like to see a medical facility in every large city or town. I believe I can train enough volunteers to be able to operate the medical machines on the simpler cases, such as illnesses and broken bones. I can be on call to come to anyone who needs more care. We've got a teleport machine on the base."

"What do you think, Queen Amy? I like her idea," Governor Katrina asked.

"I do too. This has always been a major issue with the common people. Brom Tower has been exemplary about getting their healers to those who need it, but this would be an even better system. I believe I can get the medical machines from Emperor Kino. When you have time, Doctor Whitney, start making plans for how you would like to implement it. This would be a good thing to present to the kings and queens at the High Council in June. Good idea."

The older folks took their leave, shaking hands with Whitney or hugging her in the case of Andres and Rafaela. Whitney noticed all of the women now had six inch long nails like herself and Katrina. Jan saw her making this observation and whispered, "We are all getting ready for the next High Council meeting. All of the noblewomen are sporting such claws, compliments of our Senator Zarita, who started this new craze just before she left."

"Oh, yes. Senator's wives all have them this long, but the women senators have theirs twelve inches long. I surely don't know how they can manage that; these are murder, but fun too. I hope this Zarita shortens hers, before she returns here or we may all be having them a foot long," Whitney replied.

"Good one, Whitney. Good one," Adrianna called out. "You are going to fit right in with us. We are playing cards tonight. Let's get going gang!" Turning to Whitney, she added, "Trying to shuffle the cards with these is murder. I still haven't figured that one out yet. We're all trying to get used to them before the meeting. We don't want to appear dunces in front of all the queens and noblewomen."

As they took their places, Drina barked, "Now guys, remember no cheating. No looking at another's cards through their eyes. We want a clean game here for Whitney. Don't worry, Whitney. I'll keep an eye on the guys, but we all do like to joke and kid around some."

"How about a lot, Drina?" Jan added with a wry smile.

"What? Me cheat?" Bernardo said with a coy smile. "Why, I would never dream of doing such a thing!" Several laughed, and Whitney suspected that was far from the truth. He added, "Katrina, no fair winning the large pots all of the time."

"Why would I want to win the smaller ones, Bernardo?" Katrina replied playfully. Several laughed.

Drina explained, "Whitney, you have to watch out for Lena and Katrina. Those two have *impossible* luck, especially when the pot is a rather large one. They are the best bluffers here. Trouble is, you don't know when they are bluffing and when they aren't. So be careful."

Her husband, Ben, spoke up, "Say, we could play for clothes. You know, bet the clothes we are wearing, and throw them into the pot. Wouldn't that be interesting?"

Lena laughed loudly. "Ben, I don't want you to freeze your thing off. Drina would have my butt for that! Same for you Bernardo, Henry. You three know Katrina and I would soon have your pants off. Some of us might enjoy that, but some could care less." While everyone roared, she shot a broad grin to Amy and Jan. Katrina and Whitney smiled and glanced at each other. Then the game began.

Whitney couldn't recall ever having so much pure fun. She began to realize how terrible her life had been; what she'd missed. Plus, she heard some amazing stories as Carla and Elfe, related what had happened to them, and how Elfe had been rescued. She soon saw that Lena and Katrina were the ones to beat. Lena always seemed to have an edge over Katrina, though. She suspected it had much to do with Lena having been a Sector ID Minister for so many years. More importantly, she found these people to be quite open and honest. No topic was taboo. Furthermore, she was instantly accepted as one of them, something that had *never* happened before. Whitney began to feel as though she was in heaven.

Several hours later, they ended for the night. As they broke up, Jan whispered to Whitney, "I left you and Katrina a little present on your bed. Hope you like it. Tomorrow I'll take you on a tour of the castle and tower. You can watch Henry and Adrianna, while they continue their work on the castle enlargement project."

Drina led them to their suite for the weekend, "Room 19. This is a good one. Kings stay in these. Holler if you need something. Ben and I are just next door. Glad you are with us, Whitney."

"This is something else!" Whitney exclaimed, as she and Katrina entered the spacious suite. A plush central living room had two bedrooms and a bath connected to its far side. A fire was crackling on one side of the living room. They headed to the master bedroom. Here they found a large bed with satin sheets and several layers of very beautiful quilts on top. A fire had been set, but was mostly glowing red coals. The room felt delightfully warm, filled with the odor of resinous pine. A small box lay on the bed, and Whitney opened it to discover a special toy. Katrina came over to look at it, as she opened the box.

Katrina laughed. "Jan has a sense of humor. This way we both can be the alpha dog." Both women chuckled and began to prepare for bed. Hairbrushes were right there on a night stand. An hour later, the two fully satisfied women finally fell asleep in each other's arms.

The next morning as each helped the other get dressed, Whitney jested, "I never dreamed I'd be sleeping with my boss."

Katrina chuckled. "Good one. Bernardo is rubbing off on you!"

After laughing briefly, she added seriously, "Nah, it's just I've been suppressing my sexuality for over a century, and now I'm afraid it's all coming out. Come here," Whitney explained, pulling Katrina close for another special kiss before they inserted their lip plates. Later, they made their cautious way to the small dining room, more or less following their noses. Jan was waiting them.

"I see you two love birds are finally up," she jested, but both women flushed slightly. "Come on; eat up. Lena's kindly left you a small amount of the nut bread. She's still crazy about it. I'll take you on a tour when you've eaten. Lots to see."

An hour later, Whitney exclaimed, "This is utterly amazing! I had no idea of other people's remarkable gifts — so different from mine." They were standing on the observational roof of the old tower. Off to the south, they watched, as one Circle carved out stone blocks three feet long and a foot in depth and height. Once cut, a second Circle moved them from the side of the mountain through the air and laid them into position on the new construction. Jan explained they'd already doubled the interior spaces of the castle proper, turning it into more of a maze of hallways. Now, they were building a second tower that abutted this original tower. This would allow two Circles to operate fully during the daytime. Already, Jan had shown them Capa Adrianna's Circle in operation, though there was nothing visibly to see, just nine gifted men and women sitting in a circle with a tenth acting as their Regulator. Eight of the nine flowed their combined power into the capa, who then executed the mission. Venerado Henry was controlling the laying of the stones, following the design drawn out on a large parchment next to where the trio was standing.

Jan said, "Now we can house a thousand visitors at one time. That's more than we need right now, so we've got a goodly margin of safety, if people don't get lost in the maze of halls. Well, we best get you to Brom, get Whitney going on her therapy, and her work with Rafaela. Come on. Bart's going to handle the teleport since both Circles are quite busy right now."

The large number of middle aged Underground members and their many older teen aged children left Doctor Whitney confused. "Too many names and faces to remember," she laughed, as the many introductions ended. Ken and Crystal took her on a tour of the Underground facilities. She was surprised at all that she saw, though she was most impressed with their medical facilities. "Your setup here is better than many smaller towns on well-populated planets in the Imperium. Nice going. Are all of Lilly's medical machine operators as knowledgeable about them as you are here? If so, that will make my proposal of getting a hospital installed in all larger towns on Tierra."

Jake and Misty, who were in charge of the medical facilities, shook their heads. Misty answered, "Sadly no, Doctor Whitney. They are skilled at performing the modifications and undoing some of them. You see, for safety's sake, those machines have had the extensive menu of operations hidden. A simple menu of just the few Elegant Fashions Inc stores are allowed to perform are the only visible menu choices. So they know how to do those. Still, they could well form a cadre of volunteers to learn more."

After the tour, she was led through the tunnels to the Trauma and Spiritual Rehab Center on Tierra. Jamie and Luisa, both in their middle forties, guided her through this long two-story stone building. Each floor had a hundred rooms, though the first floor was actually underground for the benefit of the many mermaids, who performed the therapy here. From there, the two took her above ground for a glimpse at Brom, the city of twenty-five thousand, its castle, Senate Building, and the enlarged Brom Tower. Then, Luisa took her into one of the ground floor rooms to begin her therapy.

Luisa anticipated a rather rough case, due particularly to two unique details. One, Whitney had accumulated over a hundred twenty years of incidents, nearly double the usual life span of most on Tierra. Two, she had been kidnaped when she was barely fourteen and taken off-world as a slave telepath. Make that three, Luisa decided after their first session. For survival, Whitney had been totally secret, never, ever sharing her own thoughts and feelings with any other person since her kidnaping.

Not surprising, loss was what was most real to Whitney. Most of the first day was spent going over lighter incident after lighter incident in which she'd been reminded of her loss and kidnaping. Only by the second day did Whitney finally unburden enough finally to face her actual kidnaping. "She must have cried a gallon of tears," Luisa explained to Rafaela later that night. The *mentales* expert was monitoring the overall progress of Luisa's new patient. "You were right about having me do it. I look older to her, and that's giving me a slight edge in getting her to open up and really face her past. She would not likely have opened up to a younger person. Good call, Rafaela."

"You'd have made, it if I hadn't," Rafaela replied with a smile. "Keep me posted."

During the next few days, Whitney uncovered some more details of her heritage. She had once lived in the old Kingdom of Oakham in a stone manor house surrounded by green pastures. Her uncle was the ruler, and she'd once been to a formal dance in a big castle higher in the foothills. She was the daughter of Ralph and Sheila Oakham, and she had two older brothers and an older sister, but she no longer recalled their names. After that session, Whitney asked Luisa, "Will this be enough for Diego to help me find this place, do you think?"

"I don't know, but if anyone can find it, Diego can. He and Nadja are more widely traveled in the south than anyone else has. We'll just have to see," Luisa answered honestly, but without making promises that might not be fulfilled.

One week was spent in getting all of the grief and traumatic loss released from Whitney's case. The second week, the underlying pain and unconsciousness began to lift. Naturally, it began with her recent body modifications. It came as a complete shock to the doctor. The amount of pain that lay buried beneath the anesthetic overwhelmed her. While it reduced considerably once she rose above antagonism, it didn't fully erase. Luisa continued to push her for something that was both similar and earlier in time, and Whitney ran smack into her birth. Once more, she was quite startled intellectually to discover such an experience could be recalled in such detail.

"As a doctor, I've delivered hundreds of babies. This is exactly right. I know. Every detail — exactly right, though I wish that midwife would have known far more about real doctoring," Whitney declared. Still, birth didn't fully erase either. Luisa pressed onwards, and, at last, Whitney ran into a series of prenatal traumas in which her mother kept banging into the corner of their family table, smashing in Whitney's head, giving her intense, but short lived headaches, which had plagued her most of her adult life.

While she got tremendous relief and immense personal satisfaction as a doctor from the discovery of the harm such prenatal incidents caused on the unborn child, it didn't erase fully. Again, Luisa pressed her for something even earlier. "How can there be anything earlier?" Whitney continued to protest. Under Luisa's gentle pressure, she continued to look. At last, she found a black mass that quickly developed into a very painful death incident. She'd been a man, who had been shot with an alien blaster, somewhere out on the rolling green grasslands of the Midlands. "This can't be happening. It's illegal," Whitney kept exclaiming. She burst into laughter, as all of the accumulated pain and trauma finally erased. Gone forever were her acute headaches.

"That's why I became a doctor. To prevent bad things from happening, like dying when you shouldn't be dying," she roared. Then, she also realized she had lived before and wasn't a body, but really something quite separate, an immortal spiritual being. She laughed even harder. Luisa quietly ended the session. Whitney's Basic Therapy was finished. She had a newfound vitality of life, as well as high enthusiasm.

"Luisa, this is utterly revolutionary, profound even! This is the greatest discovery ever! Everyone has to get this Basic Therapy, somehow, someway. How can I help?" Doctor Whitney asked.

To answer that one, Luisa, Rafaela, Katrina, and Amy met to discuss Doctor Whitney's proposal. The doctor explained, "Look, if I can get my medical facilities established in a town, why don't we also get a few trained therapy givers there as well. I can provide the space that they need and schedule the patients. You know, they come in for an injury, and, after the machines heal them, your people can heal them of the trauma too, maybe even give them Basic Therapy as well. What do you say? We can spread this far and wide."

Rafaela pointed out the biggest problem. "Our givers

live in Brom and probably don't want to move to other kingdoms. It takes a good deal of time to train good therapy givers."

"Well, it's going to take a long time to train up competent medical nurses as well. At least one person in the medical facility is going to have to be one of us *mentales* gifted so they can let me know when they get a serious case. I can then teleport there and assist. I know it's going to be hard to get this going, but the benefits make it well worth it," Doctor Whitney pleaded her case.

Queen Amy declared, "I like it. Rafaela, Luisa, check and see if some of your therapy givers and their families might be willing to move to other towns. I think it would be prudent to see if we cannot get others, who have the *mentales* healing gifts, to become the new nurses, wherever possible. Let's devote a lot to this project. It has enormous potential in more ways than one. Right now, anything we can do to promote peace, tranquility, prosperity, and health is vital."

Governor Katrina added her weight. "I couldn't agree more. The Imperium ought to provide the medical machines and perhaps even the salaries of those who work these new medical labs. We can lower the gold shipments to compensate the Imperium, though the kings might object to that. I believe we can sell them on the great benefits of having many local hospitals in their larger towns. Are we all agreed on this?" She sought confirmation and got it. "Doctor Whitney, prepare a brief announcement and description of your project. You'll get the chance to relay it to the many kings and queens. Their High Council meeting is coming up on the seventh of June, a little over a week from now."

Doctor Whitney frowned. Something was bothering her. "Excuse me, but I can't help detecting everyone here is very worried. Is there something I am missing — that I should know?"

Amy sighed, "Well, yes there is, Whitney. It's the giant germanium crystals." She launched into a lengthy explanation for the doctor's benefit, bringing her even more into her close circle. "So you see, while Venerado Henry and Capa Adrianna are using the immense power of these crystals for the benefit

68

of people, others are developing new weapons of mass destruction."

"My god! I remember now. Stories when I was a little girl. Things that could eat away the flesh from bodies. I thought those were just stories my nanny was telling me to get me to obey her," Doctor Whitney exclaimed. "It is a race against time, isn't it?"

"Astute observation, doctor," Queen Amy answered her. "It certainly is. The more good we can generate, the more we may be able to defuse the creation of such hideous weapons."

"Count me in on this battle!" Doctor Whitney declared.

Chapter 5 The High Council of June 1293

"Doctor Whitney, so pleased to meet you. I'm Queen Edda Turda. I'm so very pleasantly surprised to see you and the others have adopted one of the Easterlings' beauty suggestions. Your long nails. You see, in the past, the Easterlings women had a long tradition of binding and having nails as long as ours are now. Of course, we've had to cast aside our traditional bindings, because of the massive loss of all our young men, when that evil barbarian Damiano conscripted and killed an entire generation of our young men. We women had to take over our country and somehow survive. Bound, we could not do so, and the ancient empresses also contributed to some of us noblewomen changing the forms of our bindings. Anyway, I'm so pleased that you and Governor Katrina, Carla, and Elfe have adopted our ways. In a material way, we're now very much alike, don't you think?" Queen Edda finally allowed Whitney to get in a word. She and her Sisterhood ministers had just entered the giant Throne Room and met her along with the other three women.

"Yes, it does bring us much closer, Queen Edda. You look quite stunning yourself," Doctor Whitney responded. "I must apologize though, I'm still getting used to all of these fancy fashions. Walking is so challenging, isn't it?"

"Well, yes, but we do look good. And I do love your new style gown! I must find Lilly and find out if she has more of them," Queen Edda replied, and immediately began searching for the head of Elegant Fashions Inc. Doctor Whitney had agreed to model Nita's latest design, modeled somewhat on Whitney's personal taste. That is, she always wore a grey or black skirt hemmed just below her knees, allowing her taste in black seamed nylons to show, though this new design was done in blue satin. Now, she no longer wore her accustomed low black heels, but these new toe shoes. She was not alone in needing an arm for support. With only their toes on the floor supported by the usual tiny spiked that touched the floor almost immediately behind the back of their toes, balance and support were skimpy at best, to say nothing of the overall impact of having only about a fifth of the usual sole in contact with the ground.

As Doctor Whitney looked over the ever increasing arriving men and women, she saw the vast majority had the same problems as she did. Both men and women wore the pipe corsets and lip plates. Even some of the men wore toe boots, while most of the women wore toe shoes, much like hers. She had on her new pale blue satin gown with matching heels. At least the men didn't have to wear the very heavy and overly long dangling earrings, she thought. Nor did the men have long fingernails. Again, she thanked Senator Zarita for not having shown these women her foot long fingernails. Surely, this fashion conscious bunch of women would have demanded them as well, she concluded.

Rather quickly, the Throne Room filled up, having been converted by Amy's staff from the Great Hall just for these meetings. "We are up first," Governor Katrina whispered to her three companions. Slowly, they began moving more towards the front. When she was called upon by Queen Amy, Katrina didn't want to take "forever" to get to the platform before the throne.

Queen Amy rose catching her balance once again. "Welcome kings, queens, venerados, veneradas, aides, and guests to the High Council of the Lords. Governor Katrina and I have made some progress since our fall meeting that we wish to share with you, before I turn the meeting over to you. Governor Katrina, please make your announcements." She carefully sat down, and Governor Katrina and Doctor Whitney equally carefully stepped up onto the platform, turned, and faced the large gathering.

"Welcome one and all. First of all, let me introduce our new and highly acclaimed Doctor Whitney Jones." She motioned to Whitney with her right arm, who bowed slightly. "She is far, far older than she looks and has had a very long career in the medical field, curing and healing for over three-quarters of a century. We are very lucky to have such a competent doctor among us. Further, she is one of your own *mentales* gifted." Several gasps broke the stillness.

"Yes, she was born down in the old Kingdom of Oakham, but was kidnaped and taken off-world as a slave telepath well over a hundred years ago. At long last, she's been able to make her way back here to her own world. And we are all too thankful she has succeeded in returning to us." A round of applause caused Whitney to blush slightly.

"That said, we are working to make Tierra flourish and prosper, to help everyone survive better. To that end, we are conducting a pilot test to determine what new crops and domesticated animals would be of great benefit to you. One animal we believe will thrive well in the foothills of the Goza are called pacas. They are akin to sheep, but nearly three times their size. Their coats are highly prized, being the softest, most luxurious material for clothing within the Imperium. Harvested similar to sheep, these gentle creatures can also be used as light pack animals. They eat grass and have a kind disposition. If the pilot program is successful, at the fall council, I'll be making small herds of these valuable animals available to those who wish to experiment with them in your kingdoms."

"In addition, we are examining another dozen potential food crops we believe will do well in your various climates, from the colder north to the more arid regions. Again, I expect to have some further data on these at the next meeting."

"Third, Doctor Whitney will tell you about her current project. Doctor," Governor Katrina took a small step backwards, wobbling slightly.

"Hello everyone. I'm very pleased finally to be back on my home world. As Governor Katrina has said, I've had a very long and successful career as a top medical doctor in the Imperium. I'm bringing all that skill and knowledge here with me. Yes, my gifts lie in the healing arts, which I've used, when their medical machines and their technology all failed to cure the person," she began rather seriously.

"When I first arrived, I was appalled to discover the awful lack of medical facilities on Tierra, and I decided to use my gifts to the benefit of everyone on Tierra. I'm implementing a new program with the full approval and backing of both Governor Katrina and Queen Amy. As fast as possible, every town on Tierra with a population of five thousand or more will have their own local Hospital Facility. Each one will contain a fully equipped Imperium medical machine and a nurse trained by myself to run it. Further, if something arises the nurse cannot handle, I'll always be on call and will come at once, bringing my skills to bear."

"These new Hospital Facilities will be open to everyone, from farmer to king. Treatment will be free of charge. The Ataro Empire will be paying for the machines, and Queen Amy will be paying the salaries of the workers, the nurses. I would only ask that your local towers handle the construction of the needed stone buildings and that someone donates the small amount of land for the hospital."

"Additionally, I've just finished my Basic Therapy up in Brom at their fabulous Trauma and Spiritual Rehab Center. Honestly, there is nothing like this anywhere in the vast Imperium! I feel like I've been given back my life, and I want everyone to be able to have this too. Hence, each of these new Hospital Facilities will also be staffed with trained therapy givers, who will deliver this Basic Therapy to all those who desire it, again at no charge. Here on Tierra, some of us have been given tremendous gifts, such as me and many of you as well. These gifts are found nowhere else in the Imperium. It is our responsibility to use our gifts to help all our people, particularly those who do not have such precious gifts."

"Enough of my moralizing. Before you all head for your homes, I would appreciate you giving me a list of the larger towns in your kingdoms and perhaps noting which ones you believe should have one of the new Hospital Facilities built there first. I hope by the next meeting, we can begin to get some of these under construction and into operation by next spring. Thank you all." She stepped back. Spontaneously, a loud round of applause echoed through the great vaulted room. Whitney flushed, but graciously accepted it, stepping back beside her boss. Then, the two took careful, small steps, joining Carla and Elfe at the south side of the room, where they were holding a pair of chairs for them.

As Queen Amy again carefully rose to turn the meeting officially over to the assembled kings and queens, both she and

Governor Katrina were attacked! Unprotected, Governor Katrina felt an unknown man forcibly taking over her mind, as did Queen Amy. A voice bellowed in their heads. *Make a Formal Ruling that all guilds on Tierra are no longer subject to any taxes! Make that Formal Ruling now!* Poor Katrina's head nearly burst from the powerful energies completely overwhelming her. She tried to fight back, her crystal glowing bright blue.

Queen Amy staggered, as she felt the mental assault upon her and registered the mental command from her unknown assailant. She too fought back, her crystal glowing at its brightest, but like Katrina, the attacker's sheer psi power was far more than she could muster herself, even amplified a hundredfold by her crystal. Jan instantly sensed the attack and sent to the Gang of Nine, *Amy's under a mental attack!* Instantly, the eight others began searching the huge room, looking for the source of the attack, while Jan slipped into rapport with Amy and received the mental blast as well, along with the command. She sent, *Amy, below your throne!* That was all that Jan could send, as the mental energies overwhelmed her as well.

That was just enough for Amy though. With her remaining consciousness, she focused on the giant germanium crystal that the two of them had buried beneath the Emperor's Throne during the construction of the room well over a century ago. Like some greedy child snatching their favorite candy bar, Amy latched onto the crystal, feeling its immense powers flowing into her mind and body. *The hell I will! Take that!* She shot back a huge mental blast of raw energy straight into the mind of her attacker. Instantly, the attack on her mind and that of Katrina's vanished completely, as if it had never happened. Well, that's not entirely true, both women now had a headache, though Katrina's was quite severe.

Queen Amy hastily said, "Okay, I officially turn the meeting over to you, King Wycombe." With Jan's help, Amy sat back down.

You okay? Katrina's been attacked too, Jan sent her.

Yes, I forgot about our hidden crystal. Thanks, that was just enough to stop the attack. You saved my ass again,

Jan.

I know. Bernardo's getting Diego to assist Katrina now.

Drina sent, *Amy, we can't find the attacker! None of us saw anyone who even looked like they were doing anything. No one's crystals here were glowing, save you two's.*

Henry added, *We're still searching. Keep alert, Amy. We'll find that bastard!*

Katrina heard Diego in her mind. *Calm down. You have been mentally attacked. Someone tried to dominate you and Amy. I'm going to work my magic on you. Relax.*

But who did this? Why? My head is splitting.

We don't know. Still looking for them. You are lucky to be alive. Oh, Amy says we're all to meet in private at lunch. He began slowly removing the built up electrical charges on her neural pathways. Shortly, Whitney joined him. Together, they made fast work of it. Within five minutes, Katrina's splitting headache had vanished.

The governor looked over the crowd of attendees, but they were all either listening to the current speaker, or in the case of many wives, chatting among themselves via telepathy. She saw nothing threatening. Perhaps, this had all been some terribly bad dream, and she began to wonder if it had actually happened.

At noon, the room began to empty, heading for the large dining hall. Governor Katrina and her group hung back as did the Gang of Nine. "What was that all about? How could we be attacked? I've never been hit so damned hard. I was helpless," she whispered, although since the last person exited, there was no need.

Amy replied, "Someone tried to Dominate us to force me to issue one of my Formal Rulings that everyone on Tierra must follow — in this case the kings, queens, and senators of the many kingdoms. But that was no ordinary *mentales* Dominate! They were using one of those raw giant crystals I've told you about, Katrina. It's as I've been fearing. Someone is now using their immense power to go on the offensive."

"But they could have killed us. My head felt like it was about to explode," Katrina countered.

"Yes, a bit more power and that could well have happened to us both," Amy validated her observation. "Anyone have any clues from where the attack came?"

Many shoulders shrugged. Drina spoke up. "We looked all over this room, but no one here was doing it. I'll stake my reputation on that, Amy. So could they do it? I mean it was timed just right."

"Someone is or was spying on us," Jan declared.

"Surely not one of these kings or queens," Bernardo countered.

Lena added her thoughts. "Perhaps they took over someone else's body and observed through their eyes so they would know the precise time to launch their attack."

"Aye, that makes the most sense," Bernardo acknowledged his wife. "So what do we do now?"

Doctor Whitney asked, "What is a giant crystal? What's this all about? You all look very pale and quite worried. I'm missing something, aren't I?"

Amy decided to explain the situation fully. After all, she was using the doctor and her plans to help convince the venerados in particular to use their stones for the good of everyone. "During the war with the Federation, the Imperium fuel refinery on our moon Palidez was destroyed. The moon disintegrated into billions of fragments, which would have destroyed us all on Tierra when they landed. However, we believe one of our ancient gods, Alleric, intervened and reformed the moon, fusing the fragments back together again. Your geologist can confirm this, I think. Anyway, many smaller fragments eventually reached us and gave us a spectacular meteor shower that lasted for weeks. Some of the larger fragments reached the surface, embedding themselves a foot or so in the ground."

"These raw germanium crystals are around a foot or so in size. Each one can amplify our *mentales* powers at least a thousandfold, far beyond what our personal crystals can do. Worse, these giant crystals can be networked together by tuning them to the same unique frequency. When this is done, the potential power is staggering."

"In our ancient past, some of these giant crystals were

found in mines. The towers got a hold of them and created such weapons of mass destruction that all life on Tierra was nearly wiped out. The Age of Chaos. Elfe, that ancient tower ruins you found up north, Portillo, was one of the towers that was destroyed by these types of weapons. Way back then, there were not too many of the giant crystals around. This time, there are probably thousands of them. Most towers have hundreds of them already gathered up. Worse, the venerados and veneradas are working on ways and means of using their enormous potentials. Our fear is that sooner or later, someone is going to develop another weapon of incalculable destruction and unleash it on the rest of us."

"We've been trying to convince all the towers to devote their efforts to constructive uses of these crystals. Venerado Henry has been doing just that, using some of the power crystals to speed up vastly stone constructions all around Exchange City. Anyway, Katrina and I were attacked today by someone using the power of one of those giant crystals."

"My god! Are you both all right?" Doctor Whitney gasped, realizing now how close to death both women had been during the attack.

"Yes, barely. I was able to tap into the power of one of those giant crystals, just enough to counter the person's attack on us," Amy replied. "This is one reason why I am backing your hospital program and your plans to bring new domesticated plants and animals to Tierra. I hope to set a good example of working for the average person and not against them."

"Have I only returned to my home in time to witness its destruction?" Whitney complained. "We have to do something."

"I know. I'm open to ideas," Amy sighed. The problem seemed insurmountable to her just now.

Elfe chuckled. "You know, all this is hardly unique to Tierra, Amy. It is actually to be expected. You see, cultures who have risen to the Stone Age are basically hunters and gatherers. That means, to survive the men become expert hunters, stalkers, trappers, and killers of wild animals, as well as protectors of their clan's hunting areas from neighboring clans. Later on, they usually develop copper and bronze technology, as well as agriculture. Being able to harvest grains in abundance allows them not only to settle down in small villages, but also to greatly increase their population. You see, in hunter-gather cultures, the clan must move from area to area, as they exhaust the local game. Everything they own must be carried from one location to their next hunting locale. That means women are likely to bear a child perhaps every four years. If they had children more frequently, they wouldn't be able to move to a new area, when they'd exhausted the game in their current one."

She went on, "So with agriculture comes a dramatic increase in the available food. No longer do the clans have to move seasonally, but can reside in a given location for many years. Of course, with their typical slash and burn agriculture, they soon exhaust the soils, and then are forced to move to greener pastures. Still, agriculture and animal husbandry allows them to have vastly larger population densities. The clan or extended family gives way to a small tribe of perhaps several hundred in a hamlet. Of course, now they have to fight other tribes to be able to keep their settlement. So nearly always, we find cultures in the bronze age making use of more deadly weapons to protect their lands and to dominate or conquer neighboring hamlets. This becomes particularly critical when the population densities of the various tribes in one area become too great to support all of them."

"Warfare is commonplace and perhaps vital to their survival. Often, we see the development of wooden palisades around the hamlets, which give way to earthen walls or mud brick walls of larger and larger dimensions. Eventually, walled towns arise. As they develop further and as their forging fires get hotter and hotter, they begin to make use of iron, and thus steel weapons are invented. Stone walls replace those of mud bricks. Warfare becomes even more common and more deadly. This, in combination with better agricultural productivity, forces the people into larger towns and cities. Thus, city-states are formed, as are empires. As the population density rises, the intensive agriculture often depletes the soils. In order to have sufficient food and raw materials for construction, they have to expand their empires outward, conquering more lands, bringing the resources there into their fold."

"Of course, these empires can also collapse for various reasons. Natural disasters can wipe out agriculture for a period of time. Civil wars can erupt, especially after the death of the current ruler of the empire. Yet, there is hope for most civilizations."

She went on, "In the Stone Age, everyone was involved in hunting and gathering enough food for everyday survival. When agriculture takes over, for the first time there is more than sufficient food available. Now, some of the population can cease their daily hunt for food and begin to specialize in the making of pottery, tools, and weapons, for example. As the culture develops further, more and more of the villagers are no longer involved in food production. Millers, weavers, teamsters, and so on arise as the craftsmen and artisans. By the time that large towns and cities appear, the farmers can support a whole raft of these non-food producing elite. Some become full time warriors, educators, artists, leaders, administrative bureaucrats, as well as the craftsmen."

"Salvation from constant warfare comes from these individuals at the top, who now have time, wisdom, and the means to forge lasting peace and prosperity for a civilization. Yet, men still engage in wars no matter how sophisticated their culture becomes. Just look at our own Imperium and the Federation of Planets. Still, in more modern societies, wars are far less frequent, though vastly more dangerous. So Amy, your people here are no different than any other world. Only the means of conducting the wars are different," Elfe continued her lengthy explanation.

"Another point bears hearing, Queen Amy. As the towns develop and a separation of food-producers and the non-food-producers develops, the craftsmen, the bureaucrats, the nobles, even the kings and queens, all seek to acquire what are known in archaeology as elite goods. Such things are often rare and valuable items. Often made from gold and gems, these become status symbols that these so called 'higher class' individuals use to show their importance or wealth. Here on

Tierra, this process of acquiring elite goods has taken a different route than is more often found on other larger, more diverse worlds."

"Here, gold is almost too rare to be of any consequence. You do not have ivory, which comes from the tusks of larger mammals found on other worlds. As far as I know, your people have not developed ornamental pottery. With the vastly more limited resources on Tierra, the route of elite goods has gone in a different direction that of elaborate clothing and ornamentation, due I suspect to the heavy influence of Elegant Fashions Inc way back when it was founded."

"Here, the nobles use elegant clothing, exotic shoes, these impossibly heavy earrings, and even lip plates and pipe corsets to set themselves apart publically and quite visibly from the average person of the land. In effect, Amy, these have become the elite goods in Tierra society. This may be an important detail. The various guilds and their members are also trying to improve their own status. To do so, they'll want to acquire elite goods as well. If you have stock in Elegant Fashions Inc, you probably could make a fortune." She finished up, "So you see, many others are now trying to obtain the 'good life style' of the nobles and rulers."

Amy mused, "So this is natural. Sorry, don't know what stock is. Anyway, we have to prevent the devastating wars from happening somehow. I'll give this elite goods idea some thought. Still, all wars and conflicts are caused events. Always, someone is in the background actively fomenting the conflict, as a third party to the two combatants. The Ataro Empire has proven that law beyond a shadow of a doubt. Still, that hidden third party can be difficult to find. Just look at how hard it was to find the Gamelon-3 men, who caused the recent war."

Drina decided to speak up. "At least, we know that whoever attacked you this time was not present at the meeting. We all searched them well. So the kings, queens, and tower folks didn't directly attack you. I admit one or more of them might have been the perpetrator's eyes, though."

"I know, Drina," Amy nodded to her friend. "Good work on that. I don't think anyone who is here is behind it, based upon what they were trying to force me and Katrina to do.

Elimination of taxes on the many guilds makes me think that a guild member is behind it."

Jan commented, "But dear, the guilds don't have any of the giant crystals. Or do they?" She began to see where Amy was heading. Perhaps the tower folk were not the only ones to have discovered the power of the crystals. There were thousands of *mentales* men and women who were not part of any tower. Most were widely scattered across Tierra.

Nita volunteered, "Amy, I've noticed the guilds here in Exchange City are growing rapidly. It used to be my cloth makers, weavers, tailors, and dressmakers were mostly independent men and women. But of late, they're all joining local guilds. The guilds are then negotiating with Lilly on their wages and production quotas."

Amy sighed, "We have no choice now but to start looking into the guilds. Okay, we best join the others or they'll be asking too many questions." The group headed off to join the throng in the huge new dining hall.

"Hello Doctor Whitney. I'm Queen Agostina Terasi of the Kingdom of Domei." The tall bound woman caught her just as she was finishing her lunch.

"Pleased to meet you, Queen Agostina." She stared at this remarkable looking young woman. She wore a tight fitting brown satin gown that clearly showed that she too wore a pipe corset. She had the usual giant lip plates. Hers showed a sleigh in the snow. Her earrings were quite similar to Whitney's. What startled her was she was quite bound. A leather belt encircled her tiny waist. Attached to it, chains held her arms pinned to her sides just above her elbows, allowing her lower arms free. She too had six inch long nails that extended her restricted reach. Plus, her gown fell to her ankles but had no walking slit, forcing her to take barely two inch shuffling steps.

"We're firm believers in the Ancient Traditions," Queen Agostina explained, noticing Whitney was staring at her bindings. "The previous rulers tried to adopt all these modern ways and very nearly ruined our whole kingdom. We're trying to put things right, back to our roots, our heritage. You ought to wear far lower gowns. It is so risque to show so very much of your lower legs, you know. But I must compliment you on your toe shoes. At least, you also believe women of power must have some constraints too."

Doctor Whitney didn't quite know how to respond. "I'm trying to dress much as the many noblewomen do. Thanks for the compliment about my shoes. Walking is very difficult. I surely don't know how you can manage it in your gown. I do need my arms free to work my magic healing, though. I like your winter scene on your lip plates."

"Why thank you, Doctor Whitney. Yes, Domei has quite a lot of snow and sleighs. I guess you do need your arms free when you are healing others. Still, you ought to wear the fancy arm-fetter-gowns that Elegant Fashions Inc made at other times. You could change when you actually need to do your healing. Many women are looking to you and Governor Katrina for the latest fashions. If you wore an arm-fetter-gown, you would be letting us women of the Easterlings know you appreciate our styles too. In the north, the days are quite cold, making your short gown quite inappropriate, you see. Our longer ones keep our legs warm. At least, you have the good taste to wear the toe shoes with your short gown. I suppose it is so much warmer down here that you can get away with it. Perhaps, when winter comes, you might consider a gown more like ours."

"I can see what you mean. I've not been here during the winters, though I'm told they are quite harsh and cold. I'll chat with Lilly about such gowns later on. Thank you for the tip, Queen Agostina," Whitney replied cordially. "We best get going. I move so darn slowly."

She chuckled, "Of course we do. The men will wait for us. Look, I believe the Governor is waiting for you, as is my husband. Come. We should head back."

After the meeting, Lilly caught Doctor Whitney. "Just wanted you to know, you're new style gown has caught the attention of many others. I've got dozens of new orders for these new shorter gowns. Risque, that's what everyone is calling them. If you haven't noticed, many of the men are attracted to your legs." She chuckled some.

"I can't believe it, Lilly. I've never been a fashion model, just a plain old doctor." Both chuckled now, as did Katrina, who was glad to be sharing the duties of Tierra's fashion model.

Queen Amy asked the governor and her three companions to stick around. Finally alone with the Gang of Nine, Amy said, "After that attack on us, we are going to have to take some precautions. I believe Senator Zarita had a brilliant idea. She took one of the large crystals, had it cut into a number of smaller stones, and had each polished up to become a gemstone. She fashioned various pieces of jewelry from them. The key point is she effectively wears an entire giant crystal on her person, giving her powers an enormous boost. I'm going to hire a local jeweler to do the same for us. We women will have rings, replacement earrings, broaches, and perhaps belts with the gems in them. This way, each of us will always have the potential of an entire giant crystal available to us, if we get attacked again."

"Thanks. I'll rest a whole lot easier," Governor Katrina exclaimed, obviously greatly relieved. She had definitely had quite a shock from the attack.

Chapter 6 The Education of Zarita

"Just as soon as you two get settled in, come up to the sixtieth floor and get me," Senator Tabia ordered. "I'll take you down to the boutique and get you both fixed up. Remember, your suite is on the third floor, Senator Isabella's old suite."

Their deep space transport had landed on Proxima Prime, bringing back many memories of her Neva days on this world to Zarita. Most of the memories were not the most pleasant, however. She'd been a naive fool in those days. Now, she was going to be wholly prepared for her revenges. She was not at all surprised by the concrete and steel planet, though Senator Celenia and her assistant Lelane most definitely were. Senator Tabia had chatted during their descent, explaining the entire world was covered. The whole surface was one enormous city of hundreds of billions. Celenia and Lelane were most impressed with the sight.

They passed through customs, and the two new senators received their suite assignments and their pass codes. They shared a single shuttle craft, since Celenia had no arms with which to operate one. Senator Tabia had already arranged that detail, sparing her the embarrassment during this customs check. One shuttle would serve both, since they were both senators. By the time they arrived in their new suite, their crates had already been delivered and were sitting in the middle of their living room.

"Well, I can't move them," Zarita said rather disgustedly. She'd tried to push one of hers into her new bedroom, but her toe shoes merely slipped on the plush rug. The crate didn't budge. Darn shoes anyway, she thought.

"Leave them, dear. I think we're supposed to get a couple of servants. They can move them for us. Come on. We best go find Tabia now," Celenia suggested, trying to be as helpful as she could, considering at the moment she felt completely useless. That feeling would only escalate shortly. With Lelane holding on to each of them, the trio made their way out of their apartment and into the elevator.

Celenia thought, *I can't even open my own suite's door.*

Watching her new lover sigh slightly, Zarita sent her, *I know, but that's why you have Lelane and me.*

"Oh here you are. Okay, let's get this going," Tabia said, as the trio knocked on her door. "Huburt, be a good dear and start unpacking our things, will you?" He nodded, and she stepped out, leading them back to the elevator. A few minutes later, they entered the boutique on the first floor, where assistants were waiting for them.

The woman in charge explained they would be having two Academy students as helpers, but they already knew that from Tabia. Zarita didn't quite catch their names, but accepted the offered eighteen year old women, who headed on up to their suite to move the crates for them, as well as prepare their evening meal.

"This makes things so easy," the assistant explained, glancing at their shoes. "Why don't we all look over your choices of gowns and colors?" Indeed, with their toe shoes as one of the two accepted styles, their feet did not have to be modified. All three wore pipe corsets as well. All that needed to be done was the acquisition of proper gowns. Lelane, as a mere assistant, was allowed to wear her own Ataro dresses, but needed to keep her long talons. That she also wore toe shoes was duly noted by the assistant. Each senator picked out a dozen gowns in various colors. Zarita tended to go with shades of red, while Celenia went with blue.

Each outfit had numerous parts, bewilderingly so for both women. Lelane signed to Celenia that she had no idea how to dress her. Sensing the three's distress, she declared, "Don't worry; your two young teens are highly skilled at dressing you. That's one of their duties." Each gown nearly touched the floor. The hoop skirt flared out twelve feet across at their feet. An hour later, the store's personnel had both women dolled up in one of their new gowns, sending them on their way back up to their suite. The other outfits would shortly be delivered to them.

As Lelane, an arm around each, led them out of the boutique, Celenia whispered, "I can hardly manage this! Lelane, don't let go of me! I can't see my feet. I'm afraid I'm going to fall down." Zarita picked up some frantic images from Celenia, when in the past she'd taken a fall. She saw how terribly difficult it was for her new lover to get back up from the floor by herself. What a difference there was between the highly independent Lena and Drina and her new lover, Celenia, who had none of the training of her two Gang of Ten members, let alone Amy. Still, Zarita had her own problems now. Her nails were a foot long! While she'd been able to manage six inch talons, these were already posing problems for her, and she was only trying to manipulate her giant hoop skirt into the elevator. Poor Celenia could only try to push herself into it, hoping she'd not lose her footing or balance and take a tumble.

As they stood before their own door, Zarita struggled to get a hold of her ID card to swipe it and thus open the door. "Oh this is darn near impossible!" she exclaimed, very much annoyed. Lelane quickly intervened and swiped the card for her.

As they entered, the aroma of food cooking greeted them. Their crates were no longer in the middle of their front room. One of their new servants poked her head out of the kitchen. "Hi. Supper will be ready in about ten minutes. You're crates are in your bedrooms. Your new gowns will be arriving shortly. Boutique called. Do you want us to undress you now or will your silent one be doing that later? We both need to leave in about a half hour."

"Lelane can do it tonight. We need to get used to wearing these," Zarita answered. *I am not about to admit defeat. If the other women senators can manage, so can we.* They made their way into their new dining room. In trying to get herself seated, she managed to knock her chair over. Zarita spat out a curse, but Lelane quickly picked it back up for her. She held it secure, while Zarita fought her billowing gown and got herself seated. Then, Lelane did the same for Celenia, before taking her usual seat to the right of Celenia, where she could easily assist her.

Soon, their two new servants brought dinner to the table for the trio. One said, "You can leave everything on the table. We'll clean it up in the morning when we arrive around seven. We have to be on our way by eight, so mornings will be a bit rushed. Sundays are our off days, but we'll leave enough leftovers for you to get by without much cooking. So will that be all for today?"

"Yes, thank you," Celenia replied graciously. The two teens nodded and left. Once they heard the door closing, she added, "Gosh Zarita. How are you going to manage to eat with such impossibly long nails? I ought to ask Tabia if she has to have Huburt feed her too."

"I must find a way to manage this, dear. If the other senators manage somehow, I must as well. I don't want to look like a fool when we get invited to dinner parties."

Celenia again felt a surge of emotion. If they did, she would look like a complete fool and would be totally dependent upon Lelane. Besides, she'd have to explain she had voluntarily had her arms removed only to become a complete failure as a queen. "Everywhere I go, Zarita, I'm going to be looked upon as some freak, a total failure, and a helpless one at that. I don't know why I ever agreed to be their senator."

"You're not a freak, dear. You're a very beautiful young woman and a terribly sexy one too, as far as I'm concerned. You don't have to tell them all of the truth. You can say you lost them in an accident, and leave it at that. After all, it was an 'accident' that you didn't become a queen, right?" Zarita twisted the situation around, making it more palatable to Celenia.

"I suppose so. We best eat. If you can't handle it, dear Zarita, Lelane can help you too. This is so embarrassing to be unable to do hardly anything at all for myself."

"You have to get used to it, just like I have to get used to these new claws of mine. We both have to get used to these monster gowns too. At least, we have a couple of days before we have to go to the first Senate meeting," Zarita suggested.

It took Zarita twice as long to dine as usual, even though she ate very little compared to what she had before she was body modified. Still, she found ways to manage. Celenia and Lelane finished up long before she did, but they waited patiently for her.

After dining, they headed to their rooms to sort out all

their new clothes and stow those they had brought with them. Zarita placed her giant crystals in separate drawers of her new dresser, but not before sensing each of them to make sure they'd not somehow lost their powers during the trip. Later on, Lelane came to her and led her into their study, where she'd hooked up their small communications system and computers.

"Thanks. I do need to learn all about computers and the communications systems, Lelane. We have to become very adept with them. I've so much to learn it's not funny. Oh, you're going to show me how to turn them on. Okay, I'll Mind Link to you, and we can get started!"

A bit later, typing slowly using the very tips of her nails, Zarita began using a computer for the first time. Lelane introduced her to the vast Web of online information that was available. From that first session, Zarita was hooked.

Then curiosity rose. "What does the 5 in Ashford-5 mean?"

"Oh, I can answer that one," Celenia spoke up. She was sitting mournfully beside the two watching and trying hard not to break down and cry at her total inability to help in any way. "Some stars have planets around them but in varying numbers. When the Imperium discovers a new star that has planets, they name them after the star. Your star is called Ashford. To avoid any confusion, the planet whose orbit is the closest to the star is called 1. The next one farther out is 2. So your world of Ashford-5 is the fifth planet out from the star called Ashford. Simple."

"Interesting. Now, a lot makes sense, Celenia. Hey, wait. What's on the other four planets closer to our star?" Zarita asked a key question. "And how many more are even further away from our star?"

Lelane sent, *Type in Ashford and hit the Search button.* Carefully, Zarita did as asked, while Celenia again could only watch over her shoulder. A page soon appeared.

She read: Ashford is a red dwarf star located at. . . She ignored the unintelligible galactic coordinates. On the outer rim. Eight planets are known to circle this star, but only one, Ashford-5, is inhabited by a primitive people and is a Closed World. Click here to see images of each. At first, Zarita clicked on her own world and an image taken from far above Tierra appeared on the monitor. She could barely make out the Goza Mountains and pointed with a long nail to roughly where Exchange City must lie. "I live around there." She also saw most all information about Ashford-5 was marked "Classified."

Then, she clicked on each of the other seven planets. Celenia spoke up, "See, the ones that are closer to your star are far hotter than yours, making them uninhabitable. Look, Ashford-1's temperature is several hundred degrees! Plastics would melt in that heat. It also doesn't have any atmosphere either. Ashford-6 is extremely frigid. Wow, look at those daytime temperatures — way, way negative. It has a surface that's covered in frozen ammonia and methane. Normally, those are gasses."

"Interesting. Say, look at Ashford-4 here. It is Classified too. What's there?" Zarita exclaimed. They read further.

Celenia translated, "Yes, I see. That world rotates one time during its entire passage around Ashford. That means the same side of the world is always pointing to Ashford. The temperatures there are broiling! But on the opposite side, it is always nighttime with very frigid temperatures too. Little atmosphere. Probably the only tolerable part is that small zone between eternal day and eternal night. I wonder why it is classified?"

"Don't know. I've never heard anyone talk about Ashford-4," Zarita mused, trying to recall if she'd ever heard that before during her Neva lifetime. She hadn't. "So how do we find out more about it?"

Click on it and when the box comes up, enter your senator ID number, Lelane suggested. *It might give you a bit more information.*

Zarita very carefully typed in her number using the tips of her long nails. When she depressed the Enter key, a bit more information appeared. Classified Imperium Research Station. Security Clearance Ten required. Some numbers that Zarita didn't recognize followed this. Celenia did. "That is the date the station was built, about fourteen years ago. Let's see, that'd be during the war with the Federation, I think. Level Ten is a very high level; probably we might be able to have

Emperor Kino see if he can find out for you."

"I can ask him the next time I see him," Zarita replied. "There is so darn much for me to learn!"

I can get you a hand-held pad you can take with you. It'll do the same thing as we're doing here, if you want, Lelane sent.

"Oh please do, Lelane. You can also get us more and fancier equipment. I have to know all about these electronic machines too," Zarita proclaimed.

"It's getting late. We best get to bed, if we are to rise by seven when the new servants come," Celenia suggested.

Zarita had a hard time pulling herself away from the computer, but she sensed the rising emotions of Celenia, who could not participate. She also picked up Celenia's desires for once more sharing their bedtime pleasures. She grinned, "Okay. Tomorrow's another day. Let's get to bed and have some private fun, shall we?"

"You know I love it and can't get enough of it, dear," Celenia replied. Relief was in her voice. An hour later amid a tangle of long hair, the three women finally fell asleep in Zarita's large bed. Celenia lay snuggled between Zarita and Lelane, but rather buried beneath a mountain of their hair. The only apparel the three wore were their pipe corsets, removed only while bathing.

The next morning, the three were awakened by the arrival of their two servants. While Lelane dressed herself, the two assistants dressed Zarita and Celenia. Then, they cleaned up the table, where they'd left the supper dishes, and prepared their breakfast. "Okay, we'll be back for an hour around noon today and then at six. Remember, we won't be here tomorrow. It's Sunday," one explained.

They'd just finished eating when Senator Tabia came by. "Okay, let's get you grooved in on how to operate your shuttle to get you to the Senate and back again. The only real problem is Lelane can't accompany Celenia into the Senate building proper. So Zarita, you'll have to assist Celenia, while you are at the Senate. Okay?" Again, Celenia felt like crying, but Zarita nodded.

She led them to their balcony. "Here is your shuttle.

Lelane, you help Celenia and yourself into the two rear seats. Zarita and I'll sit in the front. I'll sit in the driver's seat and show you what to do, Zarita. Believe me, the hardest part is for us to get into and out of the shuttle in these heels and gowns! Watch how I do it. It's always a struggle, that's for sure." Poor Celenia mostly fell into the shuttle, unable to keep her balance in anyway. Even Zarita found it terribly challenging and anything but graceful.

Unplussed, Tabia said, "Okay, first, push the Enter button there. Type in your address. I'll watch over your shoulder." Zarita did as asked. "There, now enter the shortcut Home. Okay, wherever you are, when you want to fly back here, just hit the shortcut that's displayed as Home. See, simple even with these nails of ours. Not enter this series." A bit later, Zarita had entered them and following Tabia's advice, labeled it Senate. "So when you want to go to the Senate, press the shortcut Senate. Simple."

She continued, "Now press the Destination button. See, it already has the Senate shortcut there along with your condo's address. Later, I can help you enter some of the other sights you might wish to visit. All you do is scroll to the one you want and touch it. Yes, like that. Now you press the Confirm message. That's it." A metallic voice repeated the address saying take off would be in thirty seconds. An Abort message appeared on the screen, allowing them a half-minute to cancel the proposed flight. Then, the shuttle lifted gently off and joined the thousands of other shuttles zipping through the skies filled with hundred story buildings. They were on their way to the Senate building, about a half hour away. Once there, she had Zarita take them home.

Once they landed on their balcony, Celenia asked, "Tabia, what does Lelane do all the time we are at the Senate?"

"Well, I would suggest she comes there with you and helps you both out of the shuttle. Then, she can take the shuttle home or anywhere she wants and perhaps do some shopping for you, returning at five to pick you both up. How does that sound?" Tabia suggested. "I'll enter some of the other sights Lelane might wish to visit."

"Now then, let's see if you can manage to disembark

without taking a nasty tumble. Slow and easy does it. It's harder than it looks. Perhaps the wise move would be to have Lelane get out first and catch either of you, if you should take a tumble," Tabia advised.

"Tabia! I'm scared! I can't do this," Celenia exclaimed. She'd managed to wiggle herself to the door, but couldn't remotely see her feet and her billowing dress was constantly in the way of everything.

She finally managed to get out, falling into the waiting arms of Lelane, who nearly fell over herself. Her own toe shoes were not enough to keep them both steady. Fortunately, Tabia was close at hand to keep them both from falling down on top of each other. "I think Lelane should get me out first so I can help them both," Zarita suggested.

"Yes, that would be wise. Well, I'll leave you to explore now. Practice, practice, practice, Celenia, Zarita," Tabia said coyly, as she left them.

"That's an understatement!" Zarita muttered. Celenia very nearly lost it again, Lelane pressed her head into her chest, comforting Celenia. "Okay, we practice this until we can somehow manage it. Let's see if we can get inside without falling down." The three got into and out of the shuttle a dozen times, before Celenia finally felt a bit of confidence that, if the two were there to catch her, she could get out without falling down. However, they did discover it was far easier for Celenia to get into the front seats than the rear ones. Zarita declared, "From now on, Celenia, you always sit up front with me."

"But if something goes wrong, Zarita, I can't do anything to help," she protested a little.

"Then nothing had better go wrong," she replied flatly. "Hey, I think our servants just came. Lunchtime. Come on; let's get inside."

Sunday morning, the three awoke once more lying together in a tangled mass of overlapping hair. Instead of getting up, Celenia rolled slightly and gave Zarita a passionate kiss. Soon, all three picked up where they'd left off the night before. They didn't get up until close to noon. "Lounge around day," Zarita announced. "Why dress?" The three giggled and headed to the kitchen to see what they could find to eat. Later,

Lelane helped them into a simple day dress and tied their toe shoes securely. Then, Zarita got more lessons on the computer and the Web.

Monday came altogether too soon. Right on time, their servants came. Shortly, the two senators found themselves once more dressed in their huge hoop skirt gowns. After eating, Lelane helped them into the shuttle. Zarita followed Tabia's instructions, and a half hour later, their practice session paid off, as both new senators managed to get out of the shuttle without taking a nasty fall. Senator Tabia was there to greet them. "Follow me, senators," she said formally.

Today, all three wore their ULAT boxes strapped around their waists, though Zarita also wore her fancy jeweled belt as well. As they entered the building, a scanner read their ID cards allowing them inside. Zarita kept her arm around Celenia constantly, steadying both women, who followed Senator Tabia. They took an elevator down to the second subfloor and took their seats in the Ataro System. Meanwhile, the giant amphitheater filled up with several thousand senators, taking their places on some dozen tiers. The most important senators, those from Proxima Prime, sat on the first layer opposite the central platform just below them. Still, the many ULAT boxes carried all of the conversations being spoken anywhere within the theater, creating a uniform background of sounds. Far upwards on the top row sat the senators from all the Closed Worlds, except Tierra.

From where she was sitting, Zarita looked around and spotted around two dozen women senators. Most wore gowns like the one she was wearing, but three had their hair rather short and wore suits like the men. She noticed hair colors varied widely, far more so than the hues of their suits. Black, brown, blonde, and red hair predominated in a vast spectrum of shades. At last, a man rose and took the stage. Tabia whispered, "That's the current Senate President Abraham Talos."

ULAT boxes translated his words into many languages. Zarita listened. "Welcome senators one and all to our fall session. We are pleased to introduce several new senators. First, we have Senator Zarita Valen of Ashford-5 and Senator

Celenia Agahve of Winno-3. Will you two please rise?"
Dutifully the two rose and received a polite round of applause.
He went on to introduce several more new senators, before
launching into the business at hand. Almost at once, Zarita
was bored. The senators were excellent public speakers, but
they had very little of substance to actually say. As she looked
around, she noticed many other senators had small devices in
their hands and were studying them, rather than listening. She
knew she had to get one of them too or go mad. Celenia had no
such possibility for diversions, however.

Lunchtime came none too soon for the two new
senators, who followed Tabia. She led them to the spacious
underground dining hall and helped them through the buffet
line. Zarita took enough for both her and Celenia. Once they
got seated, she began to feed Celenia and herself. However,
they were continually interrupted by other senators dropping
by to meet and greet them. Tabia finished up long before the
other two and headed off to the restroom.

Just then, another pair of senators walked up to them.
Zarita blinked, the contrast between the two women was quite
startling. "Welcome senators. I'm Ari Laag from Acer-4. You
probably haven't heard of it." She was dressed in a male
senator's suit and shoes, her short black hair looked like most
men's cuts, but her foot long talons and her prominent bust
were visible proof she wasn't a man. She was holding hands
with another senator. "This is my girlfriend, Senator B'nath
Glog of Groz-3." B'nath looked like themselves, Zarita noted.
Her billowing hoop skirt was a light blue satin, and her wavy
hair was very blonde, falling nearly to the floor. Her nails were
as long as Ari's, painted to match her gown. Both women wore
toe shoes and appeared to be in their mid-twenties.

"Please, continue eating. We don't want to interrupt you
or to make you rise. Lord knows how hard it is for us in these
shoes and nails," Ari took charge. "We couldn't help noticing
you are romantically inclined, right?" Celenia flushed.

Zarita glanced at Celenia and replied, "Is it that
obvious?"

Ari giggled, "Not at all. Probably we two are the only
ones who saw the signs. It's okay for two senators to be

94

romantically involved or even married for that matter. B'nath and I wanted to make a suggestion and give you an invitation. You both are being quite practical in not going with those awful beehive fake hairdos that so many others and spouses are. Natural is the only way to go."

"Go ahead and tell her, time is running short," B'nath broke in, squeezing Ari's hand.

"Yes, well, Senator Celenia, you must have had an awful accident. Anyway, you would find everything so vastly easier to manage if you wore a man's suit as I do. We just cannot imagine how terribly difficult this must be for you, Senator Celenia. Also, we are having a small dance at our suite this Friday night around six. Wear what you have on, there's not enough time to change before the dance and party. We'll provide supper at six. Floor sixty-five at six. Women like ourselves need to stick together, if you know what I mean." She winked at the two. "We won't take no for an answer. We want to get to know you both. You'll be there, right?" Senator Ari didn't leave them any wiggle room.

Zarita looked at Celenia and then said, "Okay, we'll be there at six. Do we need to bring anything?"

"No, just yourselves and be prepared for a good time," Senator Ari replied. "As far as the men's suit goes, we both thought Senator Zarita would also look good in one, but then perhaps it's Senator Celenia who prefers to be feminine in your relationship. Still, you would find getting around far easier, senator, dressed as a man, that is. Anyway, we'll let you finish your lunch. See you then, bye." She led B'nath out of the large dining hall.

"Do you suppose this is a good idea?" Celenia asked, just a bit timidly. "We don't know them at all. I can ask Tabia if it's safe."

"Good idea. I didn't sense any hostility from them, so it's probably okay. She does have a point; you could manage far better if you wore a man's suit."

"But then I wouldn't look like a woman. I don't want to look like a man or act like one, not really, unless you want me to," she amended her declaration.

"I love you as you are. Come on; we don't want to be

late this first time. So far, we are both managing the dresses," Zarita replied. "I think she looks a little strange dressed like that." Celenia giggled, for she thought so too.

Lelane was right on time to pick them up. When they arrived home, their two servants had dinner waiting. Just as they finished eating, several of the other Closed World senators dropped by to welcome Zarita and to chat. Besides welcoming Zarita, they also asked about Ashford-5's previous Senator Isabella Valen and wanted to know if she was a relative of Isabella's. By this time, they had all heard of Senator Isabella's kidnaping and torture. They were saddened to hear of her demise and promised to keep an eye on Zarita.

Friday night came quickly. Lelane picked them up at the Senate building and drove them home, where their servants had supper waiting. By the time the two had finished, it was nearly six. Her arm securely around Celenia, Zarita led them up to the sixty-fifth floor suite. A large placard read: Senator Ari Laag. Senator B'nath Glog. Soft music could be just barely heard from the door as Zarita knocked.

"Hi! Come on in," Senator Ari greeted them enthusiastically, opening the door for the two. "We're all in the front room." The layout of all of the suites were identical, Imperium standards at work once more. They found two other young couples sitting on one sofa and B'nath sitting on a second one. She motioned for the two to come sit on hers. Zarita carefully collected Celenia's long hair out of the way and helped her sit down as gracefully as possible, before sitting herself. Ari came along in her suit and sat down beside B'nath and Celenia. She introduced Senator Klarissa Zea and her wife and Senator Dagoma Lok and her wife. These two senators also wore the billowing hoop skirts, as did their wives.

"Well, this is all of we like-minded women in the Senate," Ari said, pulling her feet up and under her on the couch, making herself comfortable, almost as if flaunting her freedom of motion in her men's suit. "Like I told you, we need to stick together and watch out for each other. Mostly from bigoted men, that is."

"So Senator Celenia, what happened to your arms, if you don't mind sharing," Senator Klarissa asked sympathetically.

"I made a bad mistake about two years ago now. I'm still trying to get used to my life like this. I'm so helpless now, but I have a personal assistant around our suite, and Zarita helps me while I'm at the Senate. Honestly, I'm mostly petrified of life now, Senator Klarissa."

"Please, let's drop the formalities. Just Klarissa. I, we just cannot imagine how awful it must be for you, Celenia. Still, you are lucky to have found Zarita; she's darn cute. If you need anything, just ask. We'd all love to help. By the way, we all just love her incredible jewelry. We've never seen anything quite like those before."

Zartia smiled. *They have no idea!* "I had them custom made for me back on Ashford-5. Thanks. I am never without them. Say, how come we senators have to have such impossibly long nails anyway? No one ever gave me a good reason why, only that it was mandatory."

Ari laughed. "Senate rules made by men millennia ago. You see, originally, all senators were men. When the first women were elected to the Senate, they created quite a stir among all the testosterone-driven men. Rumors go, they wanted to find a way to discourage women from becoming senators. They passed a law that female senators must have at least twelve inch talons, making life miserable for us. That didn't stop us, so they then tried to dictate fashions. Ha! That was a fizzle, but they did force through a law that female senators must wear either toe shoes of the Ataro Empire style — that's because those first female senators were from your system — or else wear the current styles made popular by the many wives of the senators. You can thank all of the wives for the giant platforms and those enormous hoop skirts of yours. The rules state senators must dress in the style of their wives or the men themselves. That's where they underestimated we women! Some of us have donned men's suits just to insult them. However, not every female senator who wears a man's suit is one of us. Many do it just to annoy the male senators, you see."

Ari went on, "Anyway, we don't have any choice, but to have these nails and toe shoes. I'm glad you both didn't opt for those four inch platforms with their ten inch stilettos. My god, so many women have broken their ankles or legs it's not funny. Yet, many wives still do," Ari spat out as if concluding the discussion. "Celenia, you probably could manage better if you wore a suit like mine, vastly more comfortable, but it's certainly not feminine though." She winked at both Celenia and Zarita.

Zarita replied, "No, that it isn't. Celenia is a very beautiful woman. Why hide it?" Several chuckled and grinned at the two.

Klarissa teased, "Aye, that she certainly is, a real beauty. So Zarita, you best keep an eye on her." She gave Celenia a flirting wink, and Celenia grinned.

"Well, the limo ought to be here soon. I've got tickets to the ballet tonight. After that, we'll return here for our own dance," Ari declared. Thus, Zarita and Celenia began their weekly cultural evenings with these three couples. Every Friday night, they were taken out to a formal event, followed afterwards with slow, romantic dancing to soft, wonderful music, compliments of Ari, who always knew how to find the very best in entertainment that could be found on Proxima Prime. These four couples became extremely close friends by the time of the three week long Winter Break. Of course, it was always a constant seventy-five degrees on Proxima Prime, no matter where one was at geographically. The planet-wide climate control saw to that detail.

During these many weeks, Zarita continued to learn about anything and everything, keeping Lelane very busy lining up the next topic for her to read and digest. With her new handheld mobile computer-phone, she was able to continue reading during the long and usually boring Senate meetings. Very little concerned either Celenia or Zarita's worlds, but Celenia could only sit patiently listening. Occasionally, she glanced at what Zarita was reading. More than once, she nearly burst out crying because she felt so completely helpless.

Only at night when the three of them finally got into bed did Celenia become truly alive, doing what she could to enhance the pleasures of Zarita and Lelane. She hated to have to get up in the mornings, because she loved the warmth and love the three shared together. She especially treasured waking up snuggled between the two with their long hair entwined from their night's playful romps.

The Senate discussions at the beginning of this fall session focused on preparing the budget for the coming year. Much was still being allocated for recovery from the recent war's destruction. Later, several senators brought up the relocation of their own world's population — relocations that had been ordered to make room on their worlds for the soldiers fighting the war. Now, millions wanted to return to their home worlds. Significantly, they also wanted reparation for their monetary and physical losses sustained. Lawsuits had been filed, but these senators hoped the Senate could come to an agreeable arrangement, thereby avoiding the lengthy, nasty, and prolonged litigation in the courts. Senator Celenia voted in favor of giving those who were displaced some recompense for their losses.

She was in the minority. Senate President Abraham's motion to deny them recompense passed, based on two factors. One, the Imperium was now financially strapped and could not afford to make such payments. Two, most felt these people had done their patriotic duty in moving, as their contribution to the overall war effort. "In war, everyone must do what they can to support our soldiers who do the fighting for us," he claimed. Many agreed with him.

After the voting was tabulated, Celenia commented to Zarita, "Many will find this decision a personal insult. I don't think we've heard the last of this one."

"Why do you say that?" Zarita asked, finally becoming slightly interested in the topic.

"At this time, nearly everyone has read or heard just how this war began. That is, they've heard all about the nasty business on Gamelon-3, and how Emperor Kino had to intervene to uncover the true cause of the war. I wouldn't be surprised to hear some people believing the Imperium authorities are completely incompetent and have fomented the war to line their own pockets. Many companies that deal in arms and munitions have made incredible profits. Yet, millions of people were forced to abandon their homes and lives, moved to other worlds not of their own choice or free will. Look for a backlash. That's my prediction anyway," Celenia answered.

Zarita ran her long nails through her hair. "Interesting dear. We don't have that problem on Ashford-5. Hardly any can actually read or write for that matter."

"What?" Celenia looked genuinely surprise. Then, she nodded, "Oh, I keep forgetting your world is still in the Bronze-Iron Age. Meaning most are illiterate."

Zarita let out a small huff. "Well, the nobles have the time to teach their children to read and write, especially those in the towers and the rulers. Some of us aren't illiterate, but you are right. Most everyone else is. I aim to be very educated, Celenia. There is just so much to learn, isn't there?"

Celenia smiled. "I never thought of it that way, but yes there is. No one can know everything. I mean, I don't know a darn thing about physics and chemistry. I was trying to learn all about adjudicating disputes. Well, obviously I didn't do well in that one. Now I can't do much more than sit here and listen. I have to have you press the proper voting button for me. I can't see what you see in me, Zarita. But honestly, I couldn't be doing this without you. I'd no idea being a senator would be so hard for me. I should've said no when they asked me."

"I'm glad you didn't or we'd never have met," Zarita replied and slipped her arm around Celenia, giving her a reassuring hug, while some senator was continuing to talk on the main floor.

Two weeks before the Winter Break, at their Friday night gathering, Ari asked, "So Zarita, what are you and Celenia planning to do over the three week break that's coming up soon? Going back home or do you have a vacation estate to go to?"

Rather surprised at having forgotten about it, Zarita explained, "Queen Isabella Valen willed her old estate to be used as our senator's home away from home. It used to be Senator Carlos' estate, where he tortured her and her two wives. President Snarry gave the estate to her as compensation. I certainly don't want to go there. I'm not going back to Ashford-5 during the winter. My goodness, who wants to deal with twenty feet of snow!"

Ari gasped at the snow, and Zarita digressed for several minutes outlining Tierra's strange, harsh weather. Ari's eyes flashed, reflecting her latest bright idea. She suggested, "You know, you could sell that estate and use the funds to buy one here on Proxima Prime. Then, you wouldn't have to travel far at all, when you wanted a total break from the hustle and bustle of Senate life. If you want, I can help you with that."

"Would you? I'd love the help. It sounds like a very good idea to me. Thanks Ari," Zarita replied. *It would be a good idea to have a backup place here on Proxima Prime. Having to pack up and take a deep space transport to get to that world is not only a hassle but also problematical if trouble comes.*

"Great, Zarita. Let's see what we can find for you," Ari grinned. She dove into the problem at once, though Zarita sensed that Ari wanted something more meaningful to occupy her mind than the boring Senate meetings.

"Okay, what is the prime requirement that you want?" Ari asked.

"Security. If trouble comes, I want a place where I can relax and know I'm as safe as possible here on Proxima Prime. A little grass would be nice though. I never thought I'd miss grass and trees so much," Zarita replied. Only now did she begin to realize how much she was missing Tierra. As Neva, she'd been blinded by her intense desire to be the Great Lady, working her way up the power ladder. *I've changed so much,* she thought. *Why? How?*

Mid-week, Ari and B'nath took the two to see a few possible estates that were for sale here on Proxima Prime. After entering the coordinates of their next destination, Ari explained, "We have to travel halfway around the world to get to this one. It's up at the north pole, but it is supposedly a very secure compound. Guess we'll soon see. Be there in an hour. Sit back and watch the sights."

Zarita did just that, but soon complained, "Ari, it all looks the same. Skyscraper after skyscraper. In fact, they are all laid out pretty much identical from block to block."

Ari giggled. "Silly, the whole planet is one giant city. Imperium standardization. Of course, it's all laid out the same. No creativity whatsoever. That's what I hate about Imperium civilization. Sometime, you two have to come to my world of Acer-4. Perhaps, we can spend our summer vacation there. You both have an open-ended invite to come anytime you want."

An hour later, their shuttle landed on what looked like a small spaceport pad. Zarita looked confused, but Ari explained, "We are not there yet. This compound is on Subfloor Two, that's beneath the surface two levels down. Very limited access. See, we've actually landed on an elevator. We're going down now." As Zarita looked out of the windows, the whole section of the pad began lowering; the spaceport disappeared, replaced with steel and concrete walls. Finally, the downward motion stopped. "Now we are being moved along on a mechanical conveyor system that'll stop just outside the compound's main entrance. The realtor is supposed to meet us here and show us around. This is going to be cool! Trust me, Zarita. Of course, I've never had the chance to spend someone's millions of credits before." She giggled.

The realtor was a middle aged woman, very business-like and quite knowledgeable about this property. "Senator Zarita Valen?" she asked, looking at the four. Ari pointed to her. After introducing herself, she explained, "This high security compound belonged to a former general of the Security Forces — they guard both the President and the Senate members — a very top man. Anyway, he recently died of old age, and his estate wants to settle his affairs quickly. You'll find this place is therefore extremely well equipped. This is the main entrance. A security code is required for any shuttle to activate the conveyor system that bought your shuttle here to the door. If you will follow me, these are blast-resistant doors. In fact, the entire complex is designed to withstand even a nuclear bomb." Zarita didn't know what a bomb was, but it sounded bad.

"This hallway we're entering is filled with sensors that alert you to the presence of both the usual poisons as well as blasters being brought in by whoever is entering. A secondary door right here will automatically close should such a threat be detected. While your air, water, and refuse is part of the planet-wide system, the compound filters them as well, in case of trouble."

"Now, here is the communications center. As you can see, the general has installed a massive system, all state of the art, I'm told." A wall of flat, large monitors covered one of the walls. "This video surveillance system shows all the possible entrances to the compound and from several angles. Now that one there is important. It is the entrance point for your commercial purchases. Say you order out for dinner or you have just purchased a new dress. It will be delivered to your address, which is N-2C42, North Pole, Sublevel 2, Section C, compound 42. Deliveries arrive then above ground at this elevator. Once you are satisfied the delivery is correct — again the elevator is equipped with bomb sensors and such, you press this button, and the elevator brings it down to this entrance point, just over there beyond the main entrance doors."

"Security, security. Ace Security monitors the entrances and is automatically notified whenever there is even an attempted break-in. They automatically send out a security patrol to check on things. So the place is heavily protected, even when you are away at your Senate meetings. Further, you can also take this elevator up to the first floor. A skyscraper is above you and the boutique, nail salon, hair salon, grocery store, and many other shops are there on the first and second floors, as always. Very convenient, you see. Now let's see the rest of the compound."

She led them into the Game Room, where an automatic pool table, dartboard, gaming table, and many more tables were arranged in a tasteful large room with a soft red carpet underfoot. From there, the hall led to a spacious living room, whose ceiling gave the appearance of natural sunlight coming in from overhead. Connecting with this room were the dining room, a study, and a large kitchen-pantry. Further down the hallway were a huge bathroom and the bedrooms, consisting of a spacious master bedroom with walk-in closets and four guest rooms.

"Now next, we have the cream de mint. Ta da!" They entered what looked like an outdoor patio opening onto a garden area, complete with a swimming pool. "Yes, that's real grass and dirt beneath it. Over there are the many flowerbeds. Lawn chairs. Pool. I'm told the general used to spend hours out here. I can see why, though if this were my place, I'd put in more flowers."

"Now then, the general had a staff of three to care for the place. A cook, a maid, and a gardener. They've stuck around since his death, keeping the place spotless. They're willing to stay on for the new owners, but you're under no obligation to keep them. You certainly may hire your own staff. One final feature I just *must* show you. This way please." She led them back inside.

"Of course, the general had his own deep space transport and docking facilities. Here is the elevator that takes you up one level to his ship or your ship now, if you purchase this compound, as it comes with the compound. Again, this elevator is fully equipped with bomb detectors and the like. The ship's hangar is likewise totally secure."

Next, she went through the whole process of accepting deliveries, of going up to the transport, and how flights were arranged. "It's all done by computers. From your comm center, you make all of your arrangements, and then ride the elevator up. Once inside, you merely press the Execute button, and the computers take over. The whole flight is fully automated. The general was, you see, a very important man."

Zarita was tremendously impressed with the complex. "I think it's perfect. So how are we on the financing aspect?"

"Senator Zarita, I won't lie to you. Your existing estate just outside Caltran is worth far more than this small complex. If I take it in trade for this complex, the best I can do is give you an additional ten million credits. What with my traveling expense there and back and along with my profit, ten million more is about all I dare offer you. If you wish to sell it yourself, I'm sure you could likely net perhaps as much as an additional twenty million credits," she said rather apologetically. While she was talking, Zarita picked up her surface thoughts and knew she was being fairly honest with her.

104

"As far as I'm concerned, this place is perfect for our needs. Being a senator is a full time occupation. I really don't have time to market the Caltran estate. I accept your offer. Let's do it," Zarita replied, rather excited about this whole complex. The one thing it offered was total security. Having her own deep space transport also figured into her thinking. Now, she would not be dependent on commercial flights or those of the Ataro senators. The deal offered her much more independence.

The gardener was an older man, Rupert, who came once per week to tend the lawn and gardens. The maid was a middle aged woman, Zela, who also came by once per week to clean and straighten up the compound. The cook, Allie, was a local young woman, who used to drop by and fix the general lunches and suppers. Zarita retained them all, setting up automatic payments for all three. Even though Allie's services would only be needed when she was here, this kept the woman quite pleased and helped guarantee her loyalty.

The only drawback was the compound was an hour and a half from the Senate building, far too distant for daily travel. Still, here she could be safe during breaks, if she didn't want to travel to the rim of the galaxy. Also, she could spend weekends here. Ari suggested she could host parties here as well.

During the winter break, Ari and B'nath helped the three move in and stayed with them, inaugurating one of the guest bedrooms. The three purchased additional clothing and stayed in the master bedroom, whose bed was more than large enough to hold Zarita, Celenia, and Lelane. Having Ari around for the three weeks made for a very relaxing time.

Ari loved to play pool and soon had Zarita addicted to the game, as well as darts. More importantly, Ari had some knowledge of the comm center and was able to work out details of its operation, teaching them to Zarita and Lelane. Ari was also a trove of information. It was at this point that Zarita realized just how much she really didn't know, compared to Ari and others who had formal educations. *Tierra really is a primitive world. There's so very much we're ignorant of!*

One afternoon, as Zarita was studying a bit more, Ari looked over her shoulders to see what she was reading. "Ah, how diamonds are made. Cool topic, Zarita," she commented.

"You know about these things?" Zarita asked. No longer was she surprise at all that Ari knew. It was her own ignorance showing.

"A little. It's carbon. Soft carbon is used in pencils, but if it's put under a lot of pressure and heat, it solidifies more and becomes harder. If even more pressure and heat are applied, it gets even more solid, becoming diamonds," Ari explained.

"So it takes up less space, but is still the same thing?" Zarita asked. An idea was forming in her mind. "Could it compress one of my gems into a smaller, harder gem?"

"Sure, you'd need one of the geologist's compactor machines to it. They make artificial gems that way. You know, take the raw materials, and compact them down into the gemstone form of the mineral. I bet Laniard's could do it for you. Let's check, shall we?" Ari suggested.

Two days later, Zarita sacrificed one of her spherical germanium crystals to this experiment. "Senator Zarita, you've such unusual gemstones in your jewelry. Well, Ashford-5 is known to be a big producer of fuel from such minerals. Yes, I can compact this one down. It'll be about the size of the stones in your earrings. Takes a few minutes," the geologist replied.

A half hour later, Zarita held the new stone in her palm. It was about the size of the others in her many pieces of jewelry. Furthermore, the process had not cost very much. While pretending to admire it, she found it still retained its amplification powers. However, it did require a re-tuning to her unique frequency. She arranged to have the other nine spheres also compacted. She then took them to a jewelers on the second floor of the skyscraper above her compound and had them substituted for ten that were in her earrings. When she later put them back on, her ears were really being stretched taut. They still weighted the same as they had when they were spheres a foot across! Still, the amount of power that was at her instant command was huge. And that was the entire point as far as Zarita was concerned.

With Lelane's help, she discovered a mineral site where she could purchase similar raw germanium crystals. Usually, they were sold as samples for survey geological work and for classroom use in the training of future geologists. She ordered six more, only because she had no idea if they would possess the same amplification properties as those she found on Tierra. To her amazement, they did just that. A week later, she'd replaced all of her smaller crystals with these compacted new ones, stowing the older ones in a single pod silk pouch. Although she didn't yet know the extent of her powers, she could funnel the raw power of ten Circles working together, an amazing amount of psi energies.

With her secure compound, power gems, and her own deep space transport, Zarita finally felt secure on Proxima Prime. However, it wasn't enough to enable her to make telepathic contact to Queen Amy back on Tierra, half a galaxy away. Still, she was quite satisfied now.

As their enjoyable winter break came to an end, Zarita knew quite a lot more than she had at its start. As she and her friends walked into the first Senate session after the break, she felt far more at peace and confident. In time, she thought, I'll know far more than I do now.

As the four made their slow, careful way into the large building, an enormous explosion shook the very ground. All four stumbled in their tiny toe shoes, nearly falling down. Celenia would have taken a nasty fall had not Zarita reacted and used her telekinetic powers to pull her erect. "What the hell was that?" Ari cried out, her arms waving like a windmill, as she caught her balance and steadied B'nath.

"Don't know. Are there earthquakes here?" Celenia ventured. "We have some on Winno-3."

"Hell no. This whole planet's a totally controlled environment. No such thing as earthquakes. Hell, the ground itself is miles below us, I think," Ari stated. Her voice carried a note of worry though. They four headed on inside and took their seats.

As Zarita and Celenia sat down beside Senator Tabia, she asked, "Did you two feel that? The whole building shook!"

"Yes, I almost fell, Tabia. Ari says there are no earthquakes on Proxima Prime. That sure felt like one to me," Celenia replied, rather concerned.

Senate President Abraham opened the meeting, but made no mention of the quake. The boring morning meeting was abruptly interrupted by a general from the Senate Security Forces. After whispering something to Senator Abraham, he took center stage and spoke. His bass voice carried traces of fear, Zarita noticed.

"The explosion that occurred earlier this morning just before nine was a bomb going off near the fuel depot of the spaceport close to the Presidential Office. It was definitely sabotage! The Society for Freedom claimed responsibility for the bombing. This is a terrorist organization. Thirty workers were killed and dozens taken to the hospital. The refueling depot sustained major damage. I would suggest you senators take some prompt action. That is all," he stepped down and marched out of the room, despite many questions being called out by a number of senators.

Ari sent Zarita a text message with a Web location. Using her long talons, she carefully typed it in, and began reading the Society for Freedom's web page. She then showed it to Celenia. President Abraham began speaking rather loudly. "Essentially this terrorist organization is demanding all relocated populations be moved back into their original worlds and their original homes. Obviously, that cannot be done. In some cases, homes were leveled to make army bases. Besides, we've already ruled these people must make sacrifices, just as our brave soldiers did protecting us. I would like to entertain a motion to declare this Society for Freedom to be nothing more than a terrorist organization. As such, it should be outlawed, declared illegal, and its members rounded up to stand trial for murder."

An hour passed by swiftly, as senator after senator wanted to go on record in opposition to this new terrorist group. Celenia whispered, "They are posturing, so when they return to their home worlds, they can claim they are violently opposed to this terrorist group. The real vote is hours away, I think." Tabia agreed with her assessment.

The actual voting took place shortly before the end of the day. Naturally, it passed unanimously. Lelane again picked the two up and drove them home, where their servants had dinner waiting for them. They'd only barely finished, when Ari and B'nath came knocking on their door. Both had already changed into more comfortable clothes.

"So wasn't that something. It's on the news. Come on. I'll show you," Ari gushed, heading for their small comm center. Zarita helped Celenia up, and with Lelane and Zarita on either side of her, the trio joined the other two senators, who were sitting on one of their couches, watching the news. For a few minutes, they watched the images being shown. "The reporters are making a huge deal of this bombing, because there hasn't been an incident of sabotage on Proxima Prime in ages and ages," Ari declared.

She went on, "Usually the terrorists are religious extremists, I think. Most every world has some of them. Within the Imperium, the most widespread religion is the Church of the Holy Lord, but there are also several others too. Like the Hektites, the Devil's Disciples, the Ganges, and the Unification Church. What religions do you have on Ashford, Zarita?" Ari asked curiously.

"Er, we don't have any religions that I know about. I think in ancient times there might have been one. What is a religion anyway?" Zarita asked, annoyed that here was yet another whole arena about which she knew nothing.

B'nath explained, "People believe the universe has a Supreme Being or Creator who made it and us. Of course, it's all based on faith in a power greater than ours, you see. Someone created the galaxy and us. They pray to their god or gods for nearly everything, from help, to guidance, and to be cured of an incurable illness. Some believe after we die we have this soul that then goes to some afterlife, which is heaven if you've been good or Hell if you've been bad. But the different religions differ on all such matters. The Church of the Holy Lord, for example, believes there's only one Universal God, who made the galaxies and us as well. They believe we should lead exemplary lives, so we can attain the Positive Afterlife. Should we not, then we're doomed to the Negative Afterlife. Of course, one must take this all on faith you see. No one's been to either and come back to tell the rest of us about it."

Ari broke in, "There are some splinter divisions within

the Holy Lords that believe their salvation lies through getting all others to accept their views by any means possible. They're really just thugs and terrorists really. The Hektites believe each world has its own god or goddess who watches over that world. Thus, they believe you should pray to your local deity and offer sacrifices on their behalf. The really nasty Hektites sacrifice young maidens. The Senate has outlawed that splinter group, but they've merely gone underground."

B'nath continued, "The Devil's Disciples believe we're already in Hell. These many worlds are Hell, and our goal in life is to rise above the zillions of temptations of Hell and achieve Spiritual Salvation, so when we die, we can ascend to the Positive Afterlife. If we do not, we are doomed to repeat it all again, until we do ascend. On the other hand, the Ganges believe we're gods ourselves, entombed within these physical bodies, and we're doomed to live in this Universe, until we're able to rise above all physical needs, including those of the body. You must discard all possessions, deny all carnal cravings, remain chaste and pure, and fast and meditate, until you are able to step out of this Universe and into the Positive Afterlife or the Ultimate Heaven as they call it. Of course, no one except their founder, Ganges, has ever actually done it."

Ari finished up, "The Unification Church believes each of us is a Holy Temple and that we're a god or goddess. We should strive to become one with all Nature, and thus seek a Holy Union with the Universe. B'nath and I belong to the Unification Church. So what do your people believe, Zarita?"

"Well, I can't speak for anyone but myself. I know I'm not my body. I'm an immortal spiritual being. That much I do know. Many on Tierra also know this truth about themselves. We've this thing called Basic Therapy, which I received, and, through it, discovered my true nature. As far as gods go, Tierra used to have a pantheon of gods and goddesses, but that was in ancient times. You know, a goddess of fertility and so on. No one worships them anymore, not for centuries, though some blame them when bad things happen. I think that's natural."

"Well, that's okay too. Just look out for the religious fanatics. Every religion has them, particularly the Hektites and the Holy Lords. Some of them will go to any extreme possible, even suicide bombings to try to convince others their path is the right one," Ari concluded. "I wouldn't be surprised to hear these Society for Freedom members turn out to be Holy Lords." The four then chatted about other things.

Chapter 7 Conspiracies Executed

During the ensuing weeks, additional terrorist bombings occurred. Not limited to just Proxima Prime, but ten other heavily populated worlds were struck. Worse, there was now a fuel shortage. As the Spring Break approached, Senate President Abraham explained, "Due to the enormous consumption of fuel during the war and now on all the massive reconstruction throughout the Imperium, there is a fuel shortage. It'll only get worse for the time being. I urge each and every one of you senators to visit your home worlds , explain the nature of this shortage to your people, and get their agreement to implement conservation legislation. If we all conserve fuel, we can ride this minor crisis out. President Snarry has assured me he's on top of the situation, but that we must all do our part."

That evening, Ari commented, "If President Snarry is on top of the situation, then why must we all do our part? Eh? Answer me that one if you can." The four laughed.

President Snarry had other things on his mind when he met with Legate Emeryk. "Do you know anything about this?" He slapped a pile of documents onto his desk, quite angry. "I'm being investigated!"

"By who?" asked Legate Emeryk. This was news to him. He already had as much dirt on the president as he needed.

"Emperor Kino! That's who. The man's coming after me, and I've still got six years left on my term. The new telepaths have been earning their pay, that's for sure. Just look at what Kino is looking into! The Rockham Affair. Hell, he's even looking into that whole Neva mess and even going back to that awful mess with Senator Isabella Valen. Now this damnable fuel shortage happens on my watch. Hell, we had no idea that this was even coming. What the hell do I do, Emeryk?"

"Ride it out. He can't possibly connect you to the Isabella affair. You had only a minor indiscretion with Neva.

No one will fault you over that one. You could be in trouble if the true story of the Rockham Affair becomes public, though. You might consider having a few of those who know the details have fatal accidents."

"Good god no! That could too easily be traced back to me. I tell you, this Emperor Kino is no fool. He's gunning for me, Emeryk. But you're right. He might not be able to prove anything substantial. If he presents here-say evidence, I can go after him then. You're right, calm down and ride this thing out. But what's going on with the fuel shortage?"

"I've no idea. I'll look into it," Legate Emeryk promised.

At this same time, the Consortium met again. Baal declared, "The fuel shortage is working to perfection. Well done, Yinko, well done indeed."

"Yes, but it's time to get rid of Snarry," Yinko suggested. "We need someone we can control directly, not this fool Snarry. He bends in whatever direction the wind blows. Have you looked over the Legates?"

Bindaz replied, "Yes, Legate Donat is our best candidate. However, the Senate's favorite is H-cubed, Legate Helyeon H. Hoon. He's always getting his mug on the evening news, making him rather popular with the masses. He is the likely Senate choice to fill out the remainder of Snarry's term. However, we cannot so easily manipulate him. Our best chance lies with Legate Emeryk Donat. He is a former ID Minister and knows how the game is actually played."

Baal concluded, "Okay then. It's time to call in our trump card. Force Senate President Abraham to get this Emeryk fellow chosen. I'll get in touch with the Holy Lords and arrange another 'accident' soon. Yinko, you take care of Abraham, will you?"

"Aye. Emperor Kino's investigation isn't really panning out. If it was, we could sit back and let Kino do our dirty work for us. Snarry's been too clever for Kino. I'll speak to Abraham tonight. The Senate's breaking for three weeks, so it'll be good timing indeed."

"Come on, Celenia. Come to Tierra with me. I want my

dear friends to meet you," Zarita pleaded.

"Okay, but I am obligated to stop at Winno-3 and make my official report to Queen Altha first. Are we going to go with Senator Tabia?" Celenia asked.

"No, let's try my new transport. Lelane and I have it all programmed to take us to Winno-3 and then Ashford-5 and back again. I am itching to see if this really works," Zarita countered.

"Isn't this automation something else?" Zarita exclaimed. She and Lelane sat in the pilot and navigator's seats respectively. Celenia was safely buckled in one of the passenger seats. "Let's double check the readouts; I'm a bit nervous about this." It was the next day, and they'd each brought a crate of clothing and personal items onboard. Now, they were safely inside her new deep space transport ship. The two checked over the proposed flights. In order to get to Ashford-5, they had to stop and refuel on Winno-3. This would give Celenia time to make her official report to Queen Altha before continuing on to Tierra.

"Here goes nothing," Zarita said. Holding her breath, she reached out with her long index fingernail and touched the Execute button. A monitor displayed this leg of their trip and gave them thirty seconds to abort it. Then, the elevator began rising, taking the ship up to the surface. Shortly after that, the computer controlled systems activated. Slowly, her new ship lifted off, and then jumped into hyperspace. With the new fuel restrictions in place, they took three days to get to Winno-3. They planned to spend one day there and then three more to get to Tierra, where they would spend a week before returning. Zarita wanted to at least talk to the High Council of Lords, and impress upon them the vital necessity of getting the people of Tierra literate and educated.

Emperor Kino and Queen Altha met them upon their arrival. The computer program notified them of their scheduled arrival, much to the pleasure of Zarita. "Welcome back Senator Celenia, Senator Zarita," Queen Altha greeted them. "Emperor Kino and I want to meet with you both. You can present your report first. I know Zarita needs to get going by tomorrow morning, so let's get going, shall we? By the way,

Senator Celenia, you look lovely in your fancy gown." The two had decided to continue wearing the billowing hoop skirts, if only to show the others on their worlds what they had to put up with, a particularly acute problem for Celenia.

Her report was succinct. Mostly, it centered on the fuel shortage. Once she'd given her official report, Emperor Kino then took over their meeting. He had quite a lot to say to the two senators.

"First, I've been investigating President Snarry Knoschy. He's basically a puppet leader. His rise to power seems to have some nefarious connection to a secret and illusive group known only as the Consortium. I now believe he had some role or dealings with Neva Burkhardt's rise to power. Certainly, he had a love affair with her and used her for his own ends. However, I've yet to prove just how involved he was with her mutilations and subsequent assassination. I have, on the other hand, discovered his treachery in several other earlier plots. One thing is for sure, senators, do not believe anything the man says. Always look for proof, before you act on anything he proposes, such as these conservation measures he's been insisting the Senate act upon."

"Second, I've finally traced that money trail left behind by the man, who ordered the abduction and mutilations of Amy and Jan. It's led to an even more powerful man. Legate Emeryk Donat, ex-Sector ID Minister. This man is as slippery as they come and very deadly. Before I bring charges against him in the Senate, I want to continue my investigation of him. I believe he may well have been behind the assassination of Neva Burkhardt as well. Until I bring him up on formal charges, you must be extremely careful in any dealings with that man. He's not to be trusted in the slightest."

"Third, I've been investigating this so called fuel crisis that hit the entire Imperium. Something isn't adding up right. One of the biggest consumers of fuel at this time is the vast Urzak Fabrications company. Reputedly, they're playing a major role in the rebuilding of facilities that were lost or damaged during the war. Of course, right up there with that company are the other two of the three largest enterprises in the Imperium: Baal Industries that manufactures all manner of computer systems and Mal Dynamics that builds engines that power everything from your new transport to giant earthmoving equipment. All three are current big consumers of fuel."

"I've been plotting their consumption for the last year and something has changed. Will you show them the graph please," he asked his silent assistant. "I'm tracking the amount of fuel delivered to these companies versus the calculated amount of fuel actually consumed. A year ago, the two rates are nearly identical. That is, they consumed all they took in. But look what's been going on these past six months."

Zarita stared at the graph. "They're taking in twice as much fuel as they're using."

"Precisely so, Senator Zarita. Even allowing for the maximum fuel consumption of all ships flying at top speed, I can't get the consumption figures much higher than they are. So I've been asking myself what's happening to all that extra fuel? It must be going somewhere."

"I've gotten it narrowed down to going into a company controlled by Urzak Fabrications on a small planet. That has become the focus of my attention now. What could they possibly be doing there with that gigantic amount of fuel? I can't conceive of any possible use that could use that much fuel. I'm left with only one possible conclusion."

Zarita blurted out, "They are storing it, hoarding it for when times get hard. That's what I would do if I could and if it was critical to my operations. I only need a few tanks to get back and forth from Ashford-5 though."

"Of course, you're most welcome to stop here to refuel, Senator Zarita. But you and I think alike on this. They must somehow be storing it. I've directed my investigators to look far more deeply into this anomaly. It could well be someone is trying to create a fuel crisis, probably for their own profits, but we'll see."

"Anyway, I wanted to discuss these with both of you personally. I've already briefed Senator Tabia, and I'll do so with our other senators, as they arrive for their break. Please keep all this information to yourselves for now. I don't want my investigations compromised."

116

"We will, Emperor Kino. Thanks for briefing us," Celenia replied, rather pleased her Emperor thought enough of her to take her into his confidence and tell her all these critical details, even though she'd failed miserably to become one of his queens.

Two days later and still wearing Senate gowns, the trio set foot on Tierra, landing perfectly at the spaceport on Plateau Grado. There, they were cordially met by Governor Katrina and Queen Amy. This time, Katrina hosted them in one of her larger conference rooms. For once though, Zarita and Celenia didn't feel rushed, as they followed Katrina and Doctor Whitney. They too wore the same style of toe shoes and moved quite slowly and just as carefully as the two, pleasing them.

"This is Senator Celenia Agahve of Winno-3 and my fiancé," Zarita introduced her formally. Quickly, she introduced Governor Katrina, Doctor Whitney, Carla, and Elfe. Then, she moved on to introduce Queen Amy, Jan and the rest of her Gang of Ten, calling Celenia's attention in particular to Drina and Lena.

After receiving quite a few congratulations, most notably from the governor and her three women, Zarita gave her official Senate report. She dwelled mostly on the fuel problem and the request from the Senate to implement conservation actions. While she wanted also to relay what Emperor Kino told her, she kept her word and didn't mention it.

With the formalities out of the way, Katrina announced to everyone that she and Whitney were also planning on getting married. Of course, that led immediately to Drina suggesting they have a double wedding, while Zarita and Celenia were still here. Each of the couples looked at each other and then agreed.

I need to speak with you in private, Zarita sent to Amy.

With Drina and Lena hovering over Celenia discussing wedding plans, along with the four from the spaceport, Queen Amy and Zarita slipped into a side room. "I've traded that mansion estate on Caltran for a super secure underground compound on Proxima Prime." She explained just how secure the place actually was and that she now had her own fully automated deep space transport. "I do hope what I've done is acceptable."

"Of course, it sounds perfect. That other estate holds too many bad memories and is hardly defensible or secure. I think you were very wise in making that deal, Zarita. Well done," Amy replied, validating her.

"I notice you are now wearing smaller gems like I am. Did you have a big one cut up too?" Zarita asked.

Amy frowned. "Yes, your idea was brilliant. At the last High Council meeting, Katrina and I were actually attacked mentally right there at the meeting."

"What? Domination?" Zarita guessed.

"Yes, it came from outside the castle though. They used one of the giant crystals and almost succeeded. Thank goodness, I have some of them around me too. After that, I've had some cut and made into jewelry for many of us, especially those four here at the spaceport," Amy explained.

"Well, I've another suggestion. These I'm wearing in my new earrings are actually those giant spheres!" She explained what she'd learned about geological compression. "So I'm carrying around the power of ten of those giant crystals. No one can easily get to me now. If you want, I can take some of them back with me and have them compressed too."

Amy laughed. "Isn't ten a bit of overkill? No, not really. You're out there all alone, while I have lots of backup here. Wise move, Zarita. I'll see you get two dozen spheres. Thanks, I owe you one. Oh, yes. Did Emperor Kino talk to you about this fuel shortage problem? He chatted to me about it and his suspicions that it's contrived."

"Yes, but he swore Celenia and me to silence about it. Should I have told you anyway?" she asked.

"No, never betray his confidence. I'm a queen too, so he'll keep me in the loop. Do take care out there, Zarita. There are some nasty men working behind the scenes."

"Yes. Another thing, I've come to realize just how ignorant I really am. I've been spending much time learning about many things, but there's so much to learn. Anyway, I see now that Tierra's huge problem is illiteracy. Our people need to learn to read and write, if they are ever going to learn much at all," Zarita explained.

"You're right on the money with this observation. Well done on all your studies. Yes, we need to get many more schools going. The big barrier is no textbooks. We don't have any way to mass produce any books for the kids to use in school," Amy explained.

"Hey, let me see what I can do. Maybe I can get some beginning texts converted to our three dialects and printed. If so, I'll bring them back with me on my next visit," Zarita offered. The two chatted about just what the level of the texts should be. Amy's opinion of Zarita rose considerably after this side chat. They then rejoined the others, who had the dual weddings mostly all planned out for the day before Zarita would have to leave for Proxima Prime.

The next day, Senator Zarita stood before the High Council of the Lords and gave her short presentation of what the Senate meetings held for Tierra, which wasn't much. She then explained just how vital it was to become educated, and how she was working hard to learn all she could, and that she'd promised to do her part in helping to acquire beginning texts in their own languages. To her surprise, she received a round of supporting applause.

When the group broke for lunch, Lilly came up to her. "Oh no, Zarita. Now you've gone and done it."

"Done what?" she asked, slightly worried she'd made a major blunder. Lilly looked rather annoyed with her.

"You are still wearing your Senate garb and nails. Haven't you noticed all of the noblewomen are now sporting six inch talons?"

"Well, yes, I did see that. Easterlings influence?" Zarita asked.

"Hardly. No, Zarita influence. Now, I am getting orders for gowns like those you and Senator Celenia are wearing, as well as requests for nail extensions like yours!"

Zarita relaxed and laughed, "But you'll be making money, right?"

Lilly lost her fake anger and laughed too. "Yes. That's quite true. Only I don't want to wear such billowing skirts.

Honestly, six inch nails are bad enough. I don't see how you can manage with foot long ones."

"It's not easy; I can tell you that! So I've become a fashion model now too?"

"Yes, you and Katrina and now Doctor Whitney. Between you three, you're setting new records for fashions on Tierra. Perhaps, you three should get together and agree on what to wear." Both women laughed.

On the positive side, during the remaining days, Drina and Lena took good care of Celenia. They quickly got her into a simple day dress, showing her how she could put it on herself, which totally amazed her. By the time that they left, Celenia realized she need not be totally helpless after all. She begged Zarita to return here during the three month summer vacation period so she could learn from the two who were so like herself. "I don't want to be so helpless now I've seen what all Lena and Drina can do for themselves."

"Absolutely. This is one reason why I so wanted you to come with me this time — to meet Drina and Lena. When we come this summer, I want you to get our Basic Therapy too. I do love you so." Even Lelane had tears in her eyes, finally seeing a true glimmer of hope for her Celenia.

The wedding was a simple one, with Carla and Elfe standing in as the bridesmaids for Katrina and Whitney. Lena and Drina stood in for Zarita and Celenia, with the others in the Gang of Ten acting as witnesses for both. Once they were officially married, Carla altered both their ID cards. Zarita was now also a citizen of Winno-3, and Celenia was a citizen of Ashford-5. Then, the two couples spent the rest of the time in their respective bedrooms, though Lelane was with them, as always, an inseparable trio.

The morning they were to depart, Jan came dashing into their guest suite. "Zarita, Celenia! Bad news. President Snarry has been killed. Another bombing attack killed him, several of his aides, and six Security Guards."

"Oh god. The President? We'd best get back soon," Celenia exclaimed. "If I recall right, the Senate will have to choose a temporary president to finish out his term."

"Well, this session won't be so boring for you two," Jan

teased. "You two take care and watch your backs! I told you being a politician is very dangerous to your health!"

Three days later when they stopped to refuel on Winno-3, Emperor Kino was waiting for them, along with Senator Tabia. "Nasty business, this untimely death of Snarry. While there have been other bombings on Proxima Prime, this one is rather unique. They got to him when he was in transit. Someone had to know his route of travel, which implies someone on the inside leaked the information," Emperor Kino theorized. "I'm looking into it, because I suspect it was really an assassination plot, disguised as another protest bombing."

"You three take extreme care. The Senate will have to pick a new president to finish out Snarry's term. Right now old H-cubed is the front runner, but we'll see. Keep me posted on all events and watch your backs. Oh yes, congratulations on your marriage. You have my blessings, both of you."

"But who would want President Snarry dead?" asked Celenia.

"I've asked myself that very question, senator, but as yet, I've not been able to discover who. If this was an assassination, then sooner or later, I'll get to the bottom of it and find out. Right now, I've no idea. He was a likeable president, but one who was easily pressured to follow certain courses by more powerful men. As such, it's highly unlikely he took an action against those who were pressuring him. So it makes little sense. Then again, so do most situations — not make sense, that is, until you sort out the truth, find the third party who is behind it. At the moment, I find his death suspicious, because we're facing a rather severe fuel shortage throughout the Imperium."

"You mean he could have been about to expose those who might be behind the fuel shortage?" Celenia queried him further.

Zarita smiled. *Good point! My wife is really quite bright. I didn't think of this.*

"It depends upon who was pressuring him the most — those causing the shortages or those who are being severely impacted by the shortage. The largest corporations are certainly not suffering from the shortage, which is strange.

One would anticipate they'd be severely impacted by the fuel shortage, and yet they aren't. Common folk, small businesses — the shortage affects them the most, what with the Senate issuing requests for conservation by the public. One might suspect the bomber was an ordinary person, who's been severely hurt by the shortage, except he'd have had to have inside information to know just what route the president was taking. That's the flaw in that line of reasoning. Those behind the other bombing attacks, and not just those on Proxima Prime, have been attacking relatively easy targets to reach, such as a fuel depot, which only aggravates the shortages."

"Anyway, I've got solid proof that Legate Emeryk Donat was the man who arranged for the kidnaping and mutilations of Amy and Jan. The money trail never lies. Before I go public with this, I want to see if he had any involvement in the assassination of Neva Burkhardt. I find it curious both she and President Snarry were killed by bombs. Same modus operandi at work. I'll keep you posted. You best be on your way. Please be careful, senators."

"We will. If trouble comes, I've got a very secure compound that we can use," Zarita replied. *So Legate Emeryk ordered that done to Amy and Jan! Well, well. He's going to pay for that one!*

Three days later, they landed at their private docking bay near the north pole of Proxima Prime. After refueling and paying nearly double for its cost, they had their elevator descend to Sub-level 2, and the three entered their compound. Lelane went to check their security system, paranoid the home had perhaps been compromised during their absence. Zarita and Celenia handled unpacking. Zarita had an extra crate with her that contained two dozen spherical, polished crystals. She tried to pick one crate up from the shuttle and carry it inside. She couldn't really lift it by herself. She tried pushing it, but her toe shoes had too little surface area and thus traction. Her feet slipped continuously, as if she were on ice. Frustrated, she sent for Lelane, who returned grinning. Between the two of them, they got the crates inside and into their bedroom. Lelane returned to her examination of the security logs, while Zarita did the unpacking. Celenia could only sit on their bed and watch. Her intense feelings of helplessness returned once more.

An hour later, Lelane was satisfied no one other than the gardener and the maid had been here during the past three weeks. After signaling everything was okay, she signed food and headed to the kitchen to see if she could cook up something for dinner. Zarita turned on the news channel for Celenia to watch. The death of President Snarry was still being hotly discussed by the news commentators. Speculation ran wild over who the Senate would pick to finish out his term of office. Most everyone was betting that Helyeon H. Hoon would be the likely choice, including himself.

"He's a pompous ass," Celenia called out. "This H-cubed Legate. All political sweet talk and no real action. Promise them the world seems to be his motto. Looks like it is working though."

Across the planet, a harried Senate President Abraham Talos returned to his complex a week earlier than planned. An unheard of event had occurred. A terrorist bombing had killed President Snarry Knoschy and several of his aides. The Security Guards, who were also killed, didn't matter. He was next in line, at least temporarily that is. Legally, in the event of the death or any situation in which the president was incapacitated, unable to fulfill his duties of office, and thus had to be replaced, the succession fell upon the President of the Senate, who had to lead the Senate at their very next meeting in choosing a temporary president to finish out the remainder of the current presidential term. Until that person was chosen, he, Abraham Talos, was the unofficial leader of the Imperium!

Now, he faced the biggest calamity in his political life. He'd spent his whole career working his way to the position that he coveted: President of the Senate. He had no aspirations whatsoever of stepping into the other branch of government: the Executive Zone. He saw himself as a historic "Maker of Laws," not a mere executor of them. He felt the immense pressure and stress slamming him to the ground. What to do? Action. The people, the press, everyone would be demanding immediate, swift, solid, believable actions to apprehend the terrorists responsible for the wave of unprecedented bombings on Proxima Prime no less!

The five generals of the Security Guards walked solemnly into his office, prepared to brief their temporary acting President Abraham and hand him their official resignations. Abraham snapped, "Good god! The President has just been killed and all you can think of doing is abandoning ship! Hell, I won't accept them! Give them to the new temporary President later. We need action, fast action, effective action, and yesterday! I want every known member of this Society for Freedom arrested and thrown into jail. Use every interrogation technique known, but find the perpetrators now! Find out how this could have happened. I want the most thorough investigation ever conducted in the history of the Imperium! Do it now!" The five men rushed out of his office, intent upon carrying out his orders.

He tried to calm down, but wasn't able to do so. Many arrangements had to be made. State Funeral. A firm, resolved public address, assuring the entire Imperium that everything was fully under control — so much to do and so little time. His public address didn't go over as well as he'd hoped. Reviewing the video, he thought he sounded nervous and shaky. His stress levels continued to rise. Then it came. The day he always knew was lurking nefariously in the background, the day his debts would be called in. He received a secure text message from the Consortium! His legs did give out, and he slumped into the nearest chair. The wording was brief: Meet at one at the Sportsmen's Club.

He could not ignore the summons. If he did, he was a dead man walking. He rued the day he'd accepted the assistance of this unholy Consortium, but they'd promised him what he'd sought all his life: the Senate President position. True, he'd accepted their help on far smaller matters long before that fateful day. He could not help recalling one of the three men's parting words, "One day, Senate President Abraham, we'll summon you for repayment." Now that day had come.

As he walked the short distance from his parked shuttle and the entrance of the imposing Sportsmen's Club, he tried to clear his head. What did the Consortium have to do with this calamity? Could they have had a hand in the terrorist bombing? Surely not, but then anything was possible with these men, the most powerful, wealthiest of all men in the entire Imperium. He swallowed hard, as he climbed the short series of steps to the magnificently carved double doors. Two heavily armed guard stood on either side. "I'm expected. Senate President Abraham Talos." One nodded and opened the door, but spoke into his comm device, relaying his identity.

Just inside, two more Security Guards met him and led him to a side room just off this main entrance. Ahead of him, he caught a fleeting glimpse of the splendor of the club's main gallery. A moment later, he entered a small room, where one man was sitting at a mahogany table. The odor of polish filled the air; the red carpet beneath his feet was incredibly soft and plush. Great paintings hung on the walls. "Right on time. Come, have a seat. This room is secure."

He recognized the man, Yinko Urzak, the head of Urzak Fabrications. Mechanically, he sat down and cleared his throat. "These are awful times," he attempted to make some reasonable statement.

"Yes of course they are. I'll be brief. As you are well aware, you must lead the Senate in choosing a temporary President to fill out the remainder of Snarry's term," Yinko stated factually.

"Yes, of course. I'll be leading the Senate to do this the first day they return." *What can he possibly want?*

"Of course you will," Yinko smiled disarmingly. "Might I ask who you see as the front runner for this position?"

Abraham cleared his throat, buying himself a little time to think. He'd not given this too much thought as yet. That meeting was still two weeks away. He had so much else with which to deal right now. "Well, H-cubed is the most popular Legate. He'll probably get the promotion."

"Yes, we all anticipate his push to gain that high office. But we both know that with this terrible fuel shortage, we need a man in charge of the government who can take effective action. H-cubed is a fine orator; he can move people to support him, but he never follows through and delivers the goods he's promised. In this crisis, his incompetence will bring down the entire Imperium. Let the peacock continue to strut, only not in the Presidential Office. Do I make myself clear?"

"Er, yes. H-cubed should not be elected our temporary President. But who then?" Abraham found himself asking. *What does he want of me? How bad is this going to be?*

"Legate Emeryk Donat is the man for the position. He's had a long and highly effective career as a Sector ID Minister. If anyone can lead us out of this fuel crisis, it's Donat. See that he becomes the temporary President, Senate President Abraham. Do this for us, and the ledgers are fully balanced. Understand?" He glared at Abraham.

"Yes sir. Fully balanced. Legate Emeryk — next President," he found himself saying without thinking about it.

"Precisely. If he does *not* become the President, the Consortium will have to make other arrangements for the Presidency of the Senate," Yinko said dryly, but forcefully.

Abraham swallowed. Is he threatening me? Did the Consortium have anything to do with Snarry's bombing? Oh god! Could they be behind it? "Aye sir. Legate Emeryk — next President," his voice mechanically replied.

"Good. That'll be all." Yinko pressed a button. The two Security Guards entered and summarily escorted the Senate President out of the Sportsmen's Club.

He walked slowly back to his shuttle trying to make sense of the meeting. The Consortium was certainly ahead of his own thinking. Legate H-cubed would be the logical and popular choice to fill the vacancy. No question of that. Yet, he knew Yinko was right; H-cubed was a dandy, a ladies man, and a sweet talker, who told others what they wanted to hear. Yes, that was precisely it. His beautiful orations contained just what his audience most desired to hear. Uncanny. Yet, he rarely delivered on his campaign promises. He always seemed to have a solid reason why his efforts had been thwarted. He was never at fault. No, while he was the popular choice, he would be a disastrous President. Yinko was right. Legate Emeryk Donat would be a far better choice.

As his shuttle flew him back to his office, his mind cleared. *Yes, I can easily sway the Senators into picking*

Emeryk over H-cubed. This will be relatively easy. What a relief! I was really scared back there that the Consortium was going to ask too much of me. I have the best of that deal for sure. He began to relax and focus on the myriad problems at hand.

The day that Zarita arrived back on Proxima Prime, the Consortium held an emergency meeting. Yinko complained, "All right Baal. Why this hasty meeting? Abraham will get us our new President. Everything is going according to plan." They were again in their private room deep within the very secure Sportsmen's Club.

Baal grimaced. "We need a drastic change. I've got it on good authority that Emperor Kino has discovered that Emeryk Donat paid for the hit on those women, Queen Amy and her assistant Jan. He's got irrevocable proof that Emeryk not only paid for it, but likely orchestrated the whole damned thing. Word has it that he's now suspecting Donat of being behind the assassination of the war hero Neva Burkhardt no less."

"Good god! What awful timing," Yinko scowled. "Why couldn't he discover this a year from now when it might not matter much?"

"That man is gaining too much power, if you ask me," Bindaz growled. "Yinko's right. A year from now and it wouldn't matter one iota if Donat was brought down. Our profits would be secured."

Yinko declared, "Well, hell, we had best stop Abraham from pushing Donat for the presidency and soon. The Senate will open on Monday. What do we do now?"

Baal replied, "We think this through. Obviously, we cannot use Donat. We can't use H-cubed; he is too popular and egocentric. Legate Marhildt is in charge of Finances. He'd be too darn dangerous to our plans, if he became the President. The man's a money freak."

"We can't use Dalag, he's a geologist and doesn't give a damn about the presidency or running anything but his constant search for new minerals," Yinko added.

"Hey, Jaleck and Zestial are not much better. Hand-picked for their particular Legate skills and specialties, they would make pathetic presidents. Besides, we don't have any real leverage over the other Legates. Donat was our perfect choice," Bindaz grumbled.

Baal frowned. "Look, gentlemen. This is a minor setback. We wanted our man in the presidency, one that we could control, and one that would effectively carry out the widely unpopular fuel conservation policies, while we siphon off the fuel into Yinko's reserves. That's now obviously no longer possible. What alternatives do we have to make this fuel deal pay off for us?"

Yinko pursed his lips. "You know, we could approach this from a completely opposite approach. Put a moron in as President. He'd cause so much confusion and disorder that nothing effectively could be done for quite some time. By then, we'd pass the profit-expected point and could begin to ease the fuel shortage, funneling our reserves back into the market." He hastily did some calculations on his handheld computer. "Yes, we could expect a four percent increase instead of our desired five percent. Hell, one percent isn't that big a loss, considering the mess that's occurred. What do you two think? I'm willing to lose one percent."

"Good point. One percent is nothing. Agreed. Put a moron in as President. Candidates? Hey, wait a minute. If Emperor Kino has uncovered Donat's treachery, what is to keep him from investigating this fuel shortage? If he finds out that we're manipulating the supply, he'll come after us."

"We could arrange a bomb for him," Yinko suggested.

"That would surely bring down the house on us. You forget; the man's now a War Hero. If he is assassinated, there'll be hell to pay. No, we would need far more serious reasons to stick our necks out that far," Baal countered, still thinking this new approach through. "We need to find a way to occupy his attention elsewhere. In a way, appease him. What if he were elected the new President?"

"He'd never accept it. He's the Emperor of the Ataro Empire, for heaven's sake. We can't give him that kind of power without having enough dirt on him to control him. Besides, he is anything but a moron," Yinko countered.

"Right, right. I'm thinking faster than I'm reasoning.

Still, appeasing him and directing his attention elsewhere is brilliant. Buy us one year, and we're all set. So has he got an available moron in his employ?" Baal asked.

"He and his senators do carry a disproportionate weight within the Senate," Yinko stated.

"Bring up the list of senators that are from one of the planets in the Ataro System please," Baal asked. Yinko did as asked.

"Ah, there are a hundred of them, mostly men, but a few women," Yinko commented a few minutes later.

"Find a moron among them?" Baal asked, looking over Yinko's shoulder.

"Hardly. No wait. Look at this one, an illiterate from the primitive Closed World of Ashford-5," Yinko said, pulling up her bio. "Ah, she's just married another senator from Winno-3. Hell, that one is as armless as their emperor and many queens. Here's a pair of dopes if I ever saw them."

"She's not one of them damned telepaths is she? Pull up her image, will you?" Baal asked.

"No, not a registered telepath. See, no yellow eyes. Hers are blue. Neither is the armless one, but Winno-3 has never produced an official Class V telepath yet, as far as I know," Yinko replied.

"Hell, put them both in office," Bindaz suggested. "Make the Senate a shambles, as well as the presidency." He laughed wickedly. Baal and Yinko joined him.

"My god, this is too good to be true! Sometimes adversity delivers only stellar results," Baal exclaimed. "Okay, we put the moron in as President and then put the armless one in as Senate President. That ought to keep Emperor Kino more than fully occupied, while we cash in on our fuel project. Once the confusion settles down and both are kicked out of office, Kino will have suffered a major defeat and subsequent loss of power. We've finally found a way to control Emperor Kino as well. Gentlemen, we are brilliant!"

"Aye, that we are. But how are we going to get these two morons into office? What about Abraham?" Yinko asked the key questions.

"Bring up the succession laws, please, Yinko," Baal

asked. "First things first."

"Normally, the Senate must elect a temporary President as its first action. Ah, look, they are not limited to electing only a current Legate, but the person must be a duly elected official, which includes the senators themselves. So one of them could be the next President, that much is clear," Yinko called out. "The question becomes who leads the Senate if their President is also absent?" He studied the lengthy document further. "Ah, it says in case both are absent at the same time, then one of the Legates stands in for the Senate President, gets them to elect first a new President, and then a new Senate President. This will be tricky. Time is not on our side. We must act quickly."

"Haste makes for mistakes," Baal countered. "Yet, I don't see any other way. Are we committed?" The three shook hands and set to work.

Still watching the news reports, Celenia suddenly cried out, "Zarita, Lelane! Come quick! Something else has just happened!" Both women came as fast as they could without falling down. "Look! Senate President Abraham has just been killed! My god! What's happening?" Shock and fear fought for dominance in her voice. The three stared at the images. Thick black smoke came billowing out of the top floor of one of the Senate skyscrapers.

The reported exclaimed, "A terrible accident. Just terrible. A transport ship has just run into the top floor of Senate Suites One, where Senate President Abraham Talos and his wife live. Word has it that both were home at the time of this horrific accident. Rescue personnel are fighting their way into the Senate Presidential Suite now. They must have two objectives: to contain the fires and to rescue the Senate President. In that inferno, there cannot be much hope. Who could survive such a fiery blaze? This tragic accident following so closely upon the untimely death of President Snarry will certainly create a massive gap in the government." He rattled on with his doomsday talk.

"This isn't good, Zarita. We have to elect a new temporary President on Monday, and now we don't even have a Senate President to lead us. I have to let Emperor Kino know. Can you call Tabia and have her let our other Ataro senators know about this, if they don't already know?" Celenia asked, growing more and more worried.

Zarita called Tabia, who had just heard the news as well. She promised to let the other senators know and begged her to take extreme safety precautions. As the connection ended, Ari called her. "Zarita! Have you heard the news?" She sounded terrified.

"Yes, we are in the compound. Care to join us?" Zarita offered, sensing this was the real reason for Ari's call.

"Can we? Thanks. We're terrified there'll be more bombings. We're on our way! Thanks, Zarita! Thanks!"

"Yes Emperor Kino. That's the situation here," Legate Marhildt replied. "Legate Emeryk Donat is highly likely to become the next Imperium President unless we act now. Over." The man was quite nervous. All this was happening way too fast for him. Money — that was his specialty, not politics and government. Yet, it had fallen on him to act with the sudden death of the Senate President. Indeed, the Consortium, that is, three of the most influential and powerful men in the Imperium, were here with him. What they'd told him frightened him almost as much as an economic meltdown might have. At least with that, he could deal with such an event, but this was way beyond his experience.

After the long delay, Emperor Kino replied. "Okay. I'll send you the supporting documentation outlining Legate Emeryk's complicity. I've your word then that he'll be arrested at once? Over."

"Yes, Emperor Kino. As soon as I have the documentation in my hands, I'll send the Security Guards to arrest him. All of the Imperium owes you a tremendous debt for saving us from making a terrible mistake and for the discovery of the criminal actions of Legate Donat. I'll notify you the moment we have him in custody. Over."

"Excellent. The documentation is on its way. I've attached what we've also uncovered concerning his involvement in the assassination of the war hero Neva Burkhardt as well. Mind you, my investigation is incomplete at this point. I had intended to wait on this whole thing, until I had it all sewn up. However, under these circumstances, we have to take immediate action. Keep me posted. Over and out."

"Ah, here comes the documentation. My god, who would have thought one of us Legates could ever do such things?" Legate Marhildt gushed.

Baal explained, "Some men are rotten to the core, Legate Marhildt. We knew we could trust you always to do the right thing. Now then, on Monday, you'll have to address the full Senate and take charge of them. First, per law, they must elect a new temporary President. Once that's done, they must elect a new Senate President. Then, he or she can take over, and you can return to your vitally important finance work. Lord knows, we need fiscal security right now," Baal added, playing the Legate well.

"Of course, disasters *always* shake the financial markets. I'll have my work cut out for me to keep them stable. But how am I to lead them in choosing those leaders? I've no political experience in such matters," Legate Marhildt hinted, hoping to garner some clue from these three powerful men, the Consortium.

Baal smiled, "We don't want to unduly bias you, but times have suddenly become quite dangerous, if not harried. The people need new leaders in whom they have both faith and trust. At this junction in time, Emperor Kino Sango holds that position, more than anyone we know. If I might be so bold as to make a suggestion, Legate Marhildt," Baal continued talking for quite some time, insisting that the man take notes of his arguments.

Chapter 8 New Presidents

Early Monday morning, Ari and B'nath stepped out of their shuttle and waited for Zarita and Celenia to get out of theirs. Both had been positively ecstatic, when they learned the two had gotten married while on the three week break. Ari promised them they'd hold a party for them as soon as things settled down a little. Even they were being harried by their home worlds, begging them for more information than they had. As the four senators entered the now extremely well-guarded Senate building, they felt the eyes of the Imperium were focused on them all.

Indeed, several dozen Security Guards now patrolled the perimeter of the building. Overhead, sky cams from the news outlets were showing images of the various senators as they arrived. At least the Security Guards now kept the press far away from the arriving Senate members. The four headed inside, finally splitting up to get to their respective areas within the huge amphitheater. Ari and B'nath were about midway up the many levels, while the Ataro senators were on the second level, as befitting the importance and power of that system.

As the two took their seats, everyone was talking in very hushed voices, wondering what would happen next. At nine, Legate Marhildt Chyldt, dressed in his finest business suit, walked slowly onto the raised platform and stood before the several thousand senators. He cleared his voice and began.

"Senators, it's with the greatest sorrow and sadness that I am standing here before you today, officially opening this critical session of the Senate. Recent events are threatening to undermine the very fabric of our great Imperium. On behalf of all us Legates, I want to express my deep sorrow and greatest sympathy for the untimely loss of your Senate President Abraham Talos. Per Imperium Law, in the event of the loss of both presidents, it falls upon us Legates to temporarily officiate here in the Senate."

"However, there's even more ill news I must relate to

you. Emperor Kino Sango has just presented the Imperium with concrete and irrefutable evidence that Legate Emeryk Donat arranged for the kidnaping of the Ataro Queen Amy and her personal assistant Jan and their subsequent mutilations and deaths. I've had him arrested, and I assure you he'll stand trial and pay for his crimes." Many gasps echoed in the very acoustic theater, and he paused to allow the impact and import sink into the senators' minds.

"Corruption has reached the highest levels within the Imperium. Hence, we remaining Legates have agreed that I officiate these proceedings, to help guarantee the financial and fiscal security of our Imperium in these most difficult of days. That said, we have two actions, which must be taken immediately before anything else. Per Imperium Law, a new temporary President must be elected by this body to fill out the remaining six and a half years of the late President Snarry's term. After that, new Imperium-wide elections can be held, and a new President elected. Once we have done that, then we must elect a new Senate President from among you. As soon as that is accomplished, I will step down and return to my Imperium Financial duties and obligations."

"That said, by law, I'm to begin these proceedings by presenting my choice for the new president. After I make my case for this person, I will throw the floor open for any of you, who wish to either argue for or against my choice, as well as present any of your choices. By law, the person elected must have a simple majority vote from the vote-eligible senators. I'm sorry the Closed World senators do not have an official vote in this matter. However, I encourage such senators to openly speak their minds concerning the candidates offered here."

"I've given this matter of who should become the next Imperium President considerable thought. We have entered upon harsh, if not brutal times. I can't recall when bombs ever exploded on Proxima Prime before now. Our confidence has been shaken to its very core. I can't help but recall how poorly the recent war with the Federation of Planets went. Those were grim days, as I watched helplessly, as planetary system after system fell to the Federation. In those darkest of times, *one* man stepped forward, along with three brave women, to discover the underlying cause of the war and put an end to it, at great personal risk. In those dark times, heroes appeared, unlikely heroes at best."

"I am speaking, of course, of Emperor Kino Sango, Queen Altha of Winno-3, ex-Hub Sector ID Minister Lena Squire, and Neva Burkhardt. As you know, Neva was assassinated on her return from this war-ending mission, while Lena lost her arms and her livelihood. Yet, because of their sacrifices, the war is over, one, which by many accounts, we were losing. Still, Emperor Kino continued his work and has only recently uncovered the criminal acts that Legate Emeryk Donat has committed. He continues to work tirelessly to help keep our Imperium safe."

"I personally feel an obligation to demonstrate just how much we in the Imperium appreciate all of his hard work and the many sacrifices he and his associates have made for us. Hence, my choice for the temporary President of the Imperium must go to one from the Ataro Empire. By law, our choice must be a duly elected official, meaning either the President, one of us Legates, or one of you senators. In this case, we remaining Legates are categorically withdrawing our names from any consideration of the Office of the President. What with the arrest of Legate Donat, our credibility has reached the lowest point in living memory. Hence, our choices for the temporary President must be one of you senators."

"My choice should be taken seriously by all of you. As I said, my choice comes from the Ataro Empire, as a way to honor Emperor Kino and his long efforts to save our mighty Imperium. Further, in these highly unusual times, I feel we need to make unusual choices. Choices that show the incredible flexibility of us leaders. My choice is for a woman to be the next president." He paused to allow this bit of a revelation to sink into the many minds. He very carefully followed the outline he had been given by Baal.

"Why a woman? We enter times that need a *healing* hand. We're still recovering from the devastation of the recent war. Now, assassinations, almost unheard of on Proxima Prime, has shaken the very fabric of our Imperium. I want us to turn to the nurturing hands of a woman to lead us forth out of these incredibly dark times. Women bring new life into the world, so, metaphorically, I would like a woman to lend her healing, nurturing hands to the Presidency to bring new life and vitality to our Imperium."

"I point out that Rochilda, the Second, once held the presidency, so there is historical precedence for a woman president. I believe that having a female take the reins would be the best possible choice, in light of the current mess in which we're involved. Further, we would be demonstrating to the entire Imperium that we do not ever discriminate against women. Additionally, we can show clearly, and once and for all, that we also do not discriminate against personal matrimonial choices." He chose to go with Baal's suggestion not to use the phrase sexual orientation. Such was implicit in the phrasing he used.

"Nor do we discriminate against planetary location within the galaxy. Nor do we discriminate against those whose education does not lie in political science. Look where those men have led us. Nor do we discriminate against those who are not of the wealthiest classes on our worlds. Nor do we discriminate against those worlds that do not pour billions of credits into our treasury. Yes, I am asking you to think *outside* of the usual box in this case."

"So without further preamble, my choice for the position of temporary President of the Imperium is Senator Zarita Valen of Ashford-5." Gasps echoed around the amphitheater!

Zarita nearly fainted. She was stunned; her mouth opened involuntarily, but she said nothing. Celenia shrieked, taken completely by surprise as well. She'd anticipated that it might be Tabia who was chosen, not her mate.

"But Ashford-5 is a Closed World!" some senator yelled out.

"Of course it is. All the more reason to show we support the best candidate, no matter from what world they originate," Legate Marhildt countered respectfully.

Ari's voice yelled out, "All right! It's about time for a woman president. Acer-4 fully supports your choice, Legate!"

Someone else called out, "Yeh, you would, you lesbian!"

"That's my point; we should show the universe we do not discriminate on personal matrimonial choices," Legate Marhildt spoke up, condemning the man's outburst of discrimination.

"But she doesn't even have voting rights in the Senate," another protested.

"Anyone, who is nominated before this assembly, cannot vote for the presidential choice, so that is irrelevant in this case," Legate Marhildt countered.

Ari spoke out again, "Look, everyone knows that Senator Zarita will not be unduly influenced by men. She's an ideal choice. Impartial, unbiased. She'll do what is right and just for the Imperium, not what many *vested* interests desire. She should be our next president!"

"But what does she know about running the entire Imperium? She's basically wholly ignorant, Senator Ari," another man countered.

"She is a very fast learner, senator," Ari defended Zarita again.

Senator Tabia rose. "Senators, let's make this a civil discussion, shall we? I believe we should take this one step at a time. First and foremost is the honorable Legate's suggestion that we should choose someone from the Ataro Empire. Upon that is what we should first agree. If we do not accept that proposition, all else is moot."

Another senator rose, "I agree with Senator Tabia. She's right. Do we take this golden opportunity to display honor and recognition to the Ataro Empire or not? I say yes! My god, everyone holds Emperor Kino as a bastion of truth and honor — a hero, if you please. I say let us take this opportunity to give him his long overdue honor and respect from the Senate and the Imperium. I call for a vote on this first assumption."

"Sorry. Do I take a vote on this now?" Legate Marhildt asked, rather embarrassed by his lack of knowledge of proper Senate Protocols. A senator near him coached him, and he called for a vote. It passed by an overwhelming majority. No one wanted to be seen not voting on this official display of Senate support for the hero of the recent war.

More discussions followed. There were quite a number of other Ataro Empire senators from which to choose. Several of the male senators flatly refused to be considered. Finally, Senator Tabia's next motion only to consider a female senator was called to a vote. This time, it passed by the slimmest of margins, and they adjourned for lunch.

Ari and B'nath surrounded Zarita and Celenia, as they headed to the huge lunch room. Ari could not contain her enthusiasm. "Zarita! This is the most momentous thing ever! You'll make a great president; I just know it!"

"I'm speechless. I don't know what to say. I can't imagine how this Legate Marhildt ever chose me. I've never even met him," Zarita replied. For hours, she ran through all manner of ways that he could have ended up choosing her out of the thousands of senators, most all of whom would have been a far better choice for the President of the Imperium. Surely, there had to be some other underlying plot going on. Zarita was determined to get to the bottom of it. Why pick on her? It seemed ludicrous, at least on the surface. Still, she could not help but grin. Years ago, this would have been her ultimate goal, ultimate power. Now, she calculated that something else, quite hidden, was going on, and that she was becoming a mere pawn in some giant plot of someone's.

During lunch, while she had to feed Celenia, Ari and B'nath kept at bay the many other senators, who came up to her to chat with her. "Look, she has to have time to feed Senator Celenia," Ari kept pointing out, "unless you wish to do it for her." That usually ended their attempted interruptions. Ari also knew these senators seeing Zarita doing this for the obviously helpless Celenia lent more credence to the compassion and understanding that Zarita must have, underlining what Legate Marhildt had originally suggested that Zarita possessed. As they finished up, Ari whispered to Zarita, "Get your acceptance speech ready. I bet anything that you are soon going to be President Zarita!" She gave her a hug.

In contrast to the rather heated morning session, the afternoon began much cooler. Obviously, Legate Marhildt had done some political maneuvering during the long lunch hour. "As we open this afternoon session, I call your attention to one point that was overlooked this morning. If after six months or a year or whatever, if you decide that your appointed temporary President is not fulfilling his or her duties, you can always have a recall vote. This is in stark contrast to the duly elected President. Temporary Presidents are subject to recalls." Many nodded their approval to his open declaration of this special power that the Senate held over their appointees.

Only an hour later, a final vote was taken. No one else had nominated anyone. Zarita won the appointment by some hundred votes. Legate Marhildt then asked her to come down and give an acceptance speech before the assembled Senate. Thankfully, some aide met her, as she got to the elevator, and led her to the side entrance of the center stage. She took as deep a breath as she could, cursing her tight clothing, and walked slowly and carefully out before the senators, her blue billowing gown bobbing slightly, as she took her tiny steps.

"Thank you one and all for your support. Representing my people on Ashford-5, I came here this morning to witness just how the mighty Imperium handled a crisis of this enormous magnitude. Frankly, senators you have impressed me considerably. You have risen to the task at hand. While I know I am not everyone's choice for President, I'll endeavor to be everyone's President. I'll always do my very best and work hard to earn your trust and confidence. We're facing numerous crises at this time. I swear to all of you that I will not rest until I have gotten to the truth behind them, including this fuel crisis. I'll never let myself be swayed by special interest groups or by anyone, making my own decisions based upon the facts. Working together, we can, and we must, rise above those who would destroy our great Imperium. Thank you all." She curtsied and nodded to Legate Marhildt.

"I give you President Zarita Valen," he called out loudly. Ari led the loud round of applause, as she walked off the platform.

As she got to the edge, six Security Guards surrounded her. "Madam President, we are here to escort you safely to the Presidential Office." She allowed them to escort her out of the Senate building.

Meanwhile, Legate Marhildt moved on to his second responsibility, the nomination of his choice for the Senate President. "Well done senators. Now, it is my task to nominate a candidate for Senate President to finish out the remainder of the late Senator Abraham Talos." He again made similar arguments as he had before offering up Zarita as his choice.

After repeating most of them, he added, "I believe it is high time we also demonstrate the Senate does not also discriminate against the handicapped of the Imperium. My choice for your next Senate President is Senator Celenia Agahve Valen." Once more Ari and B'nath let out cries of surprise and support. Celenia nearly fainted.

Senator Tabia put her supporting arm around her compatriot, whispering, "Shallow breaths, shallow breaths."

Many senators protested and danced around having been blindsided by this surprise move by the Legate. Yet, how could they protest without seeming to be picking on her because she was indeed handicapped. Legate Marhildt continued, "I am told she has a Personal Assistant, who cannot speak, and who can assist her as needed," countering some of their protests. "Again, I remind you that, if you discover she is unable to lead the Senate, you can vote to remove her, and vote in another of your choice to fill out the remainder of the term."

One senator called out, "I demand a half hour recess at this time."

"Hearing no objections, then it is so granted," the Legate replied.

"I can't believe this is happening to me," Celenia gushed to Senator Tabia.

"You've certainly made indelible impressions on *someone* in power," Senator Tabia stated. "I wish we could discuss this with Emperor Kino right away. Guess that will have to wait. Don't worry. I'll stay with you and make sure you get home safely. Perhaps, they will elect someone else. This day is certainly not going remotely the way I imagined it would."

During the break, Ari discretely edged her way closer to several prominent senators, who she knew coveted the Senate

Presidency, listening in on their hasty discussion. "He's boxed us in good this time! If we are seen voting against her, we'll be seen as discriminating against cripples, which she certainly is. Ideas, fellows?"

Another added, "Good god, if she gets it, then both presidencies will be in one family, wife and wife. I can't believe this is even happening!"

"Hey, she'll be the First Lady too," another pointed out.

The first mulled that over and suggested, "You know, there might be something in this for us. With the president's wife as our president, we'll have access to everything that goes on in the Presidential Office."

"Yes, but that's going to work both ways. She'll have access to our goings on as well."

"Still, we have been out-foxed by someone. Who the hell put Legate Marhildt up to these choices? The man's a financier not a politician, yet he's making some tremendous political statements here today. There's more going on behind the scenes than we are aware of. Someone is pulling the strings. We need to get to the bottom of it and fast."

"Quite true. We should form up an investigatory committee and, later on, call Legate Marhildt to task over his choices. He's right; we can't vote against her, not unless we can come up with a more viable choice."

"Yes, but it's got to be one of the Ataro System senators, and there aren't many other female choices there. Senator Tabia has already said she didn't want the position. We have been shafted big time, gentlemen!"

"Yes, but if the cripple can't handle it, we can always remove her and elect one of us," the first countered. "I sure as hell don't want to be on record as having voted against a disabled person. That'll ruin my image back home."

Ari smiled and quietly backed away, grateful for her choice of apparel. No one noticed the man standing nearby was a woman.

When the meeting resumed, a few other senators presented some feeble objections. Hearing no other candidates being nominated, Legate Marhildt called for a vote. Celenia was accepted, again by a margin of some four hundred votes this time. Few dared cast dissenting votes. Very nervously, Senate President Celenia made her way down to the central platform, thanking the aide who guided her there. Her legs felt like mush, as she began her slow walk out upon the wide platform to where the Legate was standing, waiting for her.

"I give you your new Senate President Celenia Agahve Valen, First Lady of the Imperium." Again, Ari and B'nath led the loud round of applause for her. Both of them simply could not believe what had happened today. Two of their "kind" now held the two highest offices in the Imperium!

"Thank you my fellow senators. I'm shocked and surprised by this wholly unexpected election. I'll do my very best to lead our esteemed Senate. I'll need my Personal Assistant with me at all times. Sorry about that, but she cannot speak. We senators face many critical problems that must be solved, and solved quickly before they escalate out of control. I openly admit I'm not versed on what issues were supposed to be brought before us upon our return. I do hope the late Senator Abraham has left some notes on what our immediate agenda was to be. I believe we ought to adjourn for today. Honestly, I need to do an awful lot of work before tomorrow's session. If any of you have topics or issues that you want brought up here, please jot them down and give them to me at your earliest convenience. Tomorrow, we must begin to tackle the key problems the Imperium faces. Thank you. If there are no objections, this meeting is adjourned, and Legate Marhildt can get back to his financial planning duties. Let's give him a round of applause for his diligent work in this, the darkest of times."

After a brief round of applause, the senators rose and made hasty exits. However, two aides came up to her. "We have the agenda Abraham was going to follow. How can we give it to you?" one asked rather embarrassed.

"Oh stick it in my mouth. Senator Tabia is going to help me today. Tomorrow Lelane will be with me to be my hands," she said politely.

"Will you be wanting to move into the Senate Presidential Suite? That is, the new one. The blast destroyed the old one," another aide asked.

She muttered, "No," through her clenched teeth, hoping that Tabia would come to her soon! Several Security Guards also arrived, telling her they were now responsible for her safety. She was never so glad to have Tabia slip her arm around her waist as now. She also took the paper from her mouth.

Once outside, they were surrounded by news reporters, hounding her to make a statement or give them an exclusive interview. She had no choice but to satisfy their cravings. "Hello. I am Senate President Celenia Agahve Valen. I guess that I'm also your First Lady too. I'm sworn to do my very best to lead our mighty Imperium Senate. I give you my word that we'll address and solve today's many problems. Thank you."

"Senator Celenia, do you see your obvious handicap as an impediment to your new posts?" a reported called out.

"No, do you?" she couldn't help but retort.

"But you can't even hold a document or even feed yourself," another countered.

"Senators are not elected because they have two arms, one arm, no arms or feet. We were elected because we have a mind that can reason well and think properly. We ought to have compassion and understanding for others, but we must be able to lead others as well. Arms have nothing to do with this, unless your mind resides in your hands," she countered.

"Won't some people find your marriage to another woman distasteful or even against God's Laws?" another reporter hounded her.

"Look, one's private life should remain private. I've no intention of asking who you go to bed with. That's your business. I love my wife and that should be sufficient for any sentient person. What is important here is the Senate must work to restore confidence in our Imperium leadership. We must do what is right and just for all of the many worlds we represent, playing favorites to none. Focus on what is truly important, and you will win. That's all. I really do have Senate work to do yet today. If you will excuse me, please," she replied.

The six Security Guards took that as their sign to move the reporters back, allowing the two to reach their shuttle.

Soon, the two were alone flying back to their suites in the Senatorial skyscraper. "Can I possibly do this, Tabia?" Celenia finally broke the silence.

"You have to, dear. All of the Ataro worlds are depending on you now. Here you go. Lelane's coming out to get you." She parked the shuttle on their balcony, and Lelane helped her out and into their old suite on the third floor.

"What's going on? You are home way early," Lelane wrote on a paper.

After telling Lelane about the momentous day, they could only wait to hear from Zarita. Shortly after five, she arrived escorted by a half dozen Security Guards. "Hi. Congratulations Senate President. I just heard the good news. I think you are supposed also to be the First Lady, but I'm not entirely sure of all the details yet. Now I *really* have a lot to learn. Come on; we must let Emperor Kino know what's happened," Zarita explained.

"Been waiting for you to come."

After giving her a welcoming kiss, Zarita activated the comm system. Soon, she established contact with him. She succinctly outlined all that had happened including the Legate's arguments. Then, Celenia explained what had happened after Zarita left. Finally, Celenia said, "I know this is a whole lot to digest. We're waiting for your reply. Over. There, isn't this just beyond belief? You, President Zarita, and me, Senate President Celenia?"

"Yes, it is, and that's what really has me worried, but apparently not the Security Guards and their generals. I told them we aren't going to stay in the Presidential Suite. A top floor suite is a target for bombers. We're going to be staying in our secure compound. They've set up a fast commuting shuttle for us," Zarita explained.

After a ten minute delay, Emperor Kino finally replied. "Well, this is quite a shocker. Never have I been quite so taken by total surprise as today. Much to absorb. You're quite right, Zarita. There is something going on behind the scenes, and it cannot be good. I mean no offense to either of you, but realistically, neither of you are honestly qualified for the positions you now hold. It is almost as if someone explicitly wanted to elect two leaders, who are almost certainly doomed to fail in major ways. I mean no offence, but an armless leader of the Senate will find the duties of office extremely challenging. I do hope Lelane is up to the enormous task that will land in her lap. What I find interesting is they elected members of the Ataro Empire to both positions. While on the surface, it has the appearance of honoring me for my service to the Imperium, yet it is one that is calculated to fail miserably. I suspect someone is trying their best to personally humiliate me, as well as reduce the influence of the Ataro Empire."

He continued, "I believe for the present your lives are safe. It's my suspicion that whoever is behind this will now sit back, fully expecting you both to fail miserably. Only then will recall elections be initiated. On the other hand, if you somehow succeed, that's when I believe your lives will be in extreme danger. So for now, you are likely safe. Over."

"That's my assessment too," Zarita replied. "Legate Emeryk has been arrested. He was behind the kidnaping and torture of Amy and Jan. What I don't understand is why one of the Legates wasn't chosen as president."

Celenia added, "And I don't understand why anyone of a number of other senators was not chosen for the Senate President. This is all so very weird. Over."

After the usual time delay, Emperor Kino replied, "Yes, this is all so far beyond predictable that I have no choice but to investigate. You both exercise extreme caution. I will contact you evenings at your compound. Over and out."

"We ought to pack our things and get moved yet tonight," Zarita advised. They cleverly got some of their new Security Guards to help them. Zarita sensed they were quite worried about their safety in this suite, which was rather indefensible. Later, all the men were quite pleased with their compound. Several knew it had belonged to one of their retired generals.

The next morning, two new aides came knocking around six in the morning. Both middle aged women had been assigned by the Security Generals to help the women get dressed, and into their new high speed shuttles by seven. After parting kisses, the two were whisked away by their separate

Security Guards. By eight, President Zarita was making her slow, careful walk into the Presidential Office. Her memories of this place from her Neva lifetime returned. She smiled, as she recalled many of the smaller details of the building. Even the elevator ride to the top floor was familiar to her.

Once in the huge top floor suite, everything was just as she remembered it, including the private rooms, where she'd had her affairs with Snarry, seducing him. Now all this was hers, including the oversized desk Snarry had used to intimidate others. As a host of aides followed her into the Presidential Office, she snapped, "Get rid of that abomination of a desk. I would like a regular sized desk and a wider chair that can accommodate these dresses, please."

She sat on the couch, while men bustled about, and her new personal secretary came to her to outline her day's scheduled meetings and appointments. "You need to review these papers first, President Valen." She took the stack, but had real problems with her enormous nails and page flipping. Within an hour though, she was sitting behind a normal desk, still reviewing the documents. They all seemed rather routine to her.

At ten, an aide came rushing in. "President Valen! Legate Donat has just escaped from his prison cell! A manhunt is on."

"Cancel my meetings for the moment. Leave me for a half hour. I'm not to be disturbed. I'll make some phone calls," she ordered, having no intentions at all of using the phone system. Besides not knowing how, that wasn't what she intended to do.

She sat back and focused. Her many crystals began glowing in their pale blue light. She was very familiar with Emeryk and soon made contact with him. For a brief time, she observed the man before she acted. He was being taken to the spaceport and had plans to head off-world.

Hi Emeryk. Long time no see. This is Neva Burkhardt. Remember me?

What? I had you killed! Blown up! You are dead! She felt his sudden flood of sheer panic and terror.

Sorry to disappoint you, Emeryk, but I'm hardly dead.

How did you escape this morning? She felt him trying to force himself not to remember the last few hours. That effort only brought up the images of those who had helped him to escape. She took careful note of the three men. *Whatever you do, don't remember their names,* she sent and began writing them down, as the three names popped into his mind. This is child's play, she thought. *What do you know about the assassination of President Snarry and Senate President Abraham?*

Nothing! Nothing! I swear! Yes, I wanted him dead, but someone else got to him before I could. Please, I have to get on this transport!

Zarita made an instant decision. If he got on the ship, it would be in hyperspace before she could sound the alarm. From there, he would be almost impossible to trace. After all, he knew every trick in the book from his many years as a Sector ID Minister, that is, a top spy chief. She acted. Later, Security Guards found his body on the tarmac close to a transport ship. The autopsy showed that his brains had been somehow liquefied.

When the many aides returned, she explained, "I've made some contacts. Here are the men who helped Emeryk escape. See they are fully investigated and arrested. You will find Legate Emeryk here." She slid the note over her desktop with the tip of her index finger's long nail. To say they were impressed was quite an understatement. One dashed off to carry out her orders. "How long do I have before my next meeting?"

"An hour, President Valen," her thirty year old secretary replied.

"Okay, I'm going to retire to my personal room. See that I'm not disturbed until then. I've some studying to do. Thank you." She carefully rose, got her balance, and moved slowly to the side door. An aide hastily opened it for her, and she flashed him a smile. As she exited, she sensed her personal secretary was used to having trysts with President Snarry in this very room into which she was going. Again, she smiled; that man could not control his pants, she thought.

Once settled down and with a pen and paper at hand, she again closed her eyes and focused. This time she made contact with Legate Marhildt. He was the initial source for her next investigation. He'd manipulated the Senate into making their two choices yesterday, and she wanted to know why. Still, she dare not harm him, not yet, not without proof of any crimes he'd committed. Getting the two elected certainly was not a crime.

She reached out and made contact with his mind. He was pouring over financial details. Quickly, she worked out he was worrying about the fuel shortages and how much worse it was going to become. He was trying to work out optimum distributions to keep the Imperium running as smoothly as possible. Gently, she planted the suggestion in his mind to recall the events of yesterday. He sat back doing just that. She felt his emotions he had at that time: extreme nervousness and worry. Quickly, she noticed he was following a written script, which he cleverly had held mostly concealed in his left hand. She planted the thought in his mind: I ought to send this to President Valen as a memento. She watched as he stopped and did just that.

Now, she pushed him a bit more, forcing him to recall how he'd written this crib sheet. She saw he was meeting with three men in a very fancy room. She nudged the Legate to start in at the beginning and remember that long meeting. He sighed; she picked up his distinct feeling that he didn't want to meet with these men. Then, she picked up their names along with the word Consortium. Keenly interested, she watched as Legate Marhildt recalled their extensive conversation. When he finished, she gently broke her telepathic connection and sat back. *So he was just doing what he believed was his civic duty.* She knew he truly did believe what those men had told him, that the Imperium was long overdue in honoring Emperor Kino for his many efforts on behalf of the Imperium. Legate Marhildt really did believe in all that he had said before the Senate yesterday! Zarita knew she next had to work on these three men, but first she wanted to know more about them.

Unfortunately, she had meetings until lunchtime. Right after lunch, she held a Press Conference, her first. "I would like to announce that the traitor Legate Emeryk Donat has been apprehended, after his daring escape from prison earlier this morning. As you know, he financed the kidnaping and mutilation of the Ataro Empire's Queen Amy and her personal assistant, Jan, and was responsible for their ultimate deaths. Further, we've just learned he was also behind the assassination of war hero Mrs. Neva Burkhardt. Thus, we can at long last close the books on those two outstanding, heinous crimes."

"As I've only been at work a half-day, that's all I really have to report. Questions?" she concluded.

"Will your wife, the Senate President, be your First Lady?" a reported asked.

"Certainly. She is my loving wife. The wife of the President is by definition the First Lady."

"I see you are wearing the style gown worn by female senators and their really long nails. Will you be continuing wearing them or will you be setting a different fashion trend for the presidency?" another woman reported inquired.

"Quite why the Senate laws make female senators wear such giant skirts or have to have such impossibly long nails, I surely don't know. I've not yet made any fashion decisions, but I am certainly not going to begin wearing men's suits, if that's what you are worried about. I know some female senators do, but they are wearing them in protest of these silly Senate laws."

"As a woman in the highest office, what are your plans to nurture the Imperium, as so stated during the Senate proceedings yesterday?" another asked.

"We can't grow and prosper, while corruption is running unchecked within the Imperium. Certain individuals use their power, money, and influence to try to control the Imperium from the background, such as Legate Emeryk and those who have been bombing, here on Proxima Prime and several other worlds. In a civilized society, these kinds of subversive actions cannot and will not be tolerated. My highest priority is to uncover these conspiracies and eliminate them. That way, we can all play by the same rules and prosper as never before."

She answered several more mundane questions and

then ended the conference. Her afternoon was filled with many meetings. A fair number of lesser officials just had to meet her. They were appraising their new leader, and she, they. Only by late afternoon did Zarita have another hour of private time in which to continue her "investigations."

This time, she focused on the three men, the Consortium. From the Web, she knew these were three of the richest men in the entire Imperium. Further, she now knew they were the heads of the three largest conglomerates, nearly cornering the markets on computer parts, steel fabrications from skyscrapers to spaceships, and all types of motors or engines that powered so many of the great machines of the Imperium. These three were reputedly the most powerful men anywhere.

Using the remaining private time, she focused and attempted to reach the mind of the first of these men, Baal Haug, the head of Baal Industries. Her connection solidified. He was in an office with another person. As she gently touched Baal's mind, she was suddenly aware of the other man's mind. He was a telepath! Further, he was about to alert Baal she was touching Baal's mind. In a flash, she realized Baal protected himself from telepathic mind probes by keeping a telepath with him. She also sensed this telepath had his voice box removed. Further, he was a slave telepath and rather an old one at that. She had no choice but to act, stopping the man's heart. On the flow back from the telepath, she received a short thought: *Thank you.* The telepath slumped over dead. He'd not yet contacted Baal; she was safe for the moment. However, Baal reacted and his mind became a rush of thoughts, calling out for emergency help for his telepath. She decided now was not the time to force him into careful reflections. She dropped her gentle touch for now.

"So how did your day go, dear?" Zarita asked Celenia, after giving her a warm, loving kiss. She and Lelane had just arrived at their secure compound around six. Ari and B'nath had tagged along with them.

Ari answered for Celenia, "She did great! She took total control of the meeting, in spite of several senators, who tried to get everything sidetracked and messed up for her. She showed them, didn't you, Celenia? Way to go!"

"Well I've not forgotten everything I've been taught," Celenia replied timidly. "Still, it was so scary up there. Standing for so long in these toe shoes is murder, and it's so hard for me to keep my balance. I was terrified I'd take a tumble. If I did, I couldn't even get up without help."

"I'm starving. What's for supper?" Ari asked. They headed for the dining room, where their cook had supper waiting. That she was now cooking for the President, the First Lady, and the Senate President was not lost on Allie! She went out of her way to fix them fabulous dishes. Zarita soon doubled her wages, pleasing her even more.

Over dinner, Zarita briefed Ari and B'nath on what had happened to Legate Emeryk, though she didn't reveal how she knew all that she did. "Confidential sources, you see," she gave them an appropriate explanation that satisfied them.

"So are you going to start wearing men's suits as President, Zarita? You should, you know. Celenia, you ought to as well, it would be a whole lot easier for you to manage," Ari declared.

"No, I am going to continue as I am. Perhaps, it'll get others to realize the torture we women senators have to endure. Maybe it'll get them to change their laws," Zarita answered. Celenia bravely added her "me too."

Ari grinned. "Well, I do hope you succeed. I hate looking like a man, but B'nath understands, don't you, love?" Her mate grinned and nodded. "How about a game of pool? Say, are you going to cut your nails, Zarita?"

"No, same reason."

"Whew, if you did, you'd surely beat me every time we play pool," Ari giggled.

It was late the next afternoon before Zarita had time to attempt once to more investigate Baal. This time, she found him in a business meeting, hardly the time for the reflections that she wanted him to have. She realized the best time to do her probing would be when he was asleep.

That night after a long round of three-way pleasuring, Lelane and Celenia drifted into a contented sleep, Zarita again reached out to Baal. During the remainder of that first week, she learned much, far more than she'd ever imagined. Over the weekend, she began to work out what to do about all that she'd learned.

"Emperor Kino, the problem is there isn't going to be any way to prove much of this. Over." She'd called him and carefully reported everything she'd learned from her many mind probes of the three men. Importantly, she'd learned they were behind their elections to the two presidencies and why. They had assumed she and Celenia were the two dumbest, most incapable and inept people in the Senate, a perfect setup for a crashing and dismal failure in their two top positions. When they failed and had to be removed from office, Emperor Kino would be disgraced utterly, wiping out much of his newfound popularity within the Imperium and thus his power and influence.

After the usual time delay in the transmission of the comm across half the galaxy from here in the hub, that is, halfway down the spiral arm, he replied, "The fuel storage is the entrance point. It is real. That is your entrance point, President Zarita. But do be careful. You are dealing with the three most powerful men in the Imperium! Over."

"Okay. I'll get on it on Monday. Thanks. At least, we know why Celenia and I were chosen for these positions. We won't let you down. Over and out," Zarita replied quite determined to prove these three wholly wrong.

On Monday morning, she canceled all of her morning meetings and summoned the five generals. "I need your help. Confidential sources have just told me this fuel shortage is being totally fabricated by the Consortium." She told them who was involved and just how they were manipulating the fuel shipments. "Yinko has underground storage facilities on Backner-3. There you'll find half of the fuel that has presumably been consumed this past year, a huge reserve. I want those three men arrested on treason, conspiracy, and subversion charges. Also, they're to be charged with ordering the assassinations of President Snarry Knoschy and Senate President Abraham Talos. They are here on Proxima Prime this morning at a place called the Sportsman's Club. Can you do this for me?"

"We'll send three battle cruisers to Backner-3 immediately, top speed. They should be there by noon. We'll time the arrests for the raid on the underground storage facilities," one general replied with a broad grin. "Madam President, I must tell you that I'm very much impressed with your progress! We all expected, well, you know. . ."

"Yes, I know. I'm supposed to be an illiterate primitive. I'm sorry to disappoint those who thought that. Let's get these traitors." All five grinned, saluted, and left. All morning, Zarita worried and fretted. So much could go wrong. Would someone in the Security Guards alert the three men ahead of the raids? She found herself constantly focusing and sensing the location of the three men.

As the lunch hour approached, her secretary came rushing in. "Boss, you have to turn on the news! Something major is happening right now!" She turned on the big monitor.

She saw a number of news crews outside the Sportsmen's Club. "Yes, we see General Taos over there. At least fifty Security Guards are in full battle armor, armed to the teeth. Quite what is going on here is a mystery. Are there terrorists inside this exclusive club? Are there hostages? Are they planning to bomb this establishment? We haven't been able to get any answers yet, only that this is part of a major operation taking place on several worlds. Word has it that somehow President Valen is involved with this operation. That can hardly be; she's only been in office barely a week. Still, something major is happening here. There they go. A hundred men are rushing into the club. We'll keep the cameras rolling."

"Boss, what's happening?" her secretary asked, quite concerned.

"A raid. Arrests will be forthcoming. I believe you'll need to schedule a press conference for me at say four this afternoon. I'm sure you'll be hounded for one by those newscasters."

"Look, they are coming out. Three men are in custody. Who are they? Terrorists perhaps, caught before they could blow up this magnificent club? Who? No? You sure? One has been identified as Baal Haug, head of Baal Industries! What is going on here? We'll try to get closer. Put that mike on max.

Pick up what he's saying. Do it!"

". . . charged with treason, conspiracy, and subversion and murder of President Snarry Knoschy and Senate President Abraham Talos." The microphone picked up part of what General Taos was saying to the three men, along with their retorts that this was all preposterous. The rest was cut off, as the three were shoved into waiting shuttles.

The stunned face of the reporter filled the screen. "You just heard it live! This is earthshaking news. Baal is being arrested on charges of treason, conspiracy, subversion, and the murders of President Snarry Knoschy and Senate President Abraham Talos. I can't believe I am hearing this. Someone get to President Valen quick!"

"Good, they apprehended those three. Take a note to General Taos. Thank you on a job very well done," Zarita requested. Her eyes nearly popping out of her head, the woman jotted that down and dashed off to relay it for her boss.

At four, President Zarita walked carefully out of the skyscraper and stood before a plethora of microphones, video cameras, and reporters. All were shouting questions at her. She raised her hands, and they hushed at once.

"Today, I have closed another chapter in the sad history of corruption here on Proxima Prime. These three men known as the Consortium, namely Baal Haug, Yinko Urzak, and Bindaz Rumani, masterminded the recent assassinations of President Snarry Knoschy and Senate President Abraham Talos. Further, there is no fuel shortage, despite all signs that there are. These three men hashed up a scheme to siphon off half of the fuel that has been reported as consumed during the past year, storing it in underground tanks on Backner-3. They planned to cripple the Imperium economy, and then later on, sell back the fuel at enormous profits. Greed, pure and simple. Our mighty battle cruisers have secured those facilities on Backner-3. As quickly as we can, all of that stored fuel will be put back into circulation, ending the supposed fuel shortage immediately."

"I would like to take this opportunity to deliver a message to others. Corruption and greed simply will not be tolerated within our mighty Imperium. Thank you. That is all."

Shouted questions pummeled her, but Zarita merely smiled. She had said all she intended to say. She turned and entered the building, a satisfied look on her face. General Taos was waiting for her in the Presidential Office on the hundredth floor, when she carefully entered. "Very well done, general."

He smiled, "My great pleasure indeed! However, I came to point out already they have a mountain of lawyers fighting the charges. Undoubtedly, they'll try to wrangle out of the charges. They are powerful men, and I can almost guarantee one way or another, they'll be out of jail by tonight. We'll be watching your back, President Valen."

"I understand. Time to head home. It's been quite a day, hasn't it?" she replied with a wry grin. A short while later, a heavily armed escort flew her back to her secure compound. During the flight, she focused and made contact with the three men. All had already managed to escape. Via their lawyers, some of their supporters had broken them out of their jail cells. She acted again. Later autopsies showed that the three men had mysteriously died; their brains had been liquefied.

Later Celenia, Lelane, Ari, and B'nath joined her at their compound. "Have you heard the news?" gushed Ari, the very moment she entered the compound.

Zarita smiled. "I've been rather busy today," she replied rather nonchalantly.

Part II The Rise of the Guilds

Chapter 9 The Presence of Guilds

Guilds had been a part of town and city life for over three centuries. As towns of several thousand inhabitants began to form in ancient times, so did the various guilds. In an illiterate society, knowledge of weaving, bronze making, stone masonry, milling, and so on had to be transmitted from generation to generation by person to person. This was done via the many guilds. For example, a young teen who desired to become a stonemason, joined the Stone Mason's Guild, where he worked as an apprentice for six years, learning his craft. Well over three centuries ago with the introduction of coins as a means of exchange, the many guilds expanded and began thriving.

These artisans, craftsmen, and women worked hard, trading their wares and products for coins they used to purchase agricultural products and other necessities of life. Long had these hardworking men and women watched the privileged few rise to become wealthy nobles and rulers. With the coming of the *mentales* gifted, they saw many others elevated to high status within their kingdoms. Over the centuries, they saw the shifting changes in just who ruled their kingdoms and thus their lives, from kings to the *mentales* gifted in their towers, to the *mentales* gifted lords, to simple lords, and, now in the late 1290's, to those elite, who were elected as their senators and rulers.

With the coming of the Declaration of Human Rights, many took heart. At last, they had a voice in their leaders or so they thought and hoped. And yet, what many had envisioned had still not come true. The guild members saw the same old actions being done. The wealthy continued to be wealthy. The kings continued to be kings. The *Jefe* continued to be the wealthy landowners, while they continued to have little power, save their relatively minor vote in the senate elections.

By and large, the many guilds had endured the hardships thrown upon them over the centuries, even overworked during times of war. They felt jilted. Then came the Great Meteor Shower and the subsequent explosion in the sheer numbers of the *mentales* gifted. Of course, many of these newly gifted men and women were drawn into the many towers across Tierra, with promises of a far better life, to say nothing of joining what they saw as the upper class of the world.

However, far more of these new *mentales* gifted men and women remained ordinary folk, continuing with their lives, though they all eventually received basic training from a tower, along with their prized crystals, which amplified their powers significantly. Many of these new *mentales* gifted belonged to one of the many guilds found throughout Tierra. Enter the discovery of the giant crystals. With their queen offering a bounty for any such crystal turned into her, along with similar rewards being offered by the many towers, to say nothing of the roving bands of tower folk scouring the lands looking for these buried crystals, these guilds took notice.

The *mentales* gifted within the many guilds began to find such crystals for themselves. One by one, they discovered the incredible powers that just one of these giant crystals gave them. Secretly, they began collecting them for themselves and their own guilds, to which they were quite loyal. After all, their closest friends and coworkers formed their own private worlds, their peers, with whom their guild knowledge was being passed on to their children.

By 1293, many had heard that an angry guild member in the Kingdom of Valen had used one of these giant crystals to tear down the Valen Castle's giant gates and fry half of his guards, before being killed by an alien weapon in King Alano Valen's possession. Ideas sprouted in nearly every guild house on Tierra. During 1293 and in contrast to the attacker of Valen Castle, many put these precious crystals to work within their guilds, dramatically increasing production capabilities. By this time, the *mentales* gifted within a guild had risen to positions of leadership, if not Guild Master. Further, each guild established their own communications network with their corresponding guild houses in other towns and cities around Tierra. However as of this date, there was little communication between different guilds, that is, the Stone Mason's Guild didn't communicate with the Weaver's Guild, for example.

Yet, there was a big difference between the guild leaders and the ruling elites and their towers. Each ruler only paid attention to his or her own kingdom, likewise their towers. In stark contrast, any given Stone Mason's Guild was in contact with all of the other such guilds across all of Tierra. Westerlings, Easterlings, and Midlands Stone Mason's Guilds were in frequent contact with each other. Until the arrival of these giant crystals, such communication existed, but was terribly slow; sometimes a message took a year to get from say Turda to Benito. The guilds had always worked together, developing better methods and techniques, and sharing them with their working brothers or sisters. Thus, the guilds possessed a most unique structure and organization. Combine that with their long tradition of working together, and one can see their natural evolution to power.

Additionally, over three hundred years of evolution and growth yielded strong, fortified guild houses. While the size and quality of such structures varied from town to town, city to city, and from kingdom to kingdom, usually they were quite large and made of stone, where possible. In the Easterlings, however, thick adobe bricks were used, as stone was extremely difficult to obtain there, especially in the desert regions. Furthermore, each guild employed numerous guards. Only guild members were allowed inside. It was not uncommon for a city of twenty thousand to have two dozen such mini-fortresses within its city limits.

During the summer, discontent had grown considerably, especially in the Kingdom of Valen. King Alano Valen had divided up his larger kingdom, giving away those sections of the large kingdom, whose people had insisted on following the now common ruling practices of electing their senators and kings. What remained became the new Kingdom of Valen, under his sole rule. That he was defying Queen Amy's declarations didn't faze him. He kept those lands that he and his extended family owned along with the lands owned by his loyal noblemen and women. In Valen, the guilds continued their long-time suffering, forced to meet quotas of production, while being paid far too little for their work or products.

One outraged *mentales* gifted weapons smith had

finally taken action, storming Valen Castle. He used a giant crystal to magnify his gifts, ripping the massive gates from their hinges and launching immense balls of fire onto the king's Royal Guards just inside the castle. He and his small band could well have succeeded in overthrowing King Alano had the king not used his alien hunting rifle to kill the weapons smith, ending the uprising. "Remember Jorge" became a commonplace greeting among the members of the Valen Weapons Smith Guild.

Dimas, the current guild master, exclaimed, "It's high time we take action. Remember Jorge!" Dozens of men returned his shout: Remember Jorge!

One asked, "But what can we do? He's got illegal alien weapons?"

"Look, I've a plan. The High Council will be meeting in a few days. Queen Amy and Governor Katrina will be there officiating. I'm going to get — no force those two to acknowledge our plight," Dimas explained. He outlined what he had in mind. The many members urged him on.

The next day, he sat down with his giant crystal between his legs. He focused and began observing the throng in the giant Throne Room. He located Queen Amy, she was hard to miss, standing up front. Then, he spotted Governor Katrina over at one side. He waited and then struck. Using his Domination gift, he invaded their minds and sent, *Make a Formal Ruling that all guilds on Tierra are no longer subject to any taxes! Make that Formal Ruling now!*

For an instant, he felt as if he was succeeding. Suddenly, he was hit with an enormous backlash of raw psi energies. Stunned, his concentration broke, and he slumped over, unconscious for a time. Later, he reported on his failure, hinting that somehow Queen Amy must have many of these giant crystals to protect herself. That led to a determination by all of the guild members to scour the countryside and find even more for their guild.

Dimas also learned another valuable lesson, one he would not soon forget. "We must unite all of the Weapons Smith Guilds into a single unified whole. Together, we are vastly stronger than we are alone." Thus, during the remainder of 1293, Dimas worked with all of the Westerlings Weapons Smith Guilds, preaching unification. His proposal took root and was implemented.

Unlike the many kingdoms, he divided the Westerlings into three zones, clearly demarcated by two major rivers. The Northern Westerlings Weapons Smith Guild consisted of all the guilds north of the Brozas River. The Southern Westerlings Weapons Smith Guild consisted of all the guilds south of the Alcantara River. The Central Westerlings Weapons Smith Guild contained all of the guilds between these two major rivers. Each of these three elected a Grand Master, who presided over the member guilds.

His idea was quickly adopted by the over two dozen other types of guilds during the winter of 1293-4. Further, news of his reorganization spread to the Midlands guilds and then to the Easterlings as well. During the early spring of 1294, they, too, began to adopt this new organization. The Midlands divided into two regions, the Northern Midlands Guilds and the Southern Midlands Guilds, with the demarcation being the South Fork River and the Wal River. The Easterlings formed three larger groups. The Southern Easterlings Guilds occupied Matruk and Alba. The Central Easterlings Guilds were primarily in the Arad, while the Northern Easterlings Guilds were in Domei. Each of these elected their own Grand Master.

By the summer of 1294, the twenty-five different types of guilds had adopted the regional organization, each with their own Grand Masters. Yet, Grand Master Dimas didn't stop here. Next, he proposed the various Grand Masters meet face to face and elect from among themselves a Supreme Grand Master to oversee all of them. His motto, "United as one, we stand," was soon carved into the archway entrances of all Weapons Smith Guilds across Tierra. Later on, all the other many guilds adopted it.

Where to meet took longer to decide than when or even to meet. The rulers always met at the Imperial Castle in Exchange City, under the hospitality and guidance of Queen Amy. With their open hostility to all those in power, no one wanted to meet there, though they could easily have gotten Queen Amy's support had they asked. Instead, they debated for weeks. At this time, nearly every large city had a *Círculo de la Torres*. Their distaste, bordering on anger, with the towers kept them from considering such places to meet. They feared they would be spied upon by the towers, who were obviously in league with the rulers.

They met in Carpa, Alba, Easterlings. Why? Those in the Easterlings guilds were much poorer than those in the Westerlings and Midlands. Grand Master Dimas had the good sense to take that into consideration. Besides, there wasn't a tower around for hundreds of miles; it was very much an out of the way town in central Alba. There, Dimas was elected the Supreme Grand Master of the Weapons Smith Guild, much to his pleasure.

By the end of the summer of 1294, the other twenty-plus guilds had followed suit, and now boasted their own Supreme Grand Masters. Dimas was now poised to embark on his Grand Plan. These twenty-five Supreme Grand Masters then met as a group to decide on their next step.

Chapter 10 Changes Come

During the long spring on Proxima Prime, figuratively that is, since the temperature was always a constant seventy-five degrees planet-wide, President Zarita diligently continued her work on ferreting out the last vestiges of those who had assisted the three Consortium members to escape. She saw to the even distribution of the recovered fuel supplies.

Additionally, she investigated beginning textbooks that children of the Imperium used during their early education. She picked what she thought were the best and then arranged to have them translated into the Westerlings, Easterlings, and Midlands languages, using the language disks that Nadja had uploaded to the massive linguistics database of the Imperium.

Her objective was simple. Provide textbooks for use on Tierra so true education could thrive and begin to alter their status as an illiterate society. She knew learning was the answer. Somehow, she was going to make this possible for Tierra. Via Celenia, she had the Senate pass a law to begin similar projects for the other Closed Worlds, a law Celenia pushed hard to get passed. Its passage endeared her to the many Closed World senators.

During these first few months, President Zarita enjoyed widespread popularity, because she'd been the driving force behind the revelation of the Consortium's assassinations and their fuel shortage crisis. She was seen as a force that was eliminating governmental corruption. She'd even visited the Senate requesting them to reconsider compensating in some way the millions who had been forcibly relocated to other worlds during the previous war. She made the appeal using simple language. "How would you feel if tomorrow the Imperium forced you to move to Ashford-5 and gave you no warning and no choice in the matter? Wouldn't you be angry? Our soldiers volunteered to join the army and fight. These people were summarily ordered to move. They had no choice. I feel strongly some form of compensation will go a long way to healing such deep wounds."

The Senate finally acted and offered a proportional monetary settlement, based upon the value of the property and land confiscated from each individual. While it wasn't a large amount, it was at least something to help curtail the unrest coming from the Society for Freedom.

However, for the most part, President Zarita was incredibly bored. Her idea of what the president actually did versus the reality she now had were vastly different. Fundamentally, she realized that her notions were based on what the Tierra kings did. Here, the presidential duties were very mundane and boring for the most part, unless a crisis developed. She was thankful none did. At least the bombings had ended on Proxima Prime, though at this time she had no idea why. That knowledge would come much later.

Zarita learned by and large the immense political bureaucracy handled most all of the true executive duties of the Office of the President. These nameless men and women merely went about keeping the entire Imperium running. She likened them to a miniature automated computer system, without which, the Imperium would collapse entirely. Her role as President was more that of a figurehead, except for the occasional crisis, such as those she handled during her first weeks in office. "This is ridiculous. Any moron could be the President and the Imperium would not even know!"

On the other hand, Celenia was extremely harried, as she tried to cope with running the entire Senate. Often, she complained bitterly that, if she had hands, it might be possible to hold this position, but as helpless as she was, it was a living nightmare. Still, that didn't keep her from working hard at it, along with Lelane, who often came home with writer's cramps.

The one thing Celenia became known for was maintaining order and keeping the senators on the topic at hand. That she also had an uncanny aptitude for ferreting out the truth of a matter earned her the respect of many senators.

"I can't wait for the three month summer vacation!" Celenia exclaimed one night in late April.

"It's really hard on you isn't it?" Zarita asked. Lelane nodded her head vigorously.

"Well, yes, but I must not let Emperor Kino down. He's

depending upon us. The stakes are so high, Zarita, so terribly high," Celenia answered honestly and with a deep sigh.

"I know. It's far harder on you, my love. Look, the crises are over. We've brought stability back to the Imperium. We ought to end on a positive win. I'm going to come to the Senate tomorrow and tell them so. I think it's time to elect a new President and Senate President too. We've done what we were asked to do; we've proven we can do the job, but I don't really want to be the President either," Zarita explained.

"Really? You don't mind not being the President any longer? It's such an important position, love," Celenia countered. "I'd feel just awful if you were giving it up just because of me and my helplessness."

"No, it has nothing to do with that, dear. If we can leave office now, we'll be winners in everyone's eyes, not the losers that everyone predicted. Being the President is incredibly boring, though I admit not as boring as being Ashford's senator was. If we go out now, Emperor Kino wins too. His power will remain strong, if not stronger," Zarita added.

The next day, President Zarita walked carefully onto the central platform of the Senate amphitheater. "Hello senators, one and all. I've come before you today to let you all know that the various crises we all faced have been ended. The assassinations have been solved. The fuel shortage subversion has been uncovered and ended. Fuel prices have dropped almost to pre-war levels, and supplies are well distributed. We've not had any more bombings on Proxima Prime. I've done all I can to remedy the critical issues we faced this past winter. We are at peace and once more on the road to prosperity. Thus, I believe that my work as your President is complete. I come before you today to ask that you terminate my temporary appointment as the Imperium President and elect someone, who really wishes to hold this high position. I certainly do not."

Senator Ari called out, "But you have been a great President!" She was protesting, but her words were misinterpreted. Several senators began clapping. Soon, the room exploded in a loud round of applause, which President Zarita graciously bowed and accepted. When the noise died down, another one asked how soon she wanted to leave.

"I'd like the new President to have the summer vacation period to get familiar with the job. Honestly, I was just thrown into a rather chaotic mess and left to fend for myself. I did my best and got results, but it'd be vastly smoother, if you could elect a new President soon, so he or she can far more easily make the transition," she suggested. Again, many catcalls of approval echoed around the huge chamber.

A week later, they elected Senator Balag Snod of Rimus-3 to be the new temporary President. The following week, they elected a new Senate President, Michael Sanders of Jena-4. Summer vacation for the senators began the week after that.

President Zarita held a news conference to explain her departure and to introduce formally the new President Balag. After staying on for an additional week helping smooth the transition, she finally returned to her Senate seat in time to watch the inauguration of their new Senate President. The last week before vacation, the two once more sat in their old seats beside Senator Tabia. Both had retired with high honors, which did, in fact, greatly aid Emperor Kino. The overall respect the general public had for Emperor Kino was nearly twice what he had as the "war hero." Plus, the Senate was buzzing about these two women and just how incredibly successful both had been.

With the pressures off, each evening of this final week, it was "party time," according to Ari and B'nath, who continued to spend most of their evenings in their secure compound. Ari and B'nath extended invitations for them to come visit them on their worlds. Ari explained, "The first half of the summer, we will be on my world, Acer-4. The second half, we'll be on B'nath's world, Groz-3. I wish you could come and visit each of our worlds. We'd like to come visit yours too."

Zarita laughed. "You've never seen a primitive world before, eh?" she teased Ari, who had become a very good friend of theirs, as was B'nath. Zarita felt a certain closeness to Ari, who was rather like herself — a strong, outgoing, take charge type of woman. B'nath was more like Celenia, content to play the more docile wifely role.

Ari laughed, "Oh no. Do we have to wear furs instead of

dresses?" All five roared, though Lelane's was a silent laugh.

"Okay, we'll try to visit your worlds. I want to give Celenia some time to learn how Lena and Drina manage to do things for themselves. Once that is done, we can travel some. You can contact us via Queen Amy. We'll use her comm system to chat with you two at least once a week, how's that? By the way, we don't have any pool tables on Tierra that I know about."

Ari faked a look of disappointment. "No problem. We'll make time to get together. Celenia, you're going to have to show us what all you can do at the end of summer."

She sighed, "Don't expect much. I'm, well — you know." She didn't want to come right out and say it again.

For a change, the slightly different calendar systems between the Imperium Standard Year and that of Tierra were nearly aligned. As the summer break came on the first of June 1294, it was also the last week of May on Tierra. Days later, Zarita's personal deep space transport began its descent onto the space station on Plateau Grado. Zarita was very glad to be home, but Celenia was worried about whether she could even learn to do the magical things that Drina did for herself.

Their first action was to give Governor Katrina and Queen Amy and their groups a full report. Katrina had Whitney, Carla, and Elfe with her as usual, while the Gang of Ten was with Queen Amy. All gathered in the same large conference room of Governor Katrina's. Their report took several hours. Both Katrina and Amy asked many questions, but Zarita knew Amy and Jan knew just how the four men had died — namely that she'd done the deed.

When they finished up. Governor Katrina exclaimed, "Well, you two, I'm incredibly impressed with what all you both have done these past few months! You are a credit to Tierra, Winno-3, and Emperor Kino. Frankly, I must admit I was both shocked to hear of your elections and fearful for your lives. Imperium politics can be a very dangerous profession. Well done, both of you, and you too, silent Lelane." Her personal assistant smiled broadly.

"Now you can dump those monster dresses, chop off those giant claws, sit back, and relax," Jan suggested.

"Ah, just when I am finally able to do a few things with them?" Zarita teased her.

"Don't get too used to it," Amy broke in. "According to Lilly, many noblewomen are now sporting foot long nails too."

"Oh no!" Zarita exclaimed.

"Oh yes. Thankfully, I don't have any fingers to worry about, nor does Lena or Drina," Amy added, "but don't put your hoops away. Lilly says many noblewomen are demanding similar dresses for later this summer. I don't know how you can manage them, Celenia. I may have to have you give me and Lena and Drina lessons later on." Everyone laughed again.

Drina spoke up, "We've got your guest suite all fixed up for you three. Friday nights, we all get together for fun. Katrina and her group always joins us for party time. But watch out for your money, Katrina and Lena always seem to win the large pots." Several giggled. Bernardo merely groaned.

"Ah, is it all right for Senator Ari and Senator B'nath to come here for a visit later this summer?" Zarita asked.

"Sure, senators have diplomatic immunity and can always visit Closed Worlds, though in reality, they seldom, if ever, do so," Governor Katrina answered formally.

"Great. I told them they could get a hold of us through Amy's comm center. I hope that is all right with you, Amy?" Zarita said, somewhat apologetically.

"Sure. You'll be staying with us, so of course it's perfectly fine," Amy replied. "I know Lena and Drina are eager to help Celenia learn how to do many things for herself. Now that you have three months, she ought to make very good progress."

"Can we go horse riding soon? I've really missed that, Amy," Zarita asked.

"You and me both. I've not been riding since last year. We ought to get out soon. The grass is so green and full of new life. Let's," she explained.

"Count us in too," Whitney added.

Katrina, caught up in the moment, spoke up, "Gang, this is going to be the greatest summer ever!" She had no idea how prophetic her pronouncement was.

Chapter 11 Biological Warfare

Early June 1294. Location: Classified Imperium Research Station, Ashford-4. Security Clearance Ten required. In all the hustle and bustle of the spring, Zarita had completely forgotten about Ashford-4. In hindsight, even if she had discovered more about it, that would have made no difference. Ashford-4 rotates one time during its entire passage around the sun called Ashford. With the same side of the world always pointing to Ashford, temperatures there were broiling! But on the opposite side, it is always nighttime with very frigid temperatures. The world had almost no atmosphere left. It had either evaporated or frozen out, depending. Only a very narrow strip of land that lay between the zones of eternal light and dark was marginally habitable, and then only within the self-contained biosphere that formed the research station.

The station was built fifteen years ago, during the war with the Federation. It had several basic purposes, but all were war-related. The super-secure complex housed a dozen top scientists; all were bio-engineers, some specializing in genetic modifications, and some specializing in deadly germ warfare developments. Additionally, ten support staff were permanently stationed here. Unlike the scientists, these ten were incredibly bored. Essentially marooned here for the last fourteen years, they could not leave until their contracts expired in another five years. When they did return to civilization, they would be handsomely paid, though their minds would be wiped clean.

A lucrative war contract paid the salaries of these dozen bio-engineers. Their basic charge was the development of biological weapons that could be easily unleashed upon Federation worlds as a last ditch measure. When the project began, the war was not going well. Hence, the lab was setup in complete secrecy, and the scientists were charged with developing ways and means that would enable the Imperium to somehow wipe out enemy planets wholesale. Desperate times called for desperate measures — that was the motto instilled into these dozen men and women.

Half of the researchers were involved in developing the biological weapons per se. That is, they were charged with creating a biological weapon that could be remotely inserted into a planet, and within a relatively short amount of time, kill all human beings. If they could somehow also keep it from harming wildlife and plants, so much the better. Of course, the biological weapon would also have to have a relatively short life span; otherwise the Imperium could not land and take possession of that piece of real estate.

Already, these half dozen bio-engineers had succeeded. Of the hundreds of strains they developed, two had proven outstanding. One was airborne, the other, waterborne. One small canister of each released either in the atmosphere or into the oceans would result in the human population contacting what was nicknamed, "The Black Plague," because their test victims always turned black after dying. The airborne virus was extraordinarily deadly. Estimates suggested an entire planet would be wiped out within a week of its insertion into the atmosphere of the planet. That the whole process could be done via an unmanned drone was mere frosting.

Because of the deadliness of this work in progress, extreme protocols were in place and rigidly enforced. This was also why Ashford-4 was chosen. If there were an accidental release, the extreme environment of the planet would destroy the virus within minutes.

The other half of the bio-engineers were at work on genetic modifications, designed in part to alter the bodies of their victims, making them easy prey. The field of genetics had taken a rapid advance the last century, because finally all the races of humans thus far encountered within the vast Imperium had their complete gene sequences fully mapped out. Now, the bio-engineers were working on individual genes, modifying their ACGT sequences. Already, this technology breakthrough had resulted in the vastly improved rejuvenation machines. The erroneous errors in the sequences that built up over time causing the aging process, or mutations as they are technically called, were now able to be removed. Restored genes, with some help from stem cells, quickly repaired the human body, following the repaired gene sequences.

Armed with all the latest developments in genetic research, these half dozen were experimenting by altering some very specific sequences of particular genes. They had a cadre of a hundred humans on which to experiment. These were men and women who had been sentenced to life in prison for serious crimes, the least of which was murder. Now, their bodies were being used to help the Imperium survive, or so went the justifications at the top.

Some of the sequence modifications resulted in instant death of the body, once the body began duplicating the injected modified genes. One disastrous experiment resulted in a test subject's body dissolving his lungs, because the new pattern of genes suggested lungs was no longer a needed organ. In the early years, it had been mostly trial and error, with most ending in error, that is, with the test subject dying rather rapidly. Human bodies needed certain organs to survive, such as a heart and lungs. With billions of possible variations on DNA sequences and only a vague notion of which of the twenty-three chromosomes controlled the development of what part of the human body, the research really was one of try altering this and see what happens to the test subject.

In more recent years, these bio-engineers had learned far more and were now able to make some remarkable gene alterations. More importantly, when they were injected into a human host and activated by the same activation scheme used in the rejuvenation machines, the genes rapidly took control. The body altered physically, relatively rapidly following these new blueprints. These scientists continued to follow their original charge: develop a means whereby the population of an enemy planet could be altered so that they could be easily captured by Imperium soldiers, that is, make the indigenous population basically helpless. Having given up on their attempts to have bodies grow a third arm and similar grotesque features, they focused on aspects, which if combined, would make life much more of a challenge or even impossible for their supposed enemy victims.

Early on, these researchers looked over all known worlds for inspiration for their modifications. Nearby Ashford-

5 became an unknowing model, in many ways, for ideas about how to immobilize or render helpless a human body, though many other primitive worlds contributed ideas as well. Eventually, the accidental discovery modifications were finalized.

While two of the six continued making fine tuning tweaks to the results, the other four began work on a method of delivering one of these sets to a world's population. Again, this aspect was really one of biological warfare. Even though the war was officially over, work continued here on Ashford-4. Who could say when the next war would break out? Certainly, no one had given them any orders to abandon their impressive work. These dedicated scientists wanted to be fully prepared and ready when the next war happened. After all, if the war had not ended and the Imperium depended upon their research to win, they would not have been able to assist in time. Hence, they continued their diligent work, vowing never to be caught like this again.

Like the first team of six, their goal was to be able to infect remotely a world, causing all of its inhabitants to become genetically altered according to the given master blueprint. Now, it was one thing to extract an individual's genes, modify them, insert the altered ones back into the person along with their enhancing extract, activate it properly, and then watch that individual's body rapidly modify itself to match the blueprint, and quite another to create a form that could be somehow given to a mass of individuals and have all their bodies modify themselves to match the given blueprint of the desired changes. Quite another.

The first team already solved the least significant portion of the problem. They planned to use the airborne aerosol dispersal formula that was working perfectly in delivering the deadly viruses that would easily and quickly wipe out all mammal life on a planet. The first team merely piggybacked their virus onto the aerosol dispersal chemical molecules. This second team intended to do the same thing with their genetic formula. The delivery method dictated the formula be inhaled into the victim's lungs. From there, it would be absorbed by blood capillaries in the lungs and begin to execute its intended genetic modifications on the person. That was the plan.

The second team faced setback after setback. Around the start of 1294, the already highly successful first team joined forces with the second team in an effort to bridge the gap between infecting a single individual and infecting a whole population with the genetic modifications. That's when they hit upon the neutral carrier molecule, which was able to carry the specific gene transformations but in an isolated environment. That is, the environment was not tied to any one person's individual genes, but to specific genes within the human DNA structure. Essentially, with this neutral carrier, they were able to insert the various unique ACGT sequences destined for a specific gene. When the substance was inserted into a person's bloodstream, the process was activated, much as human hands in the lab here had been done it at the research station. I say hands, but really, it was done with extremely sensitive and tiny medical equipment.

In May, the process finally worked on their single test subject, who had been subjected to a whole battery of physical alterations over the past many months. The dozen scientists now were all very excited about their results. Preparations were then made for a decisive test in which the remaining ten test subjects would be used, simulating an aerosol delivery into the atmosphere of a planet. Of note, the other ninety test subjects had already perished long ago, during previous tests. They were only hardened criminals, sentenced to death anyway.

However, some care had to be used in this extensive test. Why? This second team had compiled a rather extensive list of modifications that they could cause in any given human body. Initially, they had scoured the Web for ideas for what to modify, taking hints from some of the more primitive cultures as well as civilized ones. Some were mutually exclusive. For example, they could have a body's arms wither and drop off — the inserted genetic blueprint dictated no arms, so the test subject's modified genes quickly responded to their new orders. Or they could have the fingernails grow to a foot long, like those of their female senators. Here, they inserted a self-protecting aspect to prevent the victim from merely trimming their long nails: intense pain plus immediate regrowth. Thus, in this big test, they could not both schedule long nails and no arms, since obviously they were mutually exclusive. However, the scientists desired an extensive test, and put together a rather heady sample of modifications, some extremely significant, others more along the cosmetic lines.

Another reason this group of scientists were now very excited about this research lay in the accidental discovery of a side effect. On victim-90, they had already modified his genetic makeup no longer to have arms. Later on, they neglected to observe the current shape of victim-90 and subjected him to another test, one that attempted to have his fingernails lengthened to a foot. After the several days-long process was finished, victim-90 had the desired nails. That's when one of the scientists discovered they had inadvertently been able to restore lost limbs! This discovery would be revolutionary in the medical field, once they were able to publish their results. The dozen cracked a bottle of Champaign over this discovery.

Early June, they loaded up the neutral carrier molecules with as many compatible modifications as possible. Their last surviving ten test subjects were then going to be exposed to the prototype aerosol delivery mechanism, just as though it were being dropped onto an enemy planet. A single-man shuttle was loaded with the giant canister containing the mixture, but only a small amount of fuel was actually loaded into the shuttle. It didn't have to fly very far for this experiment. Of course, there was no atmosphere on Ashford-4 from which actually to inject the substance. While the giant canister had the proper devices attached to it so it could detect the presence of an atmosphere and automatically begin releasing the contents of the container, in this test, they would use a computer controlled manual override. As the shuttle flew over the isolated buildings housing the test subjects, they would release the gas, which would float down and be sucked into the air circulation system and thus reach the ten victims. Nothing could go wrong.

Around ten that morning, one of the support staff,

Abelard, was performing the last minute checks on the shuttle, preparatory to their big test. He knew this test run was extremely important to the many scientists. As far as he was concerned, the continual rechecking at least gave him something to do besides sit around reading the same books he'd already read a hundred times. At this moment, Ashford-4 crossed a debris field from an extinct comet. Without an atmosphere to burn up the smaller fragments, the tiny chunks struck the roofs of the many sections that made up this very secure complex, but at a very high velocity and thus momentum.

Before anyone realized what was about to happen, a chuck the size of one's thumb pierced the roof of the isolated containment building in which the highly virulent biological and genetic agents were kept under strict, tight quarantine. Continuing its downward drive, it cut through one of the cylinders holding one of the deadly new viruses. Shortly after that, ten more rained down puncturing the roof even further, damaging three more of these steel containers. Across the adjoining buildings, more stones, traveling at high velocities and at an oblique angle to the horizontal, pierced the steel roofs as well, ripping holes in the sidewalls as well. Suddenly, the automatic sensors activated, having detected the release of these deadly toxins. Red lights flashed in all areas. Automatic steel doors closed and locked to prevent the spread of the outbreak. That humans were thus trapped within various rooms was not important, only the containment of the outbreak was.

Unfortunately for everyone concerned, the extremely well designed containment systems and procedures were not designed for such a roof and wall rupture. The toxins spread rapidly into the air recycling system, supplying breathable air to all of the many rooms in this large, super-secure complex. Although no one was aware of it at the time, at the point when the sirens and flashing red lights began blaring and the containment doors shut and locked, the toxins had already spread throughout all the complex.

A minute after the sirens and lights drowned out everything, Abelard found himself suddenly cut off from the rest of the complex. The heavy steel doors had locked automatically. He raced to the nearest door and pounded on the opening latch and then the digital controls, frantically entering his access code. Biological Event Override Protocol. The words kept flashing on the digital panel, which refused to open the door. Abelard felt trapped. He knew what this emergency meant. One of the toxic creations of these scientists had somehow leaked. Everyone would die. "I don't want to die!" Abelard screamed, though there was no one around to hear his cries. The deafening noise of the continuous alarms drowned everything else out. Frantic to save himself from a horrid death, he looked around for any way out.

His eyes then fell on the partially fueled shuttle. Here was his sole chance to live! He raced to the shuttle, climbed into the driver's seat, and closed the door. Without any thought, he powered up the ship and entered the access code to open the roof doors that would allow him to take off. They didn't open, and Abelard panicked further. Then, he remembered here in the hangar bay, the dome overhead was made of a thin metal skin. Bust through! That was his only idea. He jammed the throttle to maximum acceleration, pulled back on the stick. The shuttle swooped upwards in a sharp curve, its needle-like nose pierced through the thin dome. His little shuttle shot upwards off Ashford-4 like an arrow. He was free. He was alive. He was going to survive.

Hastily, he looked at his fuel gauge and panic again swept over him. There was so little fuel. What to do? Where could he go? Ashford-5! The only inhabited planet in the Ashford system was within reach, but barely. With shaking fingers, Abelard punched in the coordinates and activated the automatic guidance system. He felt the lurch of the small shuttle as it veered onto its new course. At last, Abelard attempted to calm his racing heart, his rapid breathing. "I'll make it. I am alive. I'm going to make it to safety!" Terror and panic gave way to elation and immense relief. He shouted out various phrases, such as "Thank you shuttle!" He had no way to see the ugly red splotches that had already begun forming on his forehead or beneath his shirt on his chest.

A half hour later, he felt sick at his stomach and a bit

dizzy. He closed his eyes and never again opened them. Abelard, like everyone else at the super-secure Classified Imperium Research Station, was dead. His shuttle continued on its automated path to Ashford-5. It didn't need any human to reach its destination or even to land for that matter, another marvel of Imperium technology.

Chapter 12 Contagion

In the control tower, the Rigel-3 director spoke into the comm system, "Shuttle 239535 on approach to Ashford-5 come in please." Static. He repeated his words thrice more. Still static. Following protocol, he pressed the "Unauthorized Landing" button. Far below his tower, a red light began flashing. At once, a small detachment of Rigel-3 Security Guards rapidly buckled on their armor, grabbed their d-guns, and raced out to Landing Point 21, the indicated location where the automated guidance system would be landing this unauthorized shuttle.

Following protocols precisely, the director called Governor Katrina. "Governor, an unauthorized shuttle is about to land. They are not responding to our hails. Guards are on their way to Landing Point 21. I'm hereby notifying you of this breach of landing protocols."

"Er, thanks. What kind of craft is it? Threatening?" Governor Katrina tried to make some sense of this event.

"Shuttle type 32, very short range."

Katrina thought quickly. "Isn't that a shuttle that is used to travel around a planet?"

"Yes."

"Do we have any shuttles up now?"

"None. No flight plans have been filed for today."

"Can you id its point of origin? Is it from Ashford-5? It must certainly be from here somewhere," Katrina tried to grasp what was going on. This tiny shuttle was always used to move one or two people around a planet. It was incapable of traveling the vast distances between stars and their planetary systems. For that, one needed one of the usual models of transport ships.

"Back tracking now. It will take a while. Its ID number is apparently classified at Security Level 10. Strange."

"Give me its number again, and see if you can backtrack its trajectory and estimate a point of origin," she ordered. He repeated the number, and she jotted it down. From the invoked protocol, she knew she wasn't needed at Landing

Point 21 just yet. For now, it was in the capable hands of her Security Guards. She entered the number into her computer, using the tips of her long nails to depress the keys. Typing had now become slow and tedious with such long nails, but emulating the locals had paid royal dividends. Katrina no longer complained about such minor things. Up came Security Level 10. Enter your code. She carefully typed hers in and hit the Enter key.

Her monitor displayed: Shuttle 239535 assigned to Classified Imperium Research Station, Ashford-4. Nothing else appeared. *Well, at least I know it came from this star system. What the heck is on Ashford-4? It's not a habitable world,* she thought. Perplexed, she carefully rose to her feet, got her balance on her toes, and looked out of her window. Shortly, she spotted her Rigel-3 Security Guards moving into position. She watched, confident they had everything under control.

Not long after that, she saw the small two-man shuttle descending a bit too rapidly. It finally registered in her mind. The shuttle must be out of fuel. Its retro engines were not firing. It was going to make a fairly hard landing. "Damn!" she exclaimed, jarring her giant lip plates, which bounced a little on her upper chest. The shuttle hit hard, but did not explode, though the heavy glass windows did shatter and the underside of the shuttle was significantly crushed. She watched as her men moved forward to extricate the illegally landing personnel.

Suddenly, red warning lights and loud sirens began blaring. Over all the loud speakers, a computerized voice stated, "Warning. Biological contamination detected. Safety protocols in place. Lock down activated." All over the sprawling complex, steel doors automatically closed and locked. Some, like the Security Guards, were left stranded outside the complex. Governor Katrina was locked in her office, as were most other personnel.

"Oh! Okay," Doctor Whitney exclaimed, as the sirens and red lights activated. "I don't know if this is a drill or not, but let's get cracking, nurses. Biological attack of some kind. Into the suits everyone. Someone give me a hand, please," she added as calmly as possible. Around her, the six nurses looked startled and shocked. *They need guidance, that's my job,* she thought, moving as quickly as possible to the next room where the full-body suits were kept.

Exchanging hushed thoughts, the nurses began getting into the red suits, while Whitney removed her lip plates, knowing they would not fit inside the helmet. Thankfully, one nurse lent her a hand getting into hers. Once everyone was dressed, she spoke through the suit's intercom. "Okay. Double-check your neighbor's suit. If this is for real, I don't want to lose one of you." She proceeded to check the nurse who was helping her. Seven "Checks" came over the headsets. "All right, everyone got their detectors? Do a battery check on them. Mine checks," she ordered. Then, they made their slow way from the medical lab through the halls and out onto the tarmac. Only her pass code was able to open the barrier doors. Until she entered the all clear code, no one else in the entire spaceport could get a door open. Containment of a biological or nerve agent attack was the top priority.

As she approached the six Security Guards, she noticed five were extremely nervous, but their sergeant wasn't. He'd sounded the alarm. "Doctor, probably nothing, but you know protocols. Highly suspicious body in this shuttle. It's all yours. God, I hope this isn't an attack or we're as good as dead."

"Well done, sergeant, take your men and stand back at least fifty feet," she requested, moving slowly up to where she could take a look inside the shattered windows at the dead man in the control seat. "My god! Biological attack for sure! Okay, nurses, use the detectors. Scan the ship thoroughly, but be careful. Don't get too close. We don't want to risk a tear in our suits."

From her high vantage point, Governor Katrina watched the red suited figures moving slowly out to the shuttle. She swallowed hard. One was her mate. She spotted the slow moving Whitney. "Dear god! Keep her safe, please!" She adjusted her comm system and tuned into the seven's intercom system. She'd just heard Doctor Whitney's pronouncement and gasped. Biological attack! Then, the streaming video came through from Doctor Whitney's suit camera located on the top of her helmet. The man's ghastly looking face was covered in hideous red splotches, and the rest of his body was covered with some awful looking black patches. Governor Katrina sucked in air; this was no drill!

Swallowing hard, Governor Katrina called the control tower. "Verified Biological attack! Have you traced the origin of that shuttle yet? Are there more incoming shuttles?"

"Oh god! We're all dead!" the man cried out.

"Not yet. Get a hold of yourself. We're secure inside these doors. Are there more attacks on the way?" she barked.

"Er. No others. The alarm has gone out. Four incoming ships are in stationary orbit awaiting further orders. Still trying to track its origin. Need another half hour at least," he replied.

She looked down at Doctor Whitney again, wondering if she dared speak to her just now. Fearing to distract her, Governor Katrina sighed instead, and continued to watch the streaming video. After a long, suspense-filled half hour, Doctor Whitney turned towards the twenty-story tower and gave a thumbs-up sign. "Governor Katrina. This was a biological attack. We are in luck. The agent that killed this man as mostly been destroyed already or he was infected elsewhere and came here for help. Our detectors are registering only minute traces of some unknown biological agent, and that is coming from the corpse itself. We're going to hermetically seal the corpse, and then I want this whole shuttle moved into the containment shed. We need to go over it with a fine-tooth comb. As soon as we've sealed the corpse, I'll send the all clear codes. Stand by."

Governor Katrina watched the live video, as the nurses inserted one end of a tube through the broken window. A rush of transparent liquid sealant shot out, filling the small cabin. A minute later, it hardened into a solid block, totally encasing the corpse, preventing any possible contamination from spreading from the body. The Security Guards brought up a tractor and hauled the entire ship to the containment shed, a large hanger-like building adjacent to the main buildings. Once inside, the containment double set of doors activated, sealing the ship tight. That done, Doctor Whitney entered the proper code. All the doors automatically unlocked, the red lights and sirens ceased, much to the relief of everyone.

Governor Katrina headed down to the medical lab, figuring, as slow as she was, Doctor Whitney would be back before she got there. She was right. Doctor Whitney and her nurses were just getting out of their suits. "Well boss, that was definitely a biological attack from some unknown agent. We've got seven samples digitally recorded on our handheld detectors. Per protocols, you are going to have to inform the Sector ID Minister. Tell him I said the bio-agent is unknown at this time, but extremely deadly. I'll know more once I've done an autopsy on the corpse and examined the shuttle. Any idea where the attack came from?"

"Unclear just now. Thank god, you are all right. I was worried about all of you. Okay, I best let the Sector ID Minister know. Keep me posted, doctor," she kept her words professional, though she really wanted to say many other things to her mate. Now was not the time. She turned and headed back to her office. As she left, one nurse said, "Do we use the dog?" Doctor Whitney said yes. The dog was a mechanically controlled machine that would allow them to do the autopsy and complete examination of the shuttle remotely without any risk of getting themselves contaminated.

After making the mandatory report to the Sector ID Minister, Governor Katrina opened up a line to every speaker on the base. "This is Governor Katrina Lutgard. As you know, we've just had a scare. A shuttle crash landed. The pilot was a victim of a biological attack and was dead long before the shuttle landed. At this time, our doctor reports the biological agent that attacked the pilot of the shuttle has dissipated and poses no health risk to base personnel. I repeat, there is no immediate danger from this bio attack. The shuttle and its crew are now in a secure, quarantined shed. The proper authorities have been notified, and we are working to determine the origin of the shuttle and perhaps where the attack occurred. I'll keep you all up to date. Well done, everyone. We all responded appropriately to the emergency. Nicely done." She ended, sensing the relief coming from many minds of those on the base.

A bit later, the control tower director reported to her office. "Boss, I've got a simulation to show you. No guarantee this is entirely accurate, my best guess."

"Go ahead."

"Okay, the shuttle ran out of fuel within a half hour of its takeoff, according to telemetry data. The pilot entered our coordinates into the automatic guidance system and engaged it. Once the fuel was expended, the shuttle requested updated information from the pilot. Apparently, it got none, so the automatic safety protocols engaged."

"What does that mean?" she asked. This was out of her sphere of knowledge.

"The shuttle's computer system brought the ship to its destination. Essentially, it did a controlled glide. When it reached our upper atmosphere, the computer knew there was no fuel to land safely, so it compensated. It made a series of ten circles around Ashford-5, dropping lower and lower, using air resistance to slow the shuttle down substantially. Then, it came on in on a low glide. I'd say the safety protocols worked admirably well. The ship didn't crash, and the passengers should have survived, if they had been alive anyway. Pretty neat piece of automation, if I do say so myself. We have so darn many failsafe features in today's ships that they are incredibly safe. Amazing. Anyway, based on its trajectory, I've determined that it came from Ashford-4, strange as that sounds. Nothing is there; it's uninhabited. Now, it's on your plate, boss," he grinned.

"Excellent work. I'll relay this to the Sector ID Minister immediately. Hang around in case he has some questions about the trajectory," Governor Katrina requested. A half hour later, the two had finished their report.

"He didn't sound none too pleased, did he?" the director hinted, as he turned to leave.

"Not at all. I wonder what's going on there that we don't know," Katrina mused.

Around four that afternoon, Governor Katrina, Doctor Whitney, her six nurses, Carla, Elfe, Henkel, Jaques, and her head of security met in her office to go over the results. Doctor Whitney presented her findings, "Okay, autopsy done. It was definitely a biological attack that killed the pilot. All I was able to determine is his first name, Abelard. Everything else about the man is classified way beyond my clearance and yours too, governor. He was assigned to Ashford-4, believe it or not. Anyway, he died from an unknown biological agent long before the shuttle crash. I've not been able to identify the bio agent. It is a new one, apparently extremely virulent. My best guess is he was dead within a half hour of exposure, very virulent indeed."

"Is there any danger to us?" Governor Katrina asked, still worried about this whole nightmare affair.

"From this agent? No. We can't be infected from his corpse. We'd have to be exposed to the actual agent wherever he was exposed. From what little analysis I can do on it, the lifetime of the agent is rather short. So even, if the corpse were still contagious, by now the agent would be kaput. Nevertheless, I'm keeping the corpse sealed. Boss, there is something else that you should know."

Her face looked a little pale, Katrina thought. "We've been detecting something else in the air late this afternoon. It is registering on our detectors as an unknown agent. We've not yet done a full survey of all plant life on Tierra, so these readings could be from a local plant not in the detector's database. However, I am not so sure now."

"How come?" Katrina asked.

"Well, we discovered a giant biological agent container attached to the hold of the shuttle. The tank is empty, but we are getting the same readings from it that we are getting now from the air around us. Salaish, show her, please," she asked one of her nurses, who held one of the detectors.

She activated it, and placed the device on the table so everyone could see the readouts. Unknown agent. It then flashed a concentration level every few seconds. Doctor Whitney continued, "The readings here inside the building are only slightly lower than those in the open air on the tarmac. I sent Salaish around the entire station, having her make observations across the entire plateau. The results are pretty much the same, a rather uniform distribution. Alas, I've no idea what this may mean, other than some local plant pollen.

I'm going to set up a filtration system next to see if I can capture enough of a sample to analyze further, just to be on the safe side. Rest easy. Whatever this anomaly is, it's most definitely not the bio agent that killed the shuttle pilot."

"Damn, this isn't good news, doctor," Katrina exclaimed, growing worried. She outlined what the tower director had determined the shuttle's flight path had been. "It's circled within Ashford-5's atmosphere ten times. Is it possible the shuttle was releasing whatever was in that bio cylinder, doctor?"

"Good god I hope not! We best get to work on that one immediately," Doctor Whitney exclaimed. Katrina sensed extreme worry emanating from her mate and her six nurses as well. Doctor Whitney tried to calm nerves, "At least, it isn't whatever killed the pilot. That much we're absolutely certain of. If you have nothing further, we best get onto this at once. Have someone bring us supper in the lab, governor."

Katrina knew this was serious. Never had Whitney asked for supper in her lab! That was totally out of character for her. "Okay, keep me posted, doctor. I'll relay this on up to the Sector ID Minister. Meeting dismissed." Doctor Whitney rose at once. Accompanied by her worried nurses, they headed back down to their lab.

Later, Katrina made her slow, careful way to the mess hall. As she sat her tray down, she realized this was the first time she was dining without her lover at hand. How strange, she thought. As she looked around the mess hall, she saw far fewer than normal men and women were here eating. Curious, she thought. She was definitely hungrier than normal, eating about twice as much as she usually did. Even Carla and Elfe failed to join her, how strange. *Perhaps it's just the scare we all got this morning. Best go check on how it's coming with Whitney.*

As she walked down to the lab, there seemed to be fewer people in the halls than normal. She herself felt terribly tired and a little ill. It's just all the stress of this awful day, she told herself. When she reached the medical lab, she found fifty people were here, lying on all conceivable flat surfaces. The six nurses were tending to them. "Just a bout of flu we think," one nurse spoke up, as she spotted Governor Katrina entering. "If you aren't feeling well, best find someplace to lie down. We'll check you out as soon as we can. Nothing serious, we don't think."

"Where's Whitney?"

"In the sealed lab trying to collect up enough samples from the air to analyze. Best not go in there; it will disrupt the collection process," the nurse replied.

"Okay, I'll be in my quarters then. Have the doctor contact me as soon as she is able to." Katrina felt almost nauseous now, but guessed it was the surprise of seeing so many with the flu. She made it back to her suite and laid down. She closed her eyes and fell unconscious. One by one, the hundreds of others on at the spaceport lost consciousness as well. Some were out on the tarmac working. Those simply dropped down onto the concrete and stone. The lucky ones were already in bed like Katrina. Inside the lab, Whitney was sweating, but still trying to accumulate enough of the particles from the air to be able to do a proper analysis. Finally, her own legs gave out, and she too slumped to the floor of her lab.

Across Tierra, as night fell, most everyone headed off to bed. Only a few wasted lantern fuel to stay up later. In a way, this was an incredible blessing to the many inhabitants of Tierra. Had they collapsed during the busy daytime hours, many accidents would have resulted. Nearly everyone passed out while in their beds or at least their homes.

Further out on the rim of the galaxy, Sector ID Minister Slag Vartino of Rigel-3 poured over the recordings made of the several reports from Governor Katrina Lutgard on Ashford-5. He ran his thin, grey hands through his hair. A bio attack was extremely serious. However, before he sounded a wide alarm to all rim planets in his sector, he had to confirm the danger. His own medical staff reviewed the preliminary data sent from Doctor Jones via the governor. They confirmed the doctor's analysis; a new, unknown bio agent had killed this worker, Abelard.

At last, he had no choice but to enter his override codes that would allow him to access the actual records of Ashford-4. Only in the event of a biological or chemical weapons attack did he have the authority to override the incredible level of security surrounding this location. His emergency access code was accepted by the computer, though he knew at this instant, his doing so was being broadcast to many others around the Imperium. Well, he'd worry about the backlash later.

To his dismay, very little additional information was shown on his monitor. It did confirm the Imperium had established a top secret bio engineering research station on this uninhabited planet about fifteen years ago. It did list the personnel assigned there, and he confirmed that Abelard was one of the few who were stationed there. The only other data was its location, which, when he projected the coordinates onto a 3-d image of the planet, showed him it was located at the boundary between eternal day and night, the only possible location where a base could be constructed and run — semi-economically that is.

He sighed, and then issued orders to jump into hyperspace and get to Ashford-4 rapidly. His navigator called back, "Sir, don't you mean Ashford-5?"

"No, Ashford-4, son," he barked. *Hell, no one even knows there's anything at all on Ashford-4!* After issuing some additional orders, he headed to his briefing room. There, his staff had come running, along with his entire medical staff.

"Have a seat. We have just gotten word that there has been a biological attack on our secret research base on Ashford-4, not Ashford-5," he added. Many gasped. A biological attack was almost unheard of and instantly many unspoken fears arouse. Had the Federation already broken the treaty?

After outlining the known data that he had, he explained, "We are on our way to Ashford-4 now. We expect to arrive in another day. Strict bio protocols are to be observed at all times. Doctor, an unmanned robotic shuttle will be sent down, sending back pictures. I've already attempted to establish communications with the base personnel. They've not responded. Assume the worst. The bio agent is unknown as of this point in time. There was not enough of it left for the Ashford-5 Doctor Whitney to get a significant analysis of what we are dealing with, other than it is extremely deadly. She

187

estimated the man was dead within thirty minutes of the initial exposure. Use *extreme* caution, gentlemen. Excuse me. I've another call from Governor Lutgard." He rose and tapped his earpiece, making the connection, but only he and the recording computer could hear her report.

A bit later, he returned to his seat. "Further data. Ashford-5 may have been exposed to a second bio attack. Doctor Jones found an empty bio cylinder attached to the cargo bay of the shuttle. It was empty. Further, she has detected another unknown bio agent in the air, but the concentrations are low. However, it isn't being filtered from the air by the base filtration system, so we know the agent is extremely tiny. Her measurements suggest this unknown agent is uniformly wide spread across the entire spaceport. However, she also reports they have not done a thorough plant survey of the primitive planet, so it could well be local in origin. Still, we take no chances. *Extreme* bio containment protocols are fully in force here, gentlemen. Make your preparations. We'll be there in twenty-three hours. That is all."

Hours later, while sipping coffee in his private quarters and reviewing all the myriad details of bio containment protocols, he realized he'd not heard from Governor Lutgard for quite a few hours now. By now, Doctor Jones should have a handle on the latest bio threat. He'd reviewed her credentials. She was a highly respected and top notch doctor, especially knowledgeable in virus infections. He felt confident he had the best personnel on the ground on this one. He called Governor Lutgard. Silence. He tried a second time. Nothing. Aggravated, he called the control tower, which was always in operation. Spaceships landed twenty-four hours a day, seven days a week, mostly to refuel. Silence. After trying both another ten times, he knew that something was terribly wrong on Ashford-5!

He had no choice but to issue a full quarantine of Ashford-5. Only that would stop the many ships from landing. Then, he headed to his control center to track how many ships were about to land on the base. "Yes, no ships are allowed to take off. Full quarantine. I don't care who is on the ground. No ships are allowed to land or depart. If they do, your orders are to blast them from the sky!"

Word soon spread throughout the battle cruiser. Shortly, the commander sounded battle stations. Now, there could be no doubt that something very serious was happening! Slag had no choice but to call his boss, Legate Dalag Mulack on Proxima Prime. He felt certain he had enough information on which to base his decisions, especially the highly disruptive total quarantine of Ashford-5. Tankers would have be brought in to refuel the ships while they were still in space, an expensive proposition. Slowly the situation escalated.

"What in the name of hell is this research station? I've never heard of it, and it's in my sector! Over," barked Legate Dalag, very much annoyed at this massive disruption of his workday.

"Damned if I know either," Slag replied. "Secrets! Well, find out, will you? We'll be on site in another eighteen hours. Yes, strict bio hazard containment protocols will be used. A drone will be sent down first to ascertain the situation on the ground. I'll keep you on a live video feed. Over." They chatted a bit longer before Slag ended the transmission. He smiled; even his Legate boss didn't have a clue about this research station. Well, soon they both would.

Four hours to go. Slag climbed out of bed, glancing at his wall clock. He had slept well and felt ready for the challenge ahead. Dressing, he headed for the control room. An aide brought him a roll and coffee as he entered. The radioman looked up and said, "No word from Ashford-5 yet, sir. Been trying the governor and the tower every half hour as ordered. They've sent nothing and are not responding to our connections. Sir, does that mean they are all dead?" he asked, his voice trembling slightly.

"Who knows, son. Keep on trying. I'll be in the war room. Relay anything from Ashford-5 to me there." The man saluted, and Slag headed off to the room, followed by his aide.

He found many already assembled there. "Final inspections are being done, sir. Drone will be ready to deploy the instant we drop out of hyperspace."

"Good. Now we wait," Slag replied, finishing his roll.

Just as they were about to drop out of hyperspace, Sector ID Minister Slag received a transmission from his boss,

Legate Dalag. "I had to shake an awful lot of trees on this one, Slag. You are heading to a secret biological warfare development and research station, with a dozen top genetic engineers and ten support staff. Use extreme caution. It is possible the Federation discovered this station and wiped it out. Hell, even the president didn't know of its existence. Of course, he's new to the job. We found the records buried quite nicely. It seems no one wanted anyone at all to know about it. Why? All such research is *totally* illegal! Good god, what the hell have you stumbled into out there? Over."

"We are about to find out. Thanks for the head's up. Live drone video feed will commence shortly. Over and out. Well, you heard him. We could well be dealing with some extremely deadly things down there. *Extreme* caution, gentlemen!" Slag barked.

An hour later, many watched the live video feed coming in from the remote-controlled drone. Warning of a biological attack, the flashing red lights were still flashing. The doors were still locked shut, preventing contamination and containing the breakout. However, the roofs of the buildings looked more like Swiss cheese, tiny holes allowed interior light to shine out in small beams. One roof, the thin dome over the shuttle bay, was ripped open from the inside, not a good sign at all! There were no signs of life.

"It would help if we had a schematic layout of this place," Slag grumbled.

His doctor replied, "We're pretty sure we can isolate what's what. Give us some time to analyze these images. That there is likely the master isolation chamber, where the biological agents are stored. What we can't figure out is what made all those tiny holes in the roofs?"

"What are the bio detectors reading? How bad is it down there?" Slag ignored the unanswerable question and posed his own.

"Quite high, very deadly at the moment," the doctor replied.

"Sir, I've gotten into their master computer system. Sending our doctor the hourly bio contamination levels now," a computer technician called out.

"Well," Slag looked over the doctor's shoulders a few minutes later.

"The levels were off the charts initially, but they've been steadily dropping ever since. Based on these readings, whatever is down there will be kaput in about twenty-four hours. Much is being sucked into space and destroyed, thank god. What could have caused such a disaster? Were they attacked?" the doctor asked.

"We don't speculate, doctor. From here, there is no way to know that answer. You can rule out blaster hits, but that's the only thing that can be ruled out from here. We need ground observations, but no one is going in there until it's safe, and then only while wearing full bio hazard suits," Slag finally decided to enlighten the doctor or face that same question later on.

"Shuttle is reporting on the situation on Ashford-5, sir," his communications officer interrupted him.

"Put them on speaker phone," Slag barked.

"Sir, we are in orbit above the planet. There are ten ships also here. Their captains report that they cannot continue without refueling. I told them a tanker is on its way. Five others have already left. Three are on the base, but they got the warning just as they were landing. They have not opened their sealed hatches as yet and are standing by for orders. Am sending the drone down to the base now. Switching you to live video feed now, sir. Out."

The large group watched the streaming video coming from the unmanned drone, as it swooped down onto Plateau Grado. Many ships were there, but seemed unoccupied. Then, the drone picked up three prone Rigel-3 workers. Their bodies looked strange. A bit later, more bodies were seen lying where they had fallen. When the sweep was finished, Slag counted twenty-five bodies. He grimaced, presuming they were dead. That could only mean the entire planet may have been wiped out! Well, Ashford-5 would have to wait. First, he had to figure out what had happened here. Was it an attack by person or persons unknown? More importantly, would there be more such attacks?

As if reading his mind, Legate Dalag broke in on their

comm system. "Minister Slag, this is very serious. I have no choice but to put the entire rim on High Alert until this is resolved. I'll be sending ten battle cruisers your way immediately. Keep me posted. Out."

Slag and his group grimaced in unison. The situation seemed terribly bad just at this moment. How many more bio attacks were coming? That was on everyone's minds now. High Alert.

"Okay, the doctor suggests we have another twenty-four hours to kill. Get the ground crews ready. Full protective suits, constant communications. I'll be in my quarters," Slag announced. He could do nothing more now, not until the danger had passed. Waiting, he hated waiting, but that was all he could do without taking enormous risks.

Twenty-four hours passed slower than any day had ever done for Slag. He couldn't even sleep, but managed to doze a little. About all the ground based system could tell them was the current level of bio danger. Each hour, the doctor reported another drop, most encouraging.

Six men in their heavy, red protective suits began their slow sweep through the unfamiliar compound. The computer had finally unlocked all of the doors, but there was little atmosphere left. The air and the reserve tanks had all escaped through the tiny holes in the steel roofs. Everyone was glued to the monitors showing the live feed from the video cams on the six men's helmets. The doctor was also monitoring their vitals and the bio threat levels, while Slag was observing the overall situation.

"Show me a close up of that dead man," Slag ordered. The man bent over, bringing his head camera closer to the corpse. His face was filled with the same red splotches that Doctor Jones reported seeing on the dead Abelard. Slag began to have confidence they were dealing with a single bio agent.

A bit later, he said, "Zoom in on those small pebbles. They are wholly out of place in a bio lab," Slag ordered. Turning towards his geologist, he asked, "Don't those look like bits of a meteor?"

"Could well be debris, have them bring back a sample — in a secure container, of course," the man replied.

Slowly, Sector ID Minister Slag began to formulate a theory on just what had happened to this secret research facility. The planet may have swept across the orbit of a swarm of meteoroid particles or the refuse from a comet. Without an atmosphere, these tiny bits would come hurling down onto the roofs at a very high velocity and hence momentum. If they had sufficient momentum, they may well have pierced the steel roof. "Look for tiny holes in some of the secured bio containers, fellows," he barked his next request. Slowly, the six men made their way to the most dangerous room in the entire facility.

"Capture that image, doc; that may well be what was released on this base," Slag ordered. "See, that steel container has been punctured; probably you'll find a tiny rock inside it. I believe I know partially what has happened here. An unpredicted meteor swarm hit them, catching them totally off guard. One bit punctured that bio container releasing its bio agent into the room, causing the lock down. But with all the holes everywhere, the bio agent quickly spread throughout the entire facility. Given the lock down protocols, that man, Abelard, was probably in the shuttle hanger with this all happened. The damn fool probably thought he would be safe if he took off immediately. Whatever this all was, he's brought it to an entire inhabited world!"

"Sir, part of that may well be true, but that can't be what's happened on Ashford-5. The downed Rigel-3 workers do not show any signs of the telltale red splotches on their faces. Further, the bio agent would have mostly escaped here along with the air flowing out of the holes in the roofs and sides. Plus, it doesn't explain that empty bio canister Doctor Jones found in the shuttle's cargo bay. More likely, they were preparing for an experiment when this happened. Possibly, the shuttle was intended to be the delivery mechanism. We need to go down there and study their records."

"All right, doctor, but you have to wear a full bio hazard suit. Besides there isn't any air in the compound," Slag ordered. An hour later, the six scouts returned and were decontaminated. Now the doctor and his team suited up, preparing to go down to investigate.

"Sir, there could well be incredibly valuable research notes down there, to say nothing of additional newly developed bio agents," the doctor explained. "We may well need a full science team here sifting through what remains."

"You check it out. If so, I'll order it on your behalf, doctor. Be careful. Lord knows what nasty things are down there," Slag grimaced. Just thinking about such things knotted his stomach.

Six hours later, the doctor and his team returned from the surface and went through decontamination procedures. Then, he joined his boss in the war room. He plugged his flash drive into the computer and began scrolling through his recorded scenes. "Okay, here we go. This is their experiment log. I was right. When the accident occurred, they were about to execute another bio genetic engineering experiment. I've got the canister's number of what was going to be used. Do we have the canister number of the empty one that Doctor Jones found on the shuttle?"

"Don't know. Hold, I'll scan through her data files." Slag sifted through the various files and images she'd sent along with her report via Governor Katrina. "There. Can that image be enhanced enough to read the number on its side?" he asked.

"On it," his computer technician spoke up, taking over the console from Slag. It took him a few minutes to work his magic. "There you go, that's about as good as it is going to get."

Both Slag and his doctor compared the two sets of numbers. The doctor commented, "Well, well. Now we've a good explanation. Based on the limited data we found so far, this was to be a genetic modification experiment, one designed to prove all of their theories. Exactly what those theories are, we aren't sure at this point, only that they may have achieved a major breakthrough in genetic engineering! Somehow, they've developed a way genetically to alter all the inhabitants of a world. Aerosol delivery appears to be the mechanism. While we don't know yet precisely what was to happen, I can speculate somehow the experiment was dumped on Ashford-5 by mistake, due to the man who foolishly broke all protocols and tried to escape," the doctor advised.

"Okay, then we are certain at this point this was not an attack by some unknown party. That's a relief, just an awful accident," Slag summarized for everyone. "We can stand down on the High Alert for the Rim Sector. So the fool took the experiment to Ashford-5. What are we to expect there? They are not dead?"

"Who knows about that," the doctor hedged. "We do know they were intending to unleash an extensive test of genetic modifications on the bodies of their ten remaining test subjects. Don't worry about them; they were all criminals sentenced to death before they were brought here. If their experiment worked, we can expect some rather significant genetic modifications in the bodies on Ashford-5, sir. We'll need a full science team here to go over everything and to secure the remaining highly toxic samples that have not been compromised. I'd recommend still using full hazard suits, sir. Some of those cylinders may have been weakened and could break open at any time."

"Agreed. I'll make the calls now," Slag replied. Legate Dalag was very relieved to hear there wasn't an enemy surprise attack in progress, just a horrible accident. He promised to gather up an appropriate science team and get them on site at top speed.

A number of battle cruisers dropped out of hyperspace around his. Slag ordered two to stand guard over the site. He allowed the others to return to their stations, while he had his make the short journey over to Ashford-5. Already a tanker was on site, refueling the various ships in orbit. Those still on the ground were allowed to leave and refuel as well. Their crews showed no signs of having been infected.

At last, he had his doctor and team suit up to go down to tarmac to inspect the dozens of prone workers. Were they alive or dead? That was what Slag needed to know first and foremost. The planet total quarantine was still in effect. It had been three days since the last communication from Governor Katrina.

Chapter 13 Genetic Modifications

In her medical lab, Doctor Whitney Jones stirred and awoke to find herself lying on the floor of her lab. The equipment she had been using lay in a mess on the floor beside her. She felt funny. *What happened? Did I black out? How long? Why didn't anyone check on me? God, I am starving!* She got to her feet carefully, but her body seemed different somehow. *I've got to pee really bad!*

She moved to the side restroom as quickly as she dared in her toe shoes. She felt a bit dizzy; her breasts ached; her fingers were throbbing, as she struggled to get her gown up. Even her corset seemed loose fitting. When she removed her panties, she gasped and stared in complete disbelief! She had a small male reproductive organ between her legs! She gasped, but had to pee badly. *Well it's coming out the right place,* she thought, *not that dangling thing. What's happened to me?*

After relieving herself, Whitney carefully removed all her clothing so she could fully examine her own body. Her "doctor curiosity" had taken over from her panicked shock and surprise. "Well, I seem to be developing a full working set of male reproductive organs. Ah, they are below my female ones. Look at my waist. I swear it's lots smaller and more defined than before and my pelvis seems wider somehow." She rubbed her aching breasts and realized they were much larger. Her top had been pinching them mercilessly. Now, she noticed her long nails appeared to have grown at least another inch. "How long have I been out?" She wrapped a simple hospital gown around her, stepped back into her lab, and checked the date on her computer. "Three days? What the hell happened? Where is everyone?" She stepped out of her lab and into the main medical entrance room. She gasped.

Every bed was occupied by an unconscious man or woman. Many others were lying on make shift beds on the floor. She spotted her six nurses lying where they'd fallen. She checked a few pulses and then remembered Katrina. As fast as she dared go, she headed out of the medical lab into the halls.

196

Utter silence! Panic swept into her mind and stomach. She took the elevator up to the suite she shared with her mate. She found Katrina lying in her bed. A quick pulse check and Whitney relaxed a little. She was alive but unconscious.

Now wearing her doctor's hat, she pulled down Katrina's panties, revealing a small set of male organs, just like her own. She noticed Katrina's breasts were definitely larger too. "Best check on the others," she muttered.

She decided to return to her medical lab, because she suddenly remembered what she was doing before she'd blacked out three days ago. Counting fifty some men and women in the medical facilities, she began going from person to person, examining them. Each woman had similar male organs located behind her female ones. To her amazement, the men now seemed to have female reproductive organs just in front of their larger male ones! In addition, each man already had melon sized breasts. Then, she noticed their lips had somehow been slit, as if they also were wearing the giant lip plates that she wore. Moreover, everyone had nails that were now several inches long. On top of that, the Rigel-3 men's hair was several feet long!

As she stood there stunned, her craving hunger returned. Knowing there was nothing she could do for any of these patients, she headed off to the dining facilities, the huge mess hall. As she made her way inside, she spotted Carla and Elfe, arm in arm, making their way here too. Carla muttered quite dazed, "Whitney? You are alive too? What's happening? Our bodies — they are — well doing weird things. We're starving. No one is around. We saw unconscious people in the halls." Just talking seemed to help her regain focus.

"I don't know. Everyone's out. Our bodies are mutating somehow. I can't do anything for them, but I'm starving," Whitney said, heading for the self-serve buffet line. She punched in her order, and the machine hummed a little before the dishes appeared. Carla and Elfe joined her.

"We're ravishing! I think we've been out for three days," Elfe muttered, still groggy herself.

A bit later, the three sat together, dwarfed in the huge hall, stuffing themselves. At last, Whitney slowed down. "I haven't eaten for three days." She burped a little and began spooning her tea.

"Look at our lips! They're split like yours. We've each got something really weird growing down below," Carla hinted, but was too embarrassed to be more specific.

"I think every woman is growing a set of male organs, while the men are growing a set of female organs. In addition, everyone's lips are slit; men are definitely growing melon breasts, and we women's are getting larger. Everyone's fingernails have grown substantially. Men's hair seems to be a couple of feet long now. I've no idea what's happening. It's as if we have all somehow been genetically modified, but that's not possible. No one has developed such technology, though it's been theoretically possible on an individual basis to do some slight modifications, genetically that is," she explained.

Just then, a dazed Katrina came walking carefully into the mess hall. "Thank god someone is awake. Whitney, awful things are happening to me and to others. Everyone's unconscious. I'm starving."

"Get some food in you, and you'll feel better, love. We do. We're trying to figure out what's going on," Whitney called out. She whispered to the two, "Let her eat some; it'll clear her head. We've got a real epidemic on our hands."

After stuffing herself, Katrina finally began to get a grip on reality. Sipping her tea with a spoon, she said, "This is terribly embarrassing, but I woke up to discover I've got male organs down there!"

Whitney replied, "So far, all of the unconscious women I've check have them too. The males have female reproductive organs growing in front and above of their male organs. Plus, all manner of other alterations are occurring. We four seem to be the only ones awake on the whole base. I need your help, please. We need to make a thorough examination of our men and women. There's a goodly sample in the medical facility."

"Oh yes, I remember now. I went there to see you, but the nurses told me not to bother you. They said a large number of staff had come down with the flu. I don't think this is a flu. Just tell us what to do," Katrina stated, trying to come to grips with the situation and failing utterly.

"My feet are all screwed up," Elfe said as they were about to get up.

"Hum, they look like ours, Katrina, modified to be able to wear toe shoes. Come on; let's go by our suite and see if we can get something for Elfe to wear," Whitney suggested.

"Well, this is a whole lot better!" Elfe exclaimed, standing in a pair of Whitney's toe shoes. "But look at my waist! It's so darn tiny now."

"Even mine is so much smaller that my pipe corset is totally loose now," Carla declared, trying on a pair of Katrina's toe shoes. "Ah, now I can walk better too. Okay, let's go to the patients."

Katrina? Amy here. Something terrible is happening. We've all been unconscious. Only Jan and I are awake now. We're starving, so we must have been out of it for some time. Our bodies are somehow changing. We're developing male parts.

"Hold on a second. It's Amy," Katrina said. *Yes, a foreign shuttle crash landed here three days ago. I think it has something to do with it. Only we four are awake here. Everyone on the base is still unconscious. We're growing them too. We are about to see how extensive it is here. Touch base with you soon. Try eating; that's helped us considerably.*

Okay. Say, I'm developing tiny little arms too. Really weird. Jan can't get any response from any tower on Tierra! Are we all infected?

I think so. This is the biggest disaster I've ever heard of. More in a bit.

The four arrived in the med lab, where over fifty men and women were still unconscious. Doctor Whitney took charge. "Okay, go from patient to patient. Catalog any changes you see. I would suggest you remove everyone's tops or loosen them. Their shirts and cat suits are pinching their breasts rather significantly. That should ease their discomfort some."

An hour later, the four sat back and compared notes. Then, Katrina contacted Amy, who now felt far better. Food had helped significantly. Jan had checked on everyone else in the Imperial Castle and Tower. All were alive but were undergoing the same modifications that Whitney had jotted down from their combined notes on their many patients.

As others awake, get food in them. That's the first step. I'll know more later, Whitney advised. "We should go around to everyone we can find here at the port and help them too."

"I should let the Sector ID Minister know what's happening down here. Three days. My god, he's probably thinking we are all dead or something," Katrina exclaimed.

"Make sure he has a full quarantine in for Ashford-5," Doctor Whitney spoke formally. "We don't want this to spread beyond this world, if we can avoid it. Right now, I've no idea how it spreads or even what we are facing."

"Maybe you best come with me as I make the call. Carla, Elfe, you two start in on the top floors and work your way down. We'll join you as soon as we can. My god, Whitney, what are we going to do if the whole planet has been infected?" Katrina finally grasped the magnitude of what had happened. Worse, it had happened on her watch!

Whitney sensed her mate's sudden thought of self-recrimination. "Dear, we did everything by the book. This one is something entirely new, and, if my theories are right, there wasn't a darn thing anyone of us could have done differently. Come on. I need to talk to him too. Maybe he knows more now. It's been several days."

A half hour later, some of Katrina's fears were gone. A full quarantine was in effect for days. Her greatest fear of this thing spreading beyond this world was eliminated. Whitney finally grasped what had actually happened. "Okay, they were about to conduct a genetic modification experiment. That canister contained the material and must have been airborne. The shuttle circled Ashford-5 ten times before landing, probably releasing the gas over this entire world. It took some hours for the mixture to reach the surface. We inhaled it so we know how it enters our bodies — via the lungs and the tiny blood vessels there. Early symptoms were flu like, before everyone passed out. Sir, we are going to have a very serious, planet-wide catastrophe on our hands. If the modifications are consistent person to person, we're going to need special toe shoes for every inhabitant. Very likely, we'll need totally new clothing as well. It's too soon to say, but my god, no one can walk without these toe shoes."

"I'll see what I can do. If the entire planet has been infected, we're going to need a fabrication ship," Slag thought quickly. "Okay, doctor, keep me posted. I'll see what I can do to get one here ASAP. Over and out."

Governor Katrina then thought quickly. "You know, you'd best go visit Amy and Jan and check on them. Explain all this to them. She can alert the others via their tower comm network. I'll go help Carla and Elfe here."

"Right. My god, Katrina! We've lost all credibility with the locals! When they wake up to this mess and know it was caused by the Imperium, even though it was totally an unforeseen accident, whatever will they think of us now?"

"If I can get a fabrication ship here and provide for their physical needs, perhaps that will help keep their hatred of us to a minimum," Katrina replied. She gave Whitney a loving hug, and the two went their separate ways.

An hour later, Whitney finished her explanation to Amy and Jan. She also verified that Amy was growing a new set of arms, though currently they were the size of a newborn's. She then checked on the well-being of the remainder of their Gang of Ten. Even more surprising, both Lena and Drina also had baby arms growing from their shoulders. Other than this new and startling development, all other symptoms were identical to those at the spaceport.

Just then, Amy began to receive telepathic calls for help from some of the kings and queens, who had the *mentales* gifts. Also, Jan, who was monitoring the tower's comm network, also reported receiving many messages. After both had finished spreading the word about what had happened and the immediate action to take, namely eat a hardy meal, the three quickly compared notes.

Amy was the first to put it all together. "Hey, I think I've found the common denominator on who is waking first. Those of us who have already had the most body modifications similar to those that are happening because of this genetic virus are rousing first. Most of them have been the noblewomen, who like us, have pipe corsets, lip plates, and toe shoes. There's far less physical modifications happening to us because we've already had many of them done."

"That makes sense. It explains why only we four have awakened at the spaceport," Whitney replied enthusiastically. "Katrina and I woke before Carla and Elfe, who have far fewer modifications. Makes sense. I wonder how long it will be before the others begin coming too?"

"Why don't you head back to the base? We can handle things here, Whitney," Amy suggested. "Stay in touch. I have a bad feeling we're not out of the woods yet."

When Whitney got back, she found Katrina had created a recorded message, which Carla would have the computer system play periodically, once the others began waking. They spent the rest of the day tending to the rest of the base personnel they could find, including the couple dozen who were lying on the tarmac. In their toe shoes, the four simply couldn't bring the men inside. Their feet kept slipping out from under them.

After dark, they were exhausted and spent considerable time in the mess hall. Whitney noticed all four ate twice what they normally had, including significant protein dishes. She then suggested, "We should stay awake all night in shifts, in case some begin to wake up." All agreed, and Carla explained how to start the automated recording as soon as some woke up. Carla then volunteered to take the first shift.

Finally, the two exhausted women undressed and crawled into bed, holding each other for a time. Soon, they were sound asleep. Much later, Carla roused Elfe, but the archaeologist decided Katrina and Whitney needed their sleep, and she didn't wake them for their turn keeping watch.

The next morning, the four again ate a substantial breakfast, before commenting on the physical changes they'd noticed. "My thingy is almost the real size," Carla said, rather embarrassed by the changes she was enduring.

"Hey, so is mine. But I think it's going to work. It got big when I gave Carla here a good morning kiss," Elfe explained, far less embarrassed by all this. "Can they really be a working thing?"

Whitney shrugged her shoulders. "We are in uncharted territory. I've no idea what those genetic engineers were thinking or planning with this bug. My boobs are even larger today, as are my nails."

"Hey so are these lip loopy things of mine," Carla commented. "Any my hair seems to be thicker and a whole lot longer too."

"Okay, let's get to my lab. I'll run some diagnostics on us; Doctor Whitney took charge again.

An hour later, her face flushed, she faced her three companions. "Well, this is only getting weirder and weirder. I hate to tell you this, but our male organs are in perfect working order. We've become androgynous; we're turning into hermaphrodites! As far as I can tell, we'll be able to breed ourselves, as well as each other. I need to run some tests on one of the males, but, if this holds true, the males will be able to have babies just like we can!"

Elfe giggled. "How very strange."

"What I find most curious about the whole thing," Doctor Whitney continued, "is the way the male-female organs are situated. Katrina and I should be able to do each other simultaneously. Now that'll be something." All four giggled, somewhat embarrassed with her frankness.

"On the other hand, all the breasts show no signs of ceasing their growth. Plus, our waists haven't changed any since yesterday. According to the medical machines, our internal organs have been relocated somewhat; that's why our pelvises have been enlarged. I think our tiny waists are going to be permanent."

Katrina laughed. "Well, that'll please the noblewomen." All four laughed.

"But there is a bit more. I thought that my nails are way too long, so I tried trimming them a bit. My god, the pain! As I tried snipping a bit, it was like a bolt of lightning shooting up my finger. I endured it, and cut the tip off. Now look at it. You can't see what I cut off. It's regrown that much already."

"What? We're stuck with these things?" Elfe cried out. "How can I do my digging with these claws?"

"There is more," Whitney added. "Our hair. Once I found out we dare not cut our nails, I experimented on one of the men. I tried to cut a little off, but his body jerked from what must have been a shooting pain in his head. I'd like to verify it on one of us though."

A bit later, Carla cried out. "Well, I only cut an inch off the bottom," Whitney justified.

"Yeh, but it hurt like the devil. Crap, look, it's already regrown! What's happening to our bodies anyway?" Carla exclaimed.

"I wish I knew, Carla. I truly do. We can only wait and see," Doctor Whitney advised. "In the meantime, I want to start running a full genetic study on one of us."

"I'll volunteer. I'm in charge. It's on my head," Governor Katrina said formally.

The two headed into the lab section. After giving her a blood sample, Katrina joined the others, who were watching over the many patients in the medical lab. None has stirred yet.

Around noon, one by one, those, who were unconscious, began rousing. Carla hit the play button, and all throughout the spaceport, the recorded message blared out of the many intercom speakers. Shocked, frightened, terrified men and women struggled to their feet, urinated wherever they could, and, struggling to stand only on their toes, they did as ordered, heading to the mess hall.

By an hour later, everyone had awakened. The mess hall was packed. At this point, Governor Katrina decided to speak to everyone. After again outlining what they knew had happened, she then added, "Okay, everyone is to report to their immediate superior. I need to know if we are missing anyone. After that, go to your quarters and take a bath. Then, go through your clothes and see if there is anything you can wear at this time. I have asked that a fabrication ship come immediately to help us out. You are not alone. Everyone on Ashford-5 is in the same mess as we all are. Doctor Whitney is working on the situation now. We should know more in a few days. Until then, this whole world is under a total quarantine. So relax, and eat as much as you can, Doctor Whitney's orders. That's all."

By evening, the fear and panic had become more widespread. Their body alterations were becoming more and more pronounced, but there was little Governor Katrina could do to calm them or encourage her people. "Look, out there, the millions of Ashford-5 are experiencing the same things as we are. We are the civilized races; we must show them a good example." Her words didn't have much of an effect, especially on the men, who now looked more and more like women.

Doctor Whitney summoned her to the lab, for which she was grateful. Once there, she said, "I don't know how much longer I can keep them calmed down. What news?"

"None good, dear. I've completed your genetic work up. On the right monitor are your previous genes. On the left are your current genes. They are quite different."

"What does this mean?" Katrina asked, wishing she'd taken more biology classes at the Academy.

"It means all of us have had our very genetic makeup drastically altered. These changes, they are a permanent part of our genetic blueprints now. They aren't going away. That's the bad news. The good news is I think the process will be complete in about two more days, as long as we eat enough food for our bodies to use in the rebuilding process. I'm famished. Let's eat."

After dining, Doctor Whitney used the comm system to explain her latest results. What she had to say did not go over well at all. Many cried out, "You mean we're going to be like this forever?" Most of those doing the loudest protesting were the men, she did note. In her mind, that made perfect sense. The women were just becoming more curvaceous, if one ignored the male appendage now in their panties. The men, however, now appeared to look like women. Even those who had worn beards or moustaches found those had gone. The only redeeming feature for the men lay in their voices that had not changed. Their voices were still in the tenor to bass ranges.

By the next day, suicides began occurring among the men, who simply could not live as they now were. Governor Katrina did her best to assuage those tendencies, but her words tended to fall on deaf ears. A temporary morgue was set up. The biggest problem was with only their toes on the ground, none of the men could carry the dead. Several had to work in tandem to drag the dead to the morgue.

Finally, on the fifteenth of June, Doctor Whitney observed no further changes in anyone and decided the genetic modifications were complete. She had everyone on the base drop by her medical lab for a full examination. She also fully explained their hermaphrodite situation. Her nurses kept an accurate record of all the physical body changes among the hundreds who were here.

That evening, Doctor Whitney compiled the master list, and Governor Katrina forwarded it on up to the Sector ID Minister. Then, the two visited the Imperial Castle to show the list to Amy and Jan. However, Carla and Elfe insisted on coming along. They also felt responsible for the accident. After all, it had been their people who had made such a terrible mistake.

"What a mess of physical changes. It is like someone just wanted to see how many changes they could make to a human body," Whitney declared. "Let me go down the list. Feet. Everyone now has no choice but to wear the Ataro style toe shoes or boots. Period. Everyone now has a twelve inch waist line, with their organs relocated and hips and pelvis expanded to accommodate the changes. Everyone has breasts that are humongous in size, balls about a foot in diameter. At least, they are not the drooping kind, but everyone's backs are aching from this very heavy additional weight. Corsets are almost going to be mandatory for everyone's backs or until everyone gets their backs strengthened. Everyone is now a hermaphrodite, with perfectly working male and female organs. And yes, each one of us can impregnate ourselves and have perfectly healthy babies, though I would not recommend doing that."

"Additionally, everyone now has fingernails that are a foot long. They can't be cut shorter. Any attempt to do so results in massive pain; besides they grow back within a day. Everyone's hair has thickened substantially and now reaches the floor. Like nails, our hair cannot be cut or trimmed. Massive pain results, and the hair grows back within days. It remains to be seen if we can trim our nails and hair when they naturally grow longer. Time will tell on that one."

"Everyone now has their lips split, and the loops

thickened. It is as if someone designed them so we could wear the fancy foot-across lip plates found here on Ashford-5 and other planets. Right now, everyone has to be very careful not to get their loops caught on things or bite down on them while eating. I recommend they all acquire the lip plates that Katrina and I wear, which we got from Elegant Fashions Inc."

Amy added one more thing, "Also, anyone whose arms or hands were missing now has new arms and hands. Drina, Lena, and Celenia are quite happy about this aspect, though not with the foot long nails that came with their new arms and hands."

"Like I said, it is a complete hodgepodge of genetic alterations. I can see no rhyme or reason behind any of them, save perhaps to prove that they could be done," Whitney declared.

Katrina then brought up what had her very worried, "We've also have many suicides already. Men. They can't seem to handle all this at all well. I can't blame them; their lives are ruined. Whitney did try to alter or fix up some things. Tell them, dear."

"Well, yes. I tried the two simplest things. I used the medical machines to heal the lips and feet. As you might expect, I only had marginal success with the feet. At least, they would only have to wear six inch regular heels. However, as I said before, these are genetic modifications to our bodies, not cosmetic surgery."

"What does that mean?" Amy asked. "Didn't it work?"

"Yes, it worked; lips were healed; feet were partially restored. However, the bodies use their genetic blueprints. By the next day, all three test subjects were back as before. The healing process had been completely undone, as if I'd never done it," Whitney explained.

Jan spat on the floor, "Damn! This isn't good at all."

"I know," Doctor Whitney replied sympathetically. "Don't give up hope yet. Genetic modifications caused these. It's my hope further genetic modifications can be used to undo them. I need time to study what was done and work out ways to repair the damage."

Governor Katrina then spoke officially. "Since this

horrible mess was caused by the Imperium, I'm working to get the Imperium to at least provide emergency help for every affected person on Tierra. We have what's called a fabrication ship. Normally, it's used for heavy duty construction projects. It consists of a number of machines that can fabricate almost anything. In this case, I want the machines to make a pair of toe shoes or boots, sturdy support corsets, lip plates, suitable men's shirts and pants, and suitable apparel for women. At least with clothing that fits and supports, everyone has some chance to somehow get by while we work on a more permanent cure."

"Well, that would certainly help. Right now, most everyone is rather helpless, and they are staying home," Amy replied. "How can this be done? There are millions of people on Tierra. That's a lot of clothing."

"That's why we need a fabrication ship in orbit here. Such is well within the capabilities of such a ship, Amy. Actually, it could probably fabricate enough apparel to give everyone here a dozen outfits," Governor Katrina explained. "What do you think? Will this go over? I must do whatever I can to prevent all of Tierra from turning against us, the Imperium, wholesale. It was a most unfortunate accident, but it was an accident. No one purposely did this to us all. I'm willing to do anything to help the people of Tierra, anything."

Carla added, "She's right, Amy. We all want to do anything we can to help." Elfe concurred as well.

Chapter 14 Restoration

Ariana! Did you do this? Lysandra mentally screamed at the Goddess of Fertility. She had just discovered what was happening to all the humans on Tierra. She was fuming, angrier than she'd been in centuries. Because of the monster sized breasts and the dual, functioning reproductive organs, she'd presumed this was the work of Ariana, who she found still sitting high in the northern Goza Mountains in the abandoned cavern complex, once known as Skylar Abbey.

No, sister. Not my handiwork, but you must admit, it is genius. Why didn't we think of some of this? Hermaphrodites. That would solve so many problems, you know.

Well, if you didn't do this, who the hell did? Lysandra began toning down her anger, convinced Ariana was telling her the truth.

The aliens. Go listen in to their leader on Goza Plateau. And the one called the doctor. Let me know if we're to do anything about all this. I don't think our humans will be able to survive this time, Ariana admitted. *Perhaps, we should let them perish and go find another planet.*

The aliens? Damn them. If the humans under our care perish, they'll wish they never found our world!

I'll tag along, sister. The two beings appeared over the spaceport, and Ariana guided Lysandra to where Doctor Whitney and Governor Katrina were going over the whole mess. They listened to what the doctor was explaining. At last, Lysandra finally understood what had happened. That, however, did little to lessen her animosity to these aliens.

When the two aliens headed over to consult with Amy and Jan, the two goddesses made a spatial adjustment and joined the four in Amy's study. Again, both goddesses listened to their discussion. *Genetic modifications! Damn! Those people are getting too darn smart for their own well-being, Ariana. If I can get them to agree to have much of this mess undone, can I count on your help with the process?*

Sure, but I do think some of the humans like some of

the changes, Ariana pointed out. *I think you should take that into consideration. Am I going to have to become visible to the humans?*

Why not?

You know I like to remain invisible behind the scenes, always. Okay. This is the most serious crisis ever. You do the talking, though.

Of course, sister.

Governor Katrina had just said, "I'm willing to do anything to help the people of Tierra, anything." Lysandra took that as being her summons. Suddenly, Amy, Jan, Katrina, Whitney, Carla, and Elfe saw a yellowish glow coming from the wall opposite the door. Then, a pale whitish glow also appeared, startling all six. Slowly, the yellow glow took the shimmering shape of a lovely woman in loose fitting robes. Not long after that, the whitish glow also began to look like a shorter woman in similar robes. All six blinked several times. The forms materialized, taking on a quite solid looking form.

Amy cleared her throat and said, "Lysandra?"

"Yes, I'm here in response to Katrina's wishes. This is Ariana."

"Incredible! These are two of our ancient goddesses. Lysandra, the Goddess of Life and of Death. Ariana, the Goddess of Fertility. Wow!" Amy introduced them for the benefit of the four alien women, who were both staring at them in complete disbelief. She continued, "This is Governor Katrina and Doctor Whitney, Carla and Elfe."

Katrina swallowed hard. "Are — are — are you really goddesses?" *Now that's the stupidest question I've ever asked! My god, they just sort of appeared!*

"Yes, that's a rather stupid question, Katrina. To business. You just said you were willing to do anything to help the people of Tierra. Do you really mean that, Katrina?" Lysandra said rather solemnly.

"Yes, of course. It was a horrid accident. Everyone here is suffering terribly. Six of my own men have already killed themselves. I suspect many natives of Tierra have also done that. I can't blame them, the men that is."

"Accident? Hardly. Your scientists caused this by not

taking proper precautions. Messing with genetics is not something to be taken lightly," Lysandra could not help condemning these aliens.

"Dear, she is right. Those scientists should have realized their base was highly susceptible to meteorites and built far stronger roofs. They should not have been working in utter secrecy. If they had just been forthright about their work, kept the rest of us doctors informed of their research along the way, I would have been in a position to do something useful about this disaster," Whitney stated factually, causing Lysandra to focus her attention onto her for a minute.

"That would have been a wiser course," Lysandra admitted. *She is being honest and sincere,* she sent to Ariana.

Doesn't make it right, Lysandra, Ariana sent back.

No, it doesn't, but she's correct. I'll take that into consideration. Lysandra said, "You said you were willing to do anything to make this right. Do you still stand by your statement, Katrina?"

"Of course I do, but nothing can make it right. I'm trying to get one of our big fabrication ships here to make everyone clothing and shoes, so they can at least survive better," she explained.

"So be it. I'll make you a deal. We'll undo this mess, but there must be a price to be paid. If you six agree to pay my price, then we'll undo this mess," Lysandra spoke her offer.

"I'll pay any price, Lysandra. Only perhaps not everyone wants everything undone," Katrina agreed, thinking of Amy, Lena, Drina, and Celenia.

Whitney picked up on her mate's though and added, "The genetic modifications dictated we all have these long, cumbersome fingernails. I suspect that has played a role with some of our friends who have lost their arms. In order to have these nails, their bodies have regrown their arms, if that's the right wording. They might wish to keep their new arms. Life without them is terrible, as you must already know."

Lysandra actually laughed. "You're quite right. Others might wish to keep other changes," she winked at Whitney, who flushed, but didn't say anything. "I'll give each a personal choice in the matter, but the price you must pay will be even steeper."

"Hey, if you can restore the people of Tierra back to normal, whatever it's to be, we'll pay it. After all, it was our foolish scientists who ultimately are responsible for all this," Whitney replied.

"Then, we're agreed. Tonight when they sleep, they'll be given their choices. While they sleep, the genetic changes will be undone. When they awaken, these past few days will seem like nothing more than some horrible nightmare," Lysandra said solemnly.

"So they won't actually believe that all this happened to them?" Katrina asked.

"Precisely. Human minds are not yet capable of grasping the truth, the reality that is. The price you six must pay is to continue to live with these genetic modifications, as a constant reminder to always assume far more responsibility than you have done so far."

Amy spoke up, "Say, if there are some who wish to keep these changes, could you have them contact their nearest Elegant Fashions Inc, so that they can be provided clothing they will need? I'll see that they get them."

"Accepted," Lysandra replied.

Amy asked, "Another thing has me puzzled, goddesses. Katrina is the Imperium leader here, and this is my second run at being the leader of our people. Always, we have been trying to bring peace and prosperity to everyone, to help our people learn, and be free. I know you, Lysandra, have been helping us along these lines too, from time to time. We know you both have been around Tierra for many centuries. Why? Why are you here? Why are you helping us?"

"You are not yet ready or able to understand us or our motives, Amy. In time, we hope you will. Elfe may be able to one day guide you to some of the answers you seek. Now it's time we go. Ariana hates to be seen."

"Wait, but Amy isn't supposed to have arms. She's an Ataro Empire queen," Jan spoke up.

"Quite true. She'll lose them of course," Lysandra compromised slightly. "Perhaps in time, some good will come from all this."

Sensing this encounter was about to end, Whitney quickly asked, "I don't know how you can do this — in one night even, but I'll be eternally grateful to you both, if you can do this thing. Are we to worship you now? I'm sorry. I've never seen a goddess before. I'm not a religious woman."

Ariana laughed. "No, you should not worship us. We are. Just as you are. Get more of Benjamina's therapy, and you may find the answers you seek. At least, Lysandra here believes that is so. Me, I don't know."

"Well then from the bottom of my heart, I thank you both for your intervention," Whitney replied.

"Me too. Words cannot express how grateful I am for your help," Katrina added.

"Hey, us too," Elfe broke in; she was holding Carla's hand. "Thank you for fixing this awful Imperium blunder."

"Accepted. However, in time, you may change your minds. So be it. Tonight, it will be undone." Both solid forms began dissolving. Shortly, only the yellowish and whitish glows were visible. Then, they too vanished.

"My god, Amy! We've just been visited by Ariana too! Incredible. I don't think anyone has ever seen her — the Fertility Goddess!" Jan exclaimed. "Wait til everyone hears about this!"

Katrina swallowed hard. "Were we dreaming? Was all that real?"

"It certainly was real," Amy declared. "As far as I know, this is an historic event! Never has Lysandra appeared to you aliens, pardon the stereotype. And I don't think there has ever been a recorded sighting of Ariana!" Jan looked very pleased indeed.

"But who or what are they? Goddesses. That's the term, but who or what are they? All powerful beings? There are not such anywhere in the Imperium, not that I have ever heard of," Katrina asked, totally baffled.

"If they can undo these permanent genetic modifications to human bodies, they must be all powerful gods," Doctor Whitney declared rather formally. "But why then are they not to be worshiped? I really don't understand religion at all."

"I'm beginning to have an idea of their nature," Amy mused. "You've all had Basic Therapy and have some reality you are not your body, that you have lived other lives before this one. That alone shows us all that we are immortal spiritual beings, which now inhabit these human bodies. But Jan and I have had quite a lot of additional therapy, and our powers have grown far beyond even the ordinary *mentales* gifted. What if we once were able to have and to use all these powers *without* the necessity to have a physical body? We would then appear to be as Lysandra and Arianna are, wouldn't we? We don't consider ourselves gods, and we certainly don't want others to worship us. Nor do I think we would do so, if we had our powers and didn't need human bodies to use them."

"Are you saying we all were once like Lysandra and Arianna? That we somehow became dependent upon human bodies and have forgotten our past?" Katrina asked, trying hard to follow Amy's line of reasoning and extending it.

"I think so. I believe that is what happened to two other gods that used to be part of the original pentagram here on Tierra. Namely the gods Wystan and Calder. I know they have fallen from grace and are now like most of us, stuck in human bodies, having forgotten their past and who they were, indistinguishable from the normal people of Tierra," Amy explained.

Jan added, "Well, they deserve it. They've done so much harm to us over the centuries, causing wars and relishing over the suffering they caused us. It's like they've fallen from Grace."

"But then doesn't that mean there is a true God above them that is causing this to happen?" asked Whitney, growing more confused, not less.

Amy replied with a sigh, "I surely don't know the answer to that one, Whitney. What I want to know is what does Elfe have to do with all this?" All eyes turned to the raven haired archaeologist.

She flushed, "I have no idea what she meant. Honestly, I don't. I have no idea what she meant about me being able to guide you."

"Well, it's getting late. We best get back to the base. If

214

all this comes true, I'll have a whole lot of explaining to do tomorrow," Katrina suggested.

An hour later, Katrina and Whitney sat on the edge of their bed, brushing each other's hair. Both noticed their new arousals and gently allowed their passions to explore these new avenues opened to them. In a nearby room, Carla and Elfe did so as well, but then they'd already done so several times before now.

The next morning, still wearing makeshift clothing, hospital gowns loosely tied, the four made their slow way to the dining room. As they walked into the room, nearly a hundred men and women were wearing their usual recyclable cat suits. They all looked perfectly normal, though the four sensed a good deal of mental confusion in the room. Henkel and Jaques spotted them and motioned for the four to join them.

After getting their trays, the four quietly sat down beside their other two leaders. However, all four could not help but notice most everyone in the room covertly staring at them. "Morning boss, what a weird nightmare we've been having," Jaques spoke up. "Damnedest thing I've ever dreamt! It was as if I somehow became a woman, sort of like your four, big boobs and all that. Seemed like it went on for days. But then I woke up, and it's obviously just been a really bad dream, right boss?"

"Hey, we all had that same dream," Henkel added. He motioned around the room, indicating that others had reported similar dreams to him, before the four had gotten here.

Doctor Whitney spoke formally before Katrina could think of anything to say. "It wasn't a dream, fellows. We were the accidental victims of a biological genetic experiment that went awry. I believe the worst of it has passed now. The effects of the bio agent have mostly worn off now," she paused and looked around the room, then continued, "on most all of us. We four, unfortunately, got a far heavier dose of the bio agent. After all, we were out there working on everyone, trying to heal everyone. I do so hope it wears off us soon. I feel like a balloon that's ready to pop." The men chuckled at her obvious reference to her massive boobs.

"Thank the gods for that!" Jaques exclaimed. "I don't know if I could have lived like that! I know there are seven bodies in the morgue."

"Yes, thank the goddesses, Jaques. Yes, another must have died last night. I couldn't effectively control the bio attack on us. What a nightmare that was. I sure am glad the epidemic's now under control with only four of us left to cure," Doctor Whitney replied. She added, "Governor, I think you should make a base-wide announcement we've got this bio attack mostly under control now. I do hope our overexposure to that agent isn't going to make all this permanent on us, though."

"Brilliant, Doctor Whitney. I agree. I best make that announcement soon, and let the Sector ID Minister know about this too," Governor Katrina said formally. *Thanks dear!*

Jaques suggested, "Hey, maybe you four could go over to that fashion place in Exchange City. Maybe they would have some clothes that would more or less fit you."

"Good idea, Jaques. We can't keep wearing my hospital gowns. Too chilly," Whitney replied.

"Great going, doc! You ought to get a medal or something for getting us all cured," Henkel added.

Whitney laughed. "I'd be happier, if we'd not been so heavily exposed to that bio agent. But then, that's what we doctors always face. We leaders are asked to assume quite a lot of responsibility, you know." The two men heartily agreed with her.

An hour later, Governor Katrina made a formal announcement over the base-wide comm system. "Good morning everyone. Governor Katrina here. Yes, we were the victims of a biological agent attack. It was an unfortunate accident caused in part by that shuttle which crash landed here eight days ago. Indeed, it has been an utter nightmare for all of us. We have been working closely with Doctor Whitney these last eight days, and thankfully, a cure was found. We believe most of you have only gotten a light exposure to the bio agent. Unfortunately, she, I, and two of my staff, who were working so closely with us, have gotten a far heavier dose of the bio agent. While a cure has been found for all of you, we four are still affected. If any of you are still affected, please report to Doctor Whitney. Thank you all for persevering these past eight days, while Doctor Whitney and the rest of us did our best to care for everyone and find a cure. Hopefully, things will soon get back to normal. That's all for now. Thanks everyone. You are a good team to have supporting me."

"There, how did that sound? Think they'll buy it?" Katrina asked, having finished her announcement.

"Hope so. Now for the more difficult call," Whitney replied.

A half hour later, Governor Katrina finished her report to her Sector ID Minister Slag. "So yes, in summary, Doctor Whitney believes we all mostly received such a low dosage of the bio agent that the genetic modifications were expelled from their bodies, though it took eight days for that to happen fully. However, she and I, along with two of my ministers, worked constantly with everyone here who was infected. She believes we four got a very substantial dose of the bio agent. Time will tell if our bodies throw it off or not. The base is clear of bio contaminants, triple checked, though you are welcome to send a drone down and check further. We certainly don't want this outbreak to spread off-world, sir. Over."

After a brief delay, Slag appeared again, "Congratulations on a job well done, Doctor Jones. Simply amazing piece of work and under such hardships. Commendable indeed. I'm sorry that in doing so you and three others have been so heavily exposed, but I guess it comes with your territory and that of the governor's too. I'll go ahead and cancel the fabrication ship. After I send another drone down, if it too reports the all clear, then I'll lift the quarantine. This has been one hideous nightmare for all of us. Again, excellent work, governor, doctor. Over and out."

"Well, he bought it," Katrina whispered.

"Finally, I can relax. What a nightmare," Whitney added. "Now, all we have to do is to learn to cope with everything. How the hell I'm to do anything productive with foot long fingernails, I surely don't know yet. Besides, I can't see my feet any longer — boobs too big." Both women laughed.

Katrina suggested, "Well, on Proxima Prime, our female senators manage to get by with them, so I suppose we can too."

An hour later, two men reported to Doctor Katrina. Their modifications had not been undone. As she took their vitals and gave them an examination, she looked over their charts and smiled, though it was not invisible because her lip plates. "Well, as far as I can tell, you both have had too great an exposure to the bio agent, like I have. Perhaps in time, the changes may subside, but fellows, don't hold your breaths. I'm not. I think some of us are stuck with these genetic changes. Will you be able to handle them? Be brave, fellows."

"How unfortunate," one replied somewhat covertly. "I guess we'll have to manage, doc. At least, everyone will know that we did our part in helping everyone else and so got over-exposed."

"Yes, I'll see that Governor Katrina puts a high commendation in both of your official records. Outstanding bravery at great personal risk to your own physical well-being."

"Thank you doc! We appreciate that," he exclaimed greatly relieved. Both men then left certain now they would not be looked upon as freaks or worse, but as heroes to be respected.

As dawn came on the fifteenth of June 1294, across Tierra, men and women awoke out of a seeming eight day nightmare, thankful their hideous dreams had been just that, an awful nightmare. Work abandoned eight days ago finally began to be done. Few ever said much about their strange dreams.

Later that morning over breakfast, Lena mentioned, "What a strange dream I seemed to have lived. But last night, I simply decided I am what I am, me. I love Bernardo here, and that's all I need."

"Right my love. I had that same weird dream too, but I'm sure glad I've got you back just as you are, my gorgeous fighter," he replied, giving her a kiss on her forehead.

Drina spoke up, "Me too. I dreamt that I had arms and

claws like Jan has, and all manner of even weirder things. But hey, I just want to be little old me. I sure am glad we've all wakened from that nasty dream. How come we all had the same dream anyway? Hey, look, here comes Zarita, Celenia, and Lelane. Oops, they haven't awakened from the dream!"

"Hi'y'all. Hey, you are all normal again," Zarita observed. "Oops, sorry Amy, Jan."

"Hey, I have arms still," Celenia spoke up. "Now, I look like the senator I'm supposed to be, claws and all. Could do without the boobs though. What happened to all of you? What happened to Amy's new arms?"

Amy laughed, "Gang, that was no dream! Alien biological attack, remember?" Many suddenly did remember, and several gasps echoed around the spacious dining room. She then explained what had happened last night.

"What? Lysandra appeared here? Arianna too? Why didn't you come get me? I'd of given anything to see those goddesses!" Drina protested.

Bernardo asked, "So sis, you and Jan had to pay the price for the goddess's help?"

"Yes, and Katrina, Whitney, Carla, and Elfe too. At least, she was willing to give everyone a choice. I'm glad for you Celenia," Amy said diplomatically. "Now you have arms and hands again. You do look like a proper senator. So all this has not been for nothing. I'm so pleased that Zarita, Celenia, and Lelane have been able to reap benefits from this mess."

Celenia looked very pleased. Both Zarita and Lelane gave her a supporting hug. "Well, after we eat," Amy added, "we five ought to visit Elegant Fashions Inc and see if Lilly can get us better fitting clothes, don't you think?"

"Hey, and lip plates for Celenia and Lelane too," Zarita added.

Around ten, the nine women met with Lilly and Nita. "What an incredible nightmare we've had. I thought I and everyone else were going to be like you nine are!" Lilly admitted. "You are in luck. Thinking that, I've been frantically trying to design proper clothing. Honestly, what an awful nightmare. I can't ever recall having anything so horrible. Well, follow me, ladies. I'll show you what I've been working on."

"I sure hope they give us some back support!" Katrina exclaimed. "The weight of these is something else. My back aches terribly every night."

"I keep thinking I'm falling forward," Carla put in.

Several hours later, all nine were pleased with Lilly's emergency designs. She'd put in extra steel in the newly designed corsets. While tight and holding them quite rigid, the back support was welcomed by all. Her new gowns accentuated their incredible endowments. "Your curves are simply spectacular," Lilly declared, trying hard to find something positive to say about their altered forms, thankful she'd awaken from her similar nightmare.

With some sporting new lip plates and all wearing the first of their new outfits, the nine headed back to the Imperial Castle. "Well, now we've got a whole lot to get used to once again," Carla declared, finally able to sit down again. "Even walking that distance is challenging. Elfe, I don't know how you are going to be able to do your archaeology work."

"I'll have to manage somehow. This isn't going to stop me. Slow me way, way down, but I'm not giving up. Oh, I'm drooling. How do you all keep from making a mess?" she asked, wholly unused to wearing these lip ornaments.

Zarita suddenly remembered and spoke up, "Oh, I've those compressed crystals for you, Amy. I'd forgotten all about them. Got two dozen of them." Even during the confusing period of her presidency, she managed to get them done for Amy. At long last, the conversations returned to the real problems facing Tierra, as far as Amy was concerned.

Doctor Whitney, on the other hand, couldn't let this one go. She knew it was possible to alter an individual's genes and thus their body's structure. That this Goddess Lysandra was able to do it overnight pricked her interest. *If she can do it, so then I should be able to do something about our mess. After all, I'm a doctor.* She vowed to continue to work on the problem, wondering if she could somehow get access to the research notes from that secret research station. Even more interesting, she thought, was the side effect caused by the long nails modification. It had forced bodies somehow to regrow missing arms and hands, so that the nails could be created. She found that highly encouraging for the entire medical field. Lost appendage regrowth would be a welcome miracle cure.

So it was in June of 1294, some fifty hermaphrodites made their first appearance on Tierra. As Doctor Whitney would discover and record, when either two hermaphrodites bred each other or bred their own selves, they bred true. Children of mixed relationships of those and non-hermaphrodites were about fifty-fifty, half normal, half hermaphrodites. Over the years, the numbers of these rare human forms gradually increased substantially. However, sexual reproduction was of no concern to the rulers at this time. The giant crystals were.

Chapter 15 Internal Strife and Archaeological Beginnings

A few days before the July lease payment of iron ore and gold, Bart and Ken made a quick trip to confer with Queen Amy. The Underground had been just as mystified by the eight-day nightmare, as had everyone else. They'd taken it in stride, just as had many, though that hadn't kept them from bitterly complaining to their senator about the illegality of the bio research. That wasn't what was on Bart's mind. Rather, it was something else entirely.

"Morning Amy, Jan. Thanks for seeing us privately," Bart began, adding, "Thanks for taking the penalties for Lysandra's help this time."

"We didn't really have a choice. A cure had to be found. So why all this secrecy?" Amy asked.

"Hey, I hope you don't need me to write much," Jan teased him. "Can't hardly with these talons." She waved her foot long nails about, causing both men to grimace slightly, recalling their own eight nightmare days.

"No writing Jan. It's something highly unusual. You see, Tom and Lana have been in charge of monitoring the various communications between the many towers. Thank goodness for youthful enthusiasm. Anyway, they took it a tad farther and compiled a five year frequency analysis. Here's the graph they've come up with." He held the graph so both women could see it clearly. "Notice anything suspicious?" Bart asked.

"Well doesn't look like much is going on of late," Jan commented.

"That is peculiar, Bart," Amy mused. "There are almost no communications between the towers during the last year or so. Wonder what is up?"

"That's just it, Amy. In the past, monitoring the tower comm network used to be a huge deal, barely able to keep up at times. Now, there is hardly any. Most deal with mundane teleport requests. I don't like it when the towers are not talking to each other. Could be trouble brewing, so I thought that you ought to know," Bart said.

"Thanks, yes, this is significant. Towers no longer communicating with each other isn't good. Without meaningful communications between them, they lose reality and so goes understanding," Amy pointed out. "I wonder what is going on with the towers? Any way to eavesdrop on them?"

Bart laughed. "How many times have we wished that? No, sorry. I'll keep you posted if anything develops."

Amy thanked him, and then Ken spoke up, "Amy, things are not going so well in Brom Tower. I think you ought to have a chat with Maricela soon. Something is going on but I'm not entirely sure. I think she can use some help about now."

"Okay will do. Anything else?"

"No, I've got the travel arrangements for Elfe's expedition to those northern Goza cavern ruins made. I'm on my way to see her now," Ken replied.

"The caves where she nearly died?" Amy asked.

"Those. She wants to study them. I don't know what she can hope to find though. Cya later on." Both then left. Tom teleported his dad home, while Ken walked over to the guard station at the edge of the spaceport where he asked to see Elfe.

An hour later, Venerada Maricela walked into Amy's study, just as Jan was just pouring them some tea. She wore her simple cotton day dress and flats. She looked older, Amy thought. "Thanks for coming Maricela. Tea?"

"Sure," she replied, "if Jan doesn't mind helping me." All three women had the large lip plates, but for Maricela, that made feeding herself far too difficult.

Jan laughed, "Hope you don't mind if I accidentally poke an eye. I'm still trying to figure out how to make do with these claws," she teased, but Maricela sensed her deep frustrations buried beneath her attempts at joviality.

"Maricela, it's been some time since we had a long talk. The Underground has kept me posted on all of the construction and civic works that Brom Tower has been doing. I think that's extremely admirable of you. Surely, the citizens of Brom appreciate your good works."

"Well, yes, that's true," she sighed. She had a feeling about why Amy wanted to see her privately. "You might as well hear it from me, Amy. Things are not going so well within the tower. Politics and goals. They are not mixing well. I've received countless orders from King Bolivar to have Brom Tower construct powerful new defenses against those who might attack us with their giant crystals. His whole entourage has been hounding me something fierce. They are becoming more and more paranoid that the other kingdoms are building up their defenses and inventing new weapons for attacks. We don't know this is true, mind you. Only rumors."

"We did anticipate this would be happening. I'm not too surprised, Maricela," Amy replied.

"There's more. Politics. We have five full Circles at this time. Many are pushing hard to be allowed to do more than create Shielding Networks for protection. Honestly, they are pressuring me to resign as venerada. Frankly, I don't know how much longer I care to stay on, amid all this bickering and push to develop more and powerful weapons."

"Who is making moves to replace you?" Amy asked.

"William Brom. He claims to have inherited the right to become our next venerado. One can't deny his claim; he traces his lineage back to the legendary Felix Brom."

"I see. Powerful lineage. How much does he know about the Underground, Madiera, and such things?" Amy asked.

"Very little. He's seen the tunnels and the mermaids, but he doesn't think they are important at all. He's focused wholly on the giant crystals and the powerful potentials they can unleash for us. Shoot, he's not even interested in us katalyein anymore. Healing is not his thing, he keeps saying," Maricela explained sadly. "He has a point, Brom Tower is busting at its seams. We've far too many people there now."

"Hum, how many katalyein are there? How many healers?" Amy asked, an idea forming.

"There are fifteen of us, including Drina, who's hardly ever around the tower. I think there's about thirty others involved on the healing lines. The new hospital building is nearly done, though."

"Suppose you took all the katalyein and healers and

224

formed a healing group living and operating out of the new hospital? You could have your own small Circle there and continue serving the people of Brom."

"You mean let William take over?"

"Yes, don't tell him anything about the Underground and related things. He wouldn't be interested in them anyway, except for the damage they could possibly do. Let him dig his own grave. I don't think Brom Tower is any different from the many other towers. Bart just showed me some rather startling data. This past year, the towers have nearly ceased all communication with each other, except for mandatory teleport requests. I fear they all are going ahead with development of weapons and defenses for their kingdoms, but I've no proof of this at all, mind you," Amy advised.

"I like your idea, Amy. Theo would love to have me out of the tower work. One of my twins, Allen, is studying now with Doctor Whitney to become the head nurse of our new hospital. Of course, my Dorita can't do that. She's like me, a katalyein. The more I think about this, the more I like it. But Amy, if William takes over, you and the Underground will have a harder time dealing with them."

"That's our problem, Maricela, not yours."

"Okay then, I'll do it. The Brom Hospital is supposed to be ready for operations in August. I'll make the change then. I feel like a huge weight has just lifted from my shoulders," she exclaimed.

"You've carried the burden for far too long. I and all of us thank you for your many years of dedicated service to the people of Brom and all Tierra too," Amy declared diplomatically. She sensed Maricela smiling. She added, "Plus you can get your lips healed and never have to wear those fancy gowns again."

"I'll certainly like that; so will Theo. He hates these infernal lip plates. I'll begin making the arrangements today. Thanks, Amy. As always, we'll be ready to help out, just more secretly now."

Later that same day, twenty-five year old William Brom exclaimed, "Finally, you've come to your senses, Maricela! You should take the katalyein and the healers with you to the new

Brom Hospital. That's really where you all rightfully belong. In fact, I'll run extra shifts to get the facilities ready in two weeks. Let's make this happen!" She could tell he was quite pleased with the changes.

At supper, Drina gushed, "Hey, have you all heard the news? Maricela is retiring and heading up the new Brom Hospital! I'll lend a hand there too. Boy, am I ever glad I won't be summoned to Brom Tower to help their Circles!"

"Yes, but Venerado William Brom is something of a hawk, Drina," Bernardo cautioned her. "Expect trouble to come from him now." That was a sobering thought. "Still, I'm glad for you and all of them. Say, Lena and I are off with Elfe and her archaeological expedition tomorrow. This is going to be rather different."

"Yes but fun. I can't wait to get out on the trail again," Lena added.

"Well, gang, thanks to Zarita here, I've a present for each of you. Jan, show them, please," Amy asked. Jan struggled with the pod-silk pouches, silently cursing her long nails that made even the simplest tasks formidable. "These are replacement crystals for each of you to wear. They are actually one of the giant crystals that Zarita had compressed down to this size. They look like ordinary ones that everyone has, but they have the amplification powers of the giant crystals. I want you all to be far more protected than before."

"Wow! Thanks, Amy, Zarita!" Drina exclaimed, as Jan switched her old one with this new one. She quickly attuned it to herself.

"I want my Gang of Ten to be well protected. I still have more, but Jan and I are holding them in reserve just in case. Lena, Bernardo, you be careful out there and watch over Elfe. I'm sure she's going to have a miserable time of it," Amy asked.

"We're on it, sis. Don't fret. Worry more about what the towers are doing or planning," Bernardo replied rather cocky.

Amy then requested, "Ben, you and Drina keep an eye on Exchange City during the receipt of the lease payments. Make sure all goes well, will you?"

"On it, Amy," Ben replied.

"Henry, Adrianna, have you heard anything about what

is going on at the other towers?" she inquired, hoping perhaps they had and just hadn't gotten around to telling her.

"Nope, very strange, hardly any tower is saying much at all, except for the usual teleport requests," Venerado Henry answered. "We'll have all the castle and tower expansion work done next year. The hospital is still on schedule to be done by the first snow."

Just then, Amy's eyes fogged out for a minute. *Hi, Katrina here. My geologist Jaques had just detected an earthquake around Wye, at least he thinks that is what it is. However, something is rather strange. Too dark to see well. Can you drop over here and take a look first thing in the morning?*

After replying, Amy relayed the message to her gang. Bernardo commented, "Sis, that's flat country, farming lands. They don't have earthquakes. Something must be up. I'll come with you. Besides, I have to help Elfe with her things. We're leaving the spaceport via teleport around ten, so that will give us time."

The next morning, with a large pack slung over his back carrying his and Lena's trail gear, Bernardo put an arm around his sister on her right, while Jan took her left side. Lena followed along behind them, guarding their rear. Both she and Bernardo were wearing their leather trail clothing, while Amy and Jan wore their usual satin gowns. Amy griped, "We just can't see where we are stepping," Amy pointed out, as she and Jan both stumbled slightly. "Toe shoes don't help. You make sure that Elfe can manage, Bernardo."

"Don't fret sis. I won't let either of you take a tumble. Just glad I don't have them knockers of yours any more. What a nightmare."

"Yes, but we're still in the middle of our nightmare, so be thankful," she retorted.

"All Tierra thanks you, sis. Here we go. An electric car," he announced. A half hour later, they entered the Admin building, where a Security Guard led them to Katrina's office on the twentieth floor.

Katrina, Carla, and Elfe were waiting for them, along with Jaques. Her geologist took charge. "Our instruments indicated a small earthquake occurred around five yesterday just outside Wye. I've located what caused it, but frankly, I'm completely baffled by it. Never seen anything like this before."

He activated Katrina's computer. Presently, a series of images taken by their geo-sat system appeared on the giant monitor. "What the hell is that?" Bernardo exclaimed. They all stared at the strange images. Several were computer generations showing what the formation might look like as seen from the ground. The main images were from the top looking down. It appeared to be a giant rock finger.

"From the morning shadows, I've calculated that it is about a hundred feet across at its base and one hundred twenty feet tall. Like a giant stalagmite or something," Jaques said, clearly baffled. "Look, it's pretty well destroyed that farmhouse. Hope no one was in it when this thing came thrusting upwards."

"What the devil is it?" Bernardo asked.

"I've no idea. Do you folks? Should we send a shuttle over there to find out?" Governor Katrina asked officially.

"Best not. Let's let the Underground check it out on the quiet. The less our people see of you folks at the moment, the better," Amy replied. Katrina understood. Their bio attack was still on many minds, including her own, as she continued to try to adapt to the changes in her body.

Amy proceeded to have Bernardo hand out four new personal crystals for Katrina, Whitney, Carla, and Elfe. As soon as Katrina attuned hers, she exclaimed, "My goodness. This is a really strong one!"

"Yes, it should protect you against any more of those Domination attacks we had at the last High Council meeting. Compliments of Senator Zarita," Amy replied.

"Elfe, you ready?" Bernardo asked.

"As ready as I'll ever be," she replied. "Come on. I'll need help with my things." She and Carla, arms around each other, led Bernardo and Lena off to their room, where she had at least been able to get her things packed. Amy and Jan chatted a bit more and then left, promising to let Jaques and Katrina know what the Underground discovered about this giant rock finger.

A while later, in the Underground beneath Brom, Ken just gave his son, Ben, and Tom the assignment to go surreptitiously to Wye and check out the finger. Drina was annoyed she couldn't go, but did understand a katalyein would stick out in Wye and attract attention to them instantly. Wye didn't have any katalyein telepaths.

Bart gave them their marching orders. "Okay, I'll be teleporting you as close as I dare. I'll keep a lock on you both, in case of trouble. Holler when you want to be teleported back. Use extreme caution. We've no idea what this thing is, and the geo-sat images are showing a number of people are around it now."

Ben gave Drina a parting kiss and stepped onto the platform beside Tom, Bart's son. A moment later, they vanished, appearing behind a grove of nut trees, just on the far side of the farmstead with the strange rock formation, if rock it was. Quietly, the two began walking the two thousand yards to the rock. A number of men were hacking away at it, most peculiar, both men thought. As they drew closer, a mounted guard rode up to them. "This is as far as you go. Got orders to keep everyone back so the miners can do their thing."

"Sure, fine. Just curious," Ben replied. "What is it anyway? We heard rumors in town and came out to see for ourselves."

"Tower's pulled up a vein of iron ore. Damned near pure, I'm told. Valen keeps hogging all the good quality alien ore, so now we have our own. No more long trips up to Brom for us," he explained rather proudly.

"Hey, that's a pretty neat trick," Ben replied. He and Tom turned around and headed back to the nut tree grove. A causal backwards glance showed them the guard was keeping an eye on them. By the time they entered the grove, three others were walking up to the finger from a slightly different direction. The guard ignored the two, heading to intercept the newcomers. A moment later, the two men reappeared on the platform in the Underground.

"Iron ore? Well that's interesting," Bart and Ken both commented in unison.

"I'll let Amy know. Come on Drina dear, it's back to the

castle for us," Ben teased her.

"Well, this wasn't any big deal. We need better assignments, dear," Drina countered.

Bart smiled, as the two vanished from his platform. He commented, "Nothing seems to stop Drina and Lena. Precocious pair." Ken smiled and nodded.

"Seems innocent enough, but that's a whole lot of iron ore, especially if it's pure," Amy said to Jan, after Ben reported on his findings. She then let Katrina and Jaques know what it was. Jaques wasn't satisfied. How the heck did they find such a pure vein of iron ore, and how did it suddenly upthrust? Katrina relayed his questions, but Amy had no concrete answer for his questions.

At the same time as this conversation was occurring, another one was happening in King Wye's throne room. Guild Master Samuel Johnston was escorted into King Wye's presence. Quite a fair number of noblemen and women were here as well. Sam kept a straight face, as he observed all of the many lip plates, toe shoes, and fancy gowns and suits they wore. "Your Majesty. I am Guild Master Samuel Johnston of the Miller's Guild. I've come to launch a complaint on behalf of Emanuel Jones, the farmer whose farmhouse was destroyed. His wife and child were also killed by this giant iron finger. He should be compensated for his loss. We guilds request in the future more care be given to such magical works, and that no one's property be destroyed in the process."

"Couldn't be helped. These are harsh times, good man. Everyone is being asked to make sacrifices for the good of Wye. It's summer; this farmer has time to rebuild his farm, if he so desires. That will be all, Guild Master," King Wye declared rather sharply and harshly. Several of the noblemen chuckled.

Sam's ire rose; his face reddened, but he knew he was being dismissed. He didn't need the guard's hand on his shoulder to tell him that. He wanted to threaten this despicable king and the fools around him, but he knew would be a death sentence. Instead, he would get recompense one way or another. Once back at his mill, he sent word to his Grand Master, demanding he take some action. *We can't take this much longer,* he sent.

Over in Valen, Westerlings, a tenant farmer, who grew crops on King Alano's vast estates, was summarily ordered out of his farmhouse, along with his entire family. Venerado Arturo spoke harshly, "You've got ten minutes to get your things out of there before we run our test. Make it snappy."

"But where will we go? This has been our home for twenty years," he complained bitterly.

"You were merely a tenant farmer for King Alano. Find some other employment. Now make haste," Venerado Arturo replied harshly.

Five minutes later, a glider soared overhead. A giant wave of liquid fire dropped from its belly, drenching the farmhouse, which instantly caught fire. In only a few minutes, the fire had burned out, leaving only blackened stone walls, filthy teeth in some giant's open mouth. "Excellent, excellent. Total destruction in five minutes. Excellent," Venerado Arturo exclaimed, before he was teleported back to Valen Tower.

Around ten, Bart and Tom began the series of teleports from Elfe's workroom at the spaceport to the entrance of the cavern complex in the far northern Goza Mountains, the very cavern in which she nearly perished during her first winter on Tierra. Bernardo, Lena, and Elfe arrived first. While Bernardo entered the outer chamber with his sword drawn to make sure bears were not inside, the two women moved aside and waited for the first of their gear to arrive. Elfe was quite excited, "Lena, this is my first solo site investigation! Oh, I helped on some during my Academy days, but this is so much more fun. Who knows what we'll find."

"Dead bodies maybe?" Lena suggested. Archaeology was not her specialty, not remotely.

"Perhaps. Pollen, artifacts, cool things. Oh, here comes the first load. Damn, I'm so hobbled like this, that it isn't funny. Well, I agreed to pay the price. Guess I'll have to find ways to adapt and still get my job done."

As Lena watched, Elfe struggled to get her hands securely on the first package; her long nails continually interfered. Her huge bosom then got in the way. Once she had it gripped, she nearly fell over. Toe shoes made even walking without a load tough enough. Nevertheless, Elfe persevered, carrying the first one inside the entrance cavern. "All clear," Bernardo said, rejoining her. "Got to have some lanterns to check further."

Lena appeared behind her, using her telekinesis skills to move another of the heavier bags. Bernardo passed them and brought back two more. It took them a half hour to get their rather large number of bags brought in. While Bernardo got a lantern going, Lena assisted Elfe in getting her portable electric generator setup. Soon, she had bright lights functioning. Now the real work began.

Elfe setup her tripod and mounted her 3-d imaging and mapping camera on it. "In ancient days, one had to do all this by hand with rulers, strings, and paper drawings. With this equipment, a precise representation is captured in three dimensions and with accurate measurements as well. As soon as I photograph this empty, dusty room, we'll move deeper and setup a base camp where the floor isn't so dusty."

"Hey, is this something?" Lena pointed out, by nodding her head in the direction of the archway over the entrance to the next cavern in the complex.

"Writing. Yes. It's in a local language. I can just barely make it out. I can improve its legibility by processing some of the images I'm making. Bernardo, double-check me on this inscription. It's in Old Midlands, right? Skylar Abbey?"

"Yes, that's what it looks like to me. What's an abbey?" he asked.

"A religious retreat where monks or very religious devotees go to meditate, pray, and live, as I understand it. So this is some kind of religious place," Elfe mused. "But I thought there isn't any real religion being practiced on Tierra."

"None that I know of," Bernardo replied. "This is the room where we found you and Jaques."

"I know, see, we've really disturbed the floor. Well, I can compensate for that some in the images. Okay, let's get the portable lanterns and do a quick survey. I would like to see just what we are dealing with here," Elfe suggested.

Lena chuckled. "Well, I don't get to carry a lantern,

fellows. No arms." The two grinned, though Elfe's wasn't visible. Her giant lip plates prevented most facial expressions from showing, if they involved her mouth or lips.

They found fifteen rooms or chambers in the complex, one of which held some fifty burials. Niches had been carved in one wall. Bodies lay on the stone bed of the niche. In the dry, cold cavern, their bodies were desiccated and well preserved. "How strange. They are all men. No women, no children. Well, that fits with some type of religious orders," Elfe said.

One niche, higher and more elaborate than the others had an inscription just above it. It read: Brother Sheridan Abrams, founder of Skylar Abbey, January 10, 1002. "Sorry, never heard of him or this place," Bernardo offered even though Elfe hadn't yet asked him.

The next day, Elfe struggled with some of her equipment; her nails were continuously interfering. "Want some help?" he asked.

"No, I have to learn to do this myself, Bernardo. I'm facing this for the rest of my life, so I just have to deal with it. There. Got it. Now, we will do some dating."

"How?"

"Carbon-14 dating," Elfe explained, giving both a brief explanation. A bit later, she logged the various dates the machine displayed. "Well, it checks out, getting readings around four hundred years ago, which would make the dates around the Tierra year of 1000. Nice consistency."

They found living quarters and a kitchen with a blackened hearth. Copper pots, plates, cups, and silverware lay strewn around the room. Next to it was a dining room of sorts. The tables and chairs had been carved from the bedrock. The much smaller living quarters contained brass lamps and beds carved into a niche in the wall, much like the graves.

Eventually, Elfe found their communal latrines. "Bingo, their garbage dump. Now, we're getting somewhere."

Lena exclaimed aghast, "You aren't going digging in that foul, smelly stuff are you?"

Elfe laughed. "First, it isn't smelly any longer. Second, there's lots of useful information in there. I can determine what their diet consisted of, for example. Can you two bring me the big brown bag please? Oh and the bright lights as well. Heavenly!"

Two days later, Elfe finished her analysis. "They ate very strangely. Nuts, berries, wild grass seeds, and some meat. I believe possibly bear, though I'm not sure what some of these bone are from. We've never done a survey of your flora and fauna. I'd say they were gathers primarily, with a rare hunt. Plus, I've found the remains of a hand-written book! It's in bad shape, but it appears to be a Holy Book of some kind. Why they would have tossed it in the garbage pit doesn't make much sense, though, especially since this was obviously a men's holy retreat. Anyway, now, I must examine some of their remains. I'll not disturb them very much. I prefer to continue to honor their sacred burials. Come, let's see how their overall health was, and what some of them died of, shall we."

A day later, she listed several causes of death. "They were in poor physical health, suffering from several different vitamin deficiencies because of their sparse diet. The last man died about twenty years after the founding date of 1002. I think that about wraps this one up, gang. At least four hundred years ago, this group of fifty men came here to found this religious retreat. How they carved it from the solid bedrock remains a mystery, though, unless they had some kind of *mentales* gifts that would allow them to do that so well, and in such a short time, and with no stone cutting tools. They must have gathered what they could find to eat from around these mountains, which certainly wasn't much. That led to their overall decline in health. The one curious thing is that Holy Book, which was tossed into the garbage pit not long after the construction of the pit. So we do know there were some men who held strong religious beliefs around the year 1000 on Tierra."

"Fascinating, Elfe. Not sure if this is really of any use, but it's fascinating to know," Bernardo replied. "Now where?"

"We pack up everything, go back, and resupply. I want to go to the far south next, what everyone calls the ancient Kingdom of Bashir. It's an uninhabited desert now, but I've located what are likely smaller towns buried in the desert sands, and what looks to be a large city in the center of that land. We'll start with that city. It's most promising," Elfe declared.

Bernardo and Lena did most of the packing. They were substantially faster at it than the hobbled Elfe, whose bosom, nails, lip plates, and toe shoes continually found new ways to slow her way, way down, frustrating her immensely, though she did her best to hide it from her two companions.

The tenth of July, Bart and Tom again began the lengthy teleport operation. Re-supplied and now carrying many gallons of drinking water with them, the three arrived at the ruins of the ancient city called Valcia. Elfe had done her homework, searching the ancient records logged by the first governor of Tierra, shortly after establishing their initial spaceport on Plateau Grado. As always when in the field, Elfe had tied her floor length hair up into a tight bun. Instead of wearing their leather outfits, this time, they all wore light cotton shirts and pants. Elfe had also provided them with wide brimmed hats to help protect them from the direct rays of the orange-red sun that beat down mercilessly during the summer season this far south.

"My god! I can see why this is a desert and uninhabited!" Elfe exclaimed, as she arrived into the searing heat. "I'm sweating already, and I've just arrived!" She tried to move away from their arrival point, since Bart would soon be sending along the first of several loads of their gear. Her tiny toe shoes sank into the deep sands, sending her falling backwards onto her rump, giving her quite a jar. She let out a wicked curse.

Lena focused and used her gift to lift her gently back up, while Bernardo came to her side and put his steadying arm around her. "Got you. Looks like I'm going to get to be your support on this trip. Pretend I'm Carla," he teased, adding quickly, "Oops, forget that. Lena will have something to say about that." Elfe chuckled, glancing at the smiling Lena, wishing she had the Gang of Ten's unique attitudes towards life.

Together, they moved out of the way, and their gear

began arriving. Just inside the city, Bernardo found some relatively solid ground and left Elfe there, along with Lena. "I get to play pack horsey for a bit. You two look for some place to setup camp, before we all melt. It's hot enough to bake bread!"

Elfe surveyed what she could see of the city. While some of the buildings had been made of wood, these had somehow burned down, leaving charred posts outlining the vertical pillars supporting the destroyed walls. However, further into the city, she could see stone shells of buildings. What caught her eyes the most was perhaps the largest stone building, fairly near the center, as best she could remember from her geo-sat images she'd studied. "We should see about making our way to that tallest one. Perhaps it might provide some cover. It was likely an important building in Valcia." She had no idea it was the former founding Church of God, not yet at least.

Unable to see her feet over her bosom, Elfe was forced to take carefully measured steps, occasionally wobbling and flailing her arms to keep her precarious balance over sand covered cobblestones. Lena commented, "This is so eerie, walking through a city that's not a city. Buildings that once must have formed a magnificent city now sit here silent, like ancient specters. Creepy."

"Yes, but they tell a story. Oops," she nearly stumbled again. "Okay, I got it. Tricky. See, this used to be a market square, filled with women shopping for the day's grain. Over there, craftsmen worked, probably a blacksmith shop. There, a coppersmith. See, a few partially made bowls are sticking up from the drifting sands. Must have left in a hurry. Ah, here we are. Biggest, tallest building. Stone. The ones at the edge, where we landed, are adobe brick. Doors have dry-rotted. I need to take an image before we try to enter. They might disintegrate more."

Lena looked up at the imposing two story building and saw an engraving in the stones forming the arch over the massive double doors. "Church of God," she read aloud. "Kind of hard to read though. Sand blasted?"

"I suspect so. Centuries of blowing and drifting sands etch even the hardest stone. Church of God. So there was

236

religion on Tierra in ancient times. Interesting," Elfe commented.

"Why interesting?" Lena asked, curious.

"For some reason, this Church of God religion has totally vanished from Tierra. Inquiring minds would like to know what that was," the archaeologist replied. "Good, here comes our packhorse now," she teased Bernardo, who was lugging a number of bags, sweating profusely.

"I'm soaked. Lena, you haven't broken a sweat yet! That's not fair. I should make you pack the next load in," he grumbled, but still managed to tease his wife.

"My normal environment, silly. I grew up on a world like this. Heck, this is barely warm, and certainly the sunlight is incredibly dim," she purposely exaggerated for his expected reaction, a big groan.

"Stop playing around, Bernardo. I need my 3-d imaging system, so I can image this door before we try to enter. It'll probably disintegrate further when we do. I promise you it'll be much cooler inside," Elfe explained, though she too was sweating heavily, but glad she had her long hair tied into a bun today.

To speed things along, Bernardo got the imaging system out for her, and more or less set it up for her, knowing she would have a hard time managing it. This way, she'd get the images taken sooner. He wanted the promised relief from this unbearable heat. After she fussed he was doing it wrongly, he laughed, and let her at the equipment, while he and Lena headed back to fetch more. As the two retraced their steps, he asked, "Really? Was your home world really this unbearably hot?"

"It sure is. That's one reason for my dark skin — helps us get by in the harsh sunlight. Elfe says that building is a religious one. Church of God was carved in the arch. Have you ever heard of the Church of God?" Lena asked.

"Nope, never heard of it. Wait, maybe. Not sure. In any case, they aren't popular or a big group. Here we go. I'll hang the straps over your shoulders. Can you carry two bags? If so, I'll lug the water tins."

By the time the two returned with the next load,

Bernardo was close to a heat stroke. Lena ordered him to take a break, drink some water, and melt a bit of salt in his mouth. "You cool off some; I'll bring the next load." He didn't object this time, marveling at how well his wife was able to cope with this desert. She barely perspired so far, while he and Elfe were drenched.

Lena used her *mentales* gifts to get a pair of bag straps over her shoulders and returned with another load. To bring the remaining two water tins to the church, she had to use her telekinetic powers on them the whole way to the church. When she finally arrived, Bernardo was feeling better, and Elfe had her images. Just as the archaeologist suspected, when Lena and Bernardo attempted to open the huge, ornately carved doors, the dry rot caused them to crumble into a dusty heap at the threshold. Cooler air rushed out, blowing Bernardo's hair back some. "More like it," he grinned.

Elfe had hit the jackpot, as far as she was concerned. Inside, much had been preserved rather well. She found the archives, recovering a hundred scrolls and two copies of what was probably their religious Holy Book. As she began carefully imaging each page, she discovered they were hard to read. The language seemed to be related to Midlands, but she couldn't be sure. Hence, she sent for the linguistic expert, Nadja, knowing she would be in heaven with these documents. Nadja came at once.

"Incredible find, Elfe! Just fabulous. This is Old Midlands, rather that's what I'll call it. Some of these documents go back nearly four hundred years. These will give me vital clues on how Midlands language has evolved over time. Incredible, Elfe, just incredible. Can I study them now?" Nadja exclaimed, more excited than she'd been in years.

"Please do. That will free us to explore more of this church and the city," Elfe replied, very pleased Nadja was so enthusiastic about this new project.

The trio spent the rest of the day searching the church, taking 3-d images of whatever they found. "You see, with these special images, there is no need to actually remove any of these artifacts. I will leave them just as we find them — for future generations to study and appreciate. Come on; next room please," Elfe explained. Lena appreciated that they were not actually going to cart away the fancy pots, the tarnished but ornamental copper and bronze wares, or the few gold and silver ornaments they'd found. While Lena wasn't religious, she had a healthy respect for those who were, and felt very uneasy about disturbing or stealing objects from a holy site, which this clearly was.

As they gathered for supper, Nadja had quite a lot to report. "This is a treasure trove of information! Some go back to the first appearance of us *mentales* gifted on Tierra! And before that even! Do you realize this whole far southern peninsula was once a mighty jungle? It was. And this city, Valcia was their Holy City. Some of these documents predate the arrival of the first aliens to Tierra! They record the mighty explosion of the original Rigel-3 spaceport — it's total destruction. It outlines the strange oscillations of the planet after that, followed by the devastating climate changes that occurred. Massive wildfires spread through the jungles of Bashir. People abandoned the central highlands in droves."

"More importantly, the Church of God was actually condemning the *mentales* gifted as evil witches, burning them at the stake! But there's more. Apparently, before the aliens first arrived on Tierra, there were local witches, who were highly skilled in the healing arts. The Church of God wanted to eradicate them, substituting their own locally trained doctors for these heretical witches. That their doctors could not cure, while the witches were quite successful at it, apparently made no difference to these religious men."

"In fact, their Archbishop here made deals with the aliens to have the aliens kidnap and mind-alter the witches. Apparently, the Rigel-3's psych man was doing this without the governor's knowledge. The records indicate that just before the massive explosion, they'd wiped out all the known witches across all Tierra!"

"The *mentales* gifted first appeared somewhat after the explosion and the Great Climate Shift. During that time, the documents get very difficult to decipher. This Archbishop was probably going mad himself. The very last document states a new Archbishop was appointed, and that he was taking the

Church northward probably to a coastal city, such as Nasik. I'm going to use this material to add another huge section to my History of Tierra that I'm compiling from all available records," Nadja explained, still highly enthusiastic over this find.

Elfe pointed out, "Well, that makes sense, Nadja. When something new like the *mentales* gifted appear, people become afraid of them, because they have powers and are different from themselves. It's only natural the Church of God would view us as enemies to be destroyed. Pity we don't know more about those ancient witches and their methods of healing." The foursome talked long into the night over the significance of these discoveries and revelations. They all wondered what had happened to the Church of God. It had apparently vanished almost entirely from Tierra.

The next day, Nadja returned home with computer copies of all the documents and books, intent on making modern translations and combining them with her history book. Meanwhile, the trio spent another two weeks checking out the rest of the city and surrounding lands. Although Bernardo had constantly to keep his arm around Elfe to keep her from taking another tumble, she was able to complete her basic survey. She acquired numerous samples of the pollen from the once lush jungle vegetation, as well as animal bones. Some of these were still found on Tierra, such as horses. However, several larger animals and some snakes were no longer found anywhere on Tierra. Sadly, they had become extinct during the Great Climate Change. At least, she could now document what had been here originally. All three were very glad to return home. The heat was physically draining, though Lena enjoyed it immensely.

For her part, Elfe began to realize just how awful that first contact with the aliens had been for the people of Tierra. Dismal. She vowed to publish a full report on it in hopes others would learn from these mistakes.

Chapter 16 Genetic Digression

Early June, genetic scientist Aarok Laron received an Imperial Summons to go to the secret Genetic Laboratory on Ashford-4. The fifty-five year old man was still quite bitter. Fifteen years ago, he'd been rejected over a dozen other top geneticists, who were called up for the government funded research project — a project he'd helped formulate. With unlimited funding, he just had to be a part of it. He never forgave anyone for his rejection. Now that something bad had happened there, the Imperium was summoning him to go there and sort out the mess his fellow geneticists had made. He'd only been told that some "accident" had killed them all. That pleased him, though outwardly, he expressed the requisite sorrow for the loss of his fellow scientists.

He was to lead a team of geneticists to recover what was still there, including any and all research notes. If possible, he was to see if anything useful could still be salvaged. Better still, he was put in charge of this salvage operation, and he could hand pick his personnel. Because human genetic experiments were officially illegal within the Imperium, he had continued his own research in private all these years. His long-time assistant, Broc Lest, efficiently and quietly handled any "problems" that developed over the years. Several "samples" had died from his experiments on their bodies. Broc quietly disposed of them. Certainly, Broc would accompany him.

At this time, he had two bright and up and coming young Academy students working for him, doing their final internship before graduating as geneticists themselves. The twenty-one year olds were married. Alex and Ruth Hammil were both platinum blondes with pale blue eyes, bright and sharp, the geneticists of the future. Perhaps too bright for Aarok. He had no choice but to bring them along. He also chose two other geneticists, who had worked with him in the past, and who asked few questions.

Mid-June, their heavily loaded deep space transport arrived in orbit above Ashford-4, where it docked temporarily with the battle cruiser carrying the Sector ID Minister Slag. The group was escorted into Slag's War Room. "Welcome, Doctor Aaron, good of you to drop everything and come on such short notice. We have a situation here." He outlined what had happened in gory detail.

"We have managed to plug all of the meteorite-caused holes and restored the internal atmosphere. We've verified the complex is currently safe, but we've still got the Bio Agent Storage Building locked down. We don't know how badly damaged some of the cylinders are. Best be safe than sorry. Thank God that Ashford-5 received only a minor dose. I believe most everyone has now recovered from the temporary genetic modifications. That could have been the worst disaster in recent history. So, your task and that of your team is to first make damn sure the cylinders are secure and safe. Then, see what data, if any, can be recovered. I'm hoping it isn't a total loss. The Imperium spent a fortune on this place during the past fifteen years." He added more details, rather shocking all of the geneticists.

"Aye sir, we are up to the task. When do we begin?" Doctor Aarok asked. He knew they had made some gigantic breakthroughs down there. Now, if he did this right, he would be able to take credit for these discoveries. He'd be the most famous geneticist in the history of the Imperium!

"Now. Here's the landing coordinates. Please be extra careful. Error on the side of caution. And keep me posted. Consider everything Security Level 10 for now. Top secret. That's all."

An hour later, their ship docked on Ashford-4, the repaired dome ceiling closed overhead. Air pressure was soon restored. "Detectors on," he ordered as the small group opened their cargo doors, breathing in the recycled air of the base. While they were en route here, Doctor Aarok had studied the detailed plans of the complex. Thus, he assigned the others to search thoroughly all of the outer experimental buildings first, while he and his assistant, Broc, searched the inventory records and the actual containment building.

Quickly, he was able to find their most recent experiment and two follow up ones. These, he downloaded onto his own computer, wiping them from the research station's computer. In private, he explained what he'd found to Broc. "Look, they've made a huge breakthrough here. They are able not only to reprogram a human body's genetic makeup, but they don't need a sample of that person's genes to do it! Incredible breakthrough. Plus, they found a way to use aerosol methods of delivery. Just incredible, Broc. We don't want the others finding this out just yet. Look here, their last experiment that went wrong was designed to do all this to human bodies." He showed Broc the computer listing.

"It worked, but on the inhabitants of Ashford-5. Well, they are primitives. Either they got too low a dosage, since it was designed for ten test subjects, or the primitive's genes are somehow different than the test subjects. If this test had been successful, look at what their follow up two tests were going to be!"

His assistant mumbled something sinister.

"Yes, Broc, you are right. A cost-saving method of handling die-hard criminals! As you know, criminals are everywhere. Those, who are finally caught, are handed over to the psych men for behavior modifications. However, as you also know, about a third of them aren't phased by it, and those have to be imprisoned and heavily guarded. That costs a fortune, even though they are all sent to the prison planet. If either of these two subsequent experiments actually work, Broc, all those hardened criminals could be easily handled, saving billions of credits."

"Plus you'd be famous. But does it actually work? You know we can't get official permission to do these genetic experiments on humans now. Not since the war is over," Broc countered.

"True, true. Besides saving them billions, I'd be famous for inventing a vastly more humane way of treating the prisoners. You are right, though. I can't go trying to get permission to experiment, not unless I can already prove it produces the desired results. Catch-22. I can't get the go ahead unless I can show that the process works, but I can't show the process works unless I go ahead with it."

Broc chuckled, "Boss, when has that ever stopped you?"

243

Both men chuckled.

"We need to conduct an experiment to prove beyond any doubts that this process will work. This place here is absolutely perfect for it," Doctor Aarok replied. Slowly, an idea began forming. "Those two young interns would make perfect test subjects. Besides, they are too darn bright as it is. I don't want them getting their hands on this data. Let's see if the materials for these two next tests are still around."

"You sure it's safe in there?" Broc asked, concerned about entering the sealed chamber where the toxins were stored.

"Probably, let's suit up, just in case," Doctor Aarok advised. A half hour later, the two men entered the large storage facilities. "Look for sample 21324 or 21325," he ordered. The two men split up and began looking at the many labels.

"Hey, over here, doc, I found them. Crates?"

Doctor Aarok double-checked the numbers. "A crate goes with the cylinder? How strange. Well, let's take them out of here and see what we have."

A half hour later, having verified the cylinder was undamaged and in perfect condition, Doctor Aarok opened the crate to find clothing inside. Corsets, toe shoes, lip plates, and gowns were inside, enough for ten test subjects. Some still were in their original packaging, imported from Elegant Fashions Inc. The gowns, however, had come from another world.

"Oh I get it, boss," Broc spoke up. "Once they've had all these modifications, these are what they are going to need to wear. The fellows here thought of everything. Clever. Now what?"

Doctor Aarok grinned wickedly. "We need to arrange for a little accident, my good man."

Meanwhile, Alex and Ruth finished checking on the attached rooms. "Why does he have us checking these facilities out?" Ruth complained. "These are nothing more than living quarters. No experiments are in here. Is he hogging the real data?"

"Wouldn't put it past him. You know his record," Alex

244

grumbled. "We're done here; let's move on. If we hurry up, maybe we can get a look at the master records too." They did just that, but so did the other four geneticists. All were eager to begin the actual productive work.

At suppertime, the small crew gathered in the galley area. "Well, Alex and Ruth have verified the living chambers are in perfect order. Alex, Ruth, you two take Chamber 1 as your personal living quarters. Move your bags in there after supper," Doctor Aarok ordered. He noticed both were a bit surprise that they got the first room. He and Broc took Chamber 2, while the other four took the next four as theirs. That evening the group moved their things into their respective new quarters, planning for a very long stay indeed. There was so very much to learn here, and they were truly excited at the prospects. All had taken the opportunity to glance at the massive computer data files, meticulously kept by the dozen scientists who had died here.

After settling into their new quarters, Alex and Ruth chatted. She said, "You know, no matter how this all goes, we'll also be famous too. He can't keep all the results to himself. From what little we've seen, there are some revolutionary results here. Think of the ultimate good that can come from this disaster."

"Right sweetie pie. Regenerating lost limbs has long defied all attempts. Yet, perhaps they've developed a roundabout method that would do just that. Pretty awesome, if you ask me," Alex replied, undressing for bed.

"True, but in a way, it's unfortunate the genetic modifications were so temporary on Ashford-5. I know it would have been awful for those poor people, but they are primitives at least. If the results had been permanent, think what that would mean?" she replied, also undressing. She added, "I suppose we'll have to find a way to make them permanent. I sure want a good look at the data. Maybe tomorrow he'll let us have a good peek."

"I sure hope so. Come here, my love. I've got other things on my mind right now," he grinned mischievously.

"Men, you always have that on your minds," she countered playfully. Together, they climbed into bed and turned out the lights. After a round of lovemaking, both fell asleep. Neither heard the soft clicking of the sealing bars sliding into place. A faint hissing sound followed for about a half hour.

In the morning, after sharing passionate kisses, the two rose and dressed. "Alex! Look, we're locked inside!" Alex came over to the door. The contamination locks were in place. Both felt a surge of panic. She pressed the intercom button and called for help.

Shortly, the other six came running up to their sealed doors. Obviously, three were still eating their breakfast; they were still chewing. One held a piece of bread in his hand. "Oh my god! Contamination!" screamed Doctor Aarok cried out. Hastily, the six ran away, leaving the pair even more worried. They tried everything they could think of to release the contamination locks, but they knew they simply could not escape. After all, if this room were contaminated with a biological agent, opening the doors would expose the rest of the complex. The computer controlled systems would not permit that, even if Doctor Aarok tried to override it.

A half hour later, six suited men appeared outside their door, detectors in hand. At last, Doctor Aarok took off his helmet. Speaking into the intercom, he said, "We're all clear out here. Hang in there a bit; we're going to make further tests on your chambers. It's probably nothing more than a glitch in the computer system."

"Okay, it probably is. Otherwise, we would be dead by now," Alex replied, sounding as hopeful as he could. No need to panic yet. They had heard how the original scientists had all died within a half hour of exposure to the agent. Nervously, they paced around the confines of their twenty-foot square room.

An hour later, a grim faced Doctor Aarok appeared at their door. He pressed the intercom button. "I thought you two fully checked these rooms out! Damn it; you missed a timed release of a genetic experiment. The cylinder was attached to the air intake valve. We've got it disconnected now, but we've no idea what you've been exposed to. The computer still is registering a bio agent contamination inside. Hang in there;

we are all on it out here. Back in a while."

Now, the two did panic. "Alex! What's happening to us? Exposed? We didn't miss any cylinders. I remember checking every one of the lines. There weren't any cylinders hooked up."

"We must have missed one, somehow sweetie pie. We aren't sick yet, so maybe it's nothing at all."

"I'm scared, Alex!"

"Well, I'd be a fool, if I said I wasn't. We can't do anything about it while we're in here. I guess we have to trust in the others," Alex replied.

"Trust Doctor Aarok? Hardly," she spat, but then softened. "Well, I do trust the others. Maybe it isn't anything. We're not sick."

"Not yet at least," Alex whispered under his breath, wishing they'd not been so eager to accept this mission. He continued to pace around the small room. Finally, he felt tired and sat down beside Ruth on the bed. Suddenly, a pneumatic tube system activated, startling both of them. Over the intercom, one of the other geneticists called out, "We've figured out how to get food to you. Here's breakfast, lunch, and supper. We're still working on just what the contaminant is. Hang in there you two."

"Thanks, we're starving," Ruth called out. The two ate a goodly amount. As the outside lights dimmed for the night, the two again undressed and crawled into bed. They fell into a deep sleep, and didn't realize three days had passed before they woke up.

The second day after the exposure, one geneticist reported the two were unconscious now. That's when Doctor Aarok made his revelations to his fellow team members. "Okay, I've finally figured it out. They had a followup experiment all set up and ready to be activated when the meteor shower wiped them out. Chamber 1 was the target. They had a third followup experiment lined up after this one, but had not yet gotten a chamber hooked up for it. You see, they were on to something of monumental proportions. Look at these notes." He brought them up on a big monitor for everyone to read.

"This will revolutionize how we handle hardened

247

criminals, saving billions of credits, if it worked, of course. Their idea was genius, if you ask me. Look at what they are attempting to do to the bodies," he said rather excitedly. The list of modifications contained in experiment 21324 came up on the screen.

"My god! Is this even possible?" one asked, thunderstruck.

"Must be. It happened on Ashford-5, if only temporary for most folks there. Well, a few apparently got a heavier dose of the agent, Doctor Jones and the governor, I'm told," Doctor Aarok replied.

"But they'll be totally helpless," another exclaimed.

"Look what was planned for the follow up to this one, 21325. They were to be blinded, as well as all this. Now that would take care of even the worst criminal ever," Doctor Aarok countered. "We've discovered they also were being humane with their test subjects. They acquired new clothing and things for their subjects, assuming the tests worked. Broc and I found this crate. It has enough to clothe ten test subjects. The follow up experiment also has ten sets too."

Another geneticist spoke up, "Doctor, we should take careful notes on what happens to Alex and Ruth, and when. If this does work, we need to gather as much information as possible. I know they would want us to proceed and not lose valuable information." The others agreed.

Acting as though he were regrettable, Doctor Aarok sighed. "Well, I suppose you are right. Maybe nothing will happen to them. If it does, you are right, we should document everything that happens. Even if these changes do occur, they might not be permanent, as it was on Ashford-5." He attempted to sound hopeful. "Are they still unconscious?"

On the third day, the safety locks disengaged. Even so, Doctor Aarok had them suit up before entering and checking on the unconscious pair. They detected no signs of any bio agent remaining in the room and removed their helmets. Already massive changes were occurring in the test subject's bodies. The five geneticists took measurements and extensive notes, as well as checking their vital signs. After this point, Doctor Aarok suggested they take turns watching over the pair around the clock. No one knew how long they would remain in a semi-coma state, but the way the modifications were going, they would awake in dire need of help. Their arms were shriveled and quite withered looking.

On the morning of the fourth day, their desiccated arms fell off. One of the geneticists removed them for further study in the lab, excited to have something concrete to study. All five were absolutely astounded with the physical changes the poor pair were undergoing. Around suppertime, the two finally awoke.

Ruth felt ravenously hungry and had to urinate in the worst way. She tried to sit up, but her arms failed to operate. She looked at her right shoulder and then her left. Ruth screamed louder than she ever had in her life, waking Alex, who promptly added his cries of terror to hers. Neither had any arms left. Their shoulders looked as if their bodies had never had them to begin with! But they quickly saw that other drastic changes had occurred.

Looking at each other, they saw that their lips had been slit. Great, thick lip loops drooped down from their mouths. As they finally sat up, they could not see their own tiny waists, which were barely a foot around. The pair had enormous breasts, each over a foot in size, mammoth and blocking their view to a great extent. They had to urinate badly, and, thus, while still screaming, they got to their feet, only to fall onto the floor. Their feet had been massively altered as well. Only their toes were flat on the floor; their heels were some six inches above the floor, their arches, enormous now. Nevertheless, nature called, and they could not help but relieve themselves on the floor. That's when they noticed the other change, which only added to their shrieks. Each had both male and female sexual organs, with the male ones located below their female ones. Making matters worse, their platinum blonde hair had grown. So much so, that with both, it reached the floor when they stood. Later, they would discover it had also thickened considerably. Hers was wavy still, his fairly straight.

Just then, two of the other geneticists entered, carrying the crate of new apparel. "It's okay. We are working on a cure," one said. "We've brought you some clothes that are supposed to fit. These changes are likely only going to be temporary. Please calm down. We'll take good care of you."

"But we're helpless!" Alex yelled. As soon as he spoke, he realized he could not even understand what he was saying. So many of the phonetic sounds of his language required the use of his lips that what came out was unintelligible, not only to himself and Ruth, but to everyone else.

"Sorry, I can't make out what you are saying. See if you can get back onto the bed, Alex."

"Help us! I can't do this!" Ruth wailed, also noticing what she said was unintelligible as well. She screamed again. The two geneticists helped the two up onto the bed, but the pair was shaking visibly. Sobbing replaced their shrieking.

"Let us get some clothes on you. I bet you are starving. As soon as we get you dressed, we'll feed you. Please relax and cooperate. We aren't sure how to put all these things on you."

Valiantly, both tried to calm down, though they continued to sob. Their lives were ruined, and they knew it. After a good deal of struggling, the two geneticists got their new corsets on the pair and tightened fully. "That is supposed to be for back support," one explained.

"I can't breathe!" Ruth tried to say.

"Sorry. Can't understand you. Hang in there, Ruth." After more trial and error, the two helpers finally got them dressed. Nylons, panties, slips, and satin gowns covered them. Of note, their gown tops had no sleeves. Next, they tied their new toe shoes on securely. Finally, they fumbled about with the mouth mounting brackets for the lip plates. Eventually, they were able to snap the foot in diameter disks into place and gently stretched their lip loops over the edges.

One said, "Well, you kind of look like a pair of platypuses. Okay, food time. Stay put, food is on its way." A half hour later, the pair had eaten as much as they could. Their helpers found the only way they could drink was by spooning the liquids into their mouths. They were thankful for the overly long silverware that was also stored in that crate. The original research personnel had apparently thought of everything.

Doctor Aarok then walked in with a big smile. "Well,

you both look good. Apparently, that second follow up experiment has been successful. As you can tell, the bio agent is no longer in the room. We've determined it had a short lifetime of just several days. So you are free to come and go around the base with the rest of us. I do hope you don't mind if we take some samples from you both. You are making medical history, but I suppose that's a small consolation right now. Don't worry; these effects probably will only last a few days, like they did on Ashford-5. So up and at it. Let's get you up and walking around, shall we?"

"Doctor Aarok! We're helpless. We can't even see our feet," Ruth complained, fearing even trying to rise. "What's happened to our sex?"

"Sorry, I can't understand what you are saying, Ruth. We'll try the ULATs, when we get you into the control room. Up and at it," he added, nodding to the two original geneticists who'd dressed them. Both put their arms around the pair, forcing them to rise. Alex and Ruth wobbled wildly on their toes, trying to get their balance, as their enormously long hair fell to the floor, barely a half inch from the ground now.

"I can't see my feet! Don't let go of me!" Ruth cried out. Alex yelled similar words, but no one could understand either of them.

"Want them to hold on to you?" Doctor Aarok finally asked. Both nodded vigorously, their lip plates bobbing up and down. Slowly, with very tiny steps, the pair moved out of their bedroom, thankful to sit down at last in the control room. Eagerly, the other geneticists began examining them, taking saliva samples, as well as drawing some blood for further analysis.

Meantime, Broc brought in two ULAT boxes and had the two again attempt to speak. Everyone was dismayed. The boxes kept flashing "Error — Unknown Language" in large red letters. Alex and Ruth's hearts sank. They could not even talk to their peers now.

Eventually, the geneticists came to the most embarrassing part for both Alex and Ruth, their sexual organs. "My god! Both are fully functional!" one declared. "You're both hermaphrodites now! This is quite impressive, quite revolutionary. We need further tests!" Both Alex and Ruth faces felt like they were on fire. Never had either been so personally and profoundly embarrassed as now. A bit later, the scientist looked up, "Here, look at the results for yourselves. As geneticists, you can appreciate these changes." Both Ruth and Alex stared at the monitor, then gasped.

Both were capable of breeding themselves and bearing their own children, but they were just as capable of breeding each other as well. At the moment, they found this utterly shocking. Hermaphrodites were rare in the Imperium, but not unknown. Quite often, such people were looked upon as freaks of nature. As a result, most found employment in the sex trade, where they could please either sex of paying customers. Independently, both Alex and Ruth now clung desperately to Doctor Aarok's suggestion that these horrific changes would only be temporary ones. After all, most everyone on Ashford-5 had returned to normal after about eight days. Somehow, this just had to happen here, they prayed.

After an exhaustive series of tests, Broc led them, one by one, back into their bedroom and undressed them, helping them onto the bed. He found he had to pull their long hair to their front so each didn't either sit on it or lay on it. After finally tucking Ruth in beside Alex, he whispered, "Sweet dreams. I'll get you in the morning. Looks like I'm being assigned to be your caretaker now. The others have so much data to analyze that they will be at it for days. You are providing them with tons of useful information. So that's something positive, don't you think?"

Neither answered. Once he left them along, both wiggled and struggled to get onto their sides to face each other. Though they both wanted desperately to talk to the other, by now they knew that was impossible. Instead, Alex tried to give Ruth a loving kiss. Shortly, both became doubly aroused, confusing each of them. Each was experiencing opposite sex sensations they'd never felt before. Without much thinking, their love for each other took over, and their passions exploded as never before. Later, they fell into a much needed, deep sleep.

As the days passed, the two slowly began adjusting

somewhat. At least once dressed, they were able to walk around the complex on their own. The floor was perfectly smooth and flat. That they couldn't see their feet no longer mattered, though when Broc figured out how to lower their lip plates so that they drooped downward, they could see far better. They began to pay attention to what the five geneticists had displayed on their various computer monitors. Each was researching different aspects of their physical transformations. Unable to talk or do anything useful to help, but still budding geneticists themselves, they began to pay close attention to the various findings that appeared on the screens.

They could see quite visibly their basic genetic makeup had actually been altered. This alone was a fantastic feat in its own right. Further, each realized that these dozen researchers had gone even farther. While in a lab it was possible in some limited ways to take a sample of a person's genes, modify them, and then reinsert the genes back into the host to cause relatively minor changes, such as eye colors, this was on a whole new scale of effects. That original breakthrough had enabled a whole new generation of rejuvenation machines, which now routinely turned back the clock on human bodies.

Rather, these changes were massive genetic alterations. That alone made this groundbreaking. However, both quickly also realized these changes had been done without first having obtained their specific genes. The process had been wholly generic in nature! If that wasn't enough, the delivery mechanism was a simple airborne one, easily used on large populations. Both suddenly realized what had been the driving force behind this secret installation: the war and a way to wipe out whole Federation planets! That sobered both.

Ruth realized, if the Imperium had weaponized this and used it on a whole world, a few days later, the entire population of that world would be as helpless as she and Alex now were. Within days, billions either would die from a total inability to do anything for themselves or could be shipped off to institutions. Meantime, the Imperium forces could confiscate the planet, its wealth, its resources, it equipment, and products — all without firing a shot or fighting a single battle. Send in a small drone to release the bio agent and wait a week. The planet would be wholly theirs. She shuttered realizing just what all this actually meant. Such power, no one should have, she thought, but was helpless even to voice her concerns to Doctor Aarok.

About the only thing that kept the pair's hopes up was the eight-day limit those on Ashford-5 had endured before the effects wore off. Both kept an accurate count of the days, waiting for that all important eighth day. Still, they continued to absorb all of the findings the five other geneticists were discovering.

The all-important eighth day came and went. Tomorrow, tomorrow we will wake up from this infernal nightmare, Alex thought, as he tried to fall asleep. Beside him, her massive bosom interlocked with his, Ruth was thinking much the same thing. Both looked forward to the next day. They would be back to their old selves. Dawn came and they were not!

Both woke up and a panic crept through their stomachs. They were just as helpless as before. Patiently, they awaited Broc's assistance. He grumbled a bit about having to play nursemaid. Ruth wanted to tell him off, but had no way to do so. Grin and bear it. Perhaps the changes would occur sometime during the day, she hoped and prayed.

The ninth day came and went. The tenth, the eleventh. On the first of July some fourteen days later, both were starting to really panic. Why were they not reverting back? Surely, these horrific changes wouldn't be permanent! Doctor Aarok met them as they made their slow, careful way into the control room. After tossing their heads about to get their really long, thick hair off to one side, both sat down, where they could once more see whatever the others were doing.

"Well, I've some not so good news for you both. As far as we are able to tell, these changes seem to be rather permanent," he reported. "It's been nearly double the recovery time of those on Ashford-5. I'm truly sorry. Still, we must not lose all hope. However, I am going to have to report this accident to the Sector ID Minister Slag. I can't put it off much longer."

Now both did panic, and each tried to tell him

254

something, but soon gave up. He merely shrugged his shoulders. They had no way to communicate to him or anyone else. That only added to their panic. He and Broc left the control room.

"Boss, I'm getting mighty tired of being nursemaid to those two. How much longer until we can get rid of them?" Broc asked.

"I know. They are just in everyone's way here too. I'll put the call into Slag now. I know! We could ask him, if they could be placed under the watchful eyes of Ashford-5's Doctor Jones. She could keep us informed of their condition, should anything actually change. I'm pretty well convinced they both received sufficient bio agent to make the genetic modifications permanent. Of course, now they are totally useless. We have all the data from them we need, unless they suddenly reverse and return to normal."

"What's the odds of that happening?" Broc asked.

"Slim to none at this point. Like I told them, it's nearly double the time of Ashford-5's recovery period. I'll go make the call now, Broc. I need you on other duties, not playing nursemaid."

A short while later and after explaining the "accident" to the Sector ID Minister, he suggested, "We would like permission to have these two victims transferred to the care of Ashford-5's Doctor Jones. She can look after them and report to us, if there are any changes in their condition. Over."

After a very brief pause, Slag asked, "Is there any danger of contagion? That's my paramount consideration. We can't have this thing spreading around the Imperium, Doctor Aarok. Over."

"None at all, sir. The bio agent is long dead. Lifetime is barely four days at most. It's been nearly two weeks now. There is no chance whatsoever of this thing spreading. Someone just missed that automatic experimental setup. We believe it was triggered by the restoration of the atmosphere and the occupancy of the chamber by those two. Serves them right, they were supposed to have checked for such things that first day, and they somehow missed it completely. Over."

"Okay then, that does seem to be a reasonable way to

handle them. However, Doctor Aarok, I am holding you personally responsible. It others on Ashford-5 get this thing, this plague, this whatever it is, you'll have to personally answer to me and the Legates. I'll make the arrangements and send a shuttle for them. Over and out."

A bit later, he told Broc, and the two joined everyone in the control room. "Good news. I've told the Sector ID Minister about our unfortunate accident here. He wants Alex and Ruth to be placed under the care of Ashford-5's Doctor Jones. She's one of the most competent field doctors in the Imperium, long stellar record. She'll look after you two and maybe find a way to help you both. Meanwhile, we here will all devote our days to finding a cure for you. Count on that. Broc, go with them and help them pack their belongings, will you?"

Ruth didn't believe a single word of his promise. As a geneticist herself, she knew they would be spending their days trying to understand just how the biological weapon worked, not on any cure for them. Her life was ruined, hers and Alex's. She began crying to herself. Alex looked very frustrated and again tried to say something, but no one paid any attention to him. They couldn't understand him at all. Broc merely nudged them towards their nearby quarters.

Governor Katrina made her slow, careful way down to the medical lab on the first floor. She found Doctor Whitney once more hard at work; she'd refused to give up on finding them a cure. She looked from her electron microscope. "Hi, what brings you down here, boss?" Whitney teased her mate. Already Katrina had alerted her to what the Sector ID Minister had ordered her.

"Nurses, you ought to hear this too. It seems there has been another accident on Ashford-4. Two more were infected, a husband and wife team of genetic interns."

One nurse gasped. "Oh no! How bad is it this time?"

"Worse than we four, I'm afraid. According to Slag, who got this from their top researcher there, the two are just like we four, except they've also lost their arms as well."

"My god! They'll be completely helpless!" Doctor Whitney exclaimed, forgetting her work entirely.

256

"Precisely. They don't have the facilities nor personnel there to handle the pair, so they're sending them here. Slag wants them to be under your care, doctor. If there's any change in their bodies, we're to let the geneticists on Ashford-4 know about it at once. It's been nearly two weeks since they were exposed to this second batch, so in all likelihood, it's permanent."

"Like us, but without arms? This is downright nuts. Why?" asked Whitney.

Governor Katrina suggested, "Well, I know this much. Apparently, this was a followup experiment that was supposed to take place, once the one that accidentally infected us was done. Somehow, this pair triggered it. There was a third experiment lined up after this one, in which the victims would have been blinded on top of everything else. As to why? I believe I have a theory now. The research facility was setup during the war. I bet they developed this so the army could use a drone to wipe out an entire Federation planet without firing a shot or making any attacks. Honestly, the population would become totally helpless, allowing the Imperium to simply land and take over everything. But I picked up another unspoken thought that Slag had. They might be able to use this on their hardened criminals. Instead of wasting billions of credits running a high security penal planet, they could infect the criminals, turning them into completely helpless and totally dependent men and women. This whole thing is becoming a nightmare."

"Criminals? Well, I can understand that. But where would it stop?" Whitney asked. "If a new planet didn't want any part of the Imperium, they could just infect them and take the planet anyway. Good god, Katrina, this is becoming a nightmare of ungodly proportions. Will anyone listen to us?"

"Hardly," Katrina laughed. "It's being all kept at Security Level 10. Anyway, they should be here in an hour. We'll put them up in a dorm room on this first floor, as close to the med lab as I can find. I'll make the arrangements, and let you know when they arrive. Oh, what's apparently worse, the pair cannot even talk intelligibly, though I'm not sure what that really means."

"We'll be ready for them," Whitney replied.

When the shuttle from Ashford arrived, Katrina and Whitney, along with two Security Guards, were there to meet them. As the crew opened the doors, the two got their first look at their new patients. In most ways, the husband and wife looked remarkably like themselves, and Carla and Elfe too, for that matter. However, two things were quite striking. Their tasteful, if not elegant, satin gowns had no sleeves or even the slightest hint of them. Second, their hair was extremely blonde, nearly platinum. Both women could sense the fright that the pair was emanating.

"Fellows, will you lift our two new arrivals down to the tarmac please? Set them down gently. It's awful keeping your balance in these toe shoes," Katrina ordered. Quickly, the frightened couple were lifted out of the shuttle and positioned on their feet in front of the two. "Welcome to Ashford-5. I'm Governor Katrina, and this is our Doctor Whitney. She's also my mate, in case you're wondering about us. We have a suite prepared for you. I'm not sure why you can't speak though."

"We can, but no one can understand us," Alex said in his native language. He had no other way than to embarrass himself further in order to answer her question.

"I didn't get that. How about speaking Imperium Standard, but slowly and carefully. We both have the same lip plates that alter our pronunciations so drastically," Katrina suggested.

"No one can understand us. I am Alex Hammil. My wife, Ruth. Can you get this at all? I'm barely able to make out what you are saying," he replied.

"Yes, keep it slow. We can understand you, Alex. We're in pretty much the same boat. So are Carla and Elfe, my computer technician and archaeologist, along with two locals. These super long nails make anything a chore, but I bet you both would give anything to have our problem," Katrina added hastily. "Can you walk or would you prefer a supporting arm?"

"Arm," Ruth finally ventured to say a word. "We are so helpless." Both Katrina and Whitney sensed the volume of their suppressed grief and loss. Katrina put an arm around Alex, while Whitney did the same with Ruth.

"At least, we go at the same pace. We can't see our feet either," Katrina attempted to find common ground with Alex. Just then a gust of wind hit the four squarely; their hair flew out behind them. Both Ruth and Alex would have fallen over had not the stumbling Katrina and Whitney kept them sort of balanced. "Kind of windy. Let's get inside."

All four focused on each step. At long last, they entered Whitney's med lab, where the nurses quickly got the four seated. "That's better. Thanks. My nurses here will be assisting you. These claws of mine make that almost impossible for me," Doctor Whitney explained.

"Now then, you are geneticists?"

"Interns. We are or were on our final internship. Now we are useless," Ruth answered sadly. "Everything has been taken away from us."

"Not everything, Ruth. You still have your minds. I've been spending all of my time working on a cure. Not very successful yet," she replied.

"Can't you just cut off your nails and trim our hair for us?" Ruth asked.

"Nope. We've tried that. Even a tiny clip on nails or hair causes massive pain and besides, it grows back right away," Whitney answered honestly. "We're stuck like this for the time being. I'd appreciate it if you could lend me a hand — er symbolically that is. I've done some genetic work, but I'm not a geneticist. Maybe together, we can solve this mess that we're in."

"I don't think we can do anything," Alex said with a sigh.

"Leave the doing to me. Use your minds. My nurses and I will be your hands," Whitney suggested. "Meantime, we should show you your new quarters and give you a tour so you can get oriented a bit."

As Whitney and Katrina led the two the relatively short distance to their new suite, Katrina said sympathetically, "This must be terribly frightening to you both. Whitney and I can just barely walk, but I can't imagine how much worse this all is for you two."

"I'm terrified out of my mind!" Ruth said, trying to

remember to speak slowly. "If we fall, we cannot even get up by ourselves. We are trapped by such simple things as a closed door. We have to depend on someone else for everything. We can barely breathe, but we have to have them this tight or else our backs ache from the sheer weight of our breasts. Do you two have the same problems?"

"Yes, the same. Without the support from our corsets, our backs simply cannot hold up the sheer weight of these massive ones," Katrina admitted, backing up Ruth's opinion. She sensed both Alex and Ruth's feelings that they were not wholly alone now, at least in part.

"Here's your new quarters. We'll help you unpack your things," Katrina volunteered.

"Why bother? We can't use any of our things," Ruth sighed morosely.

"We ought to get your hairbrush out, don't you think? Toothbrush?" Whitney suggested.

"I suppose someone can use them for us," Ruth admitted. "The only clothes that we can remotely wear are what we have on. Already we've soiled our panties and our nylons are full of runs."

"Don't worry; we'll get you some new outfits soon," Katrina replied. "We have a local connection. Lilly is fabulous. I'll make us an appointment for first thing in the morning. Let's show you where the dining hall is located. Unfortunately, it's up on the second floor. Someone will assist you getting there and back. The nurses will help you dine. With these darn nails, we only can just barely manage ourselves," Katrina gently tried to build up a bit more commonality between the two and herself.

By the time that they had visited the dining hall, both of the pair's feet and knees were throbbing, and Katrina took them back to the med lab. Whitney explained, "I know you've been injected and inspected a zillion times by the geneticists, but as your doctor, I also need to examine the both of you, especially to obtain a genetic sample of where your bodies are now. I do hope you have your original DNA on file in the Imperium, so we can see what all has been modified."

"Doctor Aarok Laron has it. I don't know if ours are on

file," Alex lamented. "Ouch!" He'd forgotten to toss his long hair aside before sitting down on it. Whitney helped him up and pulled it to the front for him. He looked embarrassed, and, wisely, she didn't comment on it, but went about getting their vitals, while a nurse logged it for her. By the time Whitney was satisfied that she'd gathered all of the data possible on the two, it was time for supper.

"Would you both care to dine with Katrina, Carla, Elfe, and I?" she asked. Carla and Elfe are mates too."

"Sure. We won't stick out quite so badly," Alex admitted. "We look like total freaks, helpless freaks at that. You can't imagine how utterly embarrassed we both are."

"We know. It must be ten times worse for you, Alex, than it is for Ruth. Still, ignore the gawks. We do. Of course, we four get gawks for other reasons," she teased them slightly.

Ruth picked it up. "Say, I bet some of these modifications to your bodies have come in handy for you. I mean when you are in bed." She flushed, wondering if she was entering a very private arena.

Whitney laughed. "Yes, that part we four appreciate in some ways. Ah, here come two nurses. They'll make sure you don't take a tumble and will feed you. Mind you, you both will probably get done way ahead of us four. These long claws make eating more than a challenge." That brought a slight smile to Ruth's face. Whitney didn't miss it, though it was mostly invisible of course.

Later, the nurses got the two undressed and ready for bed, including brushing out their hair, which Broc failed to do properly. No fault of his, however; he wasn't married, and had no idea of how or what ought to be done for the pair. After tucking them both into bed, the nurses left. However, they pointed out the dimly illuminated red button they could press with any part of their anatomy to summon aid during the night, should they need it. After the two left, again Ruth and Alex wiggled about to get on their sides. This was the only time of the day they could enjoy each other, but in entirely new ways for the most part.

Later, the two snuggled as best they could. Ruth whispered, "I love you so, Alex. I don't think I could survive this without you."

"Same with me, sweetie pie. Without you, I'm lost utterly." He gave her another kiss.

After breakfast, Katrina and Whitney helped the two out to a waiting electric car, but had two Security Guards lift the two inside. A half hour later, they pulled into the Imperial Castle, explaining they needed to visit Queen Amy, who in part oversaw the entire world. Bernardo helped each woman out of the car, while Lena watched. After leading them into Amy's private study, she introduced the Gang of Ten to Ruth and Alex.

Both were very much impressed that Queen Amy's body was exactly like theirs, totally helpless. Neither knew about the *mentales* gifts as yet.

"As Ashford-5's senator, I would like to hear you whole story of what happened on Ashford-4," Zarita stated. "Amy also wants to know as well. Please, while it may be embarrassing for you, we really do want to know."

Ruth did most of the talking, however. Alex was simply too embarrassed to say much. When they finished, Zarita asked, "Wait a second. You both said you fully inspected Chamber 1 and found nothing. Yet this Doctor Aarok claims he and his assistant Broc found the bio agent cylinder all hooked up. Something's fishy here."

"I know I didn't see it," Ruth claimed.

"But we must have somehow missed it, Ruth," Alex protested. "We must have."

Zarita, her hatred of men still a hot topic, countered, "Well, perhaps those two hooked it up while you both slept. I wonder. What did they have to gain by seeing the both of you so badly altered?"

Ruth sighed, "Well, this is a huge, huge development in genetics. You see, the Imperium sends its hardened criminals to a penal world. Doctor Aarok has said, if this experiment actually works, then it could be used on all the criminals, saving the Imperium billions of credits each year. Plus, I think the original scientists there were planning to use it on Federation worlds. You know, send in the bio attack via a drone. Make all of the people of the world completely helpless like we are. Then, they could take over that world without even attacking it."

Zarita exclaimed, "My god! Yes, I see what you mean. So this doctor fellow does have a very good reason for perhaps doing this to you to verify that it does work. Bastard!"

Queen Amy said, "Senator Zarita, when the Senate reconvenes, please bring all this up and get it made wholly illegal, please!"

"You can count on that!" Zarita exclaimed.

Drina changed the topic. "When you get some time, I can show you how to do some things for yourself using your feet and toes. Lena is a master at it too. I taught her how when she first came here. I don't know what we can do to work around your lip plates though. I do use my teeth a lot too."

"I think we are going to be just plain helpless in all things," Ruth sighed, fighting from breaking down in front of all these strangers.

"We should get them over to Elegant Fashions Inc. They need new clothes," Katrina suggested.

"We'll come with you," Bernardo volunteered. He and Nita helped the four, providing an escort for the short walk. While they were inside, Bernardo promised to bring the electric car over, saving them the short walk back.

Meanwhile inside Amy's private room, Zarita and Lena conferred with Amy and Jan. "Look, if this mad doctor actually infected those two on purpose, he's got to be stopped," Zarita complained bitterly.

"Yes, but according to Ruth, the computers there contain crucial data that is needed, if ever anyone can hope to undo these genetic changes. To say nothing of the equipment and supplies to actually make this stuff," Jan countered.

Lena changed yet the topic. "You are both missing key points."

"And those are?" Jan returned somewhat defiantly.

"That these existing bio agents can be used on the hardened criminals on Xeros-1. That these agents could be used against any world or subset of people, who go against the wishes of the Imperium," Lena pointed out.

Amy added, "On the other hand, Whitney and Ruth did

suggest that this technological advance could be used for very humane purposes, such as regeneration of lost limbs, for example."

"So what do we do? It isn't bad enough that the giant crystals mess here on Tierra is getting way out of hand, and we don't have a clue of how to handle it," Jan retorted, clearly quite frustrated, "but now we have to get involved in what is rightfully Imperium business."

Zarita countered angrily, "But we're part of the Imperium. If that doctor did that to Ruth on purpose, then he doesn't deserve to live!" Amy noted she purposely didn't mention Alex.

Lena added, "Our senator is right. We're part of the Imperium now. But there is something else you should know. The Sector ID Minister. I know them. I was one of them. You can bet the entire world that Slag Vartino has really taken notice of these findings on Ashford-4. He has probably already worked out a test experiment on some of those criminals at the very least. With something this revolutionary, if he is seen as the one who found it and put it to use, and if it really does completely handle those criminals by turning them into helpless vegetables, he'll not only become extremely famous, but also his career will skyrocket. My money is on Slag having already made arrangements for this test on some criminals."

She went on, "If these geneticists are allowed to work unchecked, you can bet within a few years, they'll have it all perfected. After that, they can come here to Tierra and demand you send a thousand telepaths to work for the Imperium. When you refuse, they unleash that same bio agent again, only probably in a far higher dosage, likely way beyond Lysandra's ability to neutralize. Then, they come down and take away everyone with yellow eyes and let the others die off within a short time. After that, they can mine Ashford-5 for all the fuel they desire and at no cost or hassles."

"Good god! You really see this as a possible future, Lena?" Amy asked, rather feeling she was absolutely correct. From all her time out there in the Imperium, morals and ethics were primarily foreign to the Imperium as a collective whole.

"You know as well as I; so do you Jan. You too, Zarita," Lena said convincingly.

"Okay then we have to act," Amy decided.

"Let me go first," Zarita interrupted her. "I can find out for sure whether or not that doctor harmed Ruth on purpose, intentionally. If he did, he dies. Then, you all can take over and do what you want to do."

"While she's doing that, we need to find a way to get all that computer data downloaded to one of our computers," Jan added.

"Or steal those computers and equipment," Lena suggested.

"But we'd have to go there right under the nose of the battle cruisers," Jan protested. "I think with Carla's help, we can arrange for a full data transfer."

"But the equipment, the technology to make these bio agents would still be there, and Whitney is going to need it, if she has any chance to really help the victims," Lena countered. "Doesn't your transport have a cloaking shield on it?"

Jan grinned, but it wasn't visible. "Of course. Why didn't I think of that? We can get the computers and everything."

Chapter 17 Genetic Counter-terrorism

Ruth and Alex received royal treatment at Elegant Fashions Inc. At once, Lilly proved to them she knew precisely what they needed, apparel-wise that is. A few hours later, Katrina, Whitney, Ruth, and Alex headed back to the spaceport, their electric car packed with eight new outfits for the two, along with many extras. "I can't believe how kind Lilly was. All these clothes. They must cost a fortune," Ruth suggested, still awed by the generosity bestowed on them by these strangers.

Whitney replied, "While Ashford-5 might look to the outside world as a primitive one, once you come here, you find they have more humanity than most of the so-called civilized worlds of the Imperium. Don't worry, Ruth, Alex; right now, you can't see any way you can help others or yourself to repay all the kindness being given to you, but I assure you, in time you definitely will. For the immediate future, focus on learning to cope by any means possible. Give it time; you both have undergone a massive trauma and a total upheaval of your very lives. Time is the answer." She wanted to add and Basic Therapy, but thought better of it without asking others about that first. No need to get their hopes up only to be dashed.

As the four drove back to the castle, Zarita finally opened her eyes. For some time now, she'd been totally focused on her spying objective. Lena, Jan, and Amy had noticed the many condensed giant crystals the perky woman wore had all shone rather brightly, indicative of Zarita drawing very heavily on their amplification powers.

"Well, it is just as I thought! That bastard Doctor Aarok Laron did it to them on purpose! He wanted to test the bio agent, and he had his sneaky right hand man, that Broc fellow, hook up the bio cylinder, after Ruth and Alex had fallen asleep there that first night in Chamber 1!"

"Oh dear god!" Lena gushed.

"There's more. Lena, you are right! This Snag fellow and the doctor have already taken both remaining bio agent samples off-world. He sent two of his fellow geneticists with

Snag, along with the bio agents and their supplies, to your penal planet. They are going to conduct what Aarok is calling a 'field test,' though Slag prefers to call it a 'proof of concept.' Snag has left one battle cruiser in orbit around Ashford-4 to guard the place. There are only two geneticists left there. Aarok and Broc are now dead. I've melted their brains, but only after I let them know why I was killing them. The two others are lackeys and not in on the plot, so I've left them more or less feebleminded. I kind of temporarily dampened some of their analytical powers. They're mostly acting like little kids at the moment, but in a few weeks, it'll wear off. Now it's your turn," she ended quite satisfied with herself. She didn't say what she then thought: Never mess with Zarita!

"Okay, we can take my transport, scheduling a flight to Winno-3, but once in hyperspace, alter the coordinates to this research station. Activate cloaking. Land. Confiscate everything of value. Blow the rest to kingdom come," Jan suggested.

"Jan, you are in no physical shape to do all that," Lena countered.

Jan's face slumped. "I know that, but I can fly the ship. We'll need strong arms to move the stuff, I think."

"We'll need someone along who knows what should be taken. I know nothing about such equipment," Lena pointed out. "We can take Ben, Henry, and Bernardo, but we'll need Whitney and/or possibly Ruth and Alex; they are the geneticists. We don't have any way to blow up the facility, but Katrina's people have the explosives we would need to do the job. We're simply going to have to being them in on this raid. I don't see any other alternatives."

Amy made her decision. "Lena's right. You gather up the fellows. I'll make the arrangements with Katrina, as queen to governor. I'll have Nita help me go visit Katrina, while you get your preparations made. We simply have to step in and prevent further exploitation of this new technology for the benefit of the whole galaxy. There's nothing we can do for the criminals, who are becoming human guinea pigs, but we can stop the spread of these bio agents. Ah, Nita is on her way here now. Let's get cracking."

A half hour later, Nita assisted Amy into the spaceport and up to Governor Katrina's office on the top floor. "Yes, Governor Katrina, this has to be a formal meeting between you and me, the respective rulers, so to speak. I'll need Carla, Whitney, Ruth, and Alex here too. This concerns all them, in one way or another. There have been some developments."

Katrina laughed. "My god, Amy, we've only been gone shopping for a couple of hours, and all hell breaks loose. Okay, I'll summon them now."

A half hour later, Carla and Whitney, their arms securely around Alex and Ruth, entered her office. Both women gently pulled the pair's long hair to their front and supported them as they awkwardly sat down, then did the same with their own floor-length tresses. "Okay, this is supposed to be a formal meeting between the ruler of Ashford-5 and us," Katrina said politely. "Queen Amy, you requested this meeting. The floor is yours."

"Pardon me if I don't stand. Too much trouble." She noticed that put both Ruth and Alex more at ease. "Okay, here we go. Doctor Aarok unleashed the bio agent on both of you on purpose; he needed to test the bio agent to prove that it works." Gasps echoed around the table. Amy outlined just what the two men and done and why. She continued with what was already in progress, a field test on some criminals. "You can all see where this is going. Once they are fully able to recreate this bio agent, perhaps modifying it ever further, no one is going to be safe. While right now they want to use it on all of their criminals, I can see that in time they'll use it or threaten to use it on anyone or any world that defies or disagrees with Imperium wishes in any way."

"Dear god, we can't let them pervert this huge genetic breakthrough," Ruth exclaimed, highly animated in spite of her physical limitations.

"We don't intend to," Amy went on. She explained that Doctor Aarok and Broc were now dead, and the two remaining geneticists were temporarily incapacitated. "If Whitney, Ruth, and Alex are ever to find a cure for what was done to them and to us, they need full access to all that data, the computer notes, and even their specialized equipment."

Whitney interrupted. "She's got a point, Katrina. I'm only barely able to conduct genetic studies in my lab. Med labs just don't have the proper equipment for something like this."

"Right," Amy continued. "So we are going to go there and steal all of the computer stuff and the equipment that they need. Then, we will blow up the facility, making it unusable for such wicked purposes ever again."

"But how can you do that?" asked Whitney.

"Jan has her own deep space transport, one of the newest models with a cloaking device. She will schedule a flight to Winno-3. Once in hyperspace, she'll alter the coordinates, active cloaking, and land at the research station. Some of our men will cart off the computer systems, but we need your help. We have no idea what equipment you doctors will need brought back here so you can continue your work. We need Whitney, Ruth, and Alex to come along and tell the men what to bring back. However, we have no idea how the facility can be totally destroyed to prevent its further use."

"Good god!" Katrina sat back stunned by the sheer audacity of what Queen Amy was proposing. She took as deep a breath as she could. "Doctor Whitney. Can I trust you to see that good uses come from all this and not more bio weapons?" She already knew the answer, but wanted her to speak formally for the official record, since she had no control over Ruth and Alex.

"I give you my solemn word as a medical doctor that anything we develop will be for humane uses. As Ruth has suggested to me backing up my own thoughts, this technology may well provide the means for regeneration of lost limbs. Beyond that, the medical uses could be enormous," Doctor Whitney said formally, also knowing why Katrina had asked her this.

Ruth put in, "We want to help. I know we are completely helpless, but we are geneticists or were, and we know the equipment. We can at least tell them what to bring back. Please, we want to help. Alex, I told you we didn't miss finding that bio agent cylinder! He did this to us! I'm glad he's dead."

Katrina smiled invisibly. "Okay then, Queen Amy, we're

all onboard. If I might make one suggestion. Once you have everything you need and are out of there, I know a way we can use to get the battle cruiser to blow up the research facility for us. Protocol 89, doctor."

Whitney gushed, "Oh now that *is* devious, Katrina! I just need the proper codes."

"I'll see you have them, doctor," the governor replied. To the others, she added, "We'll signal a biological agent attack. When the battle cruiser commander receives that signal, he has absolutely no choice but to follow Protocol 89, the complete disintegration of the research facility. Of course, gang, there's no guarantee that the Imperium might come back here in a year and build a new one. When do we do this?"

"Later today. Jan and my people are making flight preparations. The transport will land here to pick up Doctor Whitney, Ruth, and Alex and then take off for Winno-3," Amy declared.

"But how can Jan fly the ship? She's almost like us," Ruth asked.

"We'll explain all that while in fight," Amy replied. "Carla, you'll be in charge of helping to dismantle and reassemble their computer system. Jan could probably do it, but I'd prefer to use a hot shot computer technician, if you don't mind being involved."

"Count me in! I was wondering why you needed me. Cool!" she replied.

"Good. I'll stay here and watch for the signal declaring the use of Protocol 89," Katrina added. "I'll make sure that commander does execute it, if he hesitates. Best get everyone ready and down to the tarmac. We take forever to walk that far."

"No kidding," Amy replied, noticing the relief that emanated from Ruth and Alex, who saw everyone else was just as slow as they were, despite having arms.

By the time the group arrived at Bay 16, Jan had landed her sleek new ship. Bernardo, Henry, and Ben climbed out to help the others board. Lena had insisted on coming along, declaring she could lend her telekinesis powers to help with the loading. The three helped Carla and Whitney on first. Once they were seated beside Lena, they lifted Ruth and Alex, carrying them up the ramp, and buckling them into their seats. Bernardo waved to Katrina and Elfe, who had come to see what was going on.

After he shut the cargo doors, Jan's voice came over the intercom. "Okay, buckle up. We're off. This is going to be a blast! Yahoo."

"Don't mind her, Ruth; she's just a bit excited to be able to fly her ship again," Bernardo joked. Once they were in flight, Bernardo began a relatively lengthy explanation of the *mentales* gifts and what that meant. Ruth and Alex were both rather startled to learn everyone they'd met so far had these incredible powers.

"Even you two, Carla, Doctor Whitney? And Governor Katrina?" Ruth asked in amazement.

"You bet. Bernardo, tell them about how the nobles on Tierra dress," Carla added. He then explained how so many of the rulers and nobles all wore pipe corsets, lip plates, and toe shoes. He also told them that it was taboo for the Easterlings to ever cut their hair and that the Westerlings women seldom cut theirs, while Midlands women's hair styles varied from short to long as they so desired. He realized Amy had wanted these two to realize that many wore the lip plates, pipe corsets, and toe shoes, plus that very long hair was commonplace. Hence, the two began to feel more comfortable about their strange appearance.

Jan's voice came over the intercom once more, "Action stations boys. We're arriving in two minutes. Activating dome opening protocol now. Remember, there are still two stunned geneticists around the place. Stay alert."

Four minutes later, the thin dome was again closed overhead, and air had refilled the landing bay. Cautiously, Bernardo opened the cargo bay doors and stepped out. His crystal activated. "They are that way, asleep I think."

"Those are the experiment chambers, which double as living quarters," Ruth explained. "The control room is just ahead, but I don't think I can get down by myself." The three men lifted the two down, and then helped Whitney and Carla as well. Jan stayed behind, monitoring everything she could dial into her onboard comm network. With Carla holding onto Ruth and Whitney doing the same with Alex, they followed the three men into the main room, which housed the computer and some of the equipment.

Ben and Carla began dealing with the computer systems, while Ruth and Alex told the others which equipment was needed. Alex added, "Of course, there is more in the vault, where the active bio agents are stored and actually manufactured. That's the dangerous place. One drop from some of the cylinders is instant death — well, maybe thirty minutes tops."

The raid was on. As Carla got a piece of the computer system unhooked, Ben carried it onto the shuttle. Meanwhile, Henry and Bernardo lugged the heavier equipment there as well. Soon, all were sweating. "This is too much like real work," Bernardo commented.

"Let a woman handle this, big man," Lena teased him. She proceeded to levitate the next heavy one, allowing Bernardo simply to push it to the shuttle.

"That's more like it, love," he grinned.

For hours, the group worked together identifying what ought to be retrieved or confiscated. Slowly, some self-respect returned to Ruth and Alex. They alone were able to identify much of the more esoteric pieces of equipment, as well as the many chemical and biological compounds that were located in the secure storage facility. Not even Doctor Whitney was sufficiently familiar with many of these; genetic research was not her specialty. It was for the pair. While they were unable actually to move anything, they soon discovered that their knowledge of what should be taken was invaluable and even indispensable.

Finally, the last of the many solutions were safely stored. The transport was packed; very little room remained for the passengers. Now came the tricky part, complicated only because they were unwilling to have the two currently sleeping and somewhat dim-witted geneticists killed. Jan got them airborne. While hovering above the dome and with her ship's cloaking device still activated, she then took control of the two men, who Zarita had mentally zapped. She forced their bodies to walk out to their small shuttle and get into it. She then used their bodies to get the ship launched out of the dome, but left the dome opened. All of her compressed germanium crystals had been glowing quite brightly as she did this, though only Bernardo in the navigator's seat saw their distinctive blue light.

"There, that's done. Okay, Bernardo, enter this sequence of numbers," Jan ordered. He did so, but had no idea what he was doing. "Press send now." As he did so, one of her long nails pressed the Execute button, and her transport slipped into hyper-drive, bound for home. They arrived a couple of minutes later, touching down near a cargo entrance of the spaceport, as previously arranged by Katrina. Here, their unloading activities would appear to be nothing more than normal base supplies being unloaded.

Back at the abandoned research facility, sirens and red lights flashed. All of the sensors there pointed to a massive breach in the chemical and biological agent containment building. Protocol 89 flashed on what remained of the warning console, indicating a massive cloud of released toxins was about to leave the surface of Ashford-4 with sufficient propulsion to allow it to go into space and beyond.

Onboard the battle cruiser parked in a high orbit, the disaster warnings from the research base were detected, causing a mad scramble to battle stations throughout the ship. The commander barked, "Situation! What's the severity?" Up on the monitors, a computer technician displayed the data coming in from the emergency systems from the research base's containment room. "My god! What's happened down there? Predictions. Predictions now!"

"Sir, their computer system shows a massive cloud of highly toxic particles leaving the surface and heading into space! Protocol 89? We have only a couple of minutes, sir," an aide exclaimed, startled by the indicated severity of the disaster. A cloud of toxins this huge would create major problems for space traffic in this area for generations until it diffused sufficiently. After all, Ashford-5 was *the* refueling center for this sector of the Imperium. The commander had no choice but to follow Protocol 89.

"Lock on all batteries! Fire at will! Someone put a tractor beam on that shuttle. Emergency chemical and biological agent protocols are in effect on that shuttle. Whoever is on it could well be contaminated," he barked.

An hour later and after extensive testing, the two surviving geneticists were pronounced free of any contamination, excepting trace amounts. The two were brought before the commander for debriefing. "What the hell happened down there?" he barked. The research station had been wholly disintegrated this time. The huge threat had been neutralized before the cloud of toxins had escaped the planet.

Both men looked terribly confused. "Where's Doctor Aarok?" the commander asked, not having gotten an answer to his first question.

"Oh, he and Broc. They are dead," one said.

"Goo was coming out of their noses, ears, and eyes. It was rather pretty goo," the other said.

"What?"

"Goo," he repeated. "Pretty goo."

"What happened down there?" the commander barked, growing annoyed with the two.

"We went to bed," the first answered.

His doctor began examining the pair. He looked up at the commander and shook his head. "Sir, they've undergone some severe brain trauma. Best sedate them and let them get some sleep."

"Sleep? Yes, that's good," one of the two mumbled.

"Where did my bed go?" the other asked, looking around the War Room, as though his cot was here, only somehow misplaced.

Several days passed before the commander got any reasonable explanations from the two men. Even though their mental facilities returned to normal, neither could cast any light on what had gone so terribly wrong. Somehow, Doctor Aarok and his assistant had suffered some severe chemical agent contamination. That was the official conclusion anyway.

Katrina met the group just inside the large entrance bay. "I've had an unused cargo hold here on the ground floor cleaned up for your new lab. I sure hope you've not brought back anything that could be a bio or chemical hazard. We don't have any large scale containment facilities here."

"Don't worry. We haven't," Doctor Whitney relieved her worries. "We've got the computers with their research notes, the equipment that we need, and the supplies. We left all of the potentially dangerous agents behind. We don't need any repeat disasters here, not on my watch," she declared.

Whitney also added, "Don't expect any miracle cures in the immediate future though. We have mountains and mountains of data to analyze first, before we even think about reversing anything. Slow and careful work will yield the best results. I do hope we can develop an easy method of limb regeneration, much like the low level cellular rejuvenation we've got now. Ruth and Alex will be critical in this work. I need them assigned to me permanently."

Xeros-1. Home of the Maximum Security Prison of the Imperium. Located on this broiling planet, the sprawling compounds of a dozen isolated prisons fanned out. Even if a prisoner could somehow escape his titanium re-enforced steel cells, get through all the guard check points, and beyond the small domed exercise area, and past the outer perimeter of the climate controlled complex, there was no place to go. Beyond these compounds, the daytime temperatures soared to well over two hundred fifty degrees. Nighttime temperatures dropped to well below a hundred-fifty below zero. No one thought about escaping these compounds, for there was no place to go on the planet. The only access was the spaceport, so well-guarded that an insect could not escape.

Here, Sector ID Minister Slag, accompanied by his two geneticists, ordered the experimental treatment of two dozen of the worst offenders. Serial psychopaths, each had more than ten murders to his or her credit. Each was sentenced to natural life here on Xeros-1. True, much of the strife and internal conflicts between gangs of prisoners had long ago been eliminated by the simple expedient of voice removal. Upon arrival here, each prisoner was put into a medical machine, and their voice boxes altered. Three centuries ago, with speech removed, the wardens noticed a tremendous drop in trouble among the prisoners. True, they still committed all manner of atrocities against one another, but with silence the norm, the wardens considered things to be quite peaceful.

Of course, running these facilities cost the Imperium a fortune each year. The pacifists had long ago gotten the Senate to pass a law forbidding outright execution of these prisoners. There was always some remote possibility of their innocence and an equally remote chance of their rehabilitation, though that had already been attempted through behavior modifications by the psych men. Those attempts had failed. That is why these men and women were here on Xeros-1.

"This new treatment will totally handle the prisoner problem, far better than the failed behavior modifications," Slag explained to the governor of the planet. "We want to test this on two dozen of your worst criminals. If this is successful, we'll move them to the psych ward, where they can get the intensive physical care they need, but at a vastly cheaper cost I might add."

He agreed and twenty-four were "treated." Eight retained their sight and looked exactly like Ruth and Alex, though they still could not talk. Sixteen others could no longer see as well, though their physical changes were explained to them, once they were properly dressed in apparel similar to what Ruth and Alex now had to wear.

"My god! They are totally helpless. They could not harm a fly now," the governor exclaimed, as he examined the two dozen totally terrified men and women sitting helplessly on a long row of benches. "This is utterly revolutionary! How soon can this be done to all of the prisoners? Heck, I can retire soon. We can close his extremely costly facility down!"

"Soon, I hope. Now that proof of concept has been done, we'll take these to the psych ward, where they can be looked after. Hell, they can't do a darn thing for themselves now. Once we get back to Doctor Aarok, I'll order enough made to handle the two thousand or so you've got locked up here," Slag replied, more than pleased with the results.

A few days later and while on his way back to Ashford-4, Slag received word of the disaster that had struck the research facilities there. "My god! Doctor Aarok dead?

Protocol 89? What went wrong?" Sector ID Minster Slag barked louder than he needed to into the microphone. The explanation he received was far from satisfactory, but the reports of goo coming from the dead man's head orifices did suggest some horrific chemical weapon had infected the facility.

Talking with the two geneticists, he said, "Okay, look, that facility has had nothing but problems since the meteor shower. Obviously, it wasn't safe, despite plugging the holes the gravel made. We ought to have moved everything out of there. Hindsight is great. The question now, geneticists, is do you have enough samples left and data to reproduce these bio agents, given another laboratory?"

Both men scratched their heads. "Possibly. It will take time and equipment and more experiments, but we can analyze what remains and work out how to duplicate it," one said.

The other added, "However, at this point in time, all such research is illegal."

"You let me worry about the legality of it. Make a list of what equipment and supplies you need. I'll get them for you. Pick your team members carefully," Slag ordered. Both men jumped at this golden opportunity — a real career maker!

Chapter 18 Escalation Begins

By mid-August, Ruth, Alex, and Doctor Whitney finally had their new lab setup. Thanks to the tireless efforts of Carla, the computer equipment was operational. Now, the three began their extensive study of just what had gone on at that research facility. "First, we must understand fully what they did, and how and why. Only then can we begin to potentially develop modifications to 'cure' what's been done," Doctor Whitney carefully explained to Governor Katrina.

"Take your time. Get it right. No accidents, please," Katrina replied, giving them the green light to proceed.

"One more thing," Whitney dropped her formal demeanor. "We're not all suffering from a bout of the flu as we all thought. Dear, we're pregnant! Yes," she added.

"Oh!" Katrina flushed. "Pregnant? Really?"

"Yes, you, I, Carla, Elfe, Amy, Jan, Ruth, and Alex. We're all pregnant, even senators Zarita and Celenia and their companion, Lelane. We're all a few weeks apart. Due dates will be next April, probably within a few weeks of each other. You and I are further along than the others. Ruth and Alex will be the last ones to give birth, assuming all goes well."

"But our babies? Will they be like us?" Katrina asked, though she already suspected the answer.

"Obviously, their bodies are formed from our genes, dear," Whitney replied. "The real problem will be telling if a newborn is a boy or a girl. The usual means won't work, obviously. I'll need to actually see them urinate to be able to tell their basic sex."

Katrina laughed a little nervously, "Well, we best pick out both a boy's name and a girl's name in that case."

Whitney laughed, "Right dear. We're going to be mothers sooner than we thought." The two hugged each other. Then, the doctor headed off to let the others know the good news.

The fall High Council of the Lords was held early the

fall of 1294. So many minor conflicts had broken out during the summer, that the kings wanted to meet sooner than normal. This appealed to Senator Zarita, because she wanted to attend to get a chance to chat with the rulers, before she headed back to the Senate on Proxima Prime. Two key features marked this council somewhat unique: fashion and conflicts.

Fashion. Senators Zarita and Celenia no longer felt out of place, wearing their billowing twelve foot hoop skirts. Already a third of the women in attendance wore somewhat similar gowns! Carla, Elfe, Whitney, Katrina, and Jan also no longer felt out of place. Around forty percent of the women now sported claws of a similar length to theirs, which remained twelve inches long. They had discovered they could file off the tips of their nails, as they continued to grow naturally. Of course, when they reached the limits of twelve inches, any further filing caused them instant pain forcing no further reductions in lengths. On top of that, another two dozen women had had their breasts enlarged, matching the monsters the group now permanently had.

During a lunch break, Elfe explained to her group and Amy's, "Look. This phenomenon is a simple one, really. On other worlds in which the population is moving upwards towards a more modern age," she put it politely, "two key features predominate everywhere. First, there is an ingrained tendency for men to fight, as I've explained before. Second, as they become wealthier by virtue of finally having sufficient food reserves, they can support artisans and craftsmen, who no longer produce their own food. As this expands, the wealthy begin to desire some way to display their superiority, their wealth, their 'nobility' and importance, such as the town leaders. With most other cultures, exotic and luxury trade goods are used. Extremely artistic pottery, finely made gold work and jewelry, exquisitely carved ivory — all manner of such things are then collected and often worn by these nobles, so the ordinary person can immediately see the importance of the person. It is as natural as the falling rain."

"However, here on Tierra, this was not so easily accomplished. With the almost total lack of all heavier elements and no ivory and the use of simple copper and bronze day-ware, what could be used or considered luxury trade goods, signifying nobility or wealth or importance? True, there is the widespread use of jewelry, but that's about all that was available here, until the coming of Elegant Fashions Inc centuries ago. At that time, fine gowns, suits, and shoes were readily adopted here as the luxury trade goods of the nobility. That process has continued here on Tierra for almost three centuries now, maybe more. So you see, the noble men and women of Tierra are using fashion to set themselves apart from the farmer, for example. Hence, they tend to adopt and emulate us and our appearances. We are obviously nobles in their eyes," Elfe explained.

She finished up, "So as miserable as we are with these boobs that get in the way of everything we do and give us back aches, as difficult as everything is with these enormous nails and lip plates and toe shoes, they emulate us, setting themselves apart from the common people of Tierra. Perfectly understandable, really. You can count on them trying their best to look like we do. Subconsciously, if not consciously, they consider us as nobles, just as they consider themselves to be. Appearance and apparel are the luxury trade goods on Tierra, plain and simple, really."

Amy asked, "So if we can eventually find a way to get our normal boobs back and have short nails again, they would soon do so too?"

"Very likely so, Amy. They've seen Senator Zarita off and on for about what, six months? Now, they are emulating her as well as us, since the bio agent attack changed us," Elfe replied.

"Am I going to have to start wearing those enormous gowns too?" Amy asked. "God, I hope not."

"As their queen, to maintain their affinity, you may well have too, Amy, but not until the majority of the women are," Elfe suggested. Amy knew Elfe was right. If they all wore the giant hoop skirts, she would also have to wear them just to maintain compatibility and thus their affinity.

Most of the meeting was nothing more than a bickering match among the many rulers. According to Ken and Ben, the Underground was detecting no real wars in progress, just minor skirmishes. However, those were becoming commonplace now and quite deadly. Some of the towers, especially the newer towers, were "testing" their newly developed weapons during these clashes, along with their proposed new defenses, all to the destruction of the nearby people and lands. The only positive thing was that such destruction was highly localized and limited.

The meeting broke down into arguments between various rulers and their supporters. When they were not arguing, they were attempting to form mutual-defense treaties. Of course, these rapidly became quite complex and involved. For example, Rusden allied itself with Matruk and Bashir. Yet Matruk allied also with Bashir and with Leedsburough and Woodhill. Bashir allied itself with Woodhill and Oakham. Rusden was currently skirmishing with its neighbors Leedsburough, Woodhill, and Oakham. Thus, it was unclear who would help whom. So it went with many of the kingdoms.

Brom allied itself with Hilliard Heights and Chester, but Walsham allied with its neighbor Chester. Still these four northernmost kingdoms stayed out of the more general conflicts of the middle and southern Midlands, much to their credit.

Repeatedly, Queen Amy begged these rulers to come to her and allow her to investigate and get to the core of the disagreements. Few did so, however. She didn't have any real way to force them to sit down and work out their difficulties peacefully. The giant crystals in their towers gave them all the power they needed right now, just as Amy and Jan had long feared would happen.

"I'm glad I'm leaving tomorrow," Zarita teased Amy, after the council finally ended. "I sure don't envy you at all. Proxima Prime and the Senate will be tame after this!"

"Thanks a lot," Amy retorted, amusing Zarita. "I'll figure something out, somehow, someway. You just keep the Imperium from developing more of those chemical and biological weapons of mass destruction, please."

"You can count on that one! What I aim to do is find out how come not even the President knew of that secret facility.

Plus, how many more of them are out there? Who is funding them? I've got plenty to do. Celenia and Lelane are going to help me. They've a vested interest in this too," Zarita declared.

After seeing Zarita off, Amy returned to find a number of people had suddenly shown up in her throne room requesting an audience with the Queen! Jan helped her to her throne, got her long hair to her front, and assisted her to sit down gracefully. "Welcome one and all. I'm Queen Amy. Who are all of you and how can I help you?" she said politely.

These were likely guilds men and women, she thought. They dressed like townsfolk, practical, but not richly. She didn't recognize any of the two dozen, split about in half between men and women. Some were older, likely their forties; some were young, perhaps in their twenties. Her curiosity was definitely roused.

One burly man stepped forward. "Your Majesty, forgive us, if we do not know how to properly address you and your court. We are from the many guilds of Tierra. In fact, we are the lawfully elected Supreme Grand Guild Masters. I am Dimas of the Weapons Makers Guild."

"Welcome Supreme Grand Guild Masters, one and all," Amy replied. "Forget formalities. I really have no use for such, though the nobles continue to insist upon such things. Please, let me summon some of my helpers and get you all some chairs. Then, let's talk as equals." She tossed that last in there, sensing this was the proper protocol to follow. Obviously, these guild leaders felt that they were all equals.

Hastily, Lena, Bernardo, Ben, and Drina came jogging in. Lena had levitated a pile of chairs. Ben and Bernardo were pushing them along. Surprisingly, the guilds folk all helped them distribute the chairs. Soon, they all sat in a semi-circle around Amy, who remained on her throne, hesitating to come down and sit among them. She decided she ought to remain above them, since they were appealing to her as a higher authority.

Dimas spoke up, "We'll get right to the point. We've had enough of the various rulers and their towers. They are building weapons of inconceivable destruction, and forging swords and armor where they can. Skirmishes have broken out in nearly all of the many small kingdoms. Our various Guild Masters have reported on all manner of atrocities that have been committed thus far. We want it stopped."

"So do I, and so does any sentient person," Amy replied.

"Well, it's not happening, and it is escalating," Dimas added.

"Tom, Supreme Grand Master of the Eagles Guild. We respect what you and Queen Isabella Valen have tried to do. Freedom. Human rights. That was the most important document ever on Tierra. But the plan has serious flaws."

"How so?" Amy asked. This was the first she'd heard of this kind of problem.

"We all agree with that document. The Senate is a good idea, but the fatal flaw in the whole thing," Tom continued, "is illiteracy. You see, in Northend, we have fifty-one elected senators, who are supposed to make the laws. Of these honorable men and women, only one of them can read and write. So despite their best intentions, there is so little they can actually do. They are dependent upon what that one person writes, and have no way to know he's actually writing what they ask him to write."

"Then the whole voting process isn't working well. Only the nobles are literate. The vast majority of our people cannot read or write. Thus, they're forced to only elect other nobles who can. Thus far, they're the worst choices possible, as we see it. These elected officials merely continue their old practices, only now with the giant crystals of power, they're forcing the towers, who by law, are supposed to answer to the rulers, to do what they ask: build hideous new weapons. True, a few are doing good deeds for the common folk, mostly helping build new stone buildings, but that has become rare this past year, as the skirmishes have escalated."

"Estella of the Weaver's Guild. We want the many rulers to cease all their continuous bickering and fighting. We want all the towers to cease building the evil weapons and to help the average people of their kingdoms. The towers should and must work for us, the people, not for the rulers and their dismal battles."

"Pastor of the Shepherd's Guild. The rulers survive only

because of our hard labor, taking taxes from us, produce, and part of our flocks to sustain themselves, giving us little in return."

"Jorge, Farmer's Guild. We work hard to produce the food they eat; yet they do nothing to help us. In most kingdoms, some of the nobles, as well as the current rulers, own some of the best croplands. They lease out parcels to farmers, providing them protection and a roof over their heads in return for half of the crops they raise by their own sweat and labors. Yet, these same nobles fail to provide the promised protection. In some recent cases, they've destroyed the homes and part of the land with their deadly skirmishes and wicked tower-spawn weapons! No compensation to the uprooted farmers, who had no say at all. Our guilds have been looking after these displaced family groups, resettling them for the most part. This has to stop now."

"Lalo, Miller's Guild. Jorge is right. We Supreme Grand Masters are in complete agreement on this, as are our many subordinate regional Guild Masters, and even our thousands of guild members. We've come here today to beg you to help us stop this madness."

"Ramiro, Stone Mason's Guild. "Right. Some of our people believe you may be able to help us, so we're here to ask for your help. In fairness, most do not believe you can help at all. They say you would have done something before now. Still, we're making the attempt. One way or another, this madness must come to an end. Some of our grandparents have told wild stories of the Age of Chaos, as told to them by their grandparents. We guild members simply refuse to relive that again."

"So will you or can you even help us?" Dimas asked politely.

Amy sighed. "We here are fully aware of just where things are headed. We know about the atrocities committed during that worst era of our history. To date, we've done just about everything we can think of to put an end to it, to set things back on a proper course. I hate to report to you that it's come to nothing at all. I've only been marginally successful in keeping the conflicts from escalating. Most, but not all, simply will not listen to reason. The root cause is these giant crystals of power that are now so widespread over Tierra."

"We know about them. Our guilds are in possession of many such crystals ourselves. After all, only a few of us *mentales* gifted ever join one of those bastard towers. We prefer to use our gifts in our trades," Dimas explained.

Tom spoke up, "Don't' worry; we have no intention of using them against the towers. We are not murderers nor do we want to stoop to their level and build vile weapons."

"We're with you on that," Amy said. "I've wracked my brain for a way to put an end to all this, but sadly, I just don't see what I can do. I haven't given up hope or trying though."

Dimas nodded. "I figured as much, Queen Amy. Officially then, we're letting you know the guilds will be taking prompt and strong action to end this madness before it gets worse."

"You're not going to fight them, battle it out? Please tell me that you aren't going to war?" Amy pleaded.

Dimas and several others laughed. "No, Queen Amy, we'll not fight them with swords or magic or evil weapons. We'll fight them where they are most vulnerable. You see, they are totally dependent upon the many guilds and our hard working members, though they know this not. Our weapon will be economics. I would suggest you lay in quite a lot of supplies. As the battle rages, may we return and have you act as our spokesperson to the rulers and nobles? To help us restructure the way things are done? We'll force them to make significant changes in the way things are handled. On that, you can count. We've taken a vote. All the Guild Masters and thousands of guild members are behind us completely. We will do what we must to force these rulers and towers to change their ways, and to work for the people, and not for themselves and their own egos and money pouches and fine clothes."

"In principle, I agree. But what exactly are you planning? The more I know, the better I can handle things," Amy replied, bringing a smile to two dozen faces. She knew this was precisely what these people had wanted to hear from her.

"All current rulers in all kingdoms will immediately

resign. New elections will be held, conducted by the local Guild Master Councils. All towers will from now on follow the orders from and be responsible to their local Guild Master Council and the Supreme Grand Master Council — that's us, by the way. Likewise, a kingdom's army will still be under the control of the duly elected king or queen, but are also subject to the higher authority of the Supreme Grand Master Council. We reserve the right to abort any king's request for his kingdom's army to attack a neighboring kingdom, without just and due cause, and first having attempted to be settled in your court. Those are our demands, which you can deliver to them when you feel the time is right. Until then, Your Majesty, stockpile is the best advice we can give you."

He added, "Now that we have met you, no matter what happens, at least one of us on this highest council will be able to communicate to you telepathically." Amy finally noticed everyone here had yellow eyes. All were *mentales* gifted. She smiled, though it was invisible.

Tom added, "Don't be alarmed at what happens in the future. We're all prepared for the worst. We're all dedicated to the cause, a just one. We, the United Guilds of Tierra, are going to force this change on the rulers and the towers for the good of all people of Tierra. We would prefer death to this continued slavery and threat of imminent destruction of all we hold dear."

Dimas added, "It will begin this fall, though it'll likely not become critical until spring or perhaps even later. However, we'll be sending our list of demands to the rulers and towers this fall, which is why we are saying it will begin then. Considering their egos, we're certain they will ignore the demands." He and the others chuckled.

Tom then said, "We've taken up too much of your time. We thank you for your gracious patience."

"Perhaps we'll meet again under better circumstances," Estella said politely. She added, "If things get too bad for you, don't hesitate to contact your local guilds here in Exchange City. They'll be able to help, on the quiet that is. They've already been notified of their obligation to make sure you do not suffer because of our actions, Queen Amy."

"Thanks for the alert. Economic warfare. Perhaps, this might just work," Amy suggested hopefully. Many grinned in response.

Dimas then added a final note. "One more thing, Your Majesty, our organizational hierarchy above the person who runs the local guild hall is, and must remain, secret. All of the guilds have adopted a very strict and secret set of leaders. It must be this way. We anticipate the rulers will be hounding the local guilds. No matter what torture they inflict, they will be unable to reach any of the actual tiers of Guild Masters, Senior Guild Masters, and we Supreme Grand Masters. The names we've used today are not our real names. We can contact you directly via telepathy, and we suspect you can now contact us, perhaps. We must do this to guarantee our safety, and the success of our mission to make Tierra free and prosperous." With that, they rose as a group, and one of Amy's guards led them out, showing them the way.

"Well, this is a total surprise," Amy commented, after the last one had left.

"No kidding," Jan added. "Economic warfare. Incredible. Why didn't we think of this?"

"We had no idea the guilds had so organized themselves, Jan. We've had tunnel vision, focusing solely on the rulers and towers. We've missed what has been going on right under our very noses and all across Tierra, it seems. These men and women are highly determined, that much I could tell," Amy replied.

"Hey, if the rulers can't get enough food, they are going to become downright nasty towards their people," Bernardo pointed out.

Lena added, "Could well be bloodshed when they try to force these guilds to hand over food and supplies."

"Let's hope not, but you may be right. Still, these people must have already considered that eventuality and have planned for it. I can't believe we've so totally missed this," Amy pointed out again, totally shocked by her failure.

"We've certainly had far worse matters on our plates these past month, love," Jan justified rather nicely.

"That's true enough. Still, I missed it, and I should not

have. I wonder what else I've missed?" Amy questioned.

Lena suggested, "Perhaps we should scout around and see if anything else has been missed."

"Agreed. Bernardo, why don't you and Lena see what you can find out. Jan, let's go see the castle steward and order him to lay in five times as much food and supplies as normal," Amy declared.

Not long after the fall harvest was over, that is, mid-October in most kingdoms, the simply written, short paragraph of demands appeared in each kingdom ruler's hands, as well as their tower's. By then, it was too late to take any effective action. What few realized was this revolt had been long in the planning. The Teamster's Guild played a vital role during late September and October. Over half of the farm produce more or less disappeared, as if the crops had not produced well at all this year. Half of the year's pod silk didn't make it to the markets. So it went that fall. Later, Amy learned the perishables, such as grain and apples, were being stored in specially prepared caverns in the Goza Mountains, as well as at certain oases within the Arad. Other items, particularly in the south were moved about from place to place in secret.

For example, a load of weapons that should have been delivered to Southbend, Easterlings, come late spring, finally ended up appearing in Govia, Westerlings, thousands of miles away. What could not be stored in secret locations locally ended up being shuffled around Tierra. Kingdom boundaries meant absolutely nothing to these guilds.

Chapter 19 Economic Warfare and Babies

As early as December 1294, the effects were being felt at the many royal castles and towers across Tierra. The Underground as well as the Gang of Ten, less Zarita of course, were busily monitoring the situations in as many kingdoms as possible. For once, the Underground members began spending more of their daytime hours above ground roaming Brom than they had ever done before.

Snug in his drafty castle, King Bolivar grumble, "Nut bread? Where's the wheat bread? Summon the steward at once!"

The older man came bustling in, but he knew why he had been sent for, the guard told him. "Sire, we've used up all of this year's shipment of wheat. We've only received about half of our usual amount. Crops must have failed this year. We're low on most everything, but I'm not sure why."

King Bolivar grumbled and excused the man. "Check if we can buy some from the local millers," he ordered. Later, he was informed they had none either. The food shortages were acutely felt within Brom Tower. The tower technicians needed to eat a good hearty meal, after expending so much psi energies during their long work periods. By January, the venerado had no choice but to begin limiting his Circle's activities.

In late January, King Bolivar sent out his Royal Guards to acquire more supplies from Brom proper. Most returned nearly empty handed. "What? Is everyone starving?" he bellowed. "Get me the venerado immediately!"

Venerado William Brom, looking the worst for wear, came at once, as fast as his toe boots would permit him. "This food crisis is becoming intolerable!" King Bolivar hollered bitterly. "What the devil is going on? Do something. We need food."

"I've checked with the other towers, My Lord. All are in the same boat. Last year must have been a really bad year. No one has much left, but we are hoping that by tightening our belts and rationing what is left, we can make it until spring. In the meantime, I suggest that hunting parties be sent out."

"Very well then. I'll order the army out to hunt for meat," King Bolivar grumbled, but accepted the venerado's words.

As the shortages in the castles and towers grew, Ken reported to Amy. "Well, this is rather interesting. The Brom castle and tower are very desperate for food supplies. They've scoured all Brom's usual locations for supplies, but they are out of food as well. However, what's amazing is the locals seem to be eating well. I did some checking. While no one household has much, whenever they are too low, they let anyone, who belongs to any guild, know about it and a small bag of food supplies mysterious appears on their doorstep in short order. It looks like these guilds have done an amazing job of preparation. They are ensuring the local people are not suffering, only the nobles. Fascinating, don't you think?"

Amy replied, "Impressive to say the very least! Come spring, the armies will have to be out foraging, and the towers will be too low on food to sustain significant actual Circle operations. Without hearty meals, the technicians will begin dissolving their own bodies to make up for the energy losses. I suspect there will be no skirmishes or devastating tower attacks this spring and well into the summer. Amazing indeed. Who would have thought something as simple as food could bring down these kingdoms?"

Ken advised, "It's only beginning. Sooner or later, the rulers are going to begin taking it out on the guilds. My guess is that half of the people in Brom proper belong to a guild."

In March, Doctor Whitney had all of the expectant mothers come by for another checkup. She was taking no chances on their physical health, not with these eight genetically altered bodies. In truth, she had nothing to guide her. There was literally no data on file about hermaphrodites and their babies. All she could do was observe the health of the parents and conduct sonograms to check on the growing fetuses within them.

While she and Katrina were due in early April, by early

March, they all were showing and having difficulties getting around. "I feel like a bloated pig," Katrina commented, holding her hands with her huge nails across her bare belly.

"Tell me about it. Walking is harder than ever, and my feet are killing me, in spite of the special soles Lilly has put in them," Whitney replied. "Well, as far as I can tell, dear, you and your baby are doing fine. Another month or so."

"It can't come soon enough for me," Katrina grumbled a little. "I know; we're all in the same boat. Honestly, I'm really looking forward to beginning our family."

"Same here, love. I've waited over a hundred years for this day. I can't think of a better mother for her or him than you," she whispered, and gave Katrina a gentle hug. With their lip plates in place, a kiss was out. "Best send Alex and Ruth in to see me next."

Katrina waddled out, taking very careful steps. A fall now could well be disastrous, that she knew from all Whitney's discussions with the eight mothers-to-be. Shortly, two nurses escorted Ruth and Alex into her exam room.

"I never knew how awful it was for mothers," Alex moaned. "This is more like torture, isn't it?"

"A loving torture, Alex," Ruth corrected him.

"I know. I love him or her already, but this is so damnably hard on us. I wasn't able to do much before, but now it's all I can do to walk, even with help," he grumbled. "How are we going to be able to care for our babies, Ruth?"

"Don't worry about that, Alex," Doctor Whitney answered for Ruth. "Mothers always find ways. I'm sure you will to."

"Don't your feet ache?" he asked.

"Of course they do. Grin and bear it. Think of how fabulous it is that you are able to bring a new life into this world. That's something almost no fathers ever get to experience," she replied. "Hold still; let's see how he or she is doing today." A bit later, she added, "As far as I can tell, you are both doing perfectly, Alex."

"Yes, but fathers don't have babies. I don't know how you women can bear this. I'll never look at a pregnant woman the same, not ever. Still, this is so wonderful, isn't it, bringing a new life into the world," Alex declared, struggling to get into a sitting position, but failing completely. A nurse quickly helped him to sit up. His face flushed with embarrassment.

"Yes, the miracle of life is still something we doctors cannot duplicate. It is wondrous indeed, Alex," Whitney replied. "Now, let's see how you are doing Ruth." She had not yet told them all she could see from the various sonograms she'd done. That is, their babies would look just like they did, that their genetic deformities were being inherited. So were hers, for that matter. She guessed, if she told them their babies would be just like them, armless as well, they would become entirely too depressed over it. She hoped once they were born, their mothering instincts would take over, and that wouldn't matter. She did wonder if Alex would have that mothering instinct though. Whitney was in unexplored territory with these eight hermaphrodites. She also couldn't help wondering how Zarita, Celenia, and Lelane were doing.

Since around early February, for the most part, their genetic research had come to a halt. Ruth and Alex simply could not move around well at all; neither could she, for that matter. For the pair, their frequent need to use the restroom was becoming something of a hassle for the nurses. Even her own frequent needs were interfering with her concentration on the research notes. The three had decided to take a break from their studies until after their babies were born.

As March drew to a close, everyone was now complaining about their swelling breasts, though they all knew birthing was close at hand. At least, Whitney could massage hers; poor Alex and Ruth could only endure it. At last, April came, as did eight babies, thankfully spread several days apart. Katrina gave birth first, followed two days later by Whitney, who put them both on a six weeks maternity leave of absence. Just as Doctor Whitney had assumed, there wasn't any sure way to tell the sex of the newborns, since they had both forms of reproductive organs. Her idea of keeping an eye on them paid off. The second day, she was able to discover that she had their son, while Katrina had their daughter. Together, the happy couple named them Hank and Rae. Both babies had an abnormally small waist. Their feet were just as distorted as their mothers were, and their lips were already slit, ready for lip plates when they grew older.

Days later, Amy and Jan each had a daughter. Amy called hers Sandy, while Jan named hers Janet. Both babies followed the pattern, born with both sexual organs, split lips, tiny waists, and distorted foot arches. At least both had their arms, for which Amy was grateful.

Carla and Elfe gave birth a few days apart the following week. Much to Elfe's pleasure, she had their son, while Carla had their daughter, pleasing both women. They agreed on names. Their son was called Lelos, after Elfe's grandfather, while their daughter was named Mindy, after Carla's grandmother. Their babies had the same genetic form as their parents had.

Near the end of April, Alex and Ruth gave birth to their babies, Alex came first. Although he very nearly had to be carried to the med lab when his time came, he commented, "Well I didn't feel much pain."

Ruth, who was sitting nearby lending morale support, replied, "Silly, Doctor Whitney hit you up with some heavy painkillers, that's why."

"It's a boy, Alex. My new genetic markers are finally able to tell," Doctor Whitney announced.

"Really? Our son, Ruth! We have a son! Oh no. He's not got any arms like us!" Whitney had just brought him over to Alex to nurse.

"You have to be very careful of his head and neck, Alex. The nurse is going to roll you on your side. I'll lay him here where he can nurse, but be careful with him. What are you two going to call your son?" She deftly ignored his sudden shock and realization.

He looked up at Ruth, smiled invisibly. "Andy. Right dear?"

"Right. He looks so much like you, Alex. I'm so proud of you," Ruth replied. "Of course, Alex, now you aren't going to get any sleep, what with all the feedings. I guess we'll be facing that together. Of course, then come the terrible two's. How are we ever going to manage all this, Whitney?"

"Hey, look! He's eating, er nursing. This is so great; look

Ruth; he's feeding; he really is," Alex exclaimed. "Come on, little Andy, eat up. You've got to grow big and strong, little guy." Ruth smiled, though she knew no one could see it. Then two days later, she had their daughter, whom they named May.

Katrina made an executive decision. With six newborns to care for, as well as the almost constant care that Ruth and Alex now needed, she moved herself and Whitney into an adjoining store room, and Carla and Elfe into the room next to theirs. This way the overworked nurses didn't have to go up to the ninth and tenth floors as well. Finally, she asked Drina if she could spare some time to come and help Alex and Ruth learn to adapt better. The katalyein was very pleased to come to help.

Quickly, Drina saw it was going to be nearly impossible for the pair to do the things she could do. Their lip plates often interfered, but most of all, with their mandatory and tight pipe corsets, they simply lacked the flexibility they needed to have. Although they did try to get by without them, their backs soon gave out from the now even heavier than normal, milk-laden breasts. Hence, she ended up just helping with the newborns, changing diapers, for example, greatly relieving the overworked nurses.

Privately, Drina chatted with Rafaela. *Honestly, if ever anyone could use the telekinesis mentales gifts, it's Ruth and Alex. They really are unable to do almost anything for themselves or their babies. Can't we give them the gifts?*

We don't know them well enough. Will they remain on Tierra or go off-world? If they have the gifts, will they continue to help Whitney find cures? Or if they have the gifts, won't they, as geneticists, try to make genetic modifications so anyone could end up with our precious gifts? I just don't know, Drina. There are too many bad aspects to this pair for me to make any call except take a wait and see approach, Rafaela replied. She'd wondered how soon this request would come and was rather surprised someone hadn't asked her before now.

Okay then. We'll make do. Had to ask, Drina replied.

"Had to ask," Bernardo smoothed his new acquaintance. "Have another ale on me." He had taken it upon himself to see what was happening at spring planting time in the Kingdom of Wye. Reports had been intercepted by the Underground and forwarded to Queen Amy. King Wye was causing a great deal of trouble with the guilds in Wye proper. Bernardo had gone there, posing as a farmhand. Having discovered who was the local guild leader, he'd run into him at a pub. Actually, he'd discretely followed the man and struck up a conversation with him.

"Yeh, that old fat man has been hassling me and our members a great deal, even had his thugs give me a good shellacking. He told me he wanted triple the production from the fields that he owns this season. I told him, if he wanted more than last year, he should get out there in his own damned fields and work them. Our members are doing all they can. He didn't take too kindly to that one. Stupid fat man. He's never done an honest day's work in his life. He sits on his throne and sucks up the labors of everyone else in his kingdom. Fool," the guild leader explained, growing more antagonistic.

"So you've told your Guild Master and those higher up about his threats and your beatings?" Bernardo asked.

"Don't be ignorant too! The guild leaders are a secret. No one knows who they are. So if I don't know them, how do you expect me to tell them? Eh? Even King Wye couldn't beat that out of me, though he tried. 'Course, that's going to cost him come harvest time this year. He'll get even less from his fields. Going to be a whole lot of insects dining on his grain fields this summer," he insinuated.

"Had to ask," Bernardo smoothed his new acquaintance. "Have another ale on me. That's sure a darn good way to protect your leaders. I bet an awful lot of insects and weeds are going to appear in many fields throughout Tierra this season."

The man laughed, "You can say that again. Going ta be a good year for insects. Weeds? Hey, I like that one. Good idea. We can use it. Going ta be some mill breakdowns this fall as well," he winked at Bernardo and took another long gulp of the free ale.

"Hope the ale holds out though," Bernardo teased him. Both laughed.

During the summer, all of the Elegant Fashions Inc stores around Tierra began limiting purchases of new gowns and suits that were made from either silk or pod-silk, citing their supplies from last year were nearly gone. Noblewomen were quite annoyed and raised a good deal of hassles for their husbands over their inability to obtain the latest fashions. While one could still purchase cotton day dresses and working leather outfits, none of the nobles desired this, not remotely. New, high quality leather shoes and toe shoes and boots were also being rationed, though work boots were not.

Shortages were found in every area of commerce that dealt directly or indirectly with items the rulers or nobility might desire to purchase. New textiles, falcons and eagles trained for hunting, horses, gems and jewelry, mine production, smelter output, and stone work — all had various shortages that appeared at different times during the summer of 1295.

The High Council of the Lords was postponed until the July lease payment date, because the various rulers were trying to get a handle on all of the shortages in their kingdoms. The meeting chaired by Queen Amy was nothing more than a mutual gripe and bickering session. The various kings and queens compared situations between their kingdoms, finding everyone was pretty much facing the same kinds of situations.

Then, they discussed the fact they could not find the actual leaders of the many guilds. At the very least, they all wanted to harass and force them to make higher production quotas. However, more wanted to arrest them, charging them with high treason, and then hang them to set examples. At least, several local guild leaders had already been hanged, but those kings saw absolutely nothing happen in response. Amy suspected they'd see the response come harvest time.

Few took King Bolivar of Brom's action seriously. He'd ordered half of the standing army out to help work the fields and orchards within the Kingdom of Brom. King Rusden, who had hanged a few guild masters, complained, "Half of the plows on my farms have gone missing, stolen!" In fact, during the critical spring planting season, various plows and harness had mysteriously disappeared from the many barns, only to be discovered by other farmers and reported to the king. Of course, once they were retrieved, the plowing time had long past, though some rushed to still try to get a crop down.

What Amy found incredible, though predictable, not one of the rulers or their tower leaders ever mentioned the short paragraph of demands the Supreme Grand Masters had given them last fall. For a moment, she thought about reminding them of it, but then thought better of it. Besides, her three-month old baby was demanding much of her time right now.

Come fall harvest time, many rulers had much of their army overseeing the field hands and escorting the many wagons, as they took their loads into the granaries of the nearest town, mill, or castle. Once more, Bernardo and several others kept a discrete watch over some of these shipments, especially in and around Wye. Later, Bernardo laughed his head off, as he tried to explain what he'd seen happening.

"The armed escorts sat on their horses and watched the field hands loading the wagons; they rode alongside of them, as though their cargo was gold or iron ore. Once in the town or at the mill or entering the castle, they then turned around and went back to the fields. As I watched, the teamsters slowed their wagons way down, as they drove along the cobblestone streets. Men would dart out, grab a sack of grain or produce from the wagon and duck down a side alley. Then, at other locations, bags seemed to rise up in the air and float away by magic. By the time the teamster reigned in at his destination, the wagon was missing half of its load, and he swore he'd seen nothing. In fact, he hadn't seen anything. He just never looked behind. Even if the towers use truth saying *mentales* on him, he'll be seen as telling the truth. This is incredibly well orchestrated, amazingly so. My god, these guild masters know what they are doing!"

Lena roared with laughter and then urged him to tell the others about it, which he did. Amy was also impressed. She commented, "This may well work!"

The next High Council of the Lords was held on the first of November 1295. At first, the many rulers griped, argued, and bitterly complained about their dismal fall harvests. They and their castle stewards had made extensive lists of their supplies, from food to ores to ale to housewares. Every kingdom was facing drastic shortages of nearly every commodity. In fact, their stewards had already begun strict rationing of food supplies in the castles and towers across Tierra! The winter promised to be quite dismal indeed.

Once they had all compared notes, they discovered each kingdom was in the same mess. They could not, for example, get an emergency loan of wheat from the Kingdoms of Rusden and Wye, as many northern Midlands rulers desired, as well as most of the Easterlings rulers. Only when the overall gravity of the situation became clear to all of these rulers, did they finally bring up the paragraph that had been mysteriously delivered to them a week ago.

It read:

All current rulers in all kingdoms will immediately resign. New elections will be held, conducted by the local Guild Master Councils. From now on, all towers will follow the orders from and be responsible to their local Guild Master Council and the Supreme Grand Master Council. Likewise, the kingdom's army will still be under the control of the duly elected king or queen, but will also be subject to the higher authority of the Supreme Grand Master Council. We reserve the right to abort any king's request for his kingdom's army to attack a neighboring kingdom, without just and due cause and first having attempted to be settled in the Supreme Court of Queen Amy.

"Just what do you know about this document?" King Rusden bellowed at Queen Amy.

"I have one too. It just appeared on my throne seat this morning. Beyond that, I know no more than you, sire," she replied politely.

"I don't believe you," he yelled back at her, his face, red with hostility.

"I don't care if you do or don't. With my own two hands, I've stolen all of your grain, and carried bags of insects and weeds, and planted them in your fields," she jested. Several broke into a nervous laugh. Obviously, she couldn't be doing these actions. She couldn't even hold her young baby.

What Amy found quite interesting was the simple fact that Bernardo and Lena had already discovered: only the fields owned by the rulers and nobles of Tierra had suffered massive losses. Privately owned lands had been unaffected, though much had disappeared from their loads being transported as well. She knew during the winter, what had been taken would be discretely returned to those who needed it, just as it had been last winter.

"This is utter treason! I won't stand for it," bellowed King Rusden. Many echoed his sentiments.

"So what can we do about it?" King Bolivar of Brom asked.

"We can kick all of our tenant farmers out and replace them with others who will obey us, that's what we can do," King Rusden argued.

"But where will we find new farmers?" asked King Wye. "We've already got every known farmer working fields as it is. I dare say we can't conscript townsfolk to farm, can we?"

Queen Amy spoke up, fearing they might try that. "Look, you know as well anyone else in this room that would lead to utter failure of next season's crops. You are talking about men and women, who have spent their lives learning their various skills well. How would you like to wear a pair of boots made by a musician? Would you trust buying a new falcon from a seamstress turned falconer? Similarly, what do you suppose a seamstress, a weapons maker, a miller knows about the proper growing of crops? Nada. And you know that as well as the rest of us here. That's a recipe for total crop failure, and we all die of starvation."

That put a damper on such notions. "But what can we do?" King Bolivar wailed. "We can't let these treasonous guild leaders get away with this. Surely, we could reason with them

299

and reach some compromise, if only we could find them."

"What compromise, King Bolivar?" asked King Alano Valen. "Their demands haven't changed in the slightest from last year's ransom note."

"Well, maybe they want more money for their work," King Bolivar suggested.

"They made no mention of money or protesting being insufficiently well paid in their ransom notes," King Alano countered. "There is no compromise for traitors. Death to them all; that's my answer! Start by killing off the tenant farmers, that'll bring them out into the open."

"To be killed themselves? I think not, King Alano," King Rusden countered. "Besides, my soldiers monitored all of my tenant farmers this past growing season. They swear they have been working as hard as possible. If we kill off our farmers, who will be left to raise our crops come spring?"

King Alano remained quiet, knowing the King Rusden had a valid point. Just then, the king of Matruk spoke up. "We've a bigger problem facing us. According to my army quartermasters, there's barely enough food in reserve to tide the army over until the next harvest. They'll be down to one ale a day during the winter, and we can't possibly spare more grain to produce more ale. Do you have any idea what will happen to the morale of our armies by summer? We're expecting desertions like mad this winter. Our soldiers expect to spend the long winters drinking ale and feasting. One ale per day and they are going to mutiny or desert. I can't say I blame them. We did promise them food and ale as part of their wages."

The rulers discussed this unfortunate aspect for some time as well, coming to no real way of handling their armies. The only idea put forth was that of Lord Alano's: make it widely known that all deserters will be publically executed. Few wanted to go that far, suspecting the army might just then overthrow them by force!

Just then, one of the venerados spoke up. "Bad news. I've just received word the noble houses in Wye have all received identical notes that the rulers have with them here. Several Wye noblemen are complaining that King Wye do something about this mess. They, too, are going to run out of food this winter, unless they implement strict rationing starting now. I suggest that the other venerados and veneradas have their Circle members check with the noblemen in their cities to see if they've received these notes as well. At least in Wye, the situation has just escalated."

By the next day, every kingdom had reported back. Their noblemen had been notified of the demands of the guilds as well. The meeting adjourned without resolving any coordinated plan of attack or even workable ideas, save to confiscate as much food supplies as they could from the townsfolk in their kingdoms. Queen Amy knew that would not go over well at all. Had the guilds thought of this eventuality? Once more, she sent as many of her Gang of Ten out to monitor the situation in several key towns and cities.

Bernardo watched, as soldiers stormed house after house in the city of Valen. He smiled, as he watched them come out with hardly anything at all. Either these people had been alerted to the raids and had hidden much of their food supplies or they, too, had little. He stuck around one block to see what happened in the ensuing days. Late at night, he observed small bags of food magically appearing on the doorsteps of those who had been robbed of their food earlier in the day by Lord Alano's soldiers. He grinned silently to himself and signaled Bart, who teleported him home.

Others reported witnessing similar re-supplies by teleportation. Queen Amy now knew beyond a doubt that many quite gifted *mentales* were behind this, as well as the obvious fact that they too were using some of the giant crystals, greatly amplifying their powers. That gave her something else to ponder. These crystals were indeed a double-edged sword. They could just as easily use them to attack the rulers, their aides, and perhaps even the towers themselves. If that happened, there would be all-out war involving all of Tierra! Yet, all she could do was fret and worry.

Chapter 20 Change Comes

By October 1295, the young mothers and their babies had settled into a workable routine. At last, Doctor Whitney and her two geneticists, Ruth and Alex, were once more able to focus a good deal of their time on the massive genetics problems they faced. So far, they had reached one significant but disheartening conclusion about the secret research that had been done on Ashford-4. It had been random trial and error, with mostly error predominating. In fact, Ruth went so far as to suggest the researchers had simply had "dumb luck" in stumbling on the current sets of modifications they'd programmed into the generic alteration genes. All three felt some sympathy for the hundred men and women upon whom the fifteen years of experiments had been performed.

According to the research notes left on the computers, each major change had simply been discovered by accident. They altered this sequence and that, adding a little of this and that, while observing the results on their experimental subjects, live humans. Many had caused the death of the subjects, sometimes painfully so. In fact, the only true breakthrough had been the straightforward adaptation of the aerosol deployment method used in the chemical warfare work.

In October, Ruth made their first real discovery. Unable to do much beyond think and observe, she had the three samples of Whitney's DNA up on her helix monitor. In the tri-view, the left panel contained Whitney's original DNA before she ever came to Ashford-5. The center panel contained her DNA after she had been here for some time and just before she'd been infected during the aerosol bio agent attack. The right panel contained her current, highly modified DNA. For hours, Ruth and Alex simply sat and watched the animated displays on the monitor. They knew how utterly limited they were physically, and that their strength now lay in observation, not in actually doing any of the work.

"Look there, on that strand, Alex. Watch it as it

develops and changes in the middle and then on the right," she suggested.

"You are right. I see it too. From normal to abnormal," he exclaimed. "Doctor Whitney, Ruth has found something you ought to see."

Whitney, rather frustrated their attempts to unravel any of these genetic alterations had yielded nothing yet, came over to have a look. Ruth patiently told her just where to look, giving a very detailed description in lieu of even being able to point to her discovery, a tiny change amid the sea of data. "I see it! I see it, too. Yes, now that's interesting. Something changed in my body's genes while I was here, but before the bio attack."

"Precisely, Doctor Whitney. Something here on Tierra changes your genes ever so slightly. What changes happened to you after you got here?" Ruth asked.

"Nothing, I just used the medical machine to alter my appearance to match the local noblewomen as Katrina suggested," she sighed. Then it struck her. "Wait! I was told that all alien women, who are here for more than six months, end up with the melon-sized breasts that my nurses now have. Let me bring up their samples too!"

An hour later, all three were quite pleased. "We've gotten our first breakthrough! That's the sequence that alters breast sizes," Doctor Whitney exclaimed. She didn't also say what she was thinking that somehow this Fertility Goddess Arianna was altering women's genes in this manner. What had been "magic" or goddess-power before now seemed quite explainable as a simple genetic alteration, again probably aerial-borne. These goddess beings, in Whitney's mind, now became nothing more than brilliant genetic scientists. She made careful notes of just what gene had been altered and what the "corrected" sequence ought to be, a return to the usual melon-sized breasts found on all Tierra women. No sense in undoing even Arianna's changes, after another six months here, they'd return anyway. She relayed their first bit of good news to Katrina and Amy.

Embolden by their discovery, Ruth and Alex continued their tri-view studies. They had one of the nurses bring up her current DNA, adding a fourth view to the monitor. Again, for hours, the two simply sat there and observed, looking for further correlations in the before and after views. Between the two views, there were many genes and some had very convoluted changes between them.

The next day, Ruth asked Carla for some help. "Can you alter this viewing program to mask out the sections that are identical in all views? That way, we can focus only on what is different between them."

"Now that's a challenge. Okay, let me give it a try," Carla volunteered. "With these stupid nails, it's going to take me a whole lot longer," she grumbled. A week later, she'd worked her programming magic. On their monitor views, only the altered sections of the many genes appeared. Now the two could track the changes much more readily.

A day later, Ruth and Alex had isolated another two very simple changes in sequencing that had occurred. However, they had no idea just what these changes had caused. Ruth argued, "Whatever these did, it has to be something relatively small. This is the problem geneticists face. We need to take normal DNA, make these changes to that blueprint, and then alter a body with it to see just what happens. But what we don't know is whether or not these changes are part of a larger change. For example, the alteration to hermaphrodites is a very complex one, obviously. These could well be just a tiny part of that modification, say for example controlling male organ erections. We undo it and now the male organ ceases to work — a catastrophic change for the worse. See why we think they just had dumb luck, and a hundred men and women suffered terribly as a result?"

Doctor Whitney replied, "I see your point. We could try to undo these small changes, but without knowing what they actually do, we risk causing further damage to ourselves, right?"

"Right," Ruth replied. "Here is where ethics collides with genetic research. We have some changes to try. Yet, without knowing in advance whether or not they're going to be what we all desire and will be beneficial to us, the risk is terribly great for the person upon whom we try these changes.

Those researchers used those poor hundred victims. Lord knows how awful it must have been for them."

Alex added, "Any yet somewhere in all this data lay some tremendous breakthroughs in genetics that could well be of immense benefit for all mankind. Admittedly, unethical experiments on humans would yield the answers in short order. I can see why temptation is so very great."

"There has to be another way," Doctor Whitney declared. "I won't allow experiments on ourselves or others."

"Quite right, we agree. However, we can't help but wonder what would happen, if we could somehow put all our genes back to the way they were originally. Would we return to the way we were before?" Alex speculated.

Ruth added, "But we've no idea how to create such a complex set of changes. Besides, there is no telling if our bodies could live through such a reversal of genetics. It's just too darn dangerous to try anything but the simplest of changes, and even those could well spell trouble. Suppose we did find a way to alter our DNA with the breast sizes. What would happen to Alex? If his breasts returned to those of a man, how could he then nurse another child that he might have? It could be disastrous, Doctor Whitney. Experiments on test subjects could give us the answers we seek, but that would be totally inhumane and unethical. We won't stand for that either, though Alex and I would desperately desire it. Our lives are so ruined now."

Alex spoke up, "Doctor Whitney, there is another way though. Study. It might take us our entire lives, but if we continue to study genes, in time, it's possible to gain enough understanding actually to know what is going on in this arena. We believe this is the right way to do it. Study, learn, and understand, not random or trial experiments on test humans. I know we are asking a lot of everyone here — we are so helpless now — but we want to stay here on Ashford-5 and devote our lives to this study."

Ruth added, "We don't have any credits to speak of; our Academy training used up all that we had. We can't even support ourselves, much less our family. I know we are taking up a huge amount of valuable spaceport personnel just caring for us and our needs. Yet, we want to continue these studies the right way."

Alex continued, "So we've come up with a plan to ease the burden we've placed upon all of you here. If we could be setup in some home in Exchange City, where we could use local help to care for our needs, and if our computers and data where there, we could continue to study and not be as much of a burden on your staff. Your nurses have been fabulous and most considerate of us, but they spend half of their days caring for us and our babies."

Doctor Whitney sighed, but agreed. "Yes, I had high hopes we'd have this solved before now. Study is the right answer. You are right; my nurses are taking the brunt of this. Let me see what I can do."

Later, she met with Katrina, explaining the situation and Ruth and Alex's proposal. "The Closed World status makes this one a challenge. Let me see what I can do," Governor Katrina said formally. In turn, she paid an official visit to Queen Amy, outlining how the genetic research was going and the plight of Ruth and Alex.

"Their sense of ethics is admirable indeed," Queen Amy began her reply. "They are quite right about tying up your nurses just to care for their needs. Whitney has a point about the Closed World status too. I'll tell you what, Katrina. I've plenty of room in my castle complex and now have a power generator from Emperor Kino. I'm a legal exception to the Closed World status. I'll take them in and their equipment, and provide for their support with some dedicated assistants from the locals here, who would love the opportunity to make descent wages. Plus, the castle would be a good place for them to raise their family too."

"I agree with that last; my spaceport is not the best place for our four babies either. If you could do this for them, I'd be eternally grateful, Amy. The Imperium ought to help finance them. Such should not be your burden alone. Whitney and I were so hopeful that she and they would quickly come up with a way to undo these genetic alterations, but it's obvious now without unethical human experiments, it is going to take a long time to learn what must be understood before taking any strides in that direction," Katrina admitted.

The two leaders chatted a bit longer. The next week was spent moving all of the computer equipment over to their new quarters in a back suite of the Imperial Castle. Two local women were hired to take care of their needs for now. The overworked base nurses finally got a well-deserved break. The move worked out well for everyone concerned. More importantly, Rafaela and Amy then decided to give Ruth and Alex the *mentales* gifts, though Rafaela tweaked their gifts to be those of telekinesis and levitation, which the two desperately needed. Thus, in November of 1295, Ruth and Alex were finally able to do some things for themselves, including handling their babies and computers, along with their own personal needs.

Late December 1295, wide spread food shortages sprang up all over Tierra, though only among the ruling castles, towers, and noble households. Of course, these people didn't know the locals were not experiencing the shortages. The northern Kingdom of Walsham was the first to accede to all the Supreme Grand Master demands. The king and queen disbanded their court and returned to their country manor house on one of his estates. As news of his accession, other kingdoms followed suit. Queen Edda did the same in Turda, Alba, followed by Sultaness Sofia of Tecuci, Arad. However, both rulers were highly loved and admired by their kingdoms and would soon be re-elected to their former posts as their kingdom's rulers.

Word soon spread that as soon as they had acceded, the food shortages eased significantly. Somehow, more food supplies were discovered and handed out. By spring, only a few of the kingdoms had not acceded to the Supreme Grand Master's demands. Rusden, Valen, and the Renegade Tower were among the more significant holdouts.

In early April 1296, King Alano Valen, King Rusden, their tower venerados, and others met in secret at Valen Castle. "What the hell are we going to do?" King Rusden bellowed. "We can't fight an enemy we can't see!"

"No we can't. Try as we might, we are nowhere closer to

discovering who these treasonous Grand Masters are," Lord Alano complained bitterly. "But we have to do something. We're being starved to death!"

Venerado Arturo suggested, "The only thing we can do is to go underground, gentlemen. We accede for now. We all have country estates. We take those who can be trusted, who are loyal to us, and move there. In secret, we build up our strength and power. One day, we'll be powerful enough to strike back and reclaim our rightful inheritances. King Wye has already done this. He's got a full Circle with him from old Bedwurth Tower. We become our own Secret Society."

"Renegade Tower has always been a renegade. We're with you on this one," Venerado Valen proclaimed. "You don't need fancy towers for Circles to operate. Hell, we'll made do with ordinary residences. Bide our time. One day, these mysterious Supreme Grand Masters will make fatal blunders, and we can regain our power and thrones."

King Alano laughed. "I like that. We become our own secret society with our own towers. My god, think of the havoc we can create! We'll undermine these traitorous Guild Masters. Hell, they know nothing of ruling a kingdom. Let's do this. We three can form our own secret society."

Venerado Arturo declared, "We shall become the Sociedad Secreta de los Reyes Ocultados!" The name stuck. "We should see about adding some others, like King Wye to our group."

After a week of planning, the men returned and formally announced their accession to the Supreme Grand Master's demands, formally abandoning their respective castles and towers. They took with them trusted tower members and a goodly supply of giant germanium crystals as well. They moved out into their various country manors and began to setup shop there.

May Day 1296, Supreme Grand Master Dimas visited Queen Amy. "Your Majesty, I've come to report that it's finally done. All of the kings and towers have acceded to our demands. While three hundred six brave men and women were killed by these murderous ex-leaders, we have persevered and won the day."

"Congratulations, Supreme Grand Master Dimas. You and your people are to be highly commended for what you've done. I feared greatly we were about to enter another massive Dark Age of Chaos with death and destruction everywhere. You've avoided all of that. Very well done indeed."

"Thank you, Your Majesty. We had no choice but to take action. The last three holdouts have acceded, and elections will soon be held there. The Towers now must answer to us. Expect far more public construction projects in the near future. The linguist and teacher, Nadja, has shown us that literacy and education are vital for our people. This will become one of our major thrusts in the immediate future. I've also come to ask if we can schedule a Joint Council of Rulers in early June? We'd like all the newly elected rulers and tower leaders to have a chance to meet their new counterparts, under your guidance, of course."

"Certainly. That's one purpose of the Imperial Castle here — to provide a safe place for all to meet. I'll make the necessary preparations. Thanks again for all your efforts and those of your many guild members. I'm absolutely floored with how well you organized this and kept the locals from suffering. Amazing," Amy replied, genuinely quite pleased indeed.

After he left, Jan commented, "Well, Amy, despite all our efforts and those of the Underground and our governor, it wasn't us who handled the kings and towers with their giant crystals, but a wholly unknown group of guild masters. We know next to nothing about them. We haven't had any close contacts with them, given them any advice or help. Yet, they've pulled this one off, leaving us wholly out in the dark. Worse, the secrecy of their organization isn't going to allow us much of an opportunity to endear us to them."

Amy commented, "I know. A new form of power structure has officially arrived on Tierra. I'm not sure what to make of it just yet. I'm not sure where they are going, though on the surface, Dimas sounds like he has the best of intentions. I don't think we've heard the last from some of the kings and their loyal tower members. There definitely has been a power shift. This time economics was the sword, but only because of their secrecy and well organized methods."

She went on, "What has me bothered the most is the Ataro Empire's belief that power corrupts, and because of that, there must be checks and balances on that power. In this case, secrecy hides those who are wielding this new-found power. There are no checks and balances on these leaders. Time will tell what effect this power will have on them. That's why I've been hesitant to bring these guild leaders in on the Underground and such things just yet. Let's keep a tight monitoring of everything on Tierra that we can."

Up in the Kingdom of Walsham with its older Bettingham Tower, the Supreme Grand Masters met in very early January. These *mentales* gifted men and women had just made use of their combined energies to teleport themselves to the secret Inner Sanctum of the Weapon Maker's Guild. They'd received word of King Walsham's accession to their demands. He and the tower's *venerado* had left the castle, returning to their own private mansions on the northern edge of the sprawling city currently buried under two feet of snow — the dead of winter.

"Now comes the hard part," Dimas explained to the two dozen other leaders. "We have to get a new king elected and soon. Plus, we have to meet with the tower and get a new leader for them chosen."

A woman spoke up, "We are limited. Whomever we nominate and get elected has to be able to read and write. How else can he be expected to follow the Senate's laws?"

Another man added, "We all know that about the only ones who can are these very same nobles who we've just usurped."

Dimas countered, "That's why we must call upon the Welsham's Guild Masters. They know their own people, their nobles. Has everyone gotten their masks?" He looked around the room. One by one, each person donned their strange looking face masks. They were made from pounded bronze. Shiny golden, impassioned faces appeared, though their yellow eyes could be seen through the openings. Their lip slits allowed their voices to be heard. No attempt was made to disguise the sex of the person. Still, this was sufficient to maintain their anonymity.

Satisfied, Dimas rose, went to the door, and told the local Guild Master to send in his first choice. The group heard him speak. "Lord Amos, you may enter now." They watched as the fifty year old Lord Amos Walsham made his slow, careful way into the room. He was obviously a nobleman. He wore polished toe boots. His bronze lip plates drooped down to his chest, showing a pair of horses in a grassy field. His strong arms and legs contrasted sharply with his slim waist. His stiff demeanor also suggested that he wore a pipe corset too. His suit was brown suede, matching his boots. In spite of his obvious physical limitations, he carried himself with pride and took the only available seat, staring out at the sea of golden masks. He did not have yellow eyes.

"Lord Amos, you are here before the Supreme Grand Masters of Tierra. At this time, we are going to choose two candidates to run for the king of Walsham. Elections will be held within a month. You have been asked to appear before us today so we may evaluate you to see if you are worthy of becoming one of those two candidates. We have a series of questions we'll be asking you first. Do not attempt to lie to us, for we can detect such. After our questions, you'll have the opportunity to say what you wish and tell us why you believe you would make a good king. Understood?" He nodded.

"A king should always have the best interests of his citizens in mind. How do you think the ex-King Walsham failed to do that?" Dimas began grilling Lord Amos. An hour later, he finally was allowed to ask his own questions.

"So if I am the elected king, am I supposed to be your puppet? Do I take my orders from the guilds? If so, I want no part of this," Lord Amos asked pointedly. From the get go, this had been his biggest concern. He'd followed the Senate legislation since its conception, and he did believe in this new form of ruling the late Queen Isabella Valen had forced upon Walsham.

"No, that would defeat the whole point of this. You obey the legally passed laws of Walsham. You enforce those laws. You don't make new policy; you don't twist those laws to suit your own ambitions," a woman answered.

Another woman added, "If you do, we'll bring you before the Supreme Court of Queen Amy and have you removed from office."

"I still get to choose my own staff?" Lord Amos asked.

Dimas replied, "Of course. We have no intention of interfering, but we'll be watching."

Lord Amos then stated, "I believe Walsham must maintain good relations with Queen Amy and the aliens as well. Look, we now have an operational hospital for the first time ever in our history. Plus, we're able to get their Basic Therapy, which I've had and found immensely useful. Will the king be allowed the flexibility to build such foreign relations as he deems appropriate? Will the king be allowed to work out mutual defense treaties, subject to Senate approval of course? Walsham is not an isolated kingdom."

"Of course, education and public health are vital to the long term survival of Walsham," a woman answered him. He asked more questions for another half hour before he finished up and was asked to leave. A half hour after that, another nobleman arrived and was likewise grilled for several hours.

After he too left, the Supreme Guild Masters accepted both candidates, but decided to back Lord Amos Walsham. They then summoned the many other local Guild Masters, who oversaw all the guilds in the kingdom and presented their two choices, along with their preference for Lord Amos. This new group was then charged with conducting the election. Because travel was most difficult here in January, it took them a month to handle this process, going from town to town, holding meetings, discussing the two candidates, and conducting a vote by a show of hands. The normal election process was impossible to conduct in the middle of the winter. They needed a new king rapidly; hence, the extreme measures taken to hold the best possible voting under the circumstances. On the first of February, Lord Amos was sworn in as the new king of Walsham.

Similar processes occurred during the long winter and very early spring of 1296. As each kingdom acceded to their demands, the Supreme Grand Masters made a trip to the capital city and made their choices, as they had done in

Walsham.

The sixth of June 1296, the High Council of the Kings of Tierra, as it was now being called, was held at the Imperial Castle. Queen Amy again presided accompanied by Governor Katrina, Doctor Whitney, Carla and Elfe, as well as the Gang of Ten members. Even Senator Zarita was present to make a full report of the past Senate meetings.

Part III Genetic Warfare

Chapter 21 Genetic Developments and the Imperium Senate

Xeros-1 held the Maximum Security Prison of the Imperium. This broiling planet held the sprawling compounds of a dozen isolated prisons. Escape was impossible. Besides being locked in titanium re-enforced steel cells along with many guard check points and the secure outer perimeter of the climate controlled complex, there was no place to go. Outside these compounds, the daytime temperatures soared to well over two hundred fifty degrees while the nighttime temperatures were well below negative hundred-fifty. Escape was impossible, and during the long history of Xeros-1, no prisoner had ever tried. Such was suicide.

Imperium justice for criminals took two forms. First, psych man behavior modifications were attempted. These procedures worked fairly well for thieves and those convicted of lesser crimes. Centuries ago, such mild procedures failed completely to take on the hardened criminals, particularly so for the psychopathic killers. These were sent to Xeros-1. Upon arrival, their voice boxes were modified, rendering all prisoners unable to speak. That alone had drastically reduced many problems inherent in previous prisons. Still, they developed their own "sign language." The toughest, as expected, became the leaders of gangs within the compounds. Rape and murder continued behind these walls. The enforced silence prevented the guards from often finding the culprits, but they didn't care too much about it. After all, these men and women were all guilty, one way or another.

Klaxton Soroyos was one of the most ruthless gang bosses in Compound A, where three hundred were held. His six-foot-six frame was all muscle. Few guards had biceps as powerful as his. He had been convicted of ten murders, but the prosecutors suspected him of at least twenty others. Klaxton had been sent here at twenty-one with a life sentence. Now nine years after he'd arrived, he'd forcibly taken control over the three hundred in Compound A, having killed three other leaders, and beaten countless others, sending them to the medical machines in the infirmary. He was the most feared man in this compound. Sector ID Minister Slag personally chose him as one of the new "test subjects" for the great genetic experiment.

In early June 1295, Sector ID Minister Slag, accompanied by his two geneticists, ordered the experimental treatment of two dozen of the worst offenders, including Klaxton Soroyos and Myrtle Tutthill. Myrtle was convicted of murdering ten men and two women. Her favorite method was drugging their wine and then cutting them up, bit by bit, beginning with their genitals. Her crime scenes were some of the bloodiest in Imperium history. Even while incarcerated here, guards had barely prevented her from dissecting two other women and one man, though she'd managed to kill them. Myrtle controlled the female population in this compound and continually made attempts and schemes to get to Klaxton, who she'd silently sworn to kill next. She dreamed of removing his genitals.

Heavily chained, Klaxton, Myrtle, and twenty-two other men and women were brought into the open courtyard, where the remaining prisoners could watch the proceedings from their cells. Two dozen beds were arranged inside two separate, transparent, biological containment constructions. Glaring at each other, Myrtle and Klaxton rattled their chains at each other, threateningly. Hatred flashed from their eyes. It was obvious these two wanted the other dead.

All were chained prone on their hospital beds. While the two geneticists prepared their bio agents, Sector ID Minister Slag addressed the two dozen criminals, the governor, the guards, and the remaining prisoners in their cells. After introducing himself, he explained, "This process is being recorded so that others can review what happens here. We have developed a new and far better method of handling you hardened criminals. The cost of housing you for the duration of your lives is prohibitively expensive. While some of you take great pride in inflicting such expenses upon the Imperium, that is about to change today. This new treatment

316

will totally handle our prisoner problem, far better than the failed behavior modifications, which all of you circumvented one way or another. Today, you're all about to witness this new process on two dozen of your worst criminals."

"As you can clearly see, we've separated them into two groups. The worst sixteen are in one tent, eight others are in the other tent. We have stripped them of their prison jump suits so they and all of you can witness these incredible changes that will occur. The process takes several days to complete, so please be patient. The results, I'm sure, you'll find most interesting, if that is the proper word for this revolutionary new process. Gentlemen, begin when you are ready."

The two geneticists opened the valves, allowing the bio agents to flood the two containment tents. All two dozen struggled against their bindings, to no avail. The tents filled up with a slightly yellow cloud. Of course, everyone watched what happened. Nothing.

Slag spoke up, "They've been infected with our latest bio-genetic engineering agents. The changes will take several days to complete. Keep watching each day." He laughed sinisterly.

Later that day, the two dozen slowly fell asleep and then drifted into a coma, as the genetic agents began modifying their bodies' genes. Periodically, the geneticists took agent readings on their monitors that were inside the sealed containment tents. Slowly the physical changes began appearing, much to the shock of everyone, except the two geneticists, who had witnessed this happening to Ruth and Alex, the two intern colleagues of theirs on Ashford-4.

The third day, the detector readings were back to normal. The bio agents were inert now. Carefully, they removed the containment tents, though the governor and guards were highly suspicious, and Slag had to convince them it was now entirely safe. By day five, the changes were complete.

Again, Slag spoke to everyone. "These sixteen, including Myrtle and Klaxton, can no longer see. Their eyes are just grey, opaque orbs now. So for their benefit, I'll explain what they all look like now."

"All of you have lost your arms. They withered up and fell off. All of you now have very tiny waists, about a foot around. All of you have extremely fine boobs; they protrude a foot in front of your chests, rather amazing endowments. Your lips are slit, and you soon will be wearing the foot in diameter lip plates found in some more primitive cultures. Your feet have also been altered. Only your toes rest on the floor now. You'll be given some of the fancy toe shoes that are also popular even among Imperium senators. Your hair has grown some; I believe you'll find it almost reaches the ground when you are standing. Careful you don't sit on it. Even more interesting, you all now have the sexual reproductive organs of both sexes. Yes, you are officially hermaphrodites. And yes, they're fully functional. Even those of you who were men are now able to bear children, so you can put those massive knockers to good use nursing them. Finally, you sixteen worst criminals — you are also blind. Don't worry; we'll soon get you all properly dressed in nice satin gowns and shoes. So Myrtle, Klaxton, your criminal days are over forever."

He turned to address the remaining criminals locked in their cells. "In time, we'll get to all of you. Have no fear. The Imperium is about to turn all you criminals into completely helpless and totally dependent men and women." He laughed, as did the guards and the prison's governor.

"My god! They're totally helpless. They couldn't harm a fly now," the governor exclaimed, as he examined the two dozen terrified men and women sitting helplessly on a long row of benches. They had been dressed, lip plates inserted, helped to get up, and moved to one long bench. "This is utterly revolutionary! How soon can this be done to all of the prisoners? Heck, I can retire soon. We can close his extremely costly facility down! Even their muscular physiques are gone now, more feminine, if that word even applies to them."

As they talked, Myrtle realized she was now sitting beside Klaxton. She tried to move her arms, but nothing happened. All she could do now was to try to bite his genitals off. She tried to knock him down, but both went sprawling onto the floor. She gnashed her teeth trying to bite him, but her lip plates prevented her from getting her teeth less than a foot from him. At last, reality sank home into her mind. She screamed, but made no sound. Someone lifted her back onto the bench and told her to behave or she'd be placed in a cell with a man. Myrtle visibly began shaking and moving her head from side to side, trying to signal No!

"Soon we can close it down, I hope. Now that proof of concept has been done, we'll take these to the psych ward, where they can be looked after. Hell, they can't do a darn thing for themselves. Once we get back to Doctor Aarok, I'll order enough made to handle the two thousand or so you've got locked up here," Slag replied, more than pleased with the results.

"Yes I agree. They can't be put back into the normal population, unless you want them raped repeatedly," the governor advised.

Klaxton was physically shaking so badly he could scarcely walk, let alone keep his balance on his toes. Someone was holding him around his waist, issuing orders he couldn't follow, not anymore. His whole world had collapsed in upon himself. Now he faced that one fear he'd fought against his entire life — a fear of complete helplessness, unable to see, speak, or physically do anything for himself. That hidden terror had been a powerful motivator all his life, since he was ten. Now, in his utter blackness, there was nothing left except this terror, about which he could do absolutely nothing. He couldn't even end his own life.

Once in the psych ward, a new problem developed. None of the inmates wore their original jump suits with their name and number on it. All their bodies now didn't resemble their former appearance. Names became confused. Not even DNA matches could be used to sort out who was who. Hence, the psychs decided to give them each a new name. After all, they reasoned, they were nothing like what they were before. Klaxton found himself being called Carla, while Myrtle was now being called Hermina.

Since beds were at a premium with the arrival of these two dozen, two were bunked together in one room. Carla and Hermina were roomed together, though they had no idea of

319

the identity of the other and now no way even to discover it. "Hold still if you want your hair brushed out, Carla," the female psych nurse ordered. "There you are done. Into bed with you." She helped the hermaphrodite into bed. Then, she did the same to the petrified Hermina. The nurse noticed when their bodies touched, especially their giant breasts, both of their male organs responded. Cleverly, she got each onto their sides. "Okay, have at each other. Here, I'll get you both properly oriented," she said mischievously. She could not help but stand back and watch the two trying hard to satisfy their physical needs. After a time, both seemed extremely contented, if she interpreted their outward signs properly. As a result, she decided to "help" the others partake of this only remaining pleasure open to these new arrivals.

Within a few days, she discovered those who could see definitely enjoyed her giving them this pleasureful opportunity. Hence, she continued this for quite some time. A couple of months later, all two dozen were pregnant, only adding to their misery. Still, the doctors were quite impressed with this new development. Up the lines came the memo that a new and productive use could be had with these modified prisoners: the creation of new individuals for the Imperium.

When Sector ID Minister Slag learned of the destruction of the research facility on Ashford-4 and the loss of Doctor Aarok, he ordered the two remaining geneticists to begin working on creating more of the bio agents. They had used up all the sample that created blindness, but still had a sufficient amount of the other bio agent. "Look, I'll get you a new facility and the equipment that you need. I want volumes of this bio agent produced as soon as possible. Can you do it?" The two jumped at this opportunity and agreed. "Don't worry; I'll handle the Senate. You make this stuff somehow, someway."

On board his battle cruiser, Slag brought up known research facilities here in the outer rim sectors. He knew he needed a reasonably secure facility, and one that didn't threaten populated planets, should something go wrong, as it had on Ashford-4. He found one that suited him, Belsarius-2. After issuing orders to go there to the ship's commander, he then headed to his planning room.

Slag was many things — organized and methodical were counted among them. He began constructing a list of "actions" that had to be taken to get this pushed through to a completion. The list turned out to be a rather long one and had several contingency options. He was not a legal expert. Thus, the first pivotal point would be the Minister of Prisons. Did he or did he not have the authority to implement these genetic changes on the prisoners on Xeros-1? If he didn't, did the Imperium President have such? Worst case scenario, he would have to get Senate approval, something that Slag wanted to avoid, if at all possible. Why? Certainly the disaster surrounding Ashford-4 and Ashford-5 would come to light. This would be a political hot potato, one that could delay the project indefinitely, if not outright terminate it.

The next day, he and his two geneticists toured the facilities on Belsarius-2. Finding them satisfactory, he issued a Sector ID Ministerial order to have his two men stationed here and given anything they desired, with the funds coming from the Bureau of Prisons' Discretionary Fund. "Okay, you are all set," Slag announced to his two men. "Now what I need is a time line on just how soon you can produce enough of this bio agent to handle the entire population of the prisons on Xeros-1."

Bazel spoke up. "Sir, we've given this considerable thought. While we realize a full study of these incredible breakthroughs in genetics is our goal, we also know it could be many years before we fully understand what was done and developed on Ashford-4. There is no question this must be undertaken in a proper scientific manner. However, we also realize just how important this particular situation is. There's always been substantial Senate disapproval of such genetic research on human test subjects, which could delay, impede, or even halt our critical research and studies."

Slag frowned. This, he already knew and was working to find a way around it, at least for the prison system. Bazel noticed this and hastily added, "So we've taken another approach. If we can get the entire prison population handled, that will save an enormous sum of money immediately. Some of the savings could then be channeled into this critical research."

Slag nodded, "That was my intention."

"So we have come up with an expedient solution," Bazel offered their best solution. "We believe we can program one of the Fabrication Machines to duplicate the bio agent along with the requisite apparel they'll need to wear. Such ignores all of the science, you see. It merely duplicates the bio agent in quantity. We couldn't make any changes in the genetic sequencing. What you get will be what you currently have with the smaller batch, those who still have their vision unimpaired. Would this be acceptable? We do apologize for having used up all the version that also blinded them, Sir."

"Excellent, excellent, Bazel," Slag brightened up. Looking at his extensive list of "to do's," he asked, "How soon?"

"Give us two weeks and the dedicated use of a Fabrication Machine," Bazel announced with a wry grin, thinking of the vast funds that would soon be freed for their genetic research.

Slag wrote that down and scratched several others from his list. "Perfect. I'll see you have the one that was brought out here to service Ashford-5. You'll have it in three days. Get to work. I'll be holding you to that two week deadline."

After making the arrangements and leaving the two geneticists on Belsarius-2, he headed directly to pay a visit to the Minister of Prisons, one Gordon Knox.

A pudgy man, though well-dressed, met him, "Come in, come in," Gordon said jovially. "To what do I owe this visit from our Sector ID Minister? Make yourself at home. Whisky? Scotch?"

"Scotch, please," Slag accepted his offer and took a seat. After the two sipped the very fine Scotch, he said, "You've undoubtedly heard of the Pilot Project I instigated on Xeros-1?"

"Ah that! Yes, truly amazing! Revolutionary. Impressive indeed. The reports are coming in almost daily. I've been following their progress closely," Gordon replied, waxing overly enthusiastic.

"Yes, well, I've come to propose in two weeks we handle all of the remaining prisoners on Xeros-1. You can then close the penal planet down. That should save you a very nice amount," Slag proposed, sensing the Minister of Prisons was eager to hear this proposal.

"What? Two weeks? Absolutely stunning! Yes, yes of course. Let's do it. I've already worked out the savings, assuming we'll then have to move them into simple, non-secure assisted living homes. It works out to an annual savings of twenty-five billion credits and some change! If we can pull this one off, Sector ID Minister, we both will be incredibly famous. No one has ever saved that much! Two weeks you say?"

"Yes, I'm told the bio agent will be ready then. Give me two days to get it to Xeros-1. The process takes around a week, after that, they can be dressed and taken to your assisted living homes. There's no way they can commit any crimes after that. It's physically impossible for them to do so," Slag pointed out.

"I'll begin making the arrangements for a dedicated assisted living facility to house these two thousand prisoners yet today! I had no idea our genetic scientists have made such remarkable discoveries. Earth-shaking discoveries. Perfectly brilliant for our hardened criminals. Centuries ago, we all thought housing them on a planet such as Xeros-1 was the solution to such society degenerates. However, the sheer cost of maintaining a livable biosphere on such a world is prohibitively expensive. This is such a simple, elegant, humane solution. Just incredible." Gordon continued expressing his enthusiasm for the proposed "solution." Slag smiled. If only everyone was this accepting, he thought. They wouldn't be, that he knew.

The two chatted about implementation details. The limiting factor was having enough personnel on hand to handle the altered men and women once the process was done. Each had to be dressed and helped with everything after that point in time. They arranged to stagger the process, doing them in batches of a hundred, beginning each new group three days apart. That would give them time to handle the ones who were done, getting them dressed, cared for, and taken off-world to their new rooms in the assisted living complex on Juno-3, a bluish planet also in the rim sector.

Gordon then said, "As Minister of Prisons, I'll have to go to Proxima Prime and make these results known to the Legates and thus the full Senate. By September, this project will be completed, and I'll have simply glowing reports to give them."

"Excellent. I'll see you have the necessary backing from the Legates as well. Never can tell with these senators," Slag advised. Seeing the signs of relief on Gordon's puffy face, he knew he'd said the precise words the minister needed to hear, but was afraid to ask.

Slag then left to handle other business. However, he conferred with his two geneticists at the end of the first week to make sure all was going according to plan. It was, their simple "duplication" process was working. The Fabrication Machine didn't have to know what it was making; rather it idiotically reproduced precisely what was in the Input Chamber, regardless of what that might be. It was pumping out half-filled canisters of the bio agent. Of course, they also had to fabricate all of the apparel that would be needed as well and in a range of sizes."

Sizes were an interesting side effect of the process. Some men had thick, burly leg muscles and others had big feet. After the genetic process was finished, those had changed as well, greatly reducing the range of sizes needed for the toe shoes, for example. Even the overweight ended up drastically reduced in size, all conforming to the genetic programmed twelve inch waist line. Constrained by the mandatory pipe corsets, they would be hard-pressed to regain the lost weight. Of course, such things would be the very least of these prisoner's concerns.

Slag took no chances. Only when the process was finished did he make the long trip to visit Proxima Prime in late August, before the Senate officially resumed from its long summer vacation period. He arrived and was escorted into the Presidential Office and met with Finance Legate Marhildt Chyldt and State Planning Legate Helyeon H. Hoon, also known affectionately as H-cubed. After cordial greetings, the three men sat down in one of the Legate's fancier meeting rooms.

"The purpose of my visit is to give you a full report on the changes that have been implemented the Minister of Prisons Gordon Knox and me," Slag began formally.

"Yes, we are familiar with these changes. Gordon has kept us both abreast of these incredible developments," H-cubed interrupted him. "What we would like is a better description of just how this came about, Sector ID Minister."

Slag spoke formally and clearly. "This is an outgrowth of the secret, wartime genetics research project on the uninhabited Ashford-4. Those dedicated researchers have made some monumental advances in the field of human genetics. Mind you, I'm not a geneticist. As I understand the findings, they were able to engineer specific modifications to anyone's genetic blueprint, which in turn causes their bodies to alter to match the new genetic model. Further, they found a way to not only make the process generic, but also to easily deploy it in the field."

"You mean to expose whole populations to it?" H-cubed interrupted, making a strong point.

"Precisely. As I understand it, this was their given wartime goal, a weapon to be used as a very last resort. If it had been used, millions of lives could have been saved. Drones would have been sent to the planet to be captured, releasing the bio agent in its atmosphere. Of course, it wouldn't matter if the drone were shot down; it would still release the bio agent. Within a week or so, the entire population of the enemy planet would be rendered nearly helpless, allowing our army to capture the planet without firing a shot or destroying any of the valuable infrastructure and resources of that world. In all honestly, that would have been one fantastic new weapon, guaranteeing Imperium victory," Slag contended.

"But there was a problem?" H-cubed again interrupted.

"Yes, the research facility was located on an uninhabited world and all manner of containment processes were implemented. What was overlooked was protection from a meteor swarm. The planet has no atmosphere to stop the small colliding grains. They ruptured the roofs and released

325

the deadly chemical toxins, killing everyone there. However, one fool jumped into their short range shuttle trying to escape. He violated all manner of protocols in a futile attempt to save himself. Probably unknown to him, the shuttle had been primed for their next experiment, the aerosol release of one of their test bio agents. The shuttle was able, by the miracle of the computer controlled, automated guidance system, to make it to Ashford-5, inhabited by a primitive population. Upon entry to its atmosphere, the experiment activated, infecting everyone on that world. A terrible accident."

"However, it did prove this method of delivery works perfectly. Fortunately, the dosage was not designed for planet-wide distribution, but only the few test subjects in their rooms on Ashford-4. Thankfully, while the changes did appear, they also went away within a week or so, except for those few who received a larger dosage while caring for others — only nine of them, mostly spaceport personnel."

"I brought in a team of top geneticists to salvage what they could from the research facility. I also recognized the tremendous benefit some of these genetic modifications could have on our hardened criminals on Xeros-1, a most costly facility to maintain for the worst scum of the Imperium. With the permission of the governor there, we conducted a pilot phase with astonishing success. The worst of the worst were rendered completely harmless. However, that research station had another unfortunate accident while I was on Xeros-1. To avoid mass contamination of the space routes, it had to be incinerated. The threat was eliminated, but so were all the records."

"However, recognizing the immense value of what we had managed to salvage, I used some discretionary funds to get more of the remaining bio agent duplicated. As of this date, all of these hardened criminals have been modified and are now completely harmless to society. They have been moved to an assisted living facility, and Xeros-1 has been closed down. I believe that Gordon has sent you the preliminary savings figures," Slag finished up.

Legate Marhildt, who had been silent, now spoke up, "Yes, I have the figures. At first, I just couldn't believe the sheer magnitude of the savings, twenty-five billion credits each year! I thoroughly reviewed all of Gordon's figures, modifying them slightly, but his final amount is close to accurate. After the tremendous expense of the war with the Federation, this could not come at a better time!"

"Ah yes, savings are valuable," H-cubed added, "but what about the lost genetic research? Can't that be somehow salvaged? Have we lost all of our money's worth from that secret research project? That'll not go over well at all."

"Not entirely, Legate Helyeon. I have set the two remaining geneticists up with a lab on Belsarius-2, again using discretionary funds. They have what data they managed to salvage from Ashford-4, as well as their samples of the bio agents. While there is an enormous amount of work to be done to recreate what was discovered, they believe that they will be able to do so, given, of course, sufficient time, funds, and test subjects. That, I'll leave to you ministers to handle. My task of preservation is now complete. Just for the official records, I used my official authority in dealing with criminals sentenced to life in prison to test the bio agent on those on Xeros-1. I alone took that gamble, and it has paid off handsomely. All further work and developments of these incredible breakthroughs in human genetics, I hereby formally give to you gentlemen. As of now, it belongs officially to you Legates," Slag said formally, releasing himself from any further responsibility in the entire matter.

H-cubed smiled broadly. Snag knew he'd hit the mark squarely. H-cubed could now go before the press and announce these startling discoveries, gaining even more publicity for himself. He'd be assured of having his face before the public for years to come, just announcing new results, as they came from this genetic research. However, it would also be *his* problem to get Senate approval for further testing and research. He didn't relish H-cubed's appearance at the Senate. Two of the senators' bodies were permanently genetically altered from the Ashford-5 accident.

Late August, the senators arrived on Proxima Prime. Senators Zarita and Celenia wore their official senate ball gowns with their twelve foot hoop skirts, while Lelane wore a form fitting pencil style gown. Hers was a pale pink, while the senators' were identical sky blue. Outwardly, only a few signs indicated to the world that their bodies had been genetically modified by the accidental exposure to the bio agent. No one really noticed their even longer, thicker hair, nearly reaching the floor. Rather their foot in diameter, drooping lip plates and gigantic bosoms did announce to any observer that they had been victims of the accident. All three were thankful that their dual sexual organs were not visible.

Holding onto each other, the three made their way through the diplomatic customs post and entered the terminal proper. There they were accosted by droves of reporters, all yelling out questions at them! "Were you the victims of the biological attack on Ashford-5?" "Isn't genetic engineering of humans totally illegal?" "Any comments on the results of the biological accident?" "How are the primitives on Ashford-5 taking the biological attack?" "Senators, any comment on the genetic experiments that took place on Ashford-4?" "How do you feel about the genetic alterations to all of the criminals on the penal planet Xeros-1?" "Senator Valen, didn't you know about this secret research station on Ashford-4 when you were President?" "Senator Valen, should genetic research on human test subjects be legalized?" "Senator, are you really now a hermaphrodite?"

Senator Zarita paused, faced the pack of reporters with their equipment pointed her way. "Yes, as a matter of fact I would like to comment. Genetic experimentation on human beings is unethical, immoral, and illegal. Not even criminals should be subjected to such things, unless the process could be undone, which in this case, it cannot. The accident on Ashford-5 should serve as a reminder to those in power that, no matter how careful one might be, accidents can happen with severe consequences." She turned away, ignoring their further questions, despite their shouting them out to her.

Chapter 22 Politics and the Senate

The first Monday in September, the Senate officially resumed. Over two thousand senators filed into the building, trying to ignore the yells from the many reporters, who continued to shout questions about genetics to them. Arm in arm, Senators Zarita and Celenia made their slow, careful way to their seats beside Senator Tabia Zuarta, trying to ignore the constant staring at their massive bosoms.

Senate President Michael Sanders of Jena-4 finally walked onto the platform at the bottom of the giant amphitheater. The general chatter died down. "Welcome to the fall session of the Imperium Senate. I hope everyone had a relaxing summer vacation. Now, it's time we got back to work once again. During our long break, there have been some very startling events occurring, primarily on the outer rim. Many deeply concern the Senate. Newscasts have not revealed everything. I feel it's vital we begin with a clear explanation of these events. I've called upon our President Balag Snod of Rimus-3 to begin these explanations. President Balag," he motioned with his hand, while moving to his seat just before the platform.

The President walked slowly to center-stage. "Senators, I have prepared a document that outlines in detail the events of this past summer. Please note it's marked Classified, so do not release this to the press outside. Sector ID Minister Slag Vartino was first on the scene. Much of what we know comes from him. During the past war, the Classified Imperium Research Station was established in secret on an uninhabited planet, Ashford-4. Their mission was to create new chemical and biological weapons of mass destruction. The level of security clearance was the very highest, Level Ten. Thus, almost no one knew of its existence. I've done a thorough search of Presidential records and have not been able to discover even who authorized or setup this base. My presumption is that it must have been done by the late President Snarry Knoschy, but I cannot verify this."

"It's my belief these geneticists were working on a last ditch war weapon to be used, should the war seriously threatened the very existence of the Imperium. After fourteen years of research, they made some amazing, startling, and vitally important discoveries that may well open new boundaries in human genetic modifications. However, they did develop a new chemical weapon and a new aerosol delivery mechanism. Apparently, the attack could be launched by a drone, releasing the airborne toxin in a planet's atmosphere. Death occurs within thirty minutes after exposure. Quite deadly. Unfortunately, this development has been totally lost, as I'll explain shortly."

"These geneticists also developed a very wide range of biological genetic alterations. Specifically, their bio agents, which I don't pretend to remotely understand, no longer needs to be tied to a specific person. I'm told in the past, they've had some slight success in taking one person's DNA and modifying it in hopes of curing some deadly disease. One of their breakthroughs has been some form of generic modifying agent, so there is no need to target one person's specific DNA. What this means is simply that these revolutionary bio agents can work their magic on whole populations at one time. Again, they somehow coupled it to their new aerosol agent for maximum dispersal."

"They had prepared three quite large experiments. Each contained rather massive amounts of physical body modifications, as I understand it. They were about to test the aerosol delivery mechanism when disaster struck the research station. While they had apparently employed the best chemical and biological agent containment, they had not considered the effect of a meteor swarm striking a planet, which has no atmosphere. In early June, Ashford-4 passed through just such a swarm right as they were preparing their latest test. As I understand it, they had a low orbit shuttle with the aerosol bio agent canister loaded up with a computer controlled activation mechanism. The meteor storm rained gravel-sized particles down on the facilities, but at tremendous velocities. These pebbles ruptured the roofs and walls of the many buildings."

"Worse, they also ruptured one or more of their stored

chemical agent containers, releasing these toxins into the entire research facilities through the many small holes. While their computer controlled containment system worked to perfection, shutting off all accesses, it was too late. They all died, I'm told, within less than a half hour after exposure. However, one worker was in the shuttle dome when the alarms went off. He broke every protocol on the books in a failed attempt to save himself. Even though he had been exposed to the chemical agent, just as all of the others there were, he got into the shuttle and smashed it through the overhead dome, which would not open because of the containment protocols. This small shuttle isn't capable of interplanetary travel, but nevertheless, he entered the coordinates of the nearest spaceport, the one on Ashford-5."

"There wasn't enough fuel to get him there, and he was dead not long after activating the automated controls. The computer guided the shuttle to the inhabited world, but then the preprogrammed bio agent dispersal program activated. The shuttle circled the planet ten times before losing sufficient speed to attempt a crash landing at the port. Thus, all of the inhabitants of Ashford-5 were infected with their experimental biological agent."

"Before long, everybody on that world began showing the signs of genetic modifications. Yes, we could be here today negotiating the largest monetary settlement in Imperium history! We were very, very lucky that the actual quantity of the bio agent was insufficient permanently to alter genetically most everyone there. We believe the quantity used was sufficient to alter the ten test subjects on Ashford-4. While the inhabitants spent a nightmare week or so, for most, the genetic modifications reversed themselves, and their bodies returned to normal."

"However, as most of you have heard, some others received significantly larger dosages. We believe those who spent most of their time assisting the infected personnel were the ones who received these larger doses. Governor Katrina Lutgard, Doctor Whitney Jones, Carla Childa, and Elfe Heilwig were those who received too high a dose. It's to their credit that these four tended to the needs of the spaceport personnel, though they have paid the price."

"Likewise, Queen Amy, her assistant, Jan, their Senator, Zarita, and her wife, Senator Celenia, and her companion were also similarly infected, as they cared for their people. I've been told by Senator Zarita that perhaps fifty others on Ashford-5 were also permanently affected, presumably because they tended to others."

"At this time, I must outline the genetic changes this experiment made in their bodies. I realize this will be highly personal to the two senators, but it's vital to your understanding of this whole process," President Balag said apologetically. "The genetic changes were impressive and far reaching. Both men and women ended up becoming hermaphrodites. Yes, they have both sexual organs, and they are fully functional." He began to outline the many other changes that had occurred.

"Why is this important? Somehow, Senator Celenia now has arms and hands once more. A miracle of genetics. We all hope that in time, we can discover just how this was done. Think of the incredible benefits to all those who have lost a limb, if such could be regenerated. Keep that in mind. I'll return to that later."

"It was at this point, that Sector ID Minister Slag got involved. He brought a group of geneticists to Ashford-4 in an attempt to salvage what could be. Such monumental advances should not be lost to us. They discovered that two additional experiments were scheduled right after the successful test that accidentally struck Ashford-5. As it turned out, we owe a great debt of gratitude to Sector ID Minister Slag, who recognized a new and vitally important use of these additional experiments, as a result of a second unfortunate accident at the research station."

"Shortly after repairing the facilities, two of those geneticists were accidentally exposed to the second bio agent experiment. In addition to their bodies being altered in the same manner as those on Ashford-5, in addition, these two lost their arms. They apparently withered away and simply fell off. The ID Minister realized that this particular modification had a very important application. Thus, he took that sample, along with the third experimental sample, and two of the geneticists with him."

"Before we go down that path, let me finish up with Ashford-4. You'll see the impact in just a moment. Not long after Minister Slag left, there was yet another unfortunate accident at the facility. We believe that the initial meteorite damage was far more severe than was at first suspected. Anyway, there was a catastrophic failure that was about to release all of the volumes of remaining chemical and biological agents into space. Had that happened, most space routes in the outer rim would have become infected. The commander of the battle cruiser had no choice but to follow Protocol 89. The entire complex was disintegrated before contaminating the surrounding space. Hence, all of the research records, data, and remaining samples have been lost."

"However, the two geneticists that went with Minister Slag did have some of those records with them, along with samples of the second and third experimental bio agents. Thus, some of that incredible genetic research has not been wholly lost to us."

"In case you've forgotten, Xeros-1 holds the Maximum Security Prison of the Imperium. This broiling planet has a very costly eco-dome system that makes life possible and escape impossible. It is the most secure prison in the Imperium. Only the hard-core criminals that have been sentenced to life are housed there. Multiple murderers predominate. As you may also know, each new arriving prisoner has his voice removed by a medical machine. That has really kept these most violent of prisoners under reasonable control. However, as Sector ID Minister Slag correctly realized, these second and third bio-genetic modification agents could be applied to these worst offenders, making it physically impossible for them to commit further crimes and hence the need to house them on this most expensive prison facility."

"The modifications are two, which go beyond the physical changes suffered by those on Ashford-5. In the first batch, they lose their arms as well, while in the second batch, in addition to losing their arms, they lose their sight. In conjunction with the prison's governor, they exposed two dozen of the worst offenders in the prison. The results were just as Sector ID Minister Slag expected. These most violent criminals are no longer capable of executing any crime at all. Further, they've been moved to assisted living housing, since they need help with everything."

"Recognizing the massive benefits, he then used some of the prison's Discretionary Funds to setup his two geneticists with a temporary lab and had them duplicate the bio agent, which they still had — the agent of the second experiment. As of this date, all of the prisoners on Zeros-1 have been treated. All now appear as senators Zarita and Celenia do, only their arms are missing. All have been moved into an assisted living complex. This not only ends all possibilities of further criminal activities on their part, but it has also resulted in a drastic monetary savings to the Imperium. To discuss this aspect, I ask the Finance Minister, Legate Marhildt Chyldt to come up here and address this."

Legate Marhildt walked onto the platform, standing beside President Balag. "Greetings senators. I've done a very careful study of the financial situation. A copy of my report is attached to President Balag's full report. In essence, we no longer need to operate that facility on Xeros-1. Factoring in the cost of the assisted living facilities, the yearly savings amounts to twenty-five billion five hundred six million four hundred sixteen thousand eighty-five credits. As of this date, I've placed these funds into a special account and will await the Senate's appropriation of these savings. If you desire, I'm prepared to meet with your Budget Committee and make some recommendations as to where I believe this sizeable amount could be best spent. For next year's budget, this amount can be redacted from your budget expense lists." As he expected, quite a few gasps echoed, when the vast figure was duplicated by the many senators.

President Balag then spoke again. "Next, I would like to call upon our State-Planning Minister, Legate Helyeon H. Hoon. He'll outline some proposals I would like the Senate at least to consider. Legate Helyeon," he again motioned for the rotund man to join him.

"Greetings senators. It's so good to see all your faces once more. As you have heard, this session we're bringing you most incredible news indeed. Let me begin by pointing out just how revolutionary this genetic research actually is. The active bio agents are generic in nature, not tied to any one person's precise DNA. It can and does affect large groups of people at one time. That alone is quite revolutionary. Further, the modifications to individual genes are likewise vitally important. As he mentioned, it holds the promise to be able to regenerate lost limbs! Impressive."

"However, since so much of the underlying research has been lost due to these three serious accidents, many long years of genetic research and study must be done to recover what has been done and lost. So first, I would like you to consider setting up an official Genetics Research Facility to pursue this research fully."

"Second, I would like you to consider expanding the scope of prisoners to be genetically altered. Xeros-1 contained only the most violent and worst criminals in the Imperium. There are many other prisons that contain other criminals, who have been sentenced to life behind bars. I would suggest we could achieve further reductions in the cost of prison operations by also subjecting all prisoners, who have been sentenced to life behind bars, to these same genetic modifications. Housing them in assisted living facilities is vastly less expensive than housing them in prisons. I'm willing to work with you and Legate Marhildt on just how much more could be saved by so doing."

"Third, if you elect to take this second action, then you might consider also subjecting other criminals, whose sentences are rather long, to these same genetic modifications. As you know, recidivism among these is extremely high. This would end all chances of repeat offenders, but this might be too severe. Nevertheless, when the population of the Imperium learns what happens to hardened criminals, this might act as a deterrent, lowering the crime rates."

"Fourth, I would like you to consider the possibility of legalizing genetic research upon willing, volunteering people. Realistically, this step will far more rapidly assist those studying and researching these amazing discoveries, perhaps even bring forth new regeneration methods within a decade. Of course, I also realize this is one very hot potato as the saying goes. Just reconsider it with an eye on what was discovered during the war effort and what could well happen in our lifetimes."

"Fifth, I would also like you to consider offering some compensation to the Ashford-5 victims of the bio agent attack. I feel that, while we cannot undo what has been permanently done to them, we can at least offer them some compensation for the tragic accident."

"Finally, I'll help drum up support for you by discussing these ideas with the many reporters. Pro or con, this will help mobilize your constituents behind your vote. As always, thank you for allowing me to explain my ideas with you today," H-cubed finally finished up, as always fishing for political support among the senators. He'd played them well, he thought. There was bound to be a huge amount of controversy over these proposals. By his going public, he hoped to raise voter emotions and opinions sufficiently, so their senators would be more inclined to appease their own voters and not make behind the scenes deals with other senators.

After the three men left the Senate, Senate President Michael Sanders again took center-stage. "Well, there, it's official. Obviously, we now have an extraordinary number of items to consider."

Senator Ari Laag rose. As always, she was dressed in a very fine business suit, her continuous slam against the Senate rules concerning the dress code for female Senators. "I believe the first action we should consider is that of compensation to those who were permanently harmed by the Imperium accident on Ashford-4. Before we create new messes, we should handle the original ones."

Senator Tabia rose, "I second Senator Ari's suggestion. Before we discuss spending the funds that have been saved on new projects, we should first compensate those who were harmed by the illegal research project. No one has yet said how those researchers managed to get around the Senate legislation that outlaws genetic experimentation on human

336

beings. I find this whole affair more than appalling. It's an outright slam in our very faces. I would also like to propose a full Senate Investigation to determine just who did this and how they were able to get around our very explicit laws concerning human experimentation."

Another senator rose. "While I appreciate Senator Tabia's outrage at this incredible violation of our previously passed legislation regarding human experimentation, at this time, I do not see that an investigation would be able to turn up much. President Snarry is dead, as are those who were involved in that research station on Ashford-4. With all knowledgeable parties dead, it would seem counterproductive to waste time on such an investigation. What's done is done. Move on. Does anyone have a suggestion for the amount of compensation that should be paid to those who were harmed? How do we compensate the primitives of Ashford-5? Certainly, our senators and Governor Katrina and her staff must be compensated, but what of the mere primitives?"

So the haggling began. After several hours, the Senate decided on two hundred thousand credits per affected Imperium citizen and fifty thousand per native Ashford-5 individuals. The latter amount would be given to Queen Amy to be distributed to those who needed it. They also gave five hundred thousand credits to the two now helpless geneticists, who had lost their arms and were being cared for on Ashford-5. The notion being this extra compensation would help defray their assisted living costs, since both were only in their early twenties. Ruth and Alex were pleased with this generosity and insisted on later paying Amy for the servants, who spent so much of their time caring for their needs.

However, now the Senate became a real hot bed of discussions, bordering on out right arguments over whether or not to even fund continuing genetic research, which was technically still outlawed. Long days of arguments followed, punctuated by continuous press, both pro and against.

One senator finally pointed out, "Look. We now have traced the names of the hundred test subjects used on Ashford-4. They were all criminals sentenced to life in prison on Xeros-1 without any chance of parole. Further, they

337

volunteered for the experiments. Minister of Prisons Gordon Knox has sent us the hundred signed documents. I say we must not just throw away any chance of recovering the knowledge that was discovered on Ashford-4. We've paid hard earned Imperium tax credits on that project. It would be criminal of us just to throw it all away. I say we simply must fund this recovery project."

"With all due respect, senator, how can they do that without conducting further tests?" another yelled back. "Are you going to volunteer to be a test subject?"

"We could offer a monetary incentive to those who volunteer," another suggested.

"And open the Imperium up to lawsuits when the subject dies from the test? I think not!" another yelled back.

"Look," another attempted to moderate the venom flying about, "there is no question these researchers have stumbled on to some vitally important knowledge. If you don't believe this, just ask how our own Senator Celenia feels about having her arms and hands regenerated by these bio agents that were discovered. Ask her. Should we just abandon all that research and forget about the enormous impact that research could well have for us all?" Many eyes turned towards Senator Celenia, who flushed.

Eventually, the Senate passed a motion to permit the ongoing study of the Ashford-4 experimental data, in hopes that, in time, it would produce results of a miracle nature. This led immediately to a lengthy debate over the need of test subjects on which to experiment. Several leading researchers were called to testify to that need. The arguments raged in the Senate and on the nightly news. If advancements were to be made, ultimately tests would have to be conducted on humans. One researcher summed it up succinctly, "All the theory in the world cannot supplant a simple test in the real world. You won't know the veracity of your theory until you can test it."

Finally, the Senate passed, but only barely, a new law allowing volunteers to become test subjects, as long as they came from the pool of criminals sentenced to life behind bars without the possibility of parole. As soon as this crack appeared, the Senate then was able to accept what had already been done to the lifers on Xeros-1, legalizing what Slag had already done there. Thus, the Senate modified the penal code for those convicted of such serious crimes that they were to be imprisoned until they died. This made headline news for days afterwards.

From there, the Senate was willing to subject all of the remaining prisoners, who were held in far less secure prisons on other planets, to the same genetic modifications as had been done to those on Xeros-1. However, they passed a provision allowing each such prisoner one opportunity for choice. When the time came for a prisoner to be genetically modified, he or she was given the option for signing up to become a human genetics test subject instead. Those who did so were then held until the new research project needed more human test subjects.

Now, Legate Marhildt was given the task of determining the savings that resulted from the closing of all the medium security "lifer" prisons, but one. That lone prison held those who opted to take their chances as human guinea pigs. Within a month, he added about another twenty billion credits into the available funds that the Senate could redirect to other projects within the Imperium.

Then, the Senate took up the highly controversial proposal of also subjecting other criminals, whose sentences were rather long to these same genetic modifications. "We have to tackle and consider the rather significant recidivism problem among these criminals. Rehab seldom works on far too many. Repeat criminals are extremely commonplace. This would end all chances of repeat offenders, as H-cubed has pointed out," Senate President Michael explained calmly.

"Yes, but some are rehabilitated. We should also consider that some are later found to be innocent and have to be released. These genetic modifications are permanent. There is no way to undo them once they've been done. We must be very careful in this arena," Senator Tabia pointed out. "Even such prisoners have human rights too."

Arguments flew in all directions for several days. Finally, Senator Tabia made an conciliatory offer. "Look, what about establishing a three conviction rule. If any criminal is convicted three times for crimes, he or she is then given the genetic modifications, ending their career in crime." The Ataro Empire fought against any and all genetic modifications, but thus far had lost the battles. Emperor Kino had finally given in to political pressure and had suggested that she make this compromise. It passed, again by a narrow margin. Now, it would be up to the Supreme Court to determine if these new laws would stand.

Finally, the Senate began lengthy discussions on how to appropriate the approximately extra fifty billion credits that were now available to be sent this physical year. Every senator now had something to say. All wanted to be seen as bringing some to their home worlds. Senator Zarita found the meetings had once more turned into utter boredom for her, though Celenia continued to work to gain some of the funds for projects on her world of Winno-3.

Into the middle of these lengthy discussions came word that many of these newly modified prisoners were now pregnant. This was followed shortly thereafter with the rather startling news that these children would be carrying forward the genetic modifications of their parent or parents. A whole new round of discussions began.

"Look, there is no truth to the saying that a child of a criminal becomes a criminal himself. Criminality isn't inherited. We should separate these children and see that they get as good an education as possible and all the help they need so that they can become productive members of the Imperium," Senator Tabia suggested. Senate President Michael Sanders threw his weight behind her suggestion.

"What can a helpless man or woman actually do that is productive?" another senator argued.

"So you believe that Senator Celenia of Winno-3 has not done anything productive until now?" Senator Tabia countered.

"Well," he sounded flustered, "she is a notable exception."

"They could well have brilliant minds; they could be geniuses," another female senator argued. Thus, the arguments began once more, lasting for an entire week. At times, the discussions were quite bitter.

At last, Senate President Michael Sanders made some deals behind the scenes. He then spoke up, "Look, we simply cannot ignore these special needs children. That won't fly on any world. I would like to make a suggestion. Let's set up a special school to service only these children and see how that goes. The school will have to provide room and board and care for these children. We can have Legates Marhildt and H-cubed work out the details and give us a preliminary cost figure. We can evaluate the program yearly."

After more discussion, his suggestion was accepted and passed, but again by only a narrow margin. H-cubed then went on several news programs to outline the new, humane program.

Senator Tabia then introduced a new bill, intentionally interrupting the ongoing arguments over the disbursement of the excess billions. "Look, we need to set strong, unquestioned limits on this genetic research. If we do not, nearly every world is going to start their own research projects. This will quickly get totally out of hand. What's going to happen if World A develops or even simply copies these genetic modifications, these bio agents? One night while we are all sleeping, they could send a few drones over Proxima Prime. A week later, we all here could be just as helpless as those prisoners of Xeros-1 are. The danger of genetic warfare is now all too real. We must enact some very strong legislation prohibiting unauthorized genetic research."

Now the arguments flew hot and heavy. Just who would grant such authorizations? No world wanted to be left out of their potential to perform genetic research studies. The world that had it could well use the threat of such bio agents against the other worlds. This was just what Emperor Kino feared most — that such weapons of mass destruction would grow and multiply on many different worlds within the Imperium. After that, one mistake could well spark a disaster of unimaginable proportions, perhaps destroying the very Imperium itself. These arguments continued unabated up to the time of the winter three-week break without showing any signs of resolution.

Chapter 23 The IBI and the Bops

Beneath the Sector ID Ministers, lay the IBI, the Imperium Bureau of Investigations, from which most of the current ID Ministers had come, rising up the ranks. This large organization's purpose was the gathering of intelligence and the prosecution of Imperium criminals. To become an Imperium Criminal, one had to commit a crime on another world than your home world. Such earned you this dubious distinction. Local crimes were handled by the individual worlds and their own police forces.

As knowledge of the newly developed genetic alteration bio weapon became known and used on the hardened criminals, the top leaders of the IBI became quite alarmed. The potential for its abuse was estimated at nearly ninety percent. The head of the IBI sent notice of this to the Commander, along with his promise to keep as many IBI field agents on the watch for such abuses among the many worlds of the Imperium.

The Commander was the only name used by the illusive head of the small and top secret sub-organization within the IBI known as the Bops. So secretive and illusive was the Bops, that only the head of the entire IBI knew of its existence. Whenever there was a change in that post, the outgoing head underwent mental modifications, eliminating his knowledge of the Bops, and the incoming head was "educated" by the current Commander of the Bops.

Just what was the Bops? Those within that organization knew it stood for Black Operations. Their mission and goals were to use any means whatsoever to stop terrorists and other large criminal organizations throughout the entire Imperium. Membership within the Bops was for life. No one ever "retired" from the Bops. When they lost their edge or were no longer fit or up to standards, they were terminated or cancelled, meaning killed.

The Bops had the latest weapons, ships, communications gear, and science laboratories. Yes, their budget seemed unlimited. The headquarters was on Proxima Prime and located on the actual surface of the planet, some three miles below the apparent surface. Actually, Bops HQ was a giant complex extending nearly a mile beneath the rocky surface. The complex was huge, containing a miniature spaceport, an equipment arsenal, living quarters, training rooms, a giant comm center, and all manner of science labs as well. There were several smaller Bops stations located on some other key planets, three within the hub of the galaxy and two in the middle of the spiral arm.

The personnel of Bops were handpicked for their special abilities and skills. They were literally "plucked out" of their old life and inserted into the Bops, without any choice in the matter and without the possibility of ever returning to their old lives. Training was intense, and many didn't pass the ultra-high standards and were cancelled. Failure on a mission was simply not an option, not ever.

It was early July. The Commander held a Divisional Status Meeting with many of his Div Heads in attendance. Without the slightest trace of human emotion, he asked, "So where are we on identifying how the Consortium was killed?"

Forty year old Leroy, head of R&D, took off his thick glasses and nodded to Doc Lambert, who was also forty and head of the Infirmary. It was his subtle hint that he was to speak first. Doc Lambert spoke equally calmly, "From the official autopsy findings and the samples recovered from the three men, COD was, how shall I put this? Severe brain degeneration. Brain ceases to function; body dies."

The Commander looked away for a second, and then his blue eyes drilled Doc Lambert. "How?"

"Now you are asking the right question, Commander. How? That's just it. I've no idea," the doctor replied, nodding to Leroy.

Leroy spoke up, "We've been conducting a number of experiments to see just how a human brain can be partially liquefied, while it's still inside the person. We've ruled out drugs. We've ruled out an injection. There were no puncture marks on their bodies. Frankly, Commander, this one has me stumped. The only way I can reproduce this effect is to microwave it. Yet, that couldn't have happened. If they'd been somehow microwaved, the doc would have seen all manner of signs elsewhere on the bodies and heads. Eyes were totally normal. Frontal lobes just behind them were partially liquefied. Cannot be electrocution; there were no contact points found on their bodies. In fact, there was absolutely nothing else amiss on their bodies."

The Commander was silent for a minute, causing the assembled department heads to squirm slightly. All knew the Commander wanted answers, not speculation, not an "I don't know answer." "So you're telling me those three men had their brains liquefied, and you don't know how that happened, Leroy?"

"Partially liquefied. Microwaved. Best guess," Leroy corrected him. He was a stickler for being precise.

The Commander gave him a long cold stare. "New weapon system?"

"Doubt it. Doc would've seen outward signs on their heads or bodies. They were entirely clean, except for their cranial cavities. Don't know of any type of weapon that can microwave the cranial cavity without also doing the same thing to the hair, skin, and face," Leroy stated factually.

After a long pause, the Commander stated, "We've seen this method of assassination before. Fifteen years ago. Legates Daag Tall and Herman Mels. Same MO. Same results. Whoever is behind this is still around, still active. Fifteen years, Leroy. How many more years until you have identified the weapon or drug?" His voice tone held a hint of condemnation.

"Yes, same MO, same results. Liquefied brains. I'm no closer to an explanation now than I was back then, Commander," Leroy admitted his failure, wondering it he was about to be terminated.

"Then, allow me to add a new dimension to this unknown assassin and their method. Lela, play the recording," the Commander ordered.

Lela was the head of the Intel Studies Department. Her group monitored literally all of the incoming field agent reports from the entire IBI, as well as those from the ID

Ministers. They also had many other sources of information they sifted through on a daily basis. She was twenty-five with short black hair and thick framed glasses, also black, perched on her nose. "Picked this up from Rim Sector ID Minister Slag," her emotionless alto voice contrasted with Leroy's bass. They watched his report of the discovery of the dead bodies of Doctor Aarok Laron and his assistant, Broc Lest. Goo coming out of their ears, noses, and around their eyes was the description used.

Both Doc Lambert and Leroy looked quite surprised. Doc Lambert hastily said, "Yes, to the untrained eye, those would be the outward signs of the liquefied brains. So it's happened again? When can I see the autopsy?"

"Can't." The Commander's stern face yielded no clue. "Their bodies were disintegrated when the battle cruiser blew up the secret research station on Ashford-4. Protocol 89 invoked."

"Ashford? Where's that world?" asked Leroy.

"Far outer rim. Just a few days ago," Lela answered.

Leroy let out a rush of air. "Wow. This assassin sure gets around! I thought it was contained to the hub, Proxima Prime. The far outer rim? What the hell is going on?"

"That's what we're here for, Leroy," the Commander's stern voice forced Leroy to lose his sudden emotional reactions.

Lela continued, "We have a connection here between the liquefied brains and chemical and biological weaponry. Could a biological or chemical agent be responsible for their deaths?"

Leroy ran his long fingers through his close cropped hair. "Could be, but not likely. Usually, such agents leave many other traces behind. This is totally isolated to the cranial cavity. Nothing else on the bodies is affected in any way. So, our assassin is still active after fifteen years, perhaps more so now than then. I don't get it."

"That's what we must discover and fast. I was hoping that there would be a tie in to these chemical and biological weapons on Ashford-4," the Commander commented dryly, though he was clearly disappointed.

Torres, the head of the Interrogation Department, spoke up. "Damn. Just when I thought I had a profile going on our assassin. Until this one, he or she has only struck men, who were guilty of very severe crimes, men in very high places. These latest killings, the genetics doctor and his assistant, don't seem to fit the pattern, unless they are guilty of crimes I'm not yet aware of."

The Commander spoke up, "Torres, don't discount that angle just yet. He was a geneticist, and he was there in that lab with the new chemical and biological weaponry."

"Right, Commander. I still think the Righteous Vigilante is our best profile on this individual," Torres stated. She was thirty, blonde with blue eyes, and extremely attractive.

Lela added, "Really gets around the entire Imperium. Need to add that to the Righteous Vigilante's profile. The only ship around Ashford-4 at the time of their deaths was a battle cruiser in high orbit, guarding the facilities. They've no record of any other ship in the vicinity of Ashford-4, let alone landing at the research facility. However, I do have one additional piece of Intel I've scrounged from that battle cruiser's surveillance of the facility. This fact was not reported by the cruiser's general. He probably wasn't aware of this or if he was, chose not to mention it in his official report. Some hours before they received the Protocol 89 signal from the research facility's computer, the landing dome opened and closed. No ship entered that was visible. Just before the signal came, the dome opened again and the shuttle came out, carrying the two stunned geneticists."

"From this, I can speculate that a cloaked ship, probably a transport, landed there and did something for several hours. Likewise, the two surviving geneticists were acting like they were idiots or morons for several days. Perhaps, their minds were also subjected to this mysterious weapon that liquefies brains, but that somehow, they escaped death," Lela speculated.

The Commander spoke up. "Won't work. Timing is off. The doctor and assistant were reported dead a day before this cloaked ship arrived, Lela. Still, it's an interesting speculation.

Could those on this mysterious cloaked ship have caused their deaths, and then raided the place, and perhaps even caused the Protocol 89 event?"

"Now we are dealing with bio terrorists," Doc Lambert blurted out the obvious conclusion.

"Perhaps they are separate events. The two Legates and the three Consortium members had no connection to this research facility or to chemical and biological weaponry," Lela pointed out dryly.

The Commander added, "I think we should consider this unknown assassin has access to one of the latest deep space transports with cloaking capabilities. Lela, I want every such transport accounted for. Meanwhile, we have more serious problems facing us. We're going to have to act quickly."

"The biological agent that's being used on Xeros-1?" asked Leroy. "I need a sample of it."

"Of course," the Commander said without emotion. "I don't have to tell you this is the most serious threat we've faced in some time. Sector ID Minister Slag is putting this bio agent to good use, but because of the accident on Ashford-5 and his prison usage, the entire Imperium will soon know about it. Lord knows what the Senate will do. Lela, what's the chatter saying?"

"Lots. Seems every dealer wants to get his or her hands on a sample. Going to be a bad one. Seems a simple Fabricator Machine can replicate it in quantity," Lela said. The Commander noticed a slight trace of nervousness in her voice.

Well, she ought to be scared of his one, he thought. "Scoby, have you got a Mission Plan for us to acquire a sample prepared?"

Scoby was the thirty year old man in charge of the Statistical and Mission Planning Division. "Yes, Commander. I have them prepared. Ninety percent chance of success. Leroy, you ready with a containment shield? God, we can't have that stuff leaking around here!" He, too, was quite worried about this mission. Bringing back that deadly bio agent here to HQ could well pose an enormous threat to everyone.

"Good. I'll assemble ST1 for this one. Lela, keep a sharp

eye on the chatter. We must be ready to stop anyone, who makes an attempt to get their hands on this stuff. You all know what will happen if we don't succeed with this one. Only takes one batch to slip through our hands. As of now, all ten of the Strike Teams are on Full Alert. Lenard, make sure that you are ready to hand out their equipment on short notice."

Lenard was the thirty-five year old head of the Equipment Department. His group handed out whatever items were needed for any mission. Guns were the least of such things. "Ready, as always, Commander. Got a Containment Field set up for each ST," he replied.

"Okay then, to your posts. Lela, Scoby, stay. ST1 is on their way here as we speak. I'll have you brief them on the details. Ah, here they come now," the Commander barked.

Strike Team 1 was the most experienced team of six in the Bops. Headed by twenty-five year old Peter, the team marched into the room. His MisCom or Mission Commander was Karkoff, twenty-four. Their sharpshooter was Ellen, also twenty-four. Hamil, twenty-three, Blackwell, twenty-two, and Jason, twenty-one, rounded out his team. Each member was highly skilled with all manner of weapons, as well as martial arts. Lightning fast reflexes and keen insights had kept this team alive on more than one mission. They worked well together, a very tight-knit group. Jason was the newest member of the team. Losses were inevitable on missions. Still, these six had managed not to lose a member during the last two years, rather a surprising length of time, compared to the other STs.

"As you know, the bio agent weapon developed on Ashford-4 has been replicated and put to use on every prisoner on Xeros-1," the Commander barked. "We need a sample of that agent. The geneticists have a lab on Belsarius-2. Your mission is to go there and secure a sample for us. Scoby has the MisDs." MisDs was short for Mission Details.

Scoby brought up three-dimensional view of the lab facilities on Belsarius-2. "Here is their containment room. It's sealed at all times. Retinal scans allow entry. Heavily guarded perimeter. This bops is going to be tricky. We can't just steal one of the cylinders and crates. That'll send up all manner of red flags. What you have to do is to retrieve one set, and then use a Fabrication Machine to duplicate it for us, returning the original to the containment room. We'll use the Fabrication Machine on site. The tricky part is that we don't want anyone to know that a sample was duplicated and taken from the facility."

He went on, "You'll arrive above the facility in a cloaked transport. Entrance will be through a storm sewer. After cutting through the grate, you'll get to this ladder here. Their comm center has a junction at Point A. Your task will be to get there, record ten minutes of surveillance video from cameras two, three, and five. Setup a playback loop. Karkoff will stay here at Point A and keep the playback going. Ellen, from Point B, you can monitor any unexpected guards entering the work room and attached Containment Room, Point C. Peter, you have ten minutes to get to Point C, get the Fabrication Machine warming up, get into the Containment Room, find one of the bio agent cylinders and the crate of apparel, get them to the machine, duplicated, and put back in place. As soon as it's duplicated, you two begin evacuation. No matter what goes down, we need those things retrieved, presumably without anyone noticing it. If you are spotted, hold the guards off long enough to retrieve the goods. The goods are all that matter on this mission. Keep that in mind."

The Commander spoke up, "Questions?" Seeing none, he added, "You leave immediately. Lenard has your equipment, including a portable containment facility. Good luck." The six rose solemn-faced and headed down the hall, where they took the elevator down to Level Three, where Lenard's Equipment Department was located. An hour later and carrying their gear, they boarded their deep space transport. After stowing their special equipment, Peter climbed into the pilot's seat, while Karkoff took the navigator's position. He punched in their two sets of coordinates. The first was their rendezvous location with a refueling tanker in deep space about halfway there. The other was Belsarius-2, their destination. If they succeeded, another refueling tanker would meet them later, not far from that world to refuel them again. Scoby had already made the refueling arrangements. These were ordinary tankers that refueled many transport ships that needed to make such long journeys. Officially, they were logged with the tankers as a merchant ship from Acer-3.

When Peter pressed the Execute button, a massive elevator slowly lifted the ship upwards to the surface, where their ship appeared on a private spaceport. A minute later, they were airborne and shifted into hyperspace at once. "Okay, autopilot is activated. We've twenty-four hours to kill before refueling," Peter announced over the intercom. "Check your gear. Then, get some shuteye. I'll take first shift."

Travel time from the hub to the rim took two days at top speed. This was always the really boring part of such missions. With time to kill, they played cards, chatted, and checked their gear several times. During the last six hours, Peter drilled each member on precisely what they were to do, going over and over each step, until he was certain each knew their part by heart. "We cannot afford to be discovered. The whole point of this mission is to retrieve the package without anyone knowing it. So no shooting unless our cover is blown. Karkoff, see that doesn't happen."

"Aye boss," he replied stiffly.

Right on schedule, they dropped out of hyperspace. Cloaked, Peter maneuvered the ship to just above the exit point of the sewer pipe, about a half mile from the actual facility. Everyone but Jason geared up. "Okay, Jason, teleport us down to the pile and stand by. Monitor all frequencies and keep the ship cloaked," Peter ordered, though Jason already had his role memorized.

A few minutes later, the black clad five appeared on the ground and ducked into the opening. Blackwell ignited his torch and began the tedious process of cutting through the steel bars that prevented access, but allowed the water to drain out. "It stinks," Ellen commented.

"Quiet," Peter barked.

Local time was around midnight. It was quite dark outside. After they made it through the grate, they turned on their helmet lights and began moving swiftly down the tunnel. From above in the ship, Jason monitored their progress on his infrared monitor, whispering instructions through their head sets, tiny transducers fastened to their ears.

Arriving at Point A, Peter and Ellen stood guard, guns with silencers pointed in opposite directions down the hall. Peter whispered to Jason, "At Point A." Safely within the cloaked ship, Jason was acting as the Mission Coordinator. He gave them an all clear signal. Quickly, Karkoff used his electronic tools to open the junction box. A few quick alligator clips later, and he began making ten minute recordings from three security cameras. One was a stationary view inside the containment vault; one was a stationary view of the working lab; one was a rotating view of the long hallway that led to this section of the facility.

With Karkoff's electronics now operational, Jason had a 3-d image of the complex. Warm bodies appeared as reddish dots. His team appeared as blue ones. "Guards are at their predicted locations. Six."

Karkoff whispered, "Loops activating now. You have ten minutes. Go!" Four silent, black garbed figures raced to their assigned positions. Soft-soled shoes made no sounds on the concrete flooring. Ellen reached Point B. From her crouched position, she could spot any guard who might walk in on the others from either guard post. She held a gun with silencer in each hand, pointed down each hallway. Now, she waited, senses alert. Peter, Hamil, and Blackwell reached the lab workroom. Peter placed a de-locking device beside the keypad entry system and activated it. A few seconds later, the latch sprung, and the door opened. The three darted inside.

Peter hand-signaled the two to get the Fabrication Machine powered up. He moved over to the heavily re-enforced containment room doors. Again, he used his de-locking device. A minute later, he was inside. Now came the hard part, finding what they came for. All manner of dangerous agents were stored in this room that was blast-proof and self-sealing in the event of even the slightest leak of the agents.

Peter was about to call for help when he finally found them. One side contained a rack of identical cylinders and a matching number of identical crates. He picked one of each and headed back out. Hamil signaled him, and he put both into the Input Bin. The second that the door closed, Hamil pressed the Duplicate button. Now they waited. Two minutes, three, four. Finally, the Completed led lights flashed. "Go!" Peter whispered. Hamil took the newly made crate; Blackwell, the cylinder. Both dashed out of the lab. Peter took the two originals and put them back exactly where he found them.

After closing the door, he used his de-locking device to relock the containment room. Then, he dashed across the lab. "Sixty seconds," Karkoff's voice entered his ear. Peter attached the de-locking device on the lab door and pressed the Lock button. After hearing the click, he grabbed it and raced down the hallway. "Twenty seconds." As he rounded a corner in the long hallway, he spotted Ellen ahead at Point B. "Ten seconds." Just as he passed by her position, she fell in line behind him. Both raced towards Point A, dashing past Karkoff, as he disconnected his alligator clips and stuffed his gear into his pack. Silently, he replaced the comm hub's cover and slipped over to the ladder. A minute later, he joined Peter and Ellen in the sewer tunnel.

After nodding, the three turned on the lamps on their headgear and made their way down the long tunnel. When they reached the entrance point, the two held the iron grate in place, while Peter used his torch to weld it back into place. Another ten minutes passed before the three black figures moved out into the open. Jason activated the teleport, and the three arrived inside the cloaked ship. Peter slipped past Jason and sat down in the pilot's chair. He pressed the Execute button, and the ship began to rise higher into the air, and then slipped into hyperspace.

"Well done," Peter spoke over the intercom. "Refueling now. Karkoff, fire off a Mission Completed Status." His Mission Communicator had just reached the navigator's seat to Peter's right. He nodded and sent the signal, an encrypted burst of sound consisting of three "dots." If the mission had failed, the burst would only have been a single sound dot.

Over the intercom, Hamil's voice reassured everyone. "Cylinder is now in the portable containment field. We're safe."

"Now that's what I want to hear!" Ellen called out, a

distinct sound of relief in her otherwise emotionless voice tone.

Beside Peter, Karkoff muttered, "You and me both, kid!" Turning to Peter, he added, "I'm not going anywhere near R&D from now on!" Peter flashed him a rare, but brief, smile. Two days later, they arrived back at Bops HQ on Proxima Prime. While Leroy was quite pleased to have this sample of the biological genetic agent, few others shared his enthusiasm.

After checking their gear with Lenard, they headed to debriefing. That done, Peter, Ellen, and Karkoff visited Lela in her Level 2 Intel Studies Department. "We miss anything?" Peter asked.

Lela flashed him a brief smile. "ST2 terminated the bombers, who took out the spaceport tanker a while back. Told you we'd get them eventually. Lot of chatter about this new bio agent, though."

As the days passed, the Commander continued to pace his office. The Senate was getting the full briefing from the President now. Lela was secretly recording that session for future reference and cross-comparisons with other Intel, looking for security breaches and other discrepancies. "Shit's really going to fly on this one," he muttered to the walls. By that, he meant that soon every crime syndicate in the Imperium would do whatever was necessary to get their own hands on samples of this new bio agent. What made matters far worse was that they only needed to get a hold of one cylinder. A Fabrication Machine could then turn that single sample into a complete biological weapon of mass destruction. Of course, many other planets would also like to get their hands on a sample as well. Same reasons. He who had it could threaten to use it. Yet, from the Commander's point of view, there would be no winners in a biological war.

When they heard the Senate passing the law legalizing the genetic alteration of the lifetime criminals on Xeros-1, the Commander's reaction was simple. He opened a complex-wide channel, "This is the Commander. The Bops is now on Alert Red. In case you've forgotten, this is our highest alert status. Don't expect it to be lowered anytime soon. The Senate has legalized genetic modification of lifers." Not long after that, the head of the IBI put the entire Imperium Bureau of Investigation also on Alert Red, all throughout the vast Imperium. Security was raised to its highest level. He also ordered three battle cruisers to hang around Belsarius-2. Not to be out done, Sector ID Minister Slag ordered security at the research facility tripled.

During the weeks that followed, everyone in power throughout the Imperium very carefully monitored the Senate's activities. This whole genetic research topic was a particularly polarizing one. Few were on the fence. Some enthusiasts swore this discovery would revolutionize human genetics, taking it a giant step beyond the up to now enormous step of complete DNA mapping, some centuries back. Regeneration of limbs and failing organs were proclaimed to be just around the corner. Others claimed cures for all manner of terminal illnesses would soon be found.

Others claimed that doomsday had finally arrived. Soon, whole cities, whole planets would be genetically destroyed, as those who had the bio agents would take over total control of the Imperium. Indeed, in some ways, the Consortium perished a year too soon, for they may well have attempted just that!

Lela could not remember a time when there was so much underground chatter occurring. Every criminal organization was trying to get their hands on a sample of the bio agent, as well as nearly every planet. The latter, of course, attempted to work through official channels, attempting to get a sample for their own geneticists. Lela complained to the Commander, "If we had a hundred STs we could not keep up with all these! I need ten times the number of agents on the monitors here, just to keep up!"

Showing no emotion, the Commander replied, "Lela, do your job; just do it."

Her face lost its brief display of emotion. "Of course," she replied calmly.

Of course was the reply that a little known criminal gave to one of his henchmen. The Chameleon was a genetic freak, a human who could change his whole appearance at will, appearing as a duplicate of any person he ever saw. Until now, he and his small gang had been content to pilfer mostly interplanetary diamond deliveries. He was quite passionate about these stones. Many criminal organizations knew of him, and even a few had made use of his unique skills at one time or another.

The ongoing debates over genetic research and the newly discovered bio agents coupled with the shocking news of its use on the lifers had not passed by the Chameleon. At first, he found the whole mess rather amusing; it didn't concern him. There weren't any diamonds involved.

By the middle of October, a dozen attempts had been made to steal samples of the bio agent cylinders. All had been handled by the stepped up security at the lab facility on Belsarius-2. There, security was at an all-time high. Still, many, many organizations desperately wanted to get their hands on a sample and were willing to take whatever risk was required and pay whatever the price might be.

One little known mafia group, the Soldiers of Fortune, based on the hub planet of Donner-3, became quite interested. General Snaggard had no real use for bio warfare, but via it, he saw his organization expanding outward to many other planets. At his weekly planning session, he explained, "Look, if we got our hands on a sample of this new bio agent, we can replicate it. We would then have other syndicates in the Imperium coming to us to purchase a sample from us. We can charge whatever we like, and they will pay."

"General, a dozen have tried to steal it already. Security is too tight. They are guarding it like it was gold or something," his Number Two countered. "It'd be suicide for us to try. Besides, the lab is way out on the rim."

"Quite true, quite. But there is another way. We don't want to get our hands dirty on this one; yet, I can't pass up the Golden Chalice. I believe I know just how we can get our hands on it. I'll need the Star of Rose. Number Two, work out how we can steal that diamond, will you, good fellow. Let me know when it is in our possession," General Snaggard ordered and left the meeting.

Two weeks later, he held the Star of Rose, reputedly one of the largest cut diamonds in the Imperium. The incredible stone was the size of his fist. Its worth, incalculable, some put it in the billions of credits. It had not been actually sold since it was first cut. After making a good video clip of the gemstone, he opened a secure line to the Chameleon. It had taken nearly a week to arrange this secure call, however. Finding this elusive man and getting him to agree to take the call had already cost him a hundred thousand in diamonds.

"Chameleon. Observe. I hold in my hand the Star of Rose." General Snaggard paused, allowing the Chameleon time to drool over this most precious stone. He then said, "I have a little job that only you can do for me. If you are successful at retrieving what I want, the Star of Rose is yours." He outlined what he needed done.

"Of course," the Chameleon replied. "Consider it done. I'll need some time. I don't even know where this Belsarius-2 is at."

"Take all the time you need, Chameleon. The Star of Rose is right here in my hand," the general replied. Even over the video comm, he could sense the desires of the Chameleon to possess this diamond.

The Chameleon and his operation were strictly "low tech." They did everything by hand, no fancy gadgets, and no super electronic devices. He knew the Imperium forces would be scouring Belsarius-2 for all such things. Even a cloaked ship could well be detected now. The Imperium forces had placed all of their most advanced electronics around that world to protect this lab. His chances lay precisely in his low tech methods.

After a week's study, the Chameleon and his three henchmen landed on Proxima Prime. There, they began their preparations. It was a simple matter for the Chameleon to shift his appearance to that of one of the Security Guards of one of Belsarius-2's senators, Senator Chambers. Soon, he realized the time to strike would be during their three-week winter break. The second week in December, he struck.

Senator Chambers walked out of the Senate at the conclusion of their last meeting. During the break, he had made plans to return to Belsarius-2 to confer with their President. These genetic research matters were taking their toll on everyone's patience. As he stepped out, his Security Detachment moved to his side and followed him to his waiting shuttle, where his long-time driver sat waiting for him. He nodded and said, "Home and then to the spaceport, please." The Security Guards nodded in turn and returned to their duties, escorting other senators safely to their waiting shuttles. Senator Chambers had no idea that his driver was not his driver. He looked and spoke just as he always did, but it was the Chameleon. He and his three henchmen had overpowered the driver and disposed of his body. The Chameleon then altered his physical form to match that of the driver.

As he drove the shuttle, though actually it was all computer controlled, he said, "There is a bottle of very fine wine there for you, senator, compliments of Senate President Michael Sanders. Help yourself. He said it was superb."

"Thank you, I will indeed," Senator Chambers replied. After taking a few sips, he drooped over, unconscious. The Chameleon altered their destination, stopping to pick up his three henchmen, now disguised as Security Guards. They stripped the senator of his clothing and all forms of identification. After injecting him with a powerful sedative, they tied him up. He would be out for days. They left him in an abandoned building. Now, the Chameleon again altered his form. His three men watched, as he became a perfect duplicate of Senator Chambers. One of his men stepped into the pilot's seat, while "Senator Chambers" and the other two climbed in as passengers. Soon, they arrived at the spaceport.

After checking his ID card, the small group walked out on the tarmac to the senator's deep space transport ship and boarded it. A half hour later, with proper clearances in order, they left for Belsarius-2, arriving in four days. There, the Chameleon went through the motions of meeting with the President, while his three henchmen cased the research facility.

Two days later, in the morning, the Chameleon appeared at the door of the home of one of the geneticists, disguised as a Security Guard. A simple black jack knocked the geneticist out and his three henchmen joined him. After drugging the geneticist, the Cameleon now altered his form yet again, appearing as the scientist. Still wearing their Security Guard's uniforms, his three henchmen escorted him to the lab, where he was allowed entry after swiping the stolen ID card. His three men took their seats outside alongside many other well-armed Security Guards, waiting to escort their charges, should they wish to travel elsewhere.

Inside, the Chameleon easily found the working lab, nodding back to all those who nodded to him or greeted him. Shortly, he entered the containment room and found the rack of cylinders and crates. He signed one pair out on the computer station there and carried them out to the lab. At the Fabrication Machine, he made a duplicate copy, dutifully logging this transaction into the workstation there. Then, he returned the original pair and again signed them back into the containment room. Back at the machine, he picked up the copies and walked to the back of the room, where a lot of equipment was busily doing things of which he knew not. Why? No one was around here. Quietly, he altered his form again; the crate and cylinder merged with his body, though he now looked like he'd gained some weight. Unobtrusively, he walked out of the lab, signing himself out as required. A bit later, his three Security Guards jumped up and took their positions around him, escorting him to his shuttle.

While in the shuttle, he again altered his form to the senator. At the spaceport, he checked in. Within a half hour, the senator's deep space transport was again in hyperspace. This time after a refueling stop, they altered their destination coordinates to Donner-3. As they landed at one of the spaceports on Donner-3, the Chameleon placed a secure call to General Snaggard. "Package delivered. Locker 218."

"Thirty minutes," General Snaggard replied and hung up. "Damn! He pulled it off! Okay, let's get going. To the spaceport, soldiers!" He wrapped the huge diamond up in a silk bag and put it into his pocket. A half hour later, he and his men arrived at the wall of public lockers at the spaceport. There was a lot of foot traffic in and around the area. One old cleaning lady was mopping the floor, but nothing seemed out of place. The general nodded to one of his men, who forced open the locker. Inside was a large bag. The two men opened it and looked inside. There was the cylinder and the crate. Satisfied, the general put the fist-sized silk bag back into the locker. After a quick glance around, they left, walking slowly to avoid attracting undo attention. The cleaning lady moved to the locker, retrieved the bag. Peering inside, she smiled, and nodded to a man reading a newspaper. He put it down and walked outside, there nodding to two other men, who were ambling along some distance from the general and his men. They turned and went another direction, shortly meeting up with the cleaning lady and the other man.

"It's done. Here is your cut. Remember, disappear," the cleaning lady whispered, handing each of the three henchmen a bag of gems. All four then walked out of the spaceport. A short while later, the Chameleon now in yet another disguise boarded a commercial flight to Centauri-3. Five more disguises later and five other worlds distant, he entered his newly purchased home, satisfied he'd disappeared sufficiently. Now, he took out his fist-sized diamond and stared into its heart for quite some time. Its beauty was not lost on this admirer.

Once the general arrived at his fortress estate, he began fabricating many copies of the pair. During the next two days, he hid five copies at various secret locations. That done, he then placed a series of secure video calls. Soon, his wealth and power would become almost unrivaled in the Imperium, or so he believed.

Within the IBI and the Bops, the chatter suddenly picked way up during late December.

Chapter 24 Strikes

In an ornate church near the South Pole of Proxima Prime, some of the more ardent Devil's Disciples met for worship. Disciple Pathagorous, the dark skinned, fifty-five year old leader of the Devil's Disciples on Proxima Prime, spoke to his followers. His long hair was white, as was his full beard and moustache, draping down to his shoulders. One could not tell what was hair and what was beard; it all blended into one white mass.

"Brethren, the Faithful, I've summoned you here today, for today the Devil hath spoken unto me yet again. Too few are of the faith. Too few are even trying to rise above the many temptations of this, Hell, this Proxima Prime. No, now the heathens are foolish enough to believe themselves to be gods. Genetic modifications. Turning people into unholy, heathen beasts, full of lust and carnal cravings that now they can satiate even by themselves. Yes and even begat more of their Unholy Forms. The Devil walks among us, my faithful, indeed he does, now so more than ever before in our long history."

"The Unholy have just make Hell even more to the Devil's liking. Soon, our worlds, our universe shall be remade in the Devil's Unholy Image. Our worlds will become more like the Negative Afterlife. Salvation is slipping from the hands of the many, greased by those that were elected to lead us all towards the Positive Afterlife. It's not enough that we are entirely surrounded by greed, lust, envy, and gluttony — the Devil's Temptations to turn us all from the path to the Positive Afterlife — nay. Tis not enough. Now, the Devil has placed into the Hands of the Unholy the very means to further our fall into temptations of the flesh. Aye, they've already done so. Have you not heard of the destruction of the prisoners' bodies on Xeros-1? Hermaphrodites one and all, the Devil's Spawn. Now, they breed more and more of their evil, wicked forms, forcing us, we the Holy, to tend to their needs."

"Helpless is their cover, their disguise. This new army of the Devil marches us all toward the Eternal Negative

Afterlife. We, the faithful, we, who have struggled mightily against all such temptations, we must fight back. Yes, it is up to us, the Faithful, to lead those who have fallen victim to the Devil's Unholy Promises. We must, we shall lead them back onto the Path of Righteousness, that we may attain the Positive Afterlife."

"Fear not death in the Holy Cause, for those who fall while striving to bring to enlightenment to those who have strayed from the Holy Path shall be risen up unto the Positive Afterlife, defeating and cheating the Devil's Due!"

"The time has come for us to force, by any means necessary, the Unholy, those who have succumbed to the Devil's Enchantments, the ignorant, the uncaring, the greedy, the gluttonous, the lustful, those who strive to satisfy carnal cravings — yes, force them back onto the Path of Righteousness."

"My Faithful. Today, we have the means! The time to strike a crushing defeat, a demoralizing blow to the Devil's Unholy Followers is now! We can, we must, we shall be victorious. We shall teach them the errors of their ways, my Faithful. Indeed, we have no other choice, if we are to attain the Positive Afterlife for our own souls. We have the means. Gather together. Let us pray that we shall not fail, that our will shall overcome the very Devil himself!"

Near the equator of Proxima Prime, the True Believers, a small sect of the Church of the Holy Lords, met with their Holy Father Jesuit. He was sixty years old or at least looked like he was. His hair and full beard had long ago turned grey. Thick, curly locks covered his face and mouth, falling to below is shoulders. His purple robes lined with gold embroidery contrasted with his "fur" and piercing, blue eyes. Some sixty faithful were carefully assembled this day to hear the Holy Words from the Holy Father Jesuit.

"Arise the Faithful, the God-fearing, those who seek Salvation and the Holy Realm of Heaven above. The long awaited time to strike has finally come unto us. For long have waited, patiently, hopefully, for the Many to cast aside their wicked, evil ways — to discard the bad for the good. While we prayed, preached, cajoled, and did our best to convert those who would propagate the Evils of the World, they have ignored us. Our Holy Words, our Holy Preaching has fallen upon ears that can no longer hear. Minds no longer want to work for the Good."

"I say unto you, the time has come. How do we know this? Look at our very own Senate. What have they done this past fall? I ask you that. Wickedness beyond our wildest imaginations. Men and women have been doomed to Utter Hell by their actions. We all know that it's never too late for the hardened criminal to repent, to see the Light of Goodness, to change their evil ways. Yet, now they no longer have that option. Their bodies have been turned into utterly helpless, corrupt, carnal houses. I speak of the so called genetic modifications done indiscriminately to both men and women, robbing them of their humanity, turning them forever into Satan's Spawn, removing forever any chance at God's Holy Redemption. Satan's Spawn cannot ever be allowed into the Positive Afterlife, for they embody all that is Negative."

"Yes, it is our very own Immoral Senators who have done this. Yet, the betrayal goes far deeper, my Faithful, far, far deeper. They've done this to every prisoner in the Imperium, who has been sentenced to life in prison, denying tens of thousands from ever having the remotest chance of repentance and acceptance of God's Holy Redemption — a chance to walk the Path of Righteous Goodness upon which we all strive to tread each and every day. Deeper still goes the betrayal! Anyone, young or old, who has been convicted of three crimes, is also so changed forever, forbidden for all eternity from entering the Positive Afterlife, condemned to eternal suffering, not only in their helpless physical bodies, but also in the Negative Afterlife as well."

"Betrayal. Betrayal. The Senate has done this to the entire Imperium. Where will it stop? I ask you that. Ponder that, my Faithful. Where will it stop? Tens of thousands have been cast aside, tossed forever into the Negative Afterlife without even the remotest possibility of redemption, of changing their paths from evil and wickedness to that of righteousness and good. Denied that forever, tens of thousands. 'Tis far worse than that; some of these may well have been innocent of one or more crimes of which they were found guilty. Humans. We are frail. We are not all knowing, as the Lord is. We make mistakes. Yet, for those upon which a terrible mistake has been made, there can now be no redemption, no possibility of salvation, of turning to the path of goodness. It has been stolen from them for all eternity!"

"Yes, stolen. Stolen by the very people that were elected to safeguard our human rights, stolen and cast asunder. Our senators. They who have chosen to betray us; they who have chosen the evil path; they who have cast religion aside for profit; they must not be allowed to continue down this path of wickedness, of pure evil. They must be not ever be allowed into God's Positive Afterlife. This, my Faithful, is something that we, God's Chosen, can ensure. We now have the means. We can teach these senators a lesson, and ensure they cannot later repent and enter God's Positive Afterlife, just as those thousands they've condemned for all eternity to the Negative Afterlife cannot repent and enter God's Positive Afterlife."

"The Lord hath said unto us: Do unto others as they have done unto thee. The time has come. The means is at our disposal. We lack only the Will to see it done. Come; let us pray together; forge our Wills into one. We must not, shall not fail to see the Lord's Commands disobeyed. Dear Holy Father," Holy Father Jesuit began his lengthy prayer. Folded hands repeated softly his words.

In January 1296, as the senators began returning from their three week Winter Break, Lela summoned the Commander to her workstation. "Commander, I've come across an anomaly I think you should see. It concerns the research facility on Belsarius-2. One cylinder and crate of the bio agent and apparel has gone missing."

"What?" the Commander exploded. "Trace it! Back-trace all activities around Belsarius-2 immediately!" He turned to the nearby Statistical and Mission Planner, Scoby. "Scoby, start working up possible scenarios. We've been breached! How could this have happened? I've got to contact Sector ID Minister Slag immediately. Keep me posted." He stormed out

of their area, heading to his own command post. Never had
Lela or Scoby seen him this emotional. Both were now quite
nervous. Something was up, but what? It was their job to find
out, before it was too late.

Too late would be his humiliating reply to the head of
the IBI and the President of the Imperium.

Laughing, Senator Ari Laag helped her wife, Senator
B'nath, out of the shuttle, while Senator Zarita did the same
with her wife, Senator Celenia. The four along with Lelane had
spent the winter break at Zarita's secure underground
compound near the North Pole of Proxima Prime. These five
had become very close friends and had truly enjoyed the
company of the others at the retreat. True, Ari and Zarita had
shot an awful lot of pool, with Ari winning most of the time, as
difficult as it was with their long nails.

Senator Ari had just had her black hair trimmed once
more, barely a couple inches long now. She wore her men's
suit as always, though her long nails and toe shoes gave her
away as not being a man. The other three wore their usual
billowing gowns, as required by Senate law. Ari said, "Thanks
Zarita, Celenia, for the best winter break we've ever had!"

"Same with us," Zarita replied. "After that nasty fall
session, we needed some rest and relaxation. I bet this winter
session will be boring once more." All four chuckled, joining
arms with their mates and making their slow, careful way into
the Senate building, past the many Security Guards.

In small groups, some two thousand plus senators filed
into the large Senate building prepared for the opening of the
Winter Session. On the agenda was the planning of the coming
year's Fiscal Budget. Far below, several dozen chefs were
beginning to prepare lunch for the group. Outside, a hundred
Security Guards stood idly by, ensuring no unauthorized
persons could gain access to the Senate or disturb their work.
Below the amphitheater, two men in work jeans pushed their
maintenance carts ahead of them.

One said quietly, "Connections are made. All praise to
the Lord God."

The other man pressed an electronic control device,

muttering, "On behalf of the Holy Father, I hereby condemn all you senators to eternal damnation of the Negative Afterlife!" Each man took out a small caliber handgun, pointed it to their heads, and pulled the triggers. At the same time, many cylinders began releasing their contents into the air intake lines that filtered the air of the amphitheater proper, keeping the senators physically cool, though not emotionally cool.

Like all major government buildings on Proxima Prime, the Senate had a failsafe mechanism in case of a chemical or biological attack. Soon, several sensors detected just such an attack. The computer controlled system activated. Without warning, sealing doors slid shut all over the complex, including all of the major exits. Outside, large red warning lights began flashing. Chemical-Biological Attack. Inside the huge amphitheater, a giant led light panel over the head of the Senate President, who had just finished his opening remarks, began to flash an identical message. All exit doors from the amphitheater slammed shut, echoing loudly around the acoustically sensitive room. The only redeeming factor fell upon the cooks, far below. Their area was sealed off from the rest of the building and had its own private air system, designed to vent the odors from all the hot stoves and cooking that went on down there. Thus, they were not infected, though they were locked inside.

"What the hell is going on?" Senate President Michael Sanders cried out, turning around to see what was behind and above him. Everyone was yelling and shouting at the same time. Many headed for the exits only to find they were sealed in, adding to the overall general panic that swept rapidly over the two thousand plus senators.

"Remain calm. This must be some kind of emergency drill," Michael yelled above the noise. Like many others, he pulled out his cell phone and began frantically making calls. Chaos reigned for some time. Senators Ari and B'nath, finding their exit blocked, carefully took the stairs down to the second level, joining Zarita and Celenia. Their faces were quite pale.

"What's going on?" Ari whispered.

"Don't know. I smell something in the air, Ari," Zarita

whispered back. "I think we're under an attack of some kind."

B'nath whispered, "If it's chemical, we'll be dead in no time. That's what I've heard. Chem attacks are really deadly. Ari, I don't want to die, not like this."

"I don't feel anything happening to my body," Zarita tried to calm the trio down. "If it was chemical, I think we'd feel sick or something by now."

"God, I feel faint!" Ari gushed.

"You're panicking. Shallow breaths. Sit down. There's nothing we can do about it now. Whatever is happening, we four must stick together," Zarita advised.

"I think the air is slightly yellow in here," Celenia whispered hesitantly.

Eventually, the senators slipped from a fear and terror flight reaction to grief and eventually apathy. Within a half hour, they had sat back down on whatever seats were closest to themselves. Many were communicating with the outside world. Shortly, Senate President Michael Sanders spoke up again. His voice trembled as he fought back his own grief.

"May I have your attention? It is official. The Senate has come under a biological attack. I'm told that sensor readings are indicating a bio attack is underway. Per containment protocols, we are locked in for the duration of the attack."

"What's going to happen to us?" a senator interrupted him.

"Are we going to die?" another yelled loudly.

"Please, please, I've no idea. The emergency responders are just now getting here. Give them time to do their work. We dare not risk opening the doors; we could spread this thing all over Proxima Prime. Be patient. If you are a praying person, now would be a good time." He sat down, his voice cracking too badly to continue speaking.

"Well, look at the crowd out there. Come to see us all die," Ari grumbled, showing her small group the images on her hand held phone. Hundreds of reporters and video cameras were plainly visible, held back by a long line of Security Guards. A dozen in red containment suits were close to the main doors, however.

While Ari kept hers streaming in the live video from

just outside the Senate building, Zarita hooked hers up to one of the local news channels. "Yes, the President has just confirmed that the entire Senate has come under a biological agent attack. He claims there is no outside danger of contamination, that the built-in containment protocols have sealed the building. We can see the red suits up close to the entrances, presumably, they are checking for leakages. The Imperium Senate has never undergone an attack before. We're all on new ground here. Mark Shields, a word. Can you tell us what is the difference between a chemical attack and a biological attack?"

A man in a business suit moved closer to the microphone. Hundreds of video cameras zoomed in on him. "Mark Shields, Bio Containment Department. Yes, a chemical attack usually kills the victims within just a few minutes. Nerve agents are the usual methods. In this case, the senators are all still alive, and it's been close to an hour now. If this were a chemical attack, they would be dead by now. Further, our internal sensors are indicating some form of biological agent is inside. A virus, who knows just what it is. Too soon to tell. We do know that as of this moment, it's an unknown bio agent. Now, if you will excuse me, I need to get back to work. There is no danger to the outside world, as long as the containment seals hold. Thank you." He stepped back, and the Security Guards allowed him to get closer, forming a blocking line preventing the reporters from getting closer to him.

By noon, everyone was getting hungry and thirsty, but also many felt rather tired. The sudden rush of adrenaline had long worn off. Many had stopped calling outside, demanding to know when the quarantine would be lifted. "The agent is still active" was the constant reply they received, not encouraging. As Zarita and Celenia watched, one by one the senators began falling asleep, some falling off their chairs. Around three, only those two remained awake.

"What's happening, Zarita? We're not falling asleep like the others are," Celenia whispered, afraid to make any loud noises, though, if you asked her why, she couldn't say.

"I don't know. It's almost like what happened to us on Ashford-5. Someone wanted to attack the whole Senate. The only biological agent we know about is that one they were using on the prisoners," Zarita speculated. "I swear to you, dearest, if anything bad happens to us, I'll make those responsible pay for it with their lives, if it's the last thing I do."

"We should maybe make Ari and B'nath more comfortable," Celenia whispered a bit later. The two slowly began moving from senator to senator, working together to get each one laid out on the floor. Several had taken nasty head wounds where they'd fallen when they passed out earlier. By the time they finished getting the two thousand unconscious men and women prone, both were quite tired themselves.

"My arms are going numb. That was more work than I'm used to," Celenia whispered. "We still aren't asleep or unconscious. Why? I don't get it."

Just then, Zarita's phone rang. Clumsily, she got it activated, again cursing her overly long nails. "Hello?"

"Mark Shields, Bio Containment Department. You and your wife — from what we can see from out here, you two are the only ones alive? Is that right? The others are dead?"

"No sir. Asleep or unconscious. We've made them as comfortable as possible," she replied. "How come we aren't being affected?"

"Don't know. We've taken a sample of the bio agent. Bad news, I'm afraid. It's the same agent that has been used on all of the hardened criminals," Mark said softly, hoping to dampen the terrible news.

"Oh! Oh, I see," Zarita replied, as she grasped the significance. "So they are going to become like Celenia and me?"

"Yes, but they will also likely lose their arms too and become completely helpless. We can't do anything to help you until the bio agent becomes inert, probably three days, we're told, maybe four," Mark replied, trying to keep his voice as calm as possible.

"Oh! Well this is bad, isn't it?" Zarita asked rhetorically. "Well, that may explain why Celenia and I aren't yet out like the others. Our bodies already have all these genetic modifications, excepting our arms, that is. We had best get their shirts loosened or they will be in trouble as the changes

368

come. Over and out," she added, thinking this was more like a comm center communication than a phone conversation.

She and Celenia spent the next two hours moving from person to person, removing their shoes and loosening or unbuttoning their shirts and tops. Then, they also realized, if the female senators lost their arms too, their giant hoop skirts would be unbearable. "We best take ours off too, in case we lose our arms as well," Celenia suggested. "It won't be so bad, Zarita, we can learn from Lena and Drina, I think." They each helped the other out of their billowing skirts and out of the giant hoops. Then, they did the same for all of the other female senators who wore them. By then, they were starving and quite tired.

Again, Mark chatted with them and validated their efforts to prepare the many senators for what he anticipated would be happening in the ensuing next few days. He added, "We might have a way to get some food and water to you. Stand by." They used a teleport to deposit a goodly amount of both near the two women. She thanked him, and the two ate their fill. Since they didn't have their special long forks and spoons, they took their lip plates completely out while they ate and drank, then put them back in for safety's sake. Tired and exhausted, the two lay down beside Ari and B'nath, covering all four with their yards of hoop skirts. Mark quietly had the Senate computer dim the inside lights for them.

They awoke several days later, minus their arms, which looked like a pair of desiccated and shriveled up sticks lying at their sides. Many men and women were going from senator to senator examining them. Using a bit of psi energy from her crystals, Zarita got herself lifted up into a sitting position. "Hello. Is it over now? Are they alive?" she called out. Several rushed over to her, just as Celenia woke and struggled to sit up, nearly impossible in her tight corset. Gentle hands helped her.

"Hello Senator Zarita, Senator Celenia. Mark Shields, Bio Containment Department. We meet at last. I must thank you both for all that you've done for the thousands of senators. You were precisely correct in what you did. How are you feeling?"

"A bit tired and hungry, and I need to use the bathroom," Zarita replied. Ari began stirring, hearing the voices around her. A nurse knelt beside her and helped her sit up. Of course, Ari merely began screaming at the top of her lungs, rousing B'nath, whose screams were added to Ari's. That roused many others. Soon the panic-stricken screams nearly deafened everyone, including the rescue workers.

Zarita activated all of her many giant crystals, sending soothing, calming waves of emotion out over all of the stricken senators. Shortly, their screams subsided, and Mark began to bring order to the chaos. Then, one man cried out, "Please, just kill me. I can't live like this!" Before anyone could reply, hundreds of others echoed his plea. Again, Zarita acted, sending out her waves of calming energies.

Mark called out, "Stay calm. We'll get to each of you in turn. Senators Zarita and Celenia had the good sense to get you partially undressed, your shoes off, and made you comfortable. Otherwise, you all would be in far worse trouble. Just lie still. We've prepared apparel for everyone. We've got temporary living facilities prepared for everyone. We know you need to use the bathroom and are starving. Be patient, if you can't wait, it's acceptable to do it where you lie. There are over two thousand of you to handle at once."

Ari whispered, "Zarita, please take B'nath and me with you, wherever you two go, please, I beg you."

"Don't worry. I won't let them separate us, Ari," she replied.

Into the confusion came a very worried Lelane. Now that the Senate had been opened back up, she was allowed to join the workers trying to assist the senators. She sought out Zarita and Celenia and quickly joined them. "Let her help Ari and B'nath," Zarita said to the nurse who was trying to get them dressed. "Are you all right?" Lelane asked worriedly. Never was she so thankful for having her voice box repaired by Doctor Jones. Now, she could express her feelings and thoughts.

"Could be a lot worse. I hope our babies aren't affected by all this," Zarita exclaimed, suddenly having a new worry. "As soon as you both get dressed, we're going to go back to my secure compound," she said to Ari.

"Thank you," Ari whispered, fighting hard to keep from breaking down completely.

Mark spoke up, "Okay. I'll send along an armed escort with you four senators. I'll be in touch. I must say, Senator Zarita, you and Senator Celenia certainly kept your heads about you, just as you both did last year as President and Senate President. Thank you for what you've done here for the others. I'll be in touch with you at your compound then."

As they got Ari to her feet, she gushed, "I've never felt so helpless in all my life! I don't think I can do this!"

"Sure you can, one step at a time," Zarita whispered back, fighting her own growing intense feelings of helplessness as well. "We must be brave," she added. She felt completely the opposite, however.

"I'm back to the way that I was, only worse now," Celenia whispered. "I'm scared too."

"I have you," Lelane whispered encouragingly. Shortly, four Security Guards joined them, putting a steadying arm around each. A half hour later, they entered the secure compound, having flown there at top speed. Two of the guards remained on duty just outside. Zarita wasn't sure why; the damage had already been done.

Once inside, Lelane helped Ari and B'nath use the bathroom, and then she heated up a hot meal for them. "This isn't going to be very easy, is it?" She realized she was going to have to feed all four of them. Just as soon as Ari and B'nath finished, both were extremely tired, and Lelane got them into their usual guest bedroom. They were asleep, as soon as she laid them down.

While Lelane was helping their two friends to bed, Zarita used her *mentales* gifts to feed herself and Celenia. "I didn't dare do this with those two here. Thanks Lelane. We've got real problems now, don't we?"

"Yes. I can't take care of four of you all that fast," Lelane admitted. "I've let Emperor Kino know what happened. It's been all over the news. He was quite upset. I think he was even angry. Whatever are we going to do now?"

"Whoever did this is going to pay," Zarita declared

vehemently. "Have they figured out who was behind it, Lelane?"

"Well, they found two dead men in the basement. They were disguised as maintenance men with fake ID cards. The reporters are saying that informed sources have identified them as members of the Church of the Holy Lords or rather a splinter sect calling themselves the True Believers," Lelane told them what she'd heard on the news. "Just a lot of generalities, Celenia."

"Can you bring up some images of these people, the True Believers, on the monitor, Lelane?" Zarita asked. "Damn, now I can't put my new computer skills to use either. Damn these men anyway!" She was growing more and more frustrated by the moment.

Lelane did as asked, surfing the Web, until she had their main church page up on the monitor. Zarita began reading. At least they haven't taken that away from me, she thought. The image of their Holy Father Jesuit was prominently displayed along with some of their religious thoughts, beliefs, and goals. "Don't disturb me for a while," Zarita asked. She closed her eyes, focused, and began expanding her awareness outward. Her many crystals began releasing their pale blue light. Concentrating on the images she had of this Holy Father Jesuit, she searched for him.

Ordinarily, this would be an easy task, if she had first met the man. All she had were vague notions of the man based on what was said on the church pages. Had she taken the time to locate geographically where their churches were located here on Proxima Prime, such would have mattered little. As she perceived telepathically the billions of minds on this world, spatial dimensions seemed vastly different to her perceptions anyway. Zarita was patient and totally dedicated to finding this one man out of all other minds on this world. As she began, she felt the loving mind of her mate, Celenia, and her good friend, Lelane, and almost at once, the minds of Ari and B'nath, so close to her heart. Grief nearly drowned both of those two minds. Knowing she could do nothing about that, she put her attention back onto the task at hand, pushing her awareness outward.

While she was probing, time also meant little. Had it been a minute or an hour? She couldn't tell and frankly didn't care. Revenge. Zarita fully intended to get revenge for what had been done to her, her mate, friends, and the many senators. On outward, she pushed. Then, she sensed him and drilled down onto that mind, Holy Father Jesuit.

From his eyes, she could see a small room, smelled incense burning, felt six other minds present, and then saw their bodies and the room. There were six cylinders and six crates stacked against one wall. The six men were sitting on rugs facing this heavily bearded man. They were praying. Perfect, she though, and invaded the bearded one's mind. She forced him to retrieve recent memories. Satisfied beyond all doubt, she sent him an appropriate thought: *You have become the Devil.* Then, she sent a huge electrical blast into his brain, her crystals briefly glowing far brighter. Ooze came from his nose, ears, and from around his eyes.

She latched onto the other six men's minds. Now, her many crystals glowed brighter than Celenia had ever seen them radiate. Identical ooze came from the orifices of these six men. The germanium crystals dimmed and became inert once more. Zarita opened her eyes. "That's done. The religious fanatics who did this to us all are dead. Never, ever mess with Zarita! Come on; let's get some sleep. Tomorrow is going to be an awful day for us all."

Chapter 25 Counterstrikes

ST1's shuttle landed a short distance from the church near the South Pole of Proxima Prime. Blackwell and Hamil, jumped out, guns at the ready, each facing a different direction, ready to shoot the enemy. Silence. Jason and Ellen hopped out, followed by their leader, Peter. Inside and hunched over his massive electronics, Karkoff whispered into their comm system, "Seven hostiles in the rear. Haven't moved."

Peter whispered. "Clear. Move to Point A." The five black clad Strike Team 1 members moved silently up to the front of the church, again taking covering fire positions. "Blackwell, Point B. Karkoff?"

Staring at the IR images that had not moved, Karkoff whispered, "Mission go!" Peter, Jason, and Hamil entered the front doors, while Ellen maintained her covering fire position.

"Take door on right. Long hall. Door on left," Karkoff continued to guide the team to their targets, the militant True Believers. As the four arrived before this last door, Peter held up his fingers, counting down from three. At one, Jason kicked open the door, and the four burst into the incense-filled room, ready to blast these men. They saw seven bodies slumped on the floor. Karkoff didn't hear any firing. "What's going on?"

Back at HQ, that was precisely what the Commander wanted to know. He, as well as half of the department heads, was closely following the events while they were unfolding in real time. Streaming video from the member's headgear was being carefully watched on five monitors, while a sixth echoed what Karkoff had on his IR setup. "What the hell is going on, Peter?" the Commander's voice bellowed in Peter's earpiece.

"Dead. Cylinders against the wall. Total containment. Someone's been here before us," Peter whispered.

Doc Lambert spoke into his microphone, "Give me a close up of their heads, Peter. Yes, like that. My god, is that ooze?"

"Looks like our Righteous Vigilante got here ahead of us," Ellen whispered.

Peter ordered, "Hamil, Jason, secure the cylinders. Get them out of here. Send the Cleanup Crew."

Doc Lambert again spoke up, "Peter. Need a body temp reading."

Karkoff replied, "I've got that, Peter. 98.6. Doc, they've only just died. Minutes ago. How is this possible?"

Peter snapped alert. "Karkoff, is the Righteous Vigilante still here? Others on the IR?"

"No, IR is showing you and the seven hostiles, just as it did when we were arriving. No change there," Karkoff answered. "Double checking now."

Back at HQ, both Lela and Scoby barked, "Double checking here, Commander!"

Meanwhile, Doc Lambert had Peter checking several other aspects, in lieu of his being personally on site. "Doc, blood is fresh, not coagulating. They've died just minutes ago. No signs of entry or exit wounds."

Ellen, waving her chem-bio detector around the room, called out, "All clear on chem weapons. Only getting a tiny trace reading from where the cylinders are located."

Doc Lambert declared, "Okay, Peter. Cleanup crew will bring the seven bodies to my station. I want to do the autopsies personally!"

The Commander was furious. "Come on, Lela, Scoby. Where the hell is this Righteous Vigilante? He's got to be on your scans somewhere? How the devil did he get to them before we did? I want answers, and I want them *now*!" The moment he was alerted to the bio attack on the Senate, the Commander had used every contact he had on Proxima Prime, pulled in every favor ever owed to him, pushed his teams harder than ever before. Everyone had been at their stations constantly for five days now, sleeping when they could. Only two hours ago, Lela had finally located what she believed were more of the cylinders, based on their RFI tags. Scoby had then worked up a Mission Profile, and the Commander had sent in his top Strike Force. And yet, this unknown, unseen Righteous Vigilante, as Lela had named him, had somehow beaten him to the terrorists! This, the Commander simply could not stomach! No one had better Intel, better manpower, better equipment, and better support than he, and yet this Righteous Vigilante had done just that. The Commander was furious.

Torres, head of the Interrogation Department, was equally furious. She desperately wanted this Jesuit man taken alive so she could interrogate him. This past week had been utter hell here at the Bops! *Well, not the hell that those poor senators faced or will be facing now. It's our fault. We should've seen this coming. How the hell did we miss it?* Her refection was interrupted by the Commander. "Department heads — meeting in one hour. I want answers, and I want them now! Do you hear me? Two thousand senators no less have paid the ultimate price for our failures this time! Heads are going to roll!" He marched out of the electronics station and headed up to his command level.

Lela and Scoby had perspiration dripping down their foreheads. Torres whispered, "I've never seen him this angry. Did you two screw up?" Neither answered her, but continued to work rather frantically at their computers. She headed over to the entrance where the Cleanup Crew would soon be bringing in the seven bodies. Torres sighed; on one of these, she'd hoped to ply her trade, obtaining the answers they desperately needed. Shortly, the doors opened, and ST1 came marching in carrying the cylinders and crates. A number of other men wheeled in seven gurneys with the dead men on them. Those, they took straight to the elevators and headed on down to Level 5, where Doc Lambert was waiting for them. Torres followed them. At least, she could lend him a hand with his autopsies. Time was ticking.

During the hour the Commander gave his personnel, he sat in his office and replayed all of the footage taken during this hideous affair, particularly the many interviews with Mark Shields of the Bio Containment Department. His attention was caught by the anomaly of Senators Zarita and Celenia. Somehow, they hadn't been knocked out as rapidly as the thousands of other senators. Indeed, this Senator Zarita woman had the sense of mind to take vitally important safety precautions, Mark had duly noted. She'd gotten them all into a prone position, their shoes off, and their shirts and blouses or tops unbuttoned. This Zarita woman certainly knew what was going to happen to these senators. When they began to transform, their feet and breasts — those would cause bad problems if their shoes and shirts not been removed. The Commander began to see this as highly suspicious. Could this Zarita have been in on the plot? Or did she have some prior knowledge this was going to happen? He knew he needed to question this senator, but such would be quite tricky. She was a senator, and from Mark's messages, she was staying in her North Pole compound now, almost impregnable.

Doc Lambert made his report first. "All seven died just a few minutes before ST1's arrival. Liquefied brains. Same exact COD as before. Absolutely no doubt of that. The same unknown weapon has been used again. Other than their brains being melted, there was nothing physically wrong with any of the seven. No signs of puncture wounds, injections, bullet holes. Not even needle marks."

The Commander frowned. "So we are dealing with this same unknown Righteous Vigilante of Lela's?"

"Unquestionably, sir," Doc Lambert replied.

"Okay," Lela sighed, knowing it was her turn in the hot seat. "I've gone over absolutely every piece of Intel we have, three times now. There's absolutely no sign whatsoever of some other agent or person having discovered the involvement of this Holy Father Jesuit, other than those who acquired the bio weapons of mass destruction. None, nada."

The Commander glared at her, as if his eyes could burn holes into her head. "How can this be? Scoby, I do hope you can shed more light than Lela."

Scoby squirmed. "Sir, I've gone over all our data from the moment we positioned the geo-sat over that church. I swear the only IR hot spots were those seven that died. I've accounted for each of their separate movements during those hours. Whoever this Righteous Vigilante is, he does not show up on any IR scan. He must therefore be at room temperature, which makes him non-human." That raised a number of eyebrows.

"I did motion sensor scans. Even if he didn't show up on IR, his movements would show up on those scans. Nada. It's as if he's wholly invisible to all of our technology. Sir, could we be chasing a ghost?" Scoby asked in complete frustration.

"A murderous ghost? That's your conclusion, Scoby?" the Commander shot back angrily.

"I'm at a loss, sir. I've never seen anything like this. He's completely invisible to us in all ways. I've even done a spectral analysis, nothing there either," Scoby admitted.

An awkward silence followed. Leroy decided to speak up. "Commander, I've done some experiments on some pigs in the lab. You know, they are somewhat similar to humans. I've been able to reproduce the liquefied brains by sending a high voltage, high amperage electric current through their brains, overloading all neurons and pathways. However, the process does leave very noticeable burn marks on their skin where I attached the contact elements. Still, I can say categorically this Righteous Vigilante has some weapon that discharges an enormous electric current into their brains. Just how that weapon works, I don't yet know."

As Leroy was discussing his recent experiments on pigs, a desperate Lela rapidly continued typing at her console. She typed in "Electrification death," but received listings that had to do with long obsolete electric chairs used to terminate criminals centuries ago. She discounted the references to lightning strikes as well. Then, she picked up on a word that Leroy had just said, overloading. She modified her search, "electrical overloading brains." Up came the usual psych men's experimentations that had all ended in complete failures. However, at the very bottom of the long list of possibilities was an anomaly. It read, Ashford-5. She clicked on that one and up came "Classified. Top Secret." She was denied access.

"Lela, are you with us?" the Commander broke in on her concentration. She looked up and saw that everyone was looking at her. She'd missed whatever had been said.

"Sorry, I need your clearance code. I might be on to something here," she replied. "I can hack it, if you prefer."

The Commander gave her a dirty look, but stepped to her console and typed in his password. Lela then brought up the document, a listing called Marisol's *Mentales* Gifts List. She scanned the list and stopped at one entry. Thought can kill. "Well?" the Commander needled her. "Holding up the meeting, are you?"

"Commander, I might have something. Here, take a look at this. It's from Ashford-5," Lela sent the document to everyone's screens. "We thought they were just Class V telepaths, but, if this document has any actual validity, these people have all manner of other skills. My god, these are almost god-like!"

Scoby jumped on this, eager to find any way out of the mess he was in. "They might not have to be physically in the same place as their victims, if it is like their telepathy thing. Isn't Senator Zarita Valen from there, Ashford-5?"

"Yes. Perhaps, we have our first clue to this Righteous Vigilante," the Commander visibly relaxed. "Let's focus now on just how these religious nuts got their hands on a dozen of these cylinders." He didn't mention his own thoughts about questioning Senator Zarita. "Heads are already rolling over this. I've got the IBI, the President, the Legates, and a host of Sector ID Ministers all hounding me for answers. ID Minister Slag is currently under arrest for failure to protect the research lab."

"Commander, I believe I might have an answer," Lela spoke up. "I've gone over and over all their data. I agree with Slag, no one assaulted that research lab. However, I've looked at several other anomalies, and I believe they tie together. Senator Chambers was kidnaped, as he left the Senate the evening of the start of their winter break. He swears it was his own driver who did it, but under grueling interrogation, the chauffeur claims he was attacked and robbed. Both men were not discovered for nearly a week. Then, according to the spaceport, Senator Chambers and three Security Guards boarded his personal deep space transport and headed for his home world. Obviously, whoever took that transport was not Senator Chambers."

She continued, "Then, we have that same ship arriving at a spaceport close to the research lab. Next anomaly. It seems one of those two researchers in charge of these bio agents and its research was also kidnaped. His body was discovered a week or so after he was kidnaped. Yet, according to all records, this same geneticist reported to work the next day. He signed out one of the cylinders and crates, used the Fabrication Machine to make a legal duplicate of it, and put the originals back in the containment room. After that, he took the copy and just disappeared. There's no trace of him after that. Weeks later, we've all that chatter about acquisition of the bio agent circulating around the underworld."

"So where does this get us, Lela?" the Commander asked.

"The Chameleon, sir. That's the only answer that fits the pieces. We know he can assume anyone's appearance. It has to have been him who stole a copy of the bio agent," Lela concluded.

"He doesn't fit the profile of a terrorist marketing bio weapons," the Commander replied.

"No he doesn't. He is only interested in diamonds, as far as we know," she countered.

"Do we know where this Chameleon is now?" he asked.

"No. He's dropped off the radar completely. Even his known gang affiliates have gone underground," she replied.

"No traces?" he asked.

"None. Burrowed under completely. But I did some additional checking last night. It seems that the Star of Rose was stolen a month or so ago. That's one of the largest cut diamonds in the Imperium. Fist-sized. Worth a fortune," she explained.

"So you think whoever stole this Star of Rose did so as payment to this Chameleon in return for the cylinder?" the Commander followed her line of thinking and asked.

"I do. We might have a line on him. If we can solve that crime, it might also lead us to whoever has and is selling these bio weapons," Lela speculated. "It's the best lead I've got so far. I know; it's all just a theory, a speculation, but what else do we have?"

Scoby, typing rapidly, spoke up, "Sir, her theory has a ninety percent chance of matching the situation with the Chameleon, and a seventy percent chance of accounting for the mysterious disappearance of that cylinder from the research lab."

"Good. Follow it up. Move fast. Everyone wants answers

yesterday. We need to know how many more radical groups now have their hands on this bio weapon and what targets they intend to hit. I don't have to impress upon you these attacks are devastating. They might as well be killing their targets. We've got an entire Senate, two thousand plus men and women, that are as good as dead now. That's what's in store for all of their targets. No one is safe as long as these bio weapons are out there. Hell, we could be next," the Commander impressed upon these department heads.

Scoby spoke up, "The Presidential Office, sir, that was the True Believer's next target. I've been going over the data ST1 brought back from the raid. They were planning to hit it on Monday. We caught a break on this one."

"Excellent. I'll put the Presidential Office on the highest alert, if it isn't already," the Commander declared. "We might have a window of some twenty hours to make some headway here. It's Sunday, and most everything is closed. Monday morning, all bets are off."

In fact, the Commander could not have been more wrong. Sunday evening, President Balag, Legate Helyeon H. Hoon, and their wives attended the Royal Imperial Opera for a special presentation in honor of the fallen senators. In part, this special showing was meant as a fundraiser to help the thousands of now helpless senators, who, in all likelihood, would need to be housed in some assisted living accommodations for the rest of their lives. Many of the wealthier and elite living on Proxima Prime were in attendance at this black tie affair. Tuxedos were mandatory. Seats were going for a thousand credits each.

Additionally, when the news of the bio attack on the Senate broke, several of the local churches on Proxima Prime decided they needed to do something to help these stricken senators. Four of the church leaders met, and Devil's Disciple Pathagorous suggested they could sponsor a private affair at the Royal Imperial Opera, using all proceeds to help defray the monumental costs the senators would be facing. Quickly, the idea took root, and word of this fund-raising event spread rapidly. Naturally, H-cubed got involved, going before the cameras, once more demonstrating his full support for this event.

Of course, immediately after the attack on the Senate, security around the Presidential Office skyscraper was so tight an ant could not get into the building without close scrutiny. Security Guards swept the Royal Imperial Opera House around noon on Sunday. After that, the many performers and stage hands began arriving, making their preparations for the gala evening's big event. Four of the top religious leaders were also in attendance, including Disciple Pathagorous himself and three of his associates.

Around seven-thirty, with reporters' cameras rolling and amid incredibly tight security, President Balag, Legate Helyeon H. Hoon, and their wives arrived, pausing for a brief cameo for the reporters. By eight, a thousand men and women were in their seats awaiting the maestro to appear and the overture to begin. A million credits had been raised for the afflicted senators this night alone. Outside, several hundred Security Guards patrolled the perimeter of the large opera house, keeping the many reporters well away from the many ornate entrance doors. A long drum roll proclaimed the overture. The full orchestra filled the opera house, masking the release of six cylinders of the bio agent, whose contents were being fed into the air circulation system. By the middle of the first Act, the dimmed giant space was filled with the faint yellow bio agent, though it wasn't visible to the thousands present.

Outside, as though on guard duty at some military base, the Security Guards marched. An hour into the production, one guard, who was posted inside, stepped out to take a smoking break. As he did so, suddenly several nearby bio-hazard alarms started clanging! Guns pointed at the Security Guard, who had stepped outside. "Get back inside or we'll shoot you!" a captain yelled. Dropping his smoke, the guard did as ordered. The portable, hand-held devices continued to blast out their warning sounds. Hastily, more guards swarmed towards the front, some holding their sensors, which also added to the noise. The captain turned on his earphone. "Sir, we have a problem. Another bio attack is underway! The opera house!"

Within a half hour, a thousand Security Guards swarmed around the facility, forcing the reporters far back. They ignored the constant volleys of questions being thrown at them. Soon, Mark Shields of the Bio Containment Department and his large team arrived in several large transports. The reporters had some of their questions answered just by seeing six men in the red containment suits, like some kind of wild spacemen, walking up to the entrance doors, devices in their hands. Two entered the building and quickly came back out. In his earpiece, Mark heard the worst. "Same biological agent as with the Senate. Massive dosage. It must be filling the entire opera house."

He replied, "Okay. Come back outside then. We've got a real problem now! Hell, how the devil do we contain this one?" Mark quickly met with his staff. "Look, we can't let them open the doors. My god, that could infect half of the city around here," Mark cried. "Ideas?"

"Hey, how about parking vehicles in front of all the exits so they can't get out?" one of his aides suggested. "We need to seal the doors and all vents."

"Okay, we'll let the opera play out. That'll give us about two hours to get this place secure. Let's not waste a second," Mark ordered. Within an hour, sealing guns arrived from the spaceport. Intended for emergency repairs in space, these guns shot a liquid sealant that hardened within a few minutes. Almost as hard as steel when dried, the sealant covered all the doors, making them impassible barriers. To guard against any eventual panic from inside, vehicles were moved up and positioned against the sealant walls. Once that was done, Mark had his men go over the plans for the opera house to find other ways out of the house and get those underground exits also sealed up.

Finally, he had his electronics man tap into the sound system inside. Soon, he was able to hear the ongoing performance as well. At long last, the thunderous applause nearly deafened his ears. He hastily turned down the volume. When the ovation ended, he switched on his microphone and made the announcement that he dreaded. As head of the Bio Containment Department, it fell upon him to do this. "May I have everyone's attention there in the opera house? This is Mark Shields of the Bio Containment Department. I have terrible news for everyone. While you were enjoying the opera, you were subjected to another one of these horrific biological agent attacks, the same agent that was used on the Senate last week. At this time, we have the opera house sealed off, in an attempt to keep the bio agent from infecting half of the city around here."

He had to pause; the screaming and yelling drowned him out completely. Several minutes later, he could speak again. "There is one thing we must ask all of you to do. For your own safety, please do three things at once. First, find some place where you can lie down and do so. Second, remove your shoes. Third, undo your shirts or blouses and tops. Within a short while, you'll all likely be falling into comas, which, if this attack is like that on the Senate, will last for three days. When it is safe for us to do so, we'll enter the opera house and rescue all of you. Until then, if you are religious, this is the time for prayer."

Not long after that, those closest to the main entrance heard loud banging upon the doors. Then, the sounds of shattering glass could be heard. Mark grimaced. Would his sealant idea hold? If not, then a goodly portion of the surrounding city had to be evacuated. Already, the skyscrapers in the surrounding block had been evacuated as a safety precaution. Ought he have evacuated more, Mark wondered? He kept his eyes focused on the six red suited men with their hand-held detectors up beside the vehicle barrier by the doors.

Disciple Pathagorous, the dark skinned, fifty-five year old leader of the Devil's Disciples on Proxima Prime, walked ceremoniously onto the stage. His long hair was white as was his full beard and moustache, draping down to his shoulders. He spoke into the microphone.

"Your attention please. The Devil hath spoken unto me yet again. Too few of you are of the faith. Too few of you are even trying to rise above the many temptations of this, Hell, this Proxima Prime. Heathens are foolish enough to believe themselves to be gods. Genetic modifications. Turning people into unholy, heathen beasts, full of lust and carnal cravings that now they can fulfill even by themselves, begetting more of their Unholy Forms. The Devil walks among us, indeed he does, now so more than ever before in our long history."

"The Unholy have just made Hell even more to the Devil's liking. Soon, our worlds, our universe shall be remade in the Devil's Unholy Image as our worlds become more like the Negative Afterlife. Salvation is slipping from the hands of the many, greased by those that were elected to lead us all towards the Positive Afterlife. It's not enough we are entirely surrounded by greed, lust, envy, and gluttony — the Devil's Temptations to turn us all from the path to the Positive Afterlife — nay. 'Tis not enough. Now, the Devil has placed into the Hands of the Unholy the very means to further our fall into temptations of the flesh. Have you not heard of the destruction of the prisoners' bodies on Xeros-1? Hermaphrodites one and all, the Devil's Spawn."

"Helpless is their cover, their disguise, as this new army of the Devil marches us all toward the Eternal Negative Afterlife. We, the faithful, we, who have struggled mightily against all such temptations, we must fight back. Yes, it is up to us, the Faithful, to lead those who have fallen victim to the Devil's Unholy Promises. We must, we shall lead them back onto the Path of Righteousness, that we may attain the Positive Afterlife."

"The time has come for us to force by any means necessary, you here, the Unholy, those who have succumbed to the Devil's Enchantments, the ignorant, the uncaring, the greedy, the gluttonous, the lustful, those who strive to satisfy carnal cravings — yes, time to force you back onto the Path of Righteousness. Taste of the very Devil that you've unleashed upon the Imperium!"

He didn't get any farther. Several angry men stormed the stage, and beat and kicked him to death.

At HQ, the many department heads were listening in to what Mark was hearing. They'd been apprised of the situation as it happened and had maximal coverage on the site, verifying over a thousand people were inside, trapped, and about to suffer the horrific genetic changes. That one was their own President and a popular Legate was not lost on the Bops personnel. Most expected another condemnation on their failure to predict and prevent this latest attack. Instead, the Commander spoke up, "Okay, ST1, you are with me. Lela, Scoby, send all other STs out to every known Devil's Disciples churches and quarters on Proxima Prime. Raid them and find any more cylinders. If they find some, I want those responsible taken alive for questioning. ST1, you are with me. We have to make a special move immediately. Details are already on your cell phones. Meet me at Transport One in ten minutes. Move!"

Peter nodded and led his team at a dash to see Lenard in the Equipment Department. "You'll be needing these," Lenard said dryly, handing them their guns with silencers on each. Ropes with battery operated body winches were issued, as well as the usual electronic surveillance gear. Their phones only showed that they would be assaulting a highly secure compound, once owned by a retired Security Guards' general. This didn't sound too promising to any of the six, certainly not on such short notice.

"We're going to need more than this to break into this kind of compound," Ellen protested.

"And whole lot more planning," Karkoff added.

Peter replied emotionlessly, "Ours is not to question, but to do. Let' go."

After boarding the transport, the Commander punched in the coordinates and Karkoff acted as pilot, though he had little to do. All was automated. The elevator system brought the ship to the surface where it lifted off and got into a high orbit, reserved for those ships that had to travel substantial distances on Proxima Prime, in this case, a quarter of the way around the world, to the North Pole.

"Okay. Our objective is Senator Zarita Valen's secure compound near the North Pole. Mark has confirmed she has taken up residence there, along with three other senators. As you can see, this compound is almost impenetrable."

"Commander? Is Senator Zarita involved in these attacks?" Peter asked.

"I have no indication that she is. Rather, I suspect she might be our mysterious Righteous Vigilante. We've may have made a major blunder in ignoring personnel from Ashford-5.

If she is one of their telepaths, *mentales* gifted I believe is their term for it, then she could well be behind the liquefied brains. This is a preventative measure. If by chance she is, then I don't want her interfering with our current raids on the Devil's Disciples. We need to take them alive and interrogate them. We must know where they got their bio weapons of mass destruction."

Peter then asked, "So how do we take her?"

Ellen, who had been studying the compound layout and specs, spoke up. "Good lord, she's inside one of the most secure compounds on Proxima Prime."

"I know," the Commander said dryly.

Ellen then said, "Well, why don't we try knocking on her door first? It's going to take more than we have with us to break inside."

The Commander flashed the very briefest of smiles. "Sounds like a workable plan to me."

The four senators spent early Sunday just trying to come to grips with what had happened to their bodies and what they could possible do now. Ari and B'nath were utterly crushed. Even though Lelane got them up, dressed more or less in some of Zarita and Celenia's dresses, their extremely long hair brushed, and fed them their breakfast, the two mostly sobbed silently to themselves for several hours. Finally, Zarita had an idea and had Lelane place a call to each senator's home world so they could report to their leaders.

At least, this brought them temporarily out of grief. Each did their best to describe in detail what had happened to the Senate. Naturally, both their leaders had already heard the news. What they needed to know immediately was twofold. First, would the current senators attempt to continue meeting? Second, did they wish to be immediately replaced as their world's senators? They had heard of Senator Celenia's brief term as Senate President. She had somehow managed to fulfill her duties well, despite her lack of arms back then. That was why they phrased their question as they did.

"I suppose I can at least try for a time," Ari admitted. "We don't know yet what the Senate is going to do." Both leaders left strict notice with each senator that, if they wanted to be replaced, they only had to let him know.

"See, they still have confidence in you, Ari," Celenia tried to sound optimistic, though she didn't feel that way at all.

"But we're helpless, Celenia," Ari protested, fighting hard to keep from another round of crying.

"So was I, but I did manage with Lelane's help. We just have to get us some more assistants," Celenia suggested. "It's anything but fun or easy. Scary actually. And yes, we are very helpless like this, more than I used to be. Back then, we didn't have these awful lip plates and boobs so large we can't see over them. Somehow, we have to keep the Senate going. The whole Imperium will be watching and praying." Everyone was speaking slowly and using IS.

Lelane headed off to fix them lunch. Around two that afternoon, mere hours before his ill-fated trip to the opera, President Balag called, setting up a video conference with Senator Celenia in particular, though the other three sat beside her on the couch, while Lelane adjusted the camera for them.

"Senator Celenia, senators, I've just talked to the former Senate President Michael Sanders. He's in bad shape and has formally resigned. In truth, no one can blame him or any of you senators. However, legally, I have to reconstitute the Senate as fast as possible. I've decided to call upon you, Senator Celenia. You graciously took over the Senate Presidency last year during one of the worst crisis we've ever had until now. I know that your current physical situation is somewhat worse than back then, but could you possibly consent once again to being the temporary Senate President and help me get the Senate functioning once more? The Imperium is at great risk as we speak. If we cannot rise to handle this disaster, other worlds may begin to secede. Civil wars could well loom on the horizon, if we don't handle this disaster rapidly and well."

"Well, of course, I'll be glad to help out again, President Balag. I'll need Lelane to be my hands as before. We should try to get all those senators, who are able to at least give it a try, together as soon as possible. I suspect some worlds will be sending replacement senators here fairly soon, don't you think?" Celenia replied and asked.

"I would expect that to be the case. I've compiled a list of all the senators and where they are staying. I'm uploading it to you now. I hereby appoint you as acting Senate President, Celenia. On behalf of the entire Imperium, we thank you for stepping up in these most impossible times," he said rather formally. She smiled, though it wasn't visible. After a bit more chatting, he ended their talk.

Celenia decided to have Ari and B'nath help her with this project. After Lelane retrieved the lengthy document, the four sat around the comm network, making call after call to the two thousand senators. Lelane got a work out dialing all the numbers for them. What promised to take over three days to do only took all the rest of that day, though they went far into the evening. Many senators were being housed together in makeshift assisted living quarters on a temporary basis. Thus, with one call, she was able to reach any number of senators. With each senator, she told them of her appointment as their temporary Senate President and suggested that the Senate formally resume work on Tuesday.

Lelane kept accurate records for Celenia. Just under half of the senators would not be coming back. Replacement senators had been requested. They would be arriving on Proxima Prime during the next few weeks. By eleven that night, Celenia finished the roll call, and Lelane pointed out they had just over half of the senators agreeing to show up on Tuesday morning. Ari commented, "Well, at least there is a quorum. Now you can hold official votes. I suppose that's something."

Around four that afternoon, three young women arrived. Mark Shields had hired them to be their temporary personal assistants. All were just eighteen and on temporary leave from the Academy. Elaine took charge of B'nath; Betsy handled Ari; while Rae agreed to assist Zarita with her needs, leaving Lelane free to continue her work with Celenia. Around the same time, their cook arrived. For the first time, dinner went well, though all three new assistants mostly fumbled their way through it. Nothing had ever prepared them for what they now had to do for these women.

While they were eating, Rae volunteered, "They've

cancelled all classes at the Academy and asked for volunteers to help all the senators. There never has been a crisis like this one before. Everyone is watching and waiting to see what happens next."

"Business as usual, well as usual as we can possibly make it," Celenia replied. "Tuesday, we are going to hold our first session somehow, someway. We have to."

Later, they sat together watching the latest news. Many reporters were predicting doomsday had come, that the entire Senate would be dissolved. Others thought the entire Senate would be wholly replaced within a few months. Celenia grimaced; the president was right; the Senate had to become operational and soon.

Suddenly, the studio reporters broke away to their field reporters. "We are at the Royal Opera House, where President Balag and Legate H-cubed are holding their fund raising event to help our stricken senators. We are told something has happened. We are trying to get confirmation, but it seems there has been another biological attack on the opera house, similar to that of the Senate. Detectors are going off as you can see; we're being pushed back for our own safety. Here comes Mark Shields, Bio Containment Department, now. Mark, what can you tell our viewers and the entire Imperium? Has there been another attack? Has the president been secured?"

Mark ignored the reporters and headed in closer. The reporters continued their wild speculation and pointing out the plainly obvious things that were happening, including the massive buildup of Security Guards. Ari cried out, "Stupid reporters. Why don't you get closer so you too can lose your arms and become as helpless as we all are? Fools!"

A bit later, they watched, as the entrances were sealed up, and vehicles rolled in to block them further. Only then, Mark did give a brief interview. "Yes, it has been verified. This is another biological agent attack; the same agents that were used on our senators are present here. Yes, the President and Legate H-cubed are inside along with a thousand others. Yes, they are some of the wealthiest men and women on Proxima Prime. There's nothing we can do now, except wait until the bio agent becomes dormant. That should be in about three days. Then, we can go in and rescue them. Right now, if we open those doors, we'll infect half the city. I've got this attack as contained as possible. If you are concerned and live within a ten block radius of this opera house, you might consider evacuating for three days. No, we don't know who is behind this latest attack. Really, no more questions. I've my hands full as it is."

"My god! Not again," Celenia exclaimed.

"Oh no! The president, we've lost our president too," Ari gushed.

"Crap. Someone's got to stop these beasts!" Zarita exclaimed, growing rather angry once more. "Men. Worthless piles of shit!" Ari chuckled at that outburst.

"Say, what's that noise?" Celenia asked.

"Oh! That's our door. Someone's there," Lelane recognized it. "I best get to the security panel and fast. Do you think someone is trying to break in here?" she asked worriedly.

Zarita lunged forward, got precariously to her feet, before her new assistant could react. "I'm going with her," she said to Rae.

As the two got to the console, they saw a strange man's face on the screen. They spotted a number of others behind him. Both grew quite worried. Lelane pushed the intercom button. "Who's there?" she said.

"I need to see Senator Zarita. Matter of extreme urgency. Oh, there you are. Senator, we would like a few words with you," the Commander stated.

Zarita looked at the console. "It says you all have guns. We don't have any guns in here, so I don't think this is such a good idea to let you in. If you don't leave, the Security Guards will be here shortly."

"We are the Security Guards," he replied, somewhat annoyed with her non-compliance. He was used to issuing orders and having them obeyed without question.

The lone woman among them stepped closer to the camera. "Let me, Commander. Senator Zarita, we don't know if you've heard the news or not. The President and a Legate, along with a thousand others, have been attacked at the opera house. It's the same biological agent that wiped out the Senate.

Please, we need to talk to you," Ellen attempted her best manners, though her voice held little actual emotion.

"What do we do?" asked a worried Lelane.

Zarita spoke up, "Okay, we'll let you in. But I'm warning you, if you try anything, you'll regret it. Men are not particularly welcome in this house. Let them in, Lelane."

"What about their guns?" she asked.

"If they try anything, Lelane, I'll kill them," Zarita replied. Lelane had forgotten to switch off the intercom. The Commander and ST1 also heard this brief exchange, but their expressionless faces gave no indication they had overheard her threat.

"Well, what do you want?" Zarita asked. She stood before the second entrance door. Lelane had her fingers on the alarm button, in case she needed to signal the Security Company that monitored the compound.

"Is there someplace where we can talk privately?" the Commander asked.

Chapter 26 Battle of Wills

"This way. My study," Zarita suggested, leading the seven into her study next to the game room. "You'll have to arrange your own chairs. I can't any longer." She tossed her head to one side, her huge earrings swinging out wide, along with her hair. With it more towards her front, she carefully sat down and watched the military precision of these seven. Six deferred to the one called the Commander; she concluded he was the most important one. Five others deferred to the one called Peter; his second in command, she assumed. None looked friendly; none showed any outward traces of emotion. What a strange group, she thought. "So what do you want?" she asked.

She noticed they were watching her very carefully, noticing everything about her, from her toe shoes all the way up her body to her giant lip plates and armless shoulders. "Well, we're all pretty darn helpless aren't we?" she said slightly testily. She'd sensed they were appraising her and found her somehow lacking. Either that or they had not seen one of the victims up close and personal. She probed slightly and picked up that surface thought from the lone woman, Ellen.

The Commander spoke sternly without the slightest trace of any emotion in his voice. "There has been another attack. The President this time. I'd rather talk about the Senate attack and what you know about it. According to Mark, you and your wife were the only two out of the two thousand plus who remained conscious for quite some time after the others went into a coma. How do you explain that? Did you have prior knowledge of the attack?"

Zarita did not like his insinuation. She retorted, "Fool. If I had, I'd have stopped it before it happened. Do you think we desire to be helpless like this? If you do, you're more than the fool I'm taking you for right now. If you had any brains, you'd know Celenia and I had already been subjected to a similar bio genetic attack on Ashford-5 half a year ago. Our bodies had already been genetically modified, except for the loss of our arms. So until our arms began going away, we had nothing to be affected."

She'd expected her retort to force some kind of emotional rise in this Commander. All she saw was a brief rise of his eyebrows, as well as several others. He countered, "But you later learned who was behind the attack on the Senate?"

"The Holy Father Jesuit and his True Believers," she answered. "It was on the news."

"And you come from Ashford-5?"

"Just how stupid are you anyway?" she blasted back at him. "No, I am a Rigel-3 native, born and raised there." Her temper was rising. She obviously wasn't. They were very tall, spindly, and had quite grey skin tones.

"Just answer the questions, senator," he countered.

"Then ask intelligent questions, stupid," she retorted. "Obviously, I'm from Ashford-5, I'm their senator, and that's on my citizen ID card. So why ask stupid questions? What the hell do you want?"

"I'll ask the questions here," he shot back. "Ashford-5 has a lot of telepaths, though you prefer to call yourselves *mentales* gifted, right?"

"Correct," she decided to give short, succinct answers, rivaling him. *Two can play the same game,* she thought.

"A *mentales* gifted can kill just with a thought, correct?" he asked.

"Of course." *What is he trying to find out? Time to find out. I've had about enough of this. Best not use my crystals, though.*

"You wanted that Holy Father Jesuit dead for what he and his men did to you and all the other senators, correct?"

"Correct."

"You saw that was done, correct?"

"Correct. You have seven dead bodies, including that evil Jesuit fellow in your morgue. You don't know how their brains were microwaved, correct?" she retorted and asked, throwing some of what she'd seen in his mind back at him, a teaser to put him on the defensive instead of herself. She watched for their reactions. Again, eyebrows flickered, but otherwise they gave no other visible reactions. She didn't need physical reactions to know she'd struck nerves. No, their minds began racing, questioning. He didn't answer swiftly enough, so she added, "Correct?"

"Correct. And you have the answer I seek in their cause of death?" he bounced it back at Zarita.

"Of course, you've already told me the cause of death, a *mentales* thought can kill."

Still no reaction. *These are damn cold people,* she thought. He countered, "So you made sure these seven terrorists couldn't harm any more innocent people?"

"No one else did it," she countered. "Ah, I see. Your people arrived on the scene shortly after they died. You feel cheated because someone else beat you to them, is that it?" Again, eyebrows rose, but only momentarily. She added, "Wait, no, you are pissed because someone found these men were behind the bio attack and got to them before you did. Men. You and your egos!" Again, eyebrows flickered slightly. She knew she'd hit a nerve in this Commander and some of those with him.

"Catching them was our job, not yours," he replied.

"Perhaps that's because you were not doing your job fast enough," Zarita countered. She added, "Others might have been harmed because you were too slow in finding them and acting." This produced a definite rise in several of them, including the Commander. She knew she'd hit it squarely this time.

"So you admit you took care of these seven men?" he insinuated.

"Someone had to stop them before they could attack other innocents. No one messes with Zarita and lives to tell about it." She thinly disguised her threat and warning to him.

"We wanted that Jesuit taken alive," he countered.

She probed a bit further then added, "Ah, so you could question him. Ah, you want to know where he got the biological agent he used in the attack on us senators. Sorry about that. Didn't know you wanted to question him."

"People should not take such matters into their own hands. Had we been able to interrogate him, we might have been able to prevent the bio attack on the president this evening," he attempted to place the blame onto her for her actions.

"Sorry, that argument doesn't hold water. Even had you gotten the information from him immediately, his group of terrorists isn't those who've attacked the president this evening. According to the news and Mark, it's this Devil's Disciple Pathagorous who's behind it. You had a week to find and interrogate Jesuit. You need to be quicker if you are going to stop these terrorists from making more attacks. How the hell did you let the terrorists get their hands on this biological agent in the first place? I think that's the real question that ought to be asked. Someone has dropped the ball big time. Perhaps the Senate should conduct a full scale investigation over this matter," she threatened him a little.

The Commander was growing more and more frustrated with Zarita. She sensed this in his mind, though his outward appearance remained as emotionless as before. The two glared at each other. Then, Ellen spoke up, "Commander, might I speak with Senator Zarita?" He glared at her, but nodded.

"Hi, I'm Ellen. We're actually trying our best to protect you and everyone else from these terrorists. We need your help. This attack on the President and Legate tonight — we need you to allow us to do our thing with the culprits and not take action on your part."

"Okay, but if you don't find them and punish them, I'll have to, as you say, take matters into my own hands, even though I don't seem to have them any longer," Zarita replied.

Her jest brought a fleeting smile to Ellen's face, as she duplicated Zarita's tease. "Thank you. So you have been reading our minds all along tonight?"

"Not at first, but he pissed me off. Why?"

"I understand. The Commander can come off rather cold at times, especially when things are as serious as they are now. Did you have to be there in the True Believer's Church to microwave their brains?"

"Not at all. It's terribly difficult for us to get around now. If I had to be there physically, I'd be unable to have done it. It's a challenge just to walk, you know. No, I can microwave their brains from anywhere on Proxima Prime, just as any telepath can send and receive from anywhere on the planet, if they are any good, that is."

"I see. So am I right in thinking you could microwave all seven of us at any time you wanted to this evening?" Ellen asked.

"Of course. Plus, now that I have met you, I could do it at any other time I wanted to do it and from wherever I was at on Proxima Prime. No one messes with Zarita," she answered Ellen. While this woman also had very little emotion visible, she was asking the right questions and not insulting her intelligence.

"We'll not give you any reason to do that to us, Senator Zarita. Might I ask if this is what happened to the three men who called themselves the Consortium after they escaped custody?"

"Yes, when I heard they'd escaped and were about to head off-world where we'd never be able to apprehend them, I had no choice but to act. I did it from my Presidential Office," she replied. *Perhaps if they know my power, they'll appreciate me and assist me. If not, they are as good as dead themselves.*

"For that, ex-President Zarita, on behalf of all on Proxima Prime, we thank you," Ellen tried a little diplomacy.

"Thanks. We should keep this tidbit just between us, though. It wouldn't be wise for others to know about it," Zarita suggested.

"Of course, our secret. In the future, might we call upon you to lend us a hand in capturing other terrorists?" Ellen asked politely.

"Oh. I see what you mean. Sorry, I couldn't help prying into your minds a little. You need to interrogate these Devil's Disciples and find out where they got the biological weapons. Oh, your methods are barbaric! There are much simpler ways of finding that out and more accurate," Zarita replied. Ellen's eyebrows rose again.

"Given enough pain, they all talk," the Commander interjected, defending his chief interrogator, Torres.

"A simple mind probe can give you far more accurate

397

information. Oh, I see. You need to know where this Disciple Pathagorous got the bio agents. You are frustrated because he's becoming a martyr himself; he's with our President and Legate H-cubed," she explained, again reading his thoughts.

"We want to interrogate him, after he becomes the same helpless vegetable he's turned the President and H-cubed and a thousand others into," the Commander replied.

"Sorry, I'm not yet a helpless vegetable. I can get you that information right now. Why wait? Besides, he might not survive the attack," Zarita countered.

"But we can't get you into the Opera House. It's totally contained at the moment," the Commander replied sternly.

"Haven't you been listening to anything I've been saying? Men! Fools one and all. I can find out right now, right from here. Only take a couple of minutes. That is, if you truly want my help," she countered.

Ellen interrupted the Commander, who was about to say something. "Yes, we certainly would like your help, Senator Zarita. If you can use your skills right now and find out if those people have more of the bio weapon cylinders that would help us prevent another attack. More importantly, we need to know where they got them. Is it possible for you to find that out now, from here?"

"Yes, give me a few uninterrupted minutes, please. Okay?"

"Agreed," the Commander said. "Peter, stand guard. Don't let anyone interrupt us." Peter rose and took a guard position at the study doorway.

Zarita focused and sent her mind's awareness outward latching onto the Opera House. That part was easy; the fear and terror emanating from the thousand plus men and women inside hit her like some brilliant beacon light. It took her a minute to find the right mind, the Holy Father Jesuit. She connected with him just as he was launching into his tirade of condemnation. He was standing center stage addressing the terror-stricken crowd, some of whom were trying to find a way out of the large building.

She witnessed the men beating him to death. *No, you don't get away so easily,* she latched on to him as he left his dead body. *I want to know two things.*

A half hour had passed. The seven had not noticed a single thing. Zarita merely had her eyes closed sitting stiffly on the couch. True, some of her jewelry briefly glowed with a pale blue light, but nothing else was observable. At last, she opened her eyes. "Well, that was a close one. The man's dead. They beat him to a pulp, after he got up on the stage and told them what he had done to them all, something about Negative Afterlife or some such nonsense. Anyway, I got what you wanted. They have six more cylinders and are planning another attack tomorrow." She gave them the location where they were being stored.

"He's gotten a dozen sets from a General Snaggard of the Soldiers of Fortune on Donner-3. I don't know where that world is, so I have to let you take care of them. If you aren't, let me know, and I'll try to go there myself and see they're killed too. Oh yes, one more thing, President Balag is dead. He shot himself and his wife, rather than become as we senators all are. Shame, now we don't have a president either. What's the Imperium coming to anyway?" she lamented.

"Thank you, Senator Zarita. We'll get on this immediately, and see if we can't prevent another attack. We'll take care of the supplier and track down all those to whom he's sold the bio agent to," the Commander replied, cordially for the first time this evening.

Just then, Lelane tried to get into the room. Peter was still blocking the doorway though. "Zarita! It's important. Legate Marhildt is calling for you. He says that it is very urgent. Please, you must take the call."

Zarita lunged forward, attempting to get to her feet, wobbling a little to get her balance. While she could have used her telekinetic powers to make a more graceful rise, she wanted the seven to see just what the victims now faced. She made her slow, careful way back out to the comm center. The seven followed behind her, curious about the Legate's call.

A very somber faced Legate Marhildt was on the monitor. "Ah Senator Zarita. I have some very bad news to relay to you. President Balag is dead. You've heard that the Opera House was attacked tonight?"

"Yes, another biological attack. He's dead?"

"Yes, H-cubed reported it to Mark Shields of the Bio Containment Department. With the Senate in total disarray and not likely to be functioning anytime soon and now with the President dead, the Imperium is facing another terrible crisis. Senator, I've called to ask big favor of you. Last year, during the crisis of leadership, you stepped forward and became our temporary President, leading us out of that disaster. Would you be willing to do so again? I'm authorized to offer you the position effective immediately. Please, the Imperium has never been as vulnerable as it is at this moment."

"The Senate will be resuming operations on Tuesday. Celenia is taking over as temporary Senate President. She's got a quorum for Tuesday. Okay, I'll do it, but only temporarily, until the Senate can choose a proper President," Zarita replied, seeing no other alternative than to accept. This way, she could bring all the force of the Imperium to bear to track down these terrorists.

"Thank you, Senator. I'll swear you into office right now. Fifty Security Guards are on their way to your compound as we speak. You'll have the highest protection we can possibly field." He proceeded to recite the official words, and she so swore.

When he hung up, Lelane dashed off to tell the others the news. The Commander looked at her and said, "Well, congratulations, President Zarita."

"Thanks, as your President, I want to be kept fully informed of these investigations. Perhaps, I can be of further use in tracking these terrorists down. I don't think we've seen the last of them. This whole notion of human genetic engineering is quite a polarizing issue."

The Commander spoke, "Normally, not even the President knows of us or how to contact us. However, in this situation, I'll give you a contact number. I don't think it would matter to you now if we didn't. You could get to us at any time you desired, right?"

President Zarita smiled, though it wasn't visible because of her lip plates. "Absolutely and at any time. Death even isn't barrier. I got that information from Pathagorous, after his body had been beaten to death." She picked up another of his thoughts and added, "Yes, you're quite right. You need to be very careful with me. There probably isn't anyone more potentially dangerous than I am, that's quite true. Let's get these terrorists soon. I don't want to be President very long. I'm expecting my first child in mid-April. Celenia and I are starting our family, you see, and we'll need a long maternity leave."

"Agreed. By the way, what we've discussed here tonight with you and even our whole organization is top secret, Level Twelve. So don't breathe a word about us to anyone," the Commander ordered.

"Agreed, as long as you keep me fully informed. I have to get this horrific situation handled soon, before others have their lives ruined," she replied. She watched, as the seven marched out of her compound, just as a large contingency of Security Guards arrived.

After the seven got into their transport, Ellen commented, "My god, Zarita is something else. If her Intel is right, we need to be very careful with her."

"Indeed. Potentially, she could be the most serious threat to the Imperium ever," the Commander replied. "First, let's see if her Intel checks out. Second, let's see if she has any ties to these organizations. There could well be a far more sinister side to this. She could be behind this whole reign of terror. She's got the Presidency again."

When Zarita joined the others in their living room, all congratulated her on becoming the President once more. "Look, I don't want to be President any longer than I have to be. So Celenia, get the senators to elect a new President very soon, please," she countered.

"I don't see how you can do it," Ari said sadly. "We're so helpless. You can't even turn a page or sign any documents. They should just shoot us as they did with President Balag. Our lives are completely ruined."

Zarita had no answer for that nor could she think of anything to say to console her either. "Men's doing. Why are all disasters men's doings?" Ari flashed a brief, but invisible, smile.

On Monday morning, surrounded by a hundred Security Guards, temporary President Zarita Valen was escorted to the Presidential Office. Outside, a huge gathering of reporters and cameras waited. A din of questions was yelled at her, and she decided to give them their first official news conference. The eyes of the Imperium were upon the ruling bodies. Still watched over by her large escort, she stepped up to the wall of microphones. Speaking slowly and in Imperial Standard, she gave her prepared address.

"Hello everyone. I'm temporary President Zarita Valen. Yes, I'm back again; this time minus my arms. We're facing a crisis far worse than that of a year ago. Biological weapons have fallen into the hands of terrorists, who want nothing more than to destroy our mighty Imperium. Today, as one of their victims, I wish to send them a message. You have failed. The Imperium is strong and vital still. While it's true, you terrorists have damaged and ruined several thousand lives, you've only strengthened the Imperium. You can take out our Senate; you can eliminate our President. Yet, we come back at once, even stronger and with a firmer resolve."

"Some often call the people of my home world of Ashford-5 uncivilized barbarians, primitives. I've news for you; my people are truly civilized. It's these terrorists of the Imperium who are the real barbarians — men and women who lack all traces of sanity, of humanity, of ethics, and of morals. To you barbarian terrorists of the Imperium, I give you my sworn word that we'll be hunting you down where you live and exterminating you, as one would squash a cockroach in your kitchen. You, of all people, do not deserve the life that is within you."

"So as of today, the Office of the President is once again functioning. Tomorrow, Senate President Celenia will open the spring session of the Senate. It'll be business as usual this week, though obviously, we both will be focusing on combating this outbreak of terrorism, as well as other normal business. The Imperium is strong and vital. The Imperium is more than those men and women who temporarily hold these offices. I'll now take a few questions."

"President Valen, how will you be able to carry out your duties as president, as crippled as you are now?"

"My mind is as clear as it ever was. Anyone can be my arms and hands. The last time I checked, my mind wasn't in my arms or hands."

"But President Valen, aren't you almost completely helpless now?" the reported persisted.

"Physically, I'm at a very distinct disadvantage, as you so carefully are pointing out. If the President were required to run a six minute mile, lift a hundred pounds, do fifty pushups, then, yes, I wouldn't be qualified to be your President. The last time I checked, none of these were the duties of the President."

"How do you respond to those who claim that you and the others are now total freaks, hermaphrodites?"

"Until this biological attack on us back on Ashford-5 and now the one on us in the Senate, I'd never even heard of hermaphrodites before. So yes, there can be no denying our bodies have been horrifically genetically altered and not for the best. Still, these are mere bodies. Our minds are wholly unaffected. Our intelligence, our knowledge, our wisdom, our ability to lead — these are fully intact. These are what are needed and wanted in both a president and a senator. These are what Celenia and I and many others still bring with us."

"President Valen, is it true that you are pregnant?"

"Why, thanks for asking. Yes, my wife and I are both expecting our first children in April. We are anxious to start our family. We fully intend to have all this wrapped up long before then."

"But aren't you concerned you'll be bringing more helpless freaks like yourself into the world?" the same reported challenged her.

"I can see you've never been a mother. I don't know of a mother anywhere who doesn't love her children, no matter what they are," she countered. It wasn't entirely true, but had enough truth in it to shut him up. She added, "Besides, in time, a cure for us all may be found. There's always hope for the future."

She decided to elaborate a little. "You see, as long as

mothers continue to bring forth new generations, there will be hope for the future. When mothers no longer create new generations, there will be no future possible."

"President Valen, considering these awful genetic modifications that have been done to so many men and women, will you be urging the Senate to legalize all forms of genetic research on humans in an attempt to find a cure for you and the others?" another reporter asked.

"Now that *is* a tough question, and a good one, I might add. Illegal experimentation on humans is what has gotten us into this mess in the first place. As is quite clear to everyone, those charged with safeguarding this biological agent in their cylinders have failed in their task. While I would dearly love someone to inject me with a miracle genetic cure, I've no intention of allowing genetic experimentation on human subjects, just in the hope that somehow, someway they'll find a cure for me. Think about the absolutely hideous intermediate effects that would likely be foisted off onto the test subjects on the way to finding that cure. I don't want a cure that's based upon the suffering and deaths of hundreds or thousands of other human guinea pigs, whether they're criminals or not. Life is within me today, and I'll live it as fully as I'm able."

"That said, I can see no reason to keep from sponsoring and promoting continuing genetic research, just not on human test subjects. While I understand this will be a far slower proposition, it's vastly more humane. That is my official position."

"President Valen, what is your position on using this same bio genetic agent on the hardened criminals that was used on you senators? Or would you rather see them put to death? What about any of these bio terrorists who get captured and convicted — should they be executed or subjected to this same bio agent?" another reported followed up.

"The Senate has already signed into Imperium Law the punishment for criminals sentenced to life. They've made their will known. As far as these bio terrorists, while I might personally like to see them dead, I must follow Imperium Law. The Office of the President is charged with carrying out the laws passed by the Senate, not in making those laws. We can take some satisfaction in that those who are captured and convicted will share the difficult life that they've sentenced us to live. Now, I best get inside, there's much work that needs to be done." She turned and allowed herself to be escorted inside and up to the top floor, the Presidential Suite. Dutifully, her Academy student assistant, Rae, followed behind her.

First on her new agenda was the selection of replacement Legate for the late Emeryk Donat. With Rae handling the computer for her, Zarita reviewed the list of candidates and then listened to their interviews that the late President Balag had conducted. None of them suited her. While these handpicked men were all obviously qualified, they were either politically motivated or thirsty for power. "I need to see a list of all current Hub Sector ID Ministers, please, Rae. Yes, that icon there." An hour later and several more bios read, she sent for Hub Sector ID Minister Mary Smith, originally from Descartes-3, whose sun was a yellow dwarf.

Late that afternoon, the fifty year old woman arrived, having dropped everything to respond to the Presidential Summons. As she walked in, President Zarita liked the woman's appearance, very businesslike and yet feminine. She wore a white silk blouse, a simple black skirt hemmed just below her knees, black stockings and matching patent leather low heels. A trim blazer with a light purple scarf rounded out her apparel. Her hair was fairly short, a wavy blonde, but her blue eyes were quite sharp. Her nose, angular. Her face, rather narrow with a pointed chin. Her skin had a distinct hint of light grey in it. "Hub Sector ID Minister Mary Smith reporting as ordered, President Valen," she said in a firm, alto voice. "I'm sorry for what happened to all you senators and now the late president and all those wealthy men and women of Proxima Prime."

"Thank you. I'll get right to the point. I need a new Legate to replace the late Emeryk Donat to oversee the Intelligence Divisions. I've reviewed all those that my predecessor had considered for the post. Frankly, I wasn't impressed with any of them. They wanted the post for political gain or personal power. That's not what I see the position as being. I've gone over your record of service. It says that Mary

Smith is not your original name?"

"Yes, I am from Descartes-3. My original name was too hard for most people to pronounce, ^Markarita Ya^maita^motia. Yes, it is a click language. Many of our women also wear lip plate ornaments, though nowhere near as large as those you and the others now wear. I believe that's the origin of our click language. I changed it to something that everyone can pronounce. It's quite effective."

"I agree. I don't think I could pronounce it either, not without a lot of practice. Okay then, Mary, I'm hereby appointing you to be our new Legate. Congratulations, Legate Mary Smith," Zarita replied.

"What? No interview? No questions?" Mary asked slightly amused and yet pleased, but confused.

"I've looked over your record. Countless times, you have tried to push through reforms within the ID, reforms I tend to agree are warranted. Each time, men have vetoed them for spurious reasons. I firmly believe, if some of your reforms had been in place, the terrorists might not have their hands on these bio weapons. Please see that your reforms are carried out. We have a tall order facing us, Legate Smith. Lord knows how many terrorist groups now have their hands on these bio weapons. They'll surely make more attempts to wreak havoc and disaster on more innocent lives. Your job, stop them. Make these bio agents secure so this cannot happen again."

A broad smile creased her lips. "Excellent! I certainly will, President Valen. I promise you we'll end this streak of terror soon. However, the damage is done, and I want you to realize that more harm may come before we can capture or kill all the terrorists."

"Of course, Legate Smith. Until they're all discovered and apprehended, some will undoubtedly strike. Let's work together and minimize the damage. Keep me informed of your progress. Come. Let's get you officially sworn in," Zarita replied.

"What about Legate H-cubed?" she asked.

"Right now, I don't know. It'll be several days before he regains consciousness. After that, I've no idea how he'll react to his body being genetically modified like this. It's damned hard to survive as we are. If he wants to resign, I'll have to replace him, but I'll not force anyone out of office simply because they've become a terrorist victim. The genetic modifications have not affected our minds, and I hope not our sense of ethics either."

"Excellent plan. I'll endeavor to bring back a sense of honor, ethics, and responsibility into the Intelligence Division," Legate Smith replied.

As Zarita suspected, during the ensuing weeks, a major overhaul of the entire Intelligence Division occurred. From her previous stint as the Imperium President, she also knew the post was primarily a figurehead. There wasn't very much to actually do. The huge staff carried out the routine business of running the vast Imperium. By presenting an image of a person very much in charge, she hoped to instill the confidence that others needed at this critical time. Hence, she handled the actual items that simply had to be done, such as picking a replacement Legate. She also lined up one to replace H-cubed, should he decide to resign his post, once he'd recovered in a few days. She figured it could go either way. He might be so humiliated that he would not dare show himself in public again or he would carry on, becoming a highly visible reminder of the fight against terrorism that was going on here on Proxima Prime.

The one thing that concerned President Valen the most was the chance that the terrorism would spread to other worlds, especially here in the densely packed hub of the galaxy. This she watched carefully during the ensuing days. When she returned home late Monday night, she found three very scared senators.

"I don't think I can do this," Ari sobbed. "I'm so helpless. I look like a freak. What possible use can I be in the Senate now?" B'nath simply sobbed quietly to herself.

"Can I make a suggestion, Ari? Tomorrow, when you all meet, propose some new legislation that allows women senators to dress anyway they desire. Get rid of those ancient laws that we were forced to follow. Leave behind that as a legacy. That's something you've been battling since I first met you," Zarita suggested. As expected, Ari brightened up and agreed to do that much.

"Look all three of you, take it one day at a time. There's no question it's going to be unbelievably rough for all of you. You aren't alone; there are hundreds of other senators in the same situation. Actually, you'll find the male senators will be having a far harder time of it. They've never worn toe shoes before," she pointed out.

Ari gave a faint chuckle. "Serves them right for having forced us to all these years."

"Right, so time to get them to change their dress codes."

Celenia spoke up, "I'm going to get an appropriations bill passed, one that gives we senators who were genetically modified a large monetary stipend so that we can get the assistants and clothing and such that we need. Not all senators are independently wealthy."

The next morning, with hundreds of reporters filming and yelling out questions from quite some distance from the entrance of the Senate Building, around a thousand senators bravely arrived for the opening session. Accompanied by wives, husbands, or newly hired assistants, they braved the public humiliation to resume their posts. Unable to see their feet over their massive bosoms, unused to walking on their toes in their new toe shoes, many stumbled on the steps. Those who were at their sides prevented them from taking nasty falls.

Once inside, some comradery began to form amid the sea of bronze giant lip plates, massive bosoms, and long hair, which were plainly visible as one looked around the amphitheater, especially from Senate President Celenia's view from the central platform looking up at all of them. Their wives, husbands, and assistants sat beside them helping as needed. Hence, the Senate gave the appearance of being quite full. Celenia first issued an official roll call, and the tabulator notified her that a quorum was present.

After announcing that, she got down to business. Quickly, they passed an appropriations bill, giving all victims of the biological attack a stipend of five hundred thousand credits, payable immediately to be used to help them survive. Next, Senator Ari introduced her new dress code bill. It passed without a single no vote, much to her surprise.

Another senator introduced a bill that would force anyone convicted of biological terrorism to be subjected to this genetic modification as well, before being sent to the assisted living quarters where the lifers were being held. Again, that passed unanimously. After that, they began the grueling work of preparing the coming fiscal year's budget.

Zarita was delayed getting home Tuesday night. Peter called her up on a secure line to relay their latest actions. They'd raided the Devil's Disciples and found the cache of six bio agent cylinders, disrupting a further plot. However, what bothered her about the call was what was left unsaid. They suspected her of somehow being involved, since she'd led them directly to this cache. By the time she got home late that night, the three senators were exhausted and had gone to bed early.

During the ensuing days, more and more replacement senators began arriving and were sworn in. Within two weeks, three quarters of the original senators, who had been attacked and genetically modified, had been replaced with new senators. Thus, early February, Senate President Celenia was able to accept nominations for a new temporary Senate President. To everyone's amazement, Senator Helmon Crack was elected. He was from one of the planets in the Ataro Empire! Emperor Kino had somehow gotten his chosen man into the leadership of the Senate.

That late afternoon, as a very pleased Celenia was making her slow, careful way out of the Senate building, with Lelane at her side helping her, and with B'nath and her assistant right behind them, a scraggly haired man broke through the line of bored Security Guards. Screaming, "Die, Devil's Spawn!" he detonated a massive bomb strapped to his chest. Suicide bombing had come to Proxima Prime. These four died instantly along with four other genetically modified senators. Senator Ari survived the blast only because someone had stopped her and her assistant over a question about her possible replacement senator from Acer-4.

Totally devastated, Ari and Zarita arrived home along with their assistants, but under very heavy guard. For hours, the two merely sat in front of the giant monitor in their living room, watching the news, though the reporters mostly repeated the same story over and over as the hours passed slowly past to two stunned women.

Finally, Ari broke down. "I wish I could just die too. I can't live like this. We are helpless freaks, Devil's Spawn. That's what we are now, Zarita, Devil's Spawn."

"No we aren't Ari. They are just intolerant and insane people out there," Zarita attempted to console her. Instead, both women broke down and began sobbing, grieving at last for their lost wives. "She was pregnant with our child too," Zarita sobbed. Quietly, their two assistants got them ready for bed and tucked in. That only brought on another round of crying; neither woman had slept alone for a very long time. Their lives seemed totally empty, drained of everything they held precious and dear.

The next day, neither went to work. Fortunately, the new Senate President hastily held a new election, and the Senate quickly elected Senator Lockley Humber, another senator from the Ataro Empire to be the next temporary President, replacing Zarita. The next few days passed by the two women as one long grey, uncomprehended mass of time. Their grief and loss was severe, and they were barely aware of the combined funerals for their lost ones.

Four days after the bombing, thirty year old Franco Hermanes arrived, replacing Zarita as Ashford-5's new senator. Queen Amy and Emperor Kino agreed; Zarita had suffered enough loss and had to have some time to recover. Besides, she was due in less than two months. As Amy well knew, getting around now was becoming harder and harder for herself. She herself was due in six weeks. Zarita had to have some help now.

"Well, I am thankful that you've come, Senator Franco. I don't think I can do this any longer," Zarita said, still mostly in a daze.

Upon hearing that Zarita too was leaving, Ari broke down completely. Sobbing, she begged, "Franco, please kill me, I beg you. Put me out of my misery. I can't take any more of this. Have mercy on me."

"Ari, come with me, please; I need you," Zarita pleaded.

Hearing the gay, fun loving Ari so completely depressed finally registered in Zarita's fogged mind. "Come with me, please."

Ari leaned her head on Zarita's shoulders and agreed. Quickly, their two helpers packed up their things into five crates. With Franco's help, they loaded them onto the waiting deep space transport that had brought him here to her compound. A few minutes later, the two grieving women were in hyperspace on their way to Ashford-5. Zarita realized there was a limit to just how much personal loss she could withstand. Now, she was way past that point.

Chapter 27 Subterfuge

"Enemy is contained," Peter spoke emotionlessly. His sub-dermal transmitter sent his words, not only to his ST1 members, but also via Karkoff's relay system back to Hans, the Comm Central Coordinator, and thus to the Commander, Scoby, and Lela, who were all monitoring this mission quite closely. He'd taken a gamble and followed up on Zarita's tip. The ST1 had raided this specific Devil's Disciples Church and found the six bio agent cylinders just as Zarita had suggested. The ST1 had eliminated six members and secured the bio agents, the meaning of his three word report.

Now, the Commander sat back to ponder the significance of this event. Either Zarita was somehow involved in this mess or she was what she claimed to be, the Righteous Vigilante, with enormous powers and the ability to kill with just a thought. Either way, Zarita was a serious threat to the Imperium. But could she be used? That was the key remaining question in the Commander's mind.

When the ST1 returned and had gone through debriefing, he summoned Lela and Scoby to his Level One office. "Okay, Zarita's Intel proved accurate. Now, we need to get onto this Soldiers of Fortune group on Donner-3. Have you the proposals, Scoby?"

"Some. A direct assault on their compound has less than a thirty percent chance of success. Too many unknowns. Where do they keep their arsenal of bio weapons? More than likely not on site. Taking one of their low level operatives is also dicey, only fifteen percent chance. General Snaggard is not likely to entrust the location of his arsenal to such operatives. Infiltration with one of our agents has an eighty percent chance of success, but will take several months at least."

"Too damn long. IBI needs results soon," the Commander commented.

"Well, posing as a buyer has a seventy percent chance of yielding definitive Intel. We'd know for sure they are the source and their modus of delivery," Scoby suggested.

"Okay, we'll use the buyer scenario. Compile your Mission Plan. Get it to me for review in six hours," the Commander ordered.

Four days later, wearing prosthetic masks, Peter and Ellen entered the Pink Flamingo, a low life bar on the edge of Dan City, Donner-3. He wore flashy neon green pants and a gaudy yellow and pink swirls silk shirt. She wore a red wig and a slinky, pink silk dress that didn't cover her knees, along with tall stilettos. Both carried d-guns strapped to their waists. The bar was filled with dozens of party revelers dressed somewhat similarly. The odor of stale beer and smoke combined with urine was almost overwhelming to the pair, who moved up to the bar and ordered a couple of beers.

"Say, heard the Soldiers of Fortune have something for sale that we want to buy," Peter said from the corner of his mouth to the bartender. Slipping him a fifty credit note; he looked the other way.

"Man in the black coat there in that corner," the bartender muttered, slipping the note into his shirt pocket, sliding the two beers over before the pair. Peter and Ellen picked up their glasses, took a sip, and sauntered in the general direction of the indicated man. He was well-armed. Several empty beer glasses littered his table, along with one that was half-full. Peter slipped into the chair opposite the man, while Ellen stood at his side, looking seductively at the man.

"Heard the Soldiers of Fortune have something for sale that we want to buy," Peter whispered.

"They might. Never seen you before," the man replied with a sneer.

"Red Ghosts. Check us out. We have big plans. Need a dozen of the stuff the Devil's Disciples got. Price is not a consideration. We're at the Nigel Hotel, Room 412," Peter replied. He rose, and the two left, leaving their beers on his table. Scoby had done his job well, fabricating an entire history of the fictitious Red Ghosts. Further, he relayed word to Karkoff in the cloaked transport ship hovering over Dan City. He was monitoring Peter and Ellen's communications.

Everything they heard or said was sent to Karkoff via the subdermal transponders imbedded in all field agents of the Bops.

Their room was filled with a distinctive stench both found revolting. Cockroaches scurried about in broad daylight, seemingly ignoring the presence of the two humans. Now they waited. A day later, someone slipped a note beneath their door. It specified a location and a time. Peter read it aloud, and Karkoff relayed it on up the line. Presently, the two heard Scoby's voice via their transponder.

"Okay, located it. Sending the data to Karkoff now."

"Got it," Karkoff soon added. "It's a warehouse six blocks from you. Bringing up the layout now. A dozen enemy are there now."

At the appointed time, Peter and Ellen walked into the warehouse. At once, four men surrounded them, guns drawn. Quickly, they took away the pair's d-guns and searched them. "Go ahead." They escorted the two to the center of a large open area near the middle of the nearly empty warehouse. There, another man sat at a table. Six more men stood behind him, guns drawn. The man looked up as the two arrived. He wore thick glasses. Through their transponders, Karkoff said, "He's not General Snaggard."

"So you checked out, Red Ghosts. Heard you want a dozen cylinders. A hundred thousand credits each," the measly voice said.

"Not a problem. How soon?" Peter replied.

"Half up front. Two days. You'll be notified where and when to pick them up."

"Missa, pay the man," Peter ordered.

Ellen pulled out a wad of large denomination credit notes from her bust line. They now smelled of cheap perfume. She counted out six hundred thousand, stuffing the remainder back into her cleavage. The man quickly counted them and nodded. The guards put their hands on the pair, nudging them back the way that they had come. The meeting was obviously over. At the door, they were given back their guns, but all ten still had theirs trained on the pair.

Now, Karkoff had work to do. If they were lucky, during the next two days, a Fabrication Machine would be used. It drew an enormous amount of power, while it replicated whatever was in the Input Basket. On the down side, Karkoff had to monitor the power consumption of an entire planet during this time. Plus, they might already have made the duplicate copies and were just bringing them to the delivery site. Thus, if Karkoff detected nothing, that wasn't definitive either way.

Two days later, another note appeared beneath their door. This time, Karkoff was waiting for him and was able to use IR to follow the deliverer back to that same warehouse. This time, the delivery note gave another location, plus instructions to bring a shuttle for transport. It also provided the overall weight and dimensions of the "package."

The two had to hurry and rent a shuttle in order to make the meeting on time. It was held in a small private hanger at the spaceport on the edge of Dan City. Again, Karkoff alerted Peter and Ellen to the number and locations of the enemy within the hangar. As they walked in, leaving their shuttle just outside, they were relieved of their d-guns and searched before being allowed inside. As they walked to the center, they saw two men wearing the familiar red containment suits. Both sat at a small table. A large crate lay to their left; its top opened.

"Pleasure to do business with the Red Ghosts," the general said, as the two walked up to the table. He wore a red containment suit. "With stuff like this, we take no chances. Cash, and it's all yours." Karkoff whispered that he was General Snaggard.

As before, Ellen retrieved and counted out the credit notes. The second man was the same one who had taken their first payment. They recognized him from his thick glasses. After he counted it out, he nodded to the general who rose. "Come; inspect the goods before we seal it." He and Peter looked into the crate. There lay a dozen of the bio agent cylinders along with a dozen apparel crates, a complete package. Peter noticed the cylinders were securely protected, a very good sign. Satisfied, the general signaled one of the guards to seal the crate.

"It's all yours now. I expect to hear great things from

the Red Ghosts in the near future," the general commented. "My men will carry it out to your shuttle for you. That'll be all." At that, four men picked up the crate, and the others escorted the pair out of the hanger. After loading it onto their shuttle, ten guards stood in front of the hanger, d-guns still pointed at the pair. Not until the two boarded and took flight did they lower their guns.

Peter had hoped to tag the general electronically, but had no chance to plant the bug. The man was wearing a full bio containment suit. However, the credit notes were tagged, and, thus, Karkoff and Scoby were able to at least monitor the movements and location of the notes, as well as the thick glasses accountant. A short while later, the shuttle docked with the deep space transport, and then headed back to HQ on Proxima Prime. The next day, Leroy confirmed that the dozen cylinders indeed contained the bio agent used in the two previous attacks on Proxima Prime.

"Well, we know the source of this stuff. Zarita was right again," the Commander commented. "I need full Intel on this entire Soldiers of Fortune organization pronto! We need a Mission Plan to capture alive this accountant and the general."

During the next several days, the Commander and Scoby ran dozens of simulations, trying to find an acceptable way to somehow "use" and yet "contain" this wild card, Zarita. To this end, he made full use of his Psych Evaluator, Pong Lu.

"She is a strong-willed woman, determined. She doesn't listen to the advice of others, but makes up her own mind," Pong Lu pointed out. "If you simply kidnap her and bring her into HQ, she's going to microwave everyone's brains. Besides, she is the President right now, untouchable."

"So how do we get to her?" the Commander asked.

"Break her down, make her want — no crave to work for us. Make it appear to her that she simply has to use us. That means we have to be in a position to provide her with the Intel she believes she needs to get her revenge. She is revenge motivated, as witnessed by her previous actions," Pong Lu stated dryly.

"How do we do that?" the Commander asked. "She went after the Consortium and the Legate because they either harmed her or her associates."

"Precisely so. She needs something similar to motivate her to seek revenge at all costs."

"What might that be? Wiping out the president, H-cubed, and the thousand at the Opera House hasn't fazed her much," the Commander replied, emotionless as always.

"Perhaps if we could get to her wife, this Celenia, that might push her over the edge."

"But she's the Senate President."

"True, but both are pregnant and expecting in two months or so. Surely, she'll step down relatively soon," Pong Lu countered. "The problem with this approach is that, if Zarita ever found out we're behind it, she'll come after us as well."

"So we need something to truly endear her to us, no matter what else happens," the Commander replied. "Put everyone onto that project. Find a way to make her beholding to us."

That answer came some ten days later and from a wholly unexpected direction. "Well, well, you'll never guess what I've uncovered," Doc Lambert said with an uncharacteristic show of emotion. "I believe I can genetically regenerate her lost arms!"

"What?" the Commander replied, also showing a brief bit of emotion.

"Yes, well, we have her original DNA on file and now her newly altered DNA. She is one very important special case. You see, the only difference being that now her genes dictate her body has no arms, whereas before it dictated that it had. I've isolated the gene changes, and I believe I can synthesize a new genetic modification that will cause her body to regenerate arms. If that would work, we could release this to the public and potentially return the arms that were lost to this biological agent."

"Incredible work, Lambert! What do you need to develop this?" the Commander asked, seeing incredible possibilities of this discovery.

"I need some expendable patients to work on and test it. Guinea pigs. It could well fail. I could be wrong, and the test subject might die," Doc Lambert replied. "The Senate has made it clear we can't use normal volunteers. Besides, this could well be fatal, if I'm not right."

"We can use prisoners. I'll arrange for several to be transported here. We should use the ones that were blinded as well. That way, there is no possibility of their ever disclosing anything about HQ," the Commander suggested.

A few days later, Doc Lambert had four prisoners in his Infirmary, and he began his experiments. Meanwhile, based on this proving successful, the Commander began laying the groundwork for the rest of the Zarita project. Scoby ran more simulations. "We must reject a direct assassination via guns," he declared. "Only can get it to forty percent at the very best. Too many things can go wrong. Besides, the senators are now under heavy guard. A sniper can't get close enough to raise the percentages."

"What about a bomb?" the Commander suggested.

"Let me run the sims," he replied, typing away. A short while later, he reported, "We could get it up to ninety-two percent, if and only if we can get the suicide bomber within a hundred feet of the target, but that means the bomber has to somehow get through the barrier line of Security Guards that are posted at the Senate exit, where the senators get into their shuttles. That's the only location where we can get a high percentage of success. Plus, it has to be done at the end of the day. Too many other variables are unpredictable during the morning arrival rush."

"Okay. Chances that Zarita will ever be able to track it back to us?" the Commander asked.

"Highly likely, unless we can get someone outside the Bops to do the deed."

"Okay, let me work on that angle. For now, prepare a Mission Plan for a suicide bomber," the Commander ordered.

He visited Lela. "I need a profile on someone within the Devil's Disciples. I'm looking for a man or woman, who is a blind follower, who hates the senators for their recent rulings, and one who is rather gullible. Find me that person."

"On it, Commander," Lela replied as emotionless as ever.

Three days later, the Commander issued his Snatch and Grab Mission to ST1. Four hours later, the grimy man was in their containment cell. Now Pong Lu worked his magic on the man. Over and over, he played the planned mission details, step by step, into the man's subconscious mind, while keeping him drugged, and consciously stating that, by becoming a martyr for the Cause, he would be sent to the Positive Afterlife. Meanwhile, down in Equipment, Lenard carefully prepared the vest bomb, designing it to explode forward and ensuring the attack would be a fatal one. He even ran several dummy tests to work out the furthest distance from the target that would still be fatal.

Meanwhile, the Commander personally worked out the means to create a break in the line of Security Guards. He arranged for a call to be placed to the Lieutenant in charge of the Security Guards in the section where the breach had to be located. A fuel spill notice would be sent, requesting him to vacate that zone and allow a cleanup man through, the bomber.

Via close monitoring of the Senate, Lela finally relayed to the Commander, "Okay, Celenia has just relinquished her post as Senate President. They've elected a new person. It's today or never!"

The Commander then issued his orders, "Mission Alpha is now a go for five today. Make it happen." His plan worked to perfection. The implanted Devil's Disciple walked through the line in the guards, began yelling his diatribe, and then detonated the bomb when he reached the programmed distance from Senator Celenia.

"Perfection," the Commander announced to all concerned a half hour later. "Monitor Zarita closely. Doc Lambert, are you ready for Phase Three?" He was, and the Commander placed ST1 on High Alert. They would need to react on a moment's notice to implement Phase Two.

Unknown to Zarita and the new Senator Franco, the pilot for the return flight to Ashford-5 had been replaced by the ST2 team leader, who Zarita had not yet met. The reason logged was pilot fatigue. Thus, after the deep space transport jumped into hyperspace, it shortly dropped out again, landing at the HQ base. The elevators quickly lowered it into the arrival bay of HQ, where the Commander stood waiting patiently.

The ST2 leader spoke over the intercom, "Zarita, the Bops Commander has asked to speak personally with you. Please step outside."

"I can't. I need help," she replied, tearfully.

"What's going on?" Ari asked, her eyes wet and red from crying.

"I don't know." Some man helped her out of her seat and carried her to where the Commander had a chair waiting for her.

"Please sit down, Zarita. I want to talk to you. I'm so sorry about the loss of your wife and unborn child." She was too encased in her own grief to notice that his sympathy was feigned.

"I'd like to make you a deal. First, we both know this Devil's Disciples group was responsible for the bombing that killed your wife and unborn child. It might be wise if all those insane church members had their brains melted. Second, we believe we have a way to regrow your arms. If we do this for you, we would like your help interrogating the men who stole the biological agent, replicated it, and sold it to all these terrorist groups. We need to locate every group that they sold some to and where they are keeping their stock of this terrible biological weapon. You help us with this, and we'll help you regrow your arms."

"Ari's too?" she looked up, barely duplicating what he said. "You can do this for real?"

"Yes, Doc Lambert has been successful at isolating and modifying the genes. If you agree, we can get started on it today. It takes months to fully regrow them."

"Okay, but where will we stay?"

"I've arranged for a room for you both and two assistants to help you. Do we have a deal?"

"Yes, yes we do. This is a miracle," she brightened up. "Can I tell Ari?"

A half hour later, both women were lying on comfortable cots in the Infirmary, isolated from the rest of the

HQ complex. IVs were hooked up to both. One of these, the doctor explained, was injecting them with his genetic cure, while the other was providing the basic nourishment their bodies would need for the regrowth process. He also had both of them on a powerful sedative, but explained to Zarita that Ari was just too emotional right now and that she needed rest. "You just lie back yourself and rest," he said as he left them alone.

"But I'm lying on my back," she thought growing a little groggy from the sedative. When she was out, Pong Lu came by and put earphones on her. He played a recording he had made especially for her, one that suggested she kill all of the Devil's Disciples, because they'd killed her wife. The Commander's idea was to keep her busy, while they raided the Soldiers of Fortune. Besides, if she did go on murdering spree, he'd have leverage over her, or so he thought.

After both women were unconscious, the Commander stepped into the Infirmary room and observed Zarita for some time. Then, he stepped back out and spoke to Doc Lambert. "I think it best for all concerned to keep her sedated as well, until ST1 returns with our Snatch and Grab Package. She's one dangerous loose cannon." The doctor nodded, and the Commander left to check on the Mission Profile.

Scoby was at Hans' Comm Center, coordinating this combined operation. Five Strike Teams were in the field. "How's it going?" the Commander asked.

"ST1 has made contact and offered to buy another dozen. They are waiting for the delivery notice now. A day or two, if they operate as before," Scoby replied with an equal lack of emotion. "The other teams are in position."

"Good. I'll be in my office. I expect hourly reports." He turned and left the busy center.

Before too long, both Pong Lu and Lela joined him. "Commander," Pong Lu spoke up, "we've just heard you are keeping Zarita sedated until the teams return. Are we not going ahead with allowing her to kill as many Devil's Disciples as she can?"

"Change of plans, Pong Lu, Lela. She's just too damned dangerous to have alert, when we have our top Strike Teams in the field. There's some percentage your implant may not be effective. There's some chance she might discover the truth behind the bombing of her wife. This Snatch and Grab is too vital to risk any interference. I reviewed the percentages. By keeping her sedated until we need her for Interrogation, we add another ten percent to our success."

"Should I attempt to undo the implanting?" Pong Lu asked.

The Commander didn't reply for a long moment. "No, I think not. The percentages are in our favor, if she becomes unmanageable. With the implant in place, she has a much higher percent chance of going after the Devil's Disciples. We'll leave it in place for now." Both nodded expressionless, turned, and left him. Now, he could only wait.

For the Commander, waiting was the part of his job he hated the most. With everyone on high alert, they took only four hour naps. Two days later, the exchange occurred. It was at the same spaceport hanger as before. Timing was critical. As before, Peter and Ellen, dressed similarly, walked into the entrance, where their d-guns were confiscated. Then, they were escorted up to the two men wearing the red biological containment suits. Once more, the dozen cylinders were packed securely in a similar shipping crate as before.

Ellen pulled out the wad of high denomination credit notes from her cleavage, proceeding to count it out before the bespectacled accountant. Overhead, the rest of ST1 along with ST2 and ST3 quietly moved out of the ribbed steelwork of the high-arched dome over the hanger. They'd been stationed there for almost a day now. Each held a gun with a silencer on it, but Jason, Hamil, and Blackwell held tranquilizer guns. The signal for action was Ellen's counting of the notes, distracting the accountant and hopefully the general.

The tranquilizer guns fired first, followed by a carefully coordinated rain of bullets, all under the direction of Karkoff, who was hovering above the port in the cloaked transport ship. He'd carefully oriented each of the dozen other team members, directing each to a specific enemy guard. Thirty seconds later, it was over. The two men in the red suits slumped to the ground, knocked out by the powerful tranquilizer; the ten guards were dead. The other team members quickly repelled down the fifty feet and moved from fallen man to man, putting a second and third bullet into them. Thus far, none of the enemy had time to either fire their d-guns or even sound the alarm.

ST2 and ST3 secured the entrance, while outside, the other Strike Teams continued to monitor the perimeter. "Targets secured. Teleporting now," Peter whispered. Overhead, Karkoff acknowledged and activated the teleport. The two unconscious men and the crate vanished from the hanger, appearing onboard the transport. A minute later, Jason and Hamil joined Karkoff. They took charge of the two "guests" and the bio agent, allowing Karkoff to return to his thermal imaging machine and the comm controls. Blackwell handed out the bio agent detectors, and the remaining ST1 members began sweeping the hanger itself. Objective: see if there were more being stored here.

Meanwhile, a dozen blue clad Cleanup crewmembers teleported down from their craft. In short order, the ten dead bodies vanished. Efficiently, the crew set about removing all traces of blood from the floor. Then, they too vanished.

"Hanger is clean. Request commencement of Phase Two," Peter spoke quietly. His transponder relayed it to all the many team members, Karkoff, and back to HQ, though there was a short time delay between Proxima Prime and Donner-3, another hub stellar system.

"Go for Phase Two," the Commander gave the order. When the teams heard it, Peter nodded to the other team leaders. Karkoff immediately teleported the rest of ST1 up to the transport. A minute later, Peter jumped them into hyperspace, heading back to Proxima Prime and HQ at top speed, bringing their precious cargo with them. The other teams then proceeded to conduct raids on other known Soldier of Fortune locations, in hopes of getting lucky and finding their stash of bio weapons. If nothing else, they would reduce the numbers of other enemy men and, with luck, sufficiently disrupting the organization. That would allow them time to interrogate the general, and then make the surgical strikes to capture the remainder of the bio agent cylinders, along with any records of sales the Soldiers of Fortune may have.

The general and the accountant were taken to two Interrogation Rooms. Each was a white sterile room with a single steel chair in the center. The men were placed in the chairs, and then heavy steel arm sleeves were slipped into place, securing their arms to the sides of the chair. Another steel band held their waists securely to the back of the chair. An attendant entered to monitor their condition.

Now, it was Doc Lambert's turn. His nurses placed the still unconscious Zarita into a wheel chair, being extra careful of her rather small, baby-like arms that were in the process of growing. They wheeled her into the Interrogation Room that held the general. Torres then joined them. Doc Lambert carefully injected another drug into Zarita, bringing her out of her sedated state.

Torres spoke, "Okay, Zarita. Time for you to do your work. Congratulations, your arms are growing."

Zarita looked down at her tiny arms. "Incredible. I feel so groggy. Guess I needed the sleep. What do you want me to do?"

"This is the man who stole the bio agent, replicated it, and sold it to all of the terrorist groups. The very ones that attacked the Senate and the Opera House," Torres explained. "We want to know first where he keeps his supply of that bio agent. Get that out of him first. Do you need him to be revived?" Torres asked. If she were doing the interrogation, he would have to be conscious.

"No, it's better this way." She focused and began probing his mind. *Where do you store your biological weapons?* She placed into his mind, knowing he probably would resist revealing that, but that very resistance would lead her to those exact memories. She was right. Her problem now was how to communicate this to these Bops people. At last, she simply Mind Joined with Torres and showed her the many images. They had a secret underground bunker built with a special bio containment section. Here's where they kept their bio agent cylinders. They also had a Fabrication Machine there as well. When orders came in, they would don their red containment suits and fabricate sufficient quantities of cylinders, though they always kept several dozen in reserve for their own use, should they be attacked.

"I need the layout of this bunker, Zarita," Torres said softly, afraid to interrupt the telepath. Zarita did her best to get the general to focus on that information and was at least partially successful.

"Okay, now we need to know everyone he sold cylinders to, Zarita," Torres whispered. She didn't realize that all she needed to do was to think her thought, not vocalize it.

Here, Zarita fumbled about a bit, before she got an image of the accountant's little black book. *The accountant has kept a log of each sale. The general isn't sure where the book is at right now.*

"Okay. We have the accountant in the next room. I'll wheel you over to him. Get that information out of him," Torres whispered. She fought hard to keep all other thoughts out of her mind. She feared the telepath.

A half hour later, she wheeled Zarita back into the Infirmary Room, where Doc Lambert took over. Torres fairly ran out of the room, so frightened of this woman! The doctor said softly, "Zarita, Ari is progressing well too. It would be best if you also go back to sleep and allow your body to continue to regrow your new arms. We don't want anything to go wrong with this process." She agreed and soon fell back into a deep sleep.

The Bops was under the gun, time-wise. At any moment, other members of the Soldiers of Fortune might notice the missing general and check on them. With thirty of their members eliminated and their bodies already disposed of, there was a fifty percent chance the remaining members would become suspicious or worse. It took Lela an hour to locate this secret bunker and another hour for her and Scoby to work up a hasty profile for the raid. Intel was scanty; much would have to be improvised by the four remaining Strike Force teams. ST1 was almost there when the raid began. Their role would be backup this time, instead of point.

From the initial infrared scans, the bunker was heavily guarded by some twenty men and many secure doors, each of which had to be breeched. Had Scoby and Lela had several days to prepare, they might have found an easier method. A firefight soon broke out. A long half hour ensued before they secured the bunker, but six team members were killed and four more wounded. While the remaining survivors secured the bunker, assisted their wounded, and stood guard, ST1 joined them to do the search and recovery phase.

An hour later, twenty-six more sets of bio agent cylinders and apparel crates were recovered and at long last the accountant's book. Once the Cleanup crew finished working, Peter personally set an explosive charge on the extremely expensive Fabrication Machine and the teams evacuated. A minute later, the charges went off, destroying the machine and much of the bio agent containment room. If they had more cylinders stored elsewhere, they wouldn't be able to replicate them. That was the plan.

Two hours later, the triumphant men and women entered HQ. Some carried the four wounded men to the Infirmary, while others carried the bio agents down to the secure containment room in R&D. Peter personally carried the black book to Lela. "Here's the book."

"Excellent. They were wise not to keep their records on a computer. We might have been able to hack into it. I'll get it scanned into the computer quickly. My crew will go over it with a fine tooth comb, but Torres also wants to study it too," Lela explained, without showing the slightest signs of any emotion.

Sometime later, Torres began reviewing the images of the pages, committing salient facts to memory. Now, she was going to interrogate the general herself, seeking confirmation of these sales, as well as what else he might be hiding from them. A nurse joined her in the Interrogation Room and injected the general with another set of drugs. "He'll be coherent in about three minutes."

"That'll be all for now," Torres replied and leaned against one of the white steel walls, waiting patiently. At last, the general woke up, dazed and confused.

"What's going on?" he mumbled and struggled futilely with his restraints and staring at the room and Torres.

"The game is over. We have you now, your accountant

426

too. Oh yes, did I mention we've raided your bunker and taken your supplies of the biological agent cylinders? No, I didn't. I hate to tell you this, General Snaggard, but your life is over. What remains is do you want a swift, painless death or would you prefer a prolonged, most painful death?"

"What do you mean? Who are you, bitch?" he spat.

"For what little it'll do you, I am Interrogator Torres. What is your choice, general?"

"Make it quick then," he spat out.

"Agreed, but in order for me to do that, you have to give me something in return. I want all of the locations where you've stored your bio agents. I want a list of everyone you've sold these weapons of mass destruction to. You give me that, and, if I can verify them, you'll have your swift, painless death. If not, you'll still give me what I want, but your suffering will be rather monumental. I'm known for being able to keep one alive for weeks if I have to, most unpleasant for the man, though. Start talking or I'll begin with pain," Torres said in a totally emotionless tone.

"If I'm dead already, I'll not tell you a god-damned thing!" the general bravely and foolishly swore, spitting towards her. She, of course, was just out of range. She snapped her fingers. Two others entered carrying black cases. She turned and started to leave, but paused demurely at the door. "Oh, if you change your mind later on, just tell them." She left and shut the door. Fortunately, these Interrogation Rooms were totally soundproof. They had to be, but an intercom system did relay what went on, but had volume filters that automatically cut in when the decibel level rose.

Six hours later, the general broke and told her what she wanted to know. It confirmed everything they'd discovered so far. She believed him, when he said that everyone they sold the bio agents to were listed in the black book. At the time, she didn't realize that she made an error in his interrogation. She had asked for a list of those to whom he'd sold the agent. She failed to ask if he had given any away at no charge. That would eventually turn out to be a horrific mistake on her part.

Now, she turned her attention onto the accountant. He readily agreed to tell all in return for a quick, painless death.

He confirmed that every sale the general had made was properly entered in his logbook and that there were no other cylinders except those within the bunker's containment lab. He and most of the men were terrified of an accidental release of the bio agent. Once she finished questioning them, she injected them with another knockout drug and awaited further orders.

A day later, the Commander was satisfied they had all that there was to obtain from the two men. "Okay, are all of the video cameras in the Interrogation Rooms working properly?" They were double checked. "Wake up Zarita. We'll let her microwave their brains. After all, she'll want to get revenge on the men who were ultimately responsible for the two biological attacks. Is everyone ready for this controlled experiment? We won't get another golden opportunity to study this." One by one, two dozen sounded off their "ready."

Doc Lambert again injected Zarita and woke her up. The Commander waited until she became coherent again. "Senator Zarita, we have the two men who originally stole the bio agent cylinder, who replicated it, and sold it to the terrorists, the ones who did this to you, to all the other Senators, to the president, and to the thousand innocent men and women at the opera house. We've confirmed their guilt. However, I thought it would only be fitting, if you took revenge for the three thousand plus who have suffered horribly because of what they've done. You can use your *mentales* thought to kill them. However, we've promised them a swift death. I would appreciate it if they died quickly. I'll wheel you into their rooms now."

"Oh you needn't bother; I can kill them from here. I feel so sleepy. My arms are growing; so are Ari's. I don't know how to thank you for this. Now, we can live again."

The Commander had to stall to give his technicians time to get extra video recordings going in this room. "Oh think nothing of it. It's the very least we can do. Our goal is to protect innocent lives and to aid where we can. Thanks to you, Zarita, we were able actually to establish a way to regenerate the lost arms. You see, you were unique in our database. We had a sample of your DNA when you came here. I mean when you were altered after that tragic accident on Ashford-5. We then took a recent sample after you were subjected to the Senate attack that also cost you your arms. So we were able to compare the two sets of genes and pinpoint precisely what was altered. Thanks to the combined work of R&D and Doc Lambert, they were able to create a method to undo just that portion. Trying to undo the rest is way beyond the level of genetic knowledge known anywhere at this time. Hence, more studies must be done. Yet, this one discovery promises to give all of you victims a much better life."

"Oh yes, indeed. I'm so very pleased. Can we get on with it? I'm rather tired, though I don't know why."

"Yes, do your thing. Eliminate those two evil men. Make them pay for what they've done to you and three thousand others, Zarita," the Commander said. As Zarita focused, she wasn't aware that three dozen others were staring at various monitors and panel readouts, of both her and the two men. All that was visible was a pale glow from the stones on her earrings. It took less than thirty seconds per man. "There, that's done."

"On behalf of the thousands, who were so horribly harmed by those men, I thank you. Now get some sleep; let those new arms of yours grow." The Commander released the intravenous sedative that put her back under in less than a minute.

Stepping out of the room, he barked, "Did we get that? Comm Center, five minutes!"

All of the department heads congregated around the Comm Center, where Hans was prepared to play back any number of recordings just made. Doc Lambert spoke first. "Commander, they are both quite dead. Microwaved brains. Ooze is coming out of their skull's orifices. Identical to the previous ones."

"Did anyone see anything?" the Commander barked.

No one had. "It's like they just died," Doc Lambert replied filling the nervous silence of the others.

Hans spoke up, "There was a massive electrical charge in their brains. It's recorded there, if you want to see it. She put a huge electrical charge in them. I've no idea how."

The Commander growled, "Well, you are supposed to be the experts. Go over all of this, and find out more. Report to me in two hours."

Two hours later, Hans reported they'd discovered absolutely nothing else, except one small thing. Her gems in her earrings had a pale blue glow for a moment. Now, the Commander was far more worried about Zarita. She wasn't even in the same room as her victims. It took almost no time for her to kill them. For the first time in a very long time, the Commander was scared. What did he have down there in the Infirmary?

He held another staff meeting, outlining his deep-seated fears about this woman. "Ordinarily, I'd simply terminate her."

"Don't think we can do that," Doc Lambert countered. "She is the one and only link on the genetic cure we've developed. Obviously, we're soon going to have to release the cure we have to regenerate the arms on those three thousand plus victims. The Imperium geneticists will be demanding to know how we developed it. She is the only unique individual we can use to show how we did it. I mean, we have her DNA with all the modifications before she lost her arms and then her DNA afterwards. It's that comparison alone that led to our breakthrough cure."

"I'm aware of that," the Commander glared at the doctor. "That's why I said ordinarily. Still, this woman is exceedingly dangerous and not only to us. What are the percentages if she has an accident during her trip home to Ashford-5?"

Scoby spoke up, "Sixteen percent, not good at all. She's part of the Ataro Empire. Emperor Kino isn't likely to accept an accident, not with everything that's been happening. He's sure to investigate. Sixteen percent is highly optimistic."

"What if we do nothing?" he asked.

"Now we are talking fifty percent," Scoby punched some numbers in his handheld calculator. "Yes, fifty. She has resigned her post as senator, planning to take maternity leave. Odds are good she'll wish to remain a mother and raise her child back on Ashford-5."

"Could we get to her on Ashford-5, if we needed to stop her," the Commander asked.

Scoby punched in more numbers before looking up, "Not so good. Eleven percent chance of that, casualties would run excessively high, unless she takes up residence outside the Imperial Castle."

Lela asked, "Is there any chance we could use her skills in the future?"

Again, Scoby entered more numbers before replying. "I'd say that there is a fifty-two percent chance of that, Lela."

The Commander sighed, a rare show of emotion, although only slight. "I can't believe we are allowing this Righteous Vigilante to go! Well, at least we've engineered her departure from Proxima Prime. Perhaps that's the best we can get out of this scenario. How soon do we dare send her on her way home?"

"Give her another two weeks. We can then make a big press deal out of this before we send her on her way," Doc Lambert suggested. "That will give us time to carefully prepare the presentation of the cure to the scientific community. The Bops cannot be seen to have anything to do with this new genetic cure. Arrangements will have to be made before hand."

Lela spoke up. "There are two affected geneticists living on Ashford-5 right now. They need the cure as well. Scoby, what are the percentages, if we use them to 'discover and announce' this breakthrough?"

"Hey, good idea. Let me crunch the numbers," he replied, typing furiously. He finally broke the long silence. Looking up, he announced, "Ninety percent chance of acceptance, if we go that route. Ninety-five percent, if we can fix it so they believe they independently discovered the cure. I can have the Mission Profile ready in a couple of hours."

"Excellent. Keep our two guests sedated until the two geneticists have it ready. Then, when we wake them up, we can tell them their Ashford-5 geneticists developed the cure and sent it to us to try out. That will be believable," the Commander replied, satisfied. "Scoby, I'll expect the Profile to be on my desk in three hours. That's all. Dismissed."

Three hours later, Doc Lambert actually grinned. "How

about this. I'm going into the field on an actual mission!" Two more hours passed, as he was drilled and drilled on just what he had to do. An additional hour to pack his things went by before he and ST1 boarded the Light Cruiser. They opted to use this much larger ship over their usual deep space transport for one main reason. The cruiser could get to Ashford-5 in two days and didn't need to refuel.

Late June, the cruiser landed at the spaceport on Ashford-5. Karkoff and the rest of the team remained on board, handling the communications, while Doc Lambert, Peter, and Ellen stepped off to be greeted by Governor Katrina and Doctor Jones. Peter and Ellen were introduced as his nurses and assistants. "Yes, I'm from the Imperium Hospital on Proxima Prime. I've come to discuss some startling findings with the geneticists, Doctors Ruth and Alex Hammil."

"Welcome to Ashford-5, Doctor Lambert. The two geneticists are staying at Queen Amy's Imperial Castle, where they are currently on maternity leave. They've used a good deal of the funds the Senate provided them to pay for personal assistants and for their research equipment. They are determined to find a cure for us all, particularly in light of the recent biological attacks on the Senate and the Opera House on Proxima Prime. If you like, I can have Doctor Jones take you to see them now. Queen Amy will provide for your room and board while you are visiting them."

"Yes, that would be excellent. I'm very excited about what I've discovered and want their opinions as soon as possible," Doctor Lambert replied. "My, it is so dark on this world."

Doctor Whitney Jones laughed. "Yes, orange-red sun. At least you've come in the summer. If it were winter, there would be many feet of snow around here. Come on; mind you, I move very slowly."

"Yes, everyone that's been infected does. We've been swamped with patients. Can you believe over three thousand senators and wealthy, including the president and one of the Legates? Terrible business, just terrible," Doc Lambert gabbed. Peter helped Whitney get into the electric car. As she drove them to the Imperial Castle, all three could not help noticing how her foot long fingernails made ordinary actions far more difficult for her.

He commented, "I must be hard for you, doctor, but at least you have hands. It's almost impossible for our patients."

Whitney laughed, "Aye, that it is. We are indeed lucky compared to so many other innocent men and women. By the way, Ruth and Alex have been diligently studying all they managed to salvage from that research station on Ashford-4 before they were infected. I am sure given enough time, those two bright geneticists will find a cure. I certainly hope so; I'm lending them all the help I can, but I'm not a geneticist."

"Right, neither am I, but I've come across some remarkable findings that may help them in their quest. Ah, a real castle. Impressive," he exclaimed. He'd never seen a real stone castle before, only images in history books.

"By the way, Alex had a little boy, Andy, and Ruth had a daughter, May. They are genetically similar to their parents, unfortunately. I knew that would be the case from their sonograms, but I didn't tell either parent. I didn't want them any more distraught than they were. All four are quite healthy and doing well. The babies are seven weeks old now. Here we are."

Queen Amy, Jan, Bernardo, and Lena met them in the courtyard. After introductions, Queen Amy said, "Bernardo and Lena will take you to their quarters. Jan and I walk too slowly. If you are planning to stay for a while, let my brother know, and I'll arrange a suite for you. Whatever you need, let him know. We are quite honored to have Ruth and Alex staying with us. They are very bright young geneticists."

"Thank you, Queen Amy. Indeed, I expect we'll be here for some days, if my theory is a correct one. Ruth and Alex will be able to make a definitive ruling on that," Doctor Lambert replied.

"I'll go with you. As a doctor, I'm really interested in all this too," Whitney added, following Bernardo and Lena, who led the trio into the maze of halls. "Don't go slow on my account." She was left behind.

They found Ruth and Alex waiting for them. Doc Lambert suspected they'd been alerted to their coming via telepathy, since there were no usual Imperium Comm systems here. After the introductions and a quick peek at their two young infants, Whitney joined them. "Sorry, Doctor Lambert, we're so darn helpless. Bernardo, can you help us get to our lab?" Alex asked.

"Don't concern yourself over that, Doctor Alex, Doctor Ruth. I do hope that you have the equipment here I'll need to show you what I've discovered. If not, there are some on the cruiser that brought us here. I'm sure the captain will allow us to use them," Doctor Lambert replied. Bernardo led them into a side room, filled with their computers and machines.

"Impressive!" Doctor Lambert commented, seeing all the latest equipment and sophisticated computer systems.

"Yes, thank the Senate for their generous gifts to us, reparations the horrible accident that we suffered. We do have a hard time working them, but we're training our local assistants to press buttons for us," Alex explained, hoping that he would buy it.

"Yes, well, let's get right to it shall we?" Doctor Lambert replied, sitting down before the computer system. He opened his brief case, took out a drive, and inserted it before continuing. "You see, for months now, I've been looking after senators Zarita, Celenia, Ari, and B'nath. All are due fairly soon. I've been really concerned, since they were genetically modified in the Senate terrorist attack. Because I've been looking after them for so long, I've got good medical records, you see. Then, it dawned on me I have more than mere health records. I have their DNA on file. One night, it struck me. I have something that no other doctor has. I have Senator Zarita's DNA both before and after that tragic Senate genetic attack. Do you see what I am getting at?"

Ruth answered. "So you have her DNA and gene structure that contains all of the genetic modifications excepting her loss of arms and those afterwards. Did you do a comparison or is that beyond your medical training?"

"Precisely so! Precisely so, Doctor Ruth. That's just what came to me. I did just that. Here is the comparison. Left is before, right is after her loss of arms. I did routine genetic comparisons. I've highlighted in green the singular changes in

434

her genes. These changes can only be the ones that caused her body to reject and dispose of her arms! Mind you, I nearly fell out of my seat when I realized what I have here!" Peter and Ellen carefully monitored Ruth, Alex, and Whitney's reactions.

"This is what we have been searching for all along! Brilliant work, Doctor Lambert! These observations, wow! This may well lead to a cure, a way for us to regenerate our lost arms," Ruth replied bursting with excitement.

Alex had tears in his eyes. "This is fantastic, Doctor Lambert, just mind blowing!"

"My reactions precisely. There are over three thousand on Proxima Prime, who would have their lives partially restored, if we can turn this into a cure. I've done a bit more research into how it might be done, but as I said, I'm not a geneticist. That's why I've come to you two. You are tremendously involved in this line of research. One might say you have a vested interest in finding a cure. Let me show you what I came up with, and then let you have at it. I am probably way off base, but we simply have to find a cure, a way for so many to regenerate their arms."

"Yes, of course. If we only had our arms and hands back, we could at least live fairly well. The other modifications don't make us helpless like their lack does," Alex declared.

"Here's my initial theory and thinking about this regeneration process," Doctor Lambert began feeding them his "cure," that he already knew was working. "As a medical doctor, I know the regrowth process will almost certainly require certain building blocks, such as calcium and various vitamins and minerals. I've put together this intravenous feeding formula, but I'm sure you two can vastly improve upon it." He chatted away for an hour, while Ruth and Alex continued to ask questions and make suggestions.

"We have the ability to synthesize the genetic cure here, but we don't have the hands with which to operate the machines," Alex finally said. "Could we beg you to stick around a while and be our hands on this project, Doctor Lambert?"

He readily agreed, but only, if he could take a sample back to use on Zarita and Ari, hopefully before Zarita gave birth. His worry was for her baby. There probably would not be sufficient time for the unborn child to regenerate, while still in the womb.

"The process can be accelerated, if we add this amino acid to the mix," Ruth suggested. For two days, the trio worked on perfecting the formula. Finally, when all was ready, Doctors Whitney and Lambert implemented the process on Ruth and Alex. They kept the pair bedridden for quite some time, but by the second day, the four saw results. Tiny arms and hands were growing, similar to their development within a womb. For a week, the two doctors handled the pair with the gentlest possible care.

"Well, congratulations, Doctors Ruth and Alex! Your new formula is working! Your discovery will give life back to over three thousand senators and others on Proxima Prime!" Doctor Lambert exclaimed.

"But we owe it all to your initial discoveries," Alex countered.

"No, I am just a mere OBGYN, who happened to stumble on Zarita's DNA as part of my prenatal care for her. This is really all your doing. I'll see that you both get full credit for this amazing and revolutionary development. I'm sure you will next be expanding your research to help others, who have lost a limb, to regenerate it." He continued to insist they take full credit for the discovery, over their protests. "Look, you both have suffered terribly because of the accident. This is the very least that the Imperium can do for you both. You, more than any others, deserve the full credit."

He went on, "I would like to take a batch of this back with me to treat senators Zarita and Ari, before they gives birth. I'll send along more samples and the full documentation to those on Proxima Prime, and get them to begin developing enough quantities to heal the other three thousand plus, who are desperate for the cure as well. We should first hold a formal news conference before I leave. I'll arrange it for you. On behalf of Senators Zarita and Ari and the three thousand others, I thank you from the bottom of my heart for what you've done!"

There weren't any reporters or news outlets on Ashford-5, naturally; it was a Closed World. Karkoff pretended to be an independent journalist, and he conducted the interview with Doctors Ruth and Alex Hammil. He also cleverly edited out of the video any references to Doctor Lambert. Two weeks after they arrived, ST1 and Doc Lambert finally left, taking with them the many samples and the formal papers outlining the procedures to follow. Once they were back at HQ, Karkoff released the edited interview to the news reporters, while Doc Lambert delivered the goods to the giant Imperium Hospital. Within days, treatments began. This was the hottest news story in weeks. Some three thousand people received a new lease on life as a result.

Meanwhile, Doc Lambert formally roused both Zarita and Ari, whose arms were now those of a young child, fully functional to their great pleasure. He carefully explained how he'd come up with this cure, showing them the video Karkoff had made, where Ruth and Alex announced to the world their genetic discovery and cure. He did his best to tweak their sense of time, convincing them he'd gotten the formula he'd used on them from those two genetic doctors. As confused as the two women were, they accepted his explanation.

"Now, it's time you head back to Ashford-5. You'll be giving birth in a few more weeks, Senator Zarita. It would be best for both of you to be in your own home when the time comes. Doctor Jones will take excellent care of you both. She'll be able to work the miracle cure on your child if need be. I believe she is already doing that for the Hammil's two infants." Two confused women soon found themselves back on their deep space transport headed for Ashford-5.

After the transport had left Proxima Prime, the Commander asked, "Well, do you think those two bought it all?"

Scoby replied, "There is a fifty-two percent chance that they have. Best we can hope for now."

Chapter 28 Unraveling

Zarita and Ari arrived on Ashford-5 on the twentieth of June 1297. Both were still heavily in grief over the loss of their marital partners and confused about what had been going on the past many weeks. Yet, their arms were doing well, developing along nicely. Upon arrival, Katrina and Whitney got them both over to the Imperial Castle, and Amy put them into a suite together, assigning a couple of assistants to help them.

Doctor Whitney had been kept very busy and was spending most of her days watching over Ruth and Alex, as well as implementing the cure on their two babies. As soon as Zarita and Ari arrived, she gave them both a full physical and then prepared for the delivery of her baby, which could happen in mere days. She then discussed her findings with Amy and Jan.

"Look, both are suffering from the loss of their wives. Their physical health is acceptable; their new arms are coming along nicely, though they are both ahead of Ruth and Alex, and I'm not sure why. Both are mentally confused. Zarita keeps saying she hears voices in her head, first telling her it's okay for her to kill all the Devil's Disciples she can find, and then not to do that. Strange. They both need Basic Therapy right away."

"But is that wise for Zarita right now?" Amy asked, knowing that her birth was likely at any time now.

"No it isn't. My professional recommendation is to hold off on that, until after she gives birth. Then, it can all be handled. But Ari is another case. She's absolutely devastated over her genetic modifications and the loss of her long time mate, Senator B'nath. I really think she ought to get therapy very soon," Whitney replied.

"Okay, I'll get someone here to do it on Ari tomorrow, if possible. Keep me posted. You are really busy now," she teased.

"Duh, understatement. But then, that's what I want to

do, as you well know. Got to make my rounds now. I'll keep you posted."

The next day, Amy introduced twenty-six year old Ari Laag to Drina, who proceeded to give her Basic Therapy. This was a good match; their personalities were quite similar. It took Ari nearly three weeks to handle all of the emotional trauma and physical losses she'd suffered. In the end, she was back to her old self, playful, fun loving, a prankster when appropriate, and loving. However, she now felt a very strong bond with Zarita, to whom she looked upon as her savior.

"Look Zarita, if it hadn't been for you looking after me, I'd have killed myself. I just could not go on alone, not after all that."

She also became invaluable to Zarita, helping her with the care of her new daughter, whom she named Ruthy in honor of Ruth and Alex. Zarita gave birth to Ruthy on the first of July. A few days later, Doctor Whitney began working the new miracle cure on Ruthy as well. After finishing up Ari's therapy, Drina began on Zarita, while Ari looked after Ruthy as much as possible. Once more, it took over three weeks to handle the emotional and physical trauma Zarita endured. She was very pleased finally to have the source of the man's voice in her head completely gone.

By early October, things finally quieted down around the castle. At long last, Doctor Whitney had everything running smoothly. Now, she had time to reflect on the momentous events of the past months. Coupled with what she learned about the two from discussions Zarita and Ari had with her after their therapy was done, she had grave suspicions something wasn't quite right. She called a meeting with Katrina and Amy, though Jan attended as always.

"Look, I smell something foul. Things just don't add up properly," Whitney began. "First, this miracle cure. That Doctor Lambert showed up with the entire problem solved really, if the truth be told. Sure, Alex and Ruth made some necessary improvements, but he had a workable cure already. So why come here? Why did he insist that those two take full credit for his discovery? It doesn't add up."

"I see what you mean. Did he really have it solved?"

Amy asked, growing suspicious herself.

"Yes. I'm not a geneticist, but from what I saw, he had it wrapped up before he came here."

"Perhaps, he wanted real geneticists to back him up," Amy suggested.

"Likely, but why was he so insistent they take full credit and leave him out completely? That doesn't make sense. I know many of us doctors prefer to cure and not be in the limelight; still, something this major would bring him fame and recognition throughout the entire Imperium and for decades to come. It doesn't make sense. So I did some digging."

"The Imperium Hospital does have records of him working for them, but he doesn't seem to have any patients. His name isn't on any patient records. Why would a hospital have a doctor on staff who didn't see any patients? Yet, he claimed to have been Zarita's doctor during her pregnancy. I checked. She saw another doctor a few times. He lied. So why would he lie about that?" Whitney asked.

"And another anomaly. Zarita and Ari's arms are far more developed than Ruth and Alex's arms. It is almost as if Doctor Lambert treated those two long before he came here and presumably returned with the cure. That's backed up somewhat by Zarita and Ari. Now that they've had their therapy, both claim that they were given the cure by Doctor Lambert probably several weeks before he came here. Again, why? On top of that, why would he travel from the hub of the galaxy out here to the very rim? It makes no sense at all."

"And another thing that doesn't sit right with me, Amy, according to both Zarita and Amy, he kept them totally sedated for most of the time. He did revived Zarita twice, though, but only briefly. Why? There's nothing in this new treatment that requires the patient to be totally sedated all of the time. The only justification I can find is that they were in a terrible emotional state at the time. Still, totally sedated?"

"I see your point," Amy concurred.

"Then, there is the matter of the voice in Zarita's head. According to her, she doesn't know the man nor has she met him. Yet, the man first told her to go ahead and kill every

Devil's Disciple she could find, claiming that religious group was behind the assassination of her wife. According to the news, the assassin belonged to that church. Still, one cannot blame an entire church for the insane actions of one member. Then, days later, this same man told her not to kill these church members. I swear this was a mild form of attempted brain washing. It left her in a complete confusion. On the one hand, she wanted nothing more than to kill all of them in retribution for killing Celenia and her unborn child and the others, including B'nath. Then, she has the impulse not to do that. It makes no sense at all. One would think telling her not to go on a killing rampage would be the only thing told to her. Still, telling her all this while she is sedated and unconscious can only be an attempt at brain washing."

"Insidious at best," Amy replied, growing more concerned.

"Precisely. And then there is this whole mysterious group she was with, while this Doctor Lambert was treating them. As far as I can tell, they don't exist. Yet, they must exist. Both claim they do exist, and their therapy backs them up," Whitney continued.

"Zarita did say she was asked to help them interrogate two men who originally stole the bio agent from the research facility, duplicated it, and then sold it to all of the terrorist groups, who proceeded to use it. After she did so and got that Intel, she was allowed to kill them. Again, why were those two not sent to the penal colony or given the bio agent like all of the criminals, who are serving a lifetime sentence were?" Doctor Whitney asked.

"There is enough here to warrant a complete investigation," Queen Amy replied formally. "I'll get all this documented and sent to Emperor Kino. I'm certain he'll conduct a formal investigation. Something is definitely not on the up and up here, Whitney. I smell a whole pile of rats." Both women chuckled.

So what are we going to do now, Zarita?" Ari asked. Zarita lay on their bed nursing Ruthy. "Where you go, so go I. At least, we can play pool again, if only we can find a pool table."

"I don't know, Ari. I'm a mother now. I've got little Ruthy here to look after. Going back to the Senate is not an option. It's way too risky. I never dreamed being in politics could be this dangerous to us all."

"Me either. I'll never go back to the Senate. It's pretty much a pointless job anyway. Plus, you and I, we're pretty much freaks now. I can't go back to my home world, not looking like this. Everywhere I'd go, people would stare and talk behind my back. Some would say that I deserved it because of my sexual preferences. Can we stay here on Tierra? At least here, we are not looked upon as freaks."

Zarita laughed. "No, we aren't. They are fashion nuts here, at least the nobles are. I'd like a nice home of my own, where we can live at peace and raise Ruthy right. I never thought that I'd be saying things like this though. Maybe you'll feel the same way when you have a baby of your own, Ari. I'd be lost without having you around me too. I've had enough adventure in my life now."

Ari chuckled, "You have a strange sense of what constitutes an adventure, dear. I call it torture. Can we possibly pool our money and buy a place somewhere around here?"

"Sure. Let's. Probably should stay pretty close to the castle here. It's too hard to walk far on our own, and Amy might need us from time to time. We best get you some language disks. Not many beyond the castle speak Imperium Standard," Zarita suggested. "We don't have to decide anything until spring. Snow will be coming soon. We'll have to winter over here, but it'll be fun. Amy likes to play cards."

Emperor Kino replied to Queen Amy's secure but lengthy document. "Yes, this does have the makings of something far deeper and more sinister. I'll look into it, but not on formal lines. I think it best to conduct this investigation on the quiet. There's an awful lot at stake at the moment. We anticipate more of the biological attacks. I'll keep you informed."

Emperor Kino knew times were tough. They had to be

for his men to be picked for both the Senate President and the Imperium President as well, replacing Zarita and Celenia. Because of what had happened to the two women, he sent along two private detachments of Security Guards and two teams of competent investigators. He knew some of the underlying causes, most of which stemmed from the nearly two decades long war with the Federation of Planets — a war which the Imperium may well have lost, had he not intervened. Now freed from the immense pressures and austerity measures imposed during the war, political elements, businessmen, organized crime, and even religious groups were attempting to expand their control, influence, profits, and dogmas. This was the officially held and widely proclaimed reality among the Senate, Presidential Office, and the various planetary government officials.

Yet, he and his investigators knew this was only an apparency. The truth of the matter was that someone or several someones were working both sides, secretly and behind "closed doors" actively to foment these uprisings. It was also quite true that, if unchecked soon, they could well bring down the entire Imperium as a ruling institution, throwing the thousands of worlds into smaller alliances and independent empires. Naturally, this would inevitably lead to many smaller internal wars between them, all vying for more resources, wealth, power, and influence, just what the situation had been two millennia ago, when the Ataro Empire first forged what would become this Imperium.

This time, matters had become vastly more complicated because of the rapid spread of the new biological-genetic terrorism. So far, each attack left the victims very nearly helpless vegetables, totally dependent upon others to survive. Some gave up and found ways to terminate their lives, but few even had the ability to do that much on their own. Through sheer effort, the late Senate President Celenia had managed to keep the Senate in operation, while President Zarita had done the same with the Executive Branch of the Imperium. At least at this point in time, July, the Senate had been mostly reconstituted with able bodied, newly elected Senators.

Still, more of these biological attacks occurred.

President Lockley ordered every Sector ID Minister to put every field agent to work, gathering Intel on any conceivable group that might foster hatred against the Imperium or other large institutions. Never in its long history had the IBI been as active as it now became in 1297.

Likewise, armed with the anomalies that Queen Amy reported surrounding the incidents involving the two largest bio terrorist attacks and Zarita and Celenia, he instructed his investigators on Proxima Prime to focus on those first. Quietly and efficiently, they went about their business of fact-finding. Quickly, they traced the "gap in the Security Guard's line" to the fictitious orders that their leader had been given. It was through this breach that the suicide bomber had made his close approach to the senators.

A follow up on this Doctor Lambert at the Imperium Hospital on Proxima Prime yielded more proof that something was amiss. No one there ever heard of this doctor, though their own computer records showed that he was currently on their staff. A computer analysis showed their records system had been hacked into, and the file on Doctor Lambert had been inserted only few months ago. Further, a search of all the doctors registered on Proxima Prime yielded no one by that name. True, there were three men with the first name of Lambert and two with that last name. None fit the description and none was remotely involved with genetics. The only conclusion possible was that he was using an alias, which only added more credence that something was very wrong about the whole affair.

Convinced that something was going on behind the scenes, the investigators dug into the past of the actual Devil's Disciple's suicide bomber. They learned the man was very unstable, if not outright insane. Further, he had somehow vanished some two weeks before he reappeared blowing up himself, the senators, and assistants. Again, this was highly suspicious. Someone had snatched him up and probably brainwashed him into becoming a mad bomber. By late August, the emperor's investigators were convinced there was a secret organization behind all this.

The next phase of their investigation focused on

obtaining proof of the existence of this secret organization. They did it by clever means. Pouring over all the massive amount of Intel being funneled into the IBI by all of the thousands of ID field agents, a pattern quickly developed. Certain organizations or groups suddenly had a significant number of their leaders and followers simply vanish. One day they were there planning and sometimes carrying out their plots, and the next day they were gone, never to be heard of again. Conclusion: since these organizations with the missing were either known criminal organizations or had espoused anti-Imperium feelings or even serious threats, the secret group was targeting groups and individuals that threatened the stability and existence of the Imperium itself.

In early October, the head of the IBI was called into President Lockley's office. Armed with the voluminous reports from the emperor's investigators, President Lockley acidly fired off datum after datum, all the while watching the growing reactions from the IBI head. The overwhelming evidence could not be ignored. The man had no choice but to reveal the existence of the Bops to President Lockley. "Honestly, I have no control over the Bops. They are here to do what must be done to protect us all," he justified.

"I expect their leader to report here to me in two hours. If not, I'll instruct the entire armed forces to hunt them down and exterminate them," President Lockley fumed. "If anything happens to me before then, I assure you copies of everything I've presented here today will be given to all press outlets in the entire Imperium. It's on an automatic timer. If I don't enter the proper codes at the proper times, it'll be automatically sent." He'd covered himself, via Emperor Kino's orders. It was the emperor himself, who would be sending the documents, if his man were somehow taken out by this Bops organization or anyone else for that matter.

Precisely two hours later, the Commander walked into President Lockley's office. His face showed no emotion whatsoever. "I am reporting as ordered, President Humber Lockley. I do hope you've taken sufficient security protocols or you'll be destroying our organization, which is dedicated to the preservation of the Imperium and its leaders," the

Commander said gruffly.

"Of course. And you are?" he replied just as gruffly.

"The Commander. That's all anyone knows. Why have you risked revealing our organization to the world by summoning me here?"

"You already know that, Commander. As I understand your charter, your organization is dedicated to preserving the lives and well-being of the innocent of the Imperium, no matter on what world they live. Is that not true?"

"It is."

"Then, tell me why you engineered the execution of Senate President Celenia, Senator B'nath, and several others? Tell me why you attempted to force President Zarita Valen to go on a murdering campaign against the Devil's Disciples? Tell me why you went to all that trouble to get the miracle genetic cure to Ruth and Alex Hammil on Ashford-5!"

"We developed the cure in house in our labs. We could not be seen as presenting this invaluable cure to the Imperium. That would have exposed us. We allowed those two geneticists to become the heroes and present this astounding breakthrough in genetics to the Imperium," the Commander replied.

"I can accept that. What about the more serious charges?" the President countered. He'd suspected that would be the man's answer to the genetics issue.

"President Zarita is no innocent. Indeed, she was identified by us as the Righteous Vigilante. She was the one who murdered the three Consortium members," he justified.

The President countered again, "After they had escaped and were about to vanish into hyperspace. Had that happened, they would likely still be at large and wreaking havoc upon us all," the President countered.

"Who can say?"

"I can say. You made a big mistake."

"We needed to get her out of the picture. The only way to do that without killing her was the route that we took," the Commander justified, still wholly emotionless.

"Yet, you then used her special skills to interrogate two men?"

"True, we used her to rapidly obtain key and particularly valuable Intel. Intel, I might add, that we used to retrieve the key distribution source of the bio agent cylinders. We prevented countless bio agent attacks as a result," the Commander continued to justify his position.

"Did you think to just ask her for her help?"

The Commander didn't reply.

After a long pause, President Lockley asked, "Well?"

"Look, that Intel allowed us to raid and seize fifty-six more bio agent cylinders from ten more renegade groups, preventing another ten massive biological terrorism attacks," he replied.

"Still biological attacks have occurred," he countered. He was referring to several more. In one instance, five hundred sixty wealthy men and women were genetically modified while they were gambling at the exotic Space Paradise, an elegant space station in orbit above Proxima Prime. Here, the very wealthiest went to gamble in the most luxurious settings within the Imperium. A similar biological attack occurred within the Sportsmen Club, wiping out three hundred six of the wealthiest men in the Imperium. That attack had been responsible for the current disintegration of the three largest corporations, namely Baal Industries, Urzak Fabrications, and Mal Dynamics. The former heads of these giants had been the late Consortium members, convicted of creating the fictitious Fuel Crisis that President Zarita had uncovered. The fallout was far reaching. Already a dozen other large conglomerates had splintered into smaller corporations. The giant monopolies were rapidly becoming history.

"Yes, we have limited resources and could not get to all of those to whom General Snaggard and his Soldiers of Fortune had sold the bio agent to in time to prevent all of them from carrying out their acts of terrorism. We did stop and prevent ten others, Mr. President," the Commander justified.

"And yet only yesterday the luxury spa, Water Home, on Zeta Minor was attacked, leaving three hundred sixteen women genetically altered," President Lockley countered.

"We now suspect other groups may have gotten their hands on this bio agent as well. We suspect General Snaggard

447

gave away some cylinders to his close friends and associates, rather than selling them. We have his accounting ledger that details every sale that was made. We did not anticipate he would have given this stuff away."

"So you made yet a second mistake."

"Yes."

"And a third. You coerced Zarita into killing the general and his accountant. If you had followed protocol and had them imprisoned for life, which now means they would have been subjected to this same genetic modifications and had their voices removed, they would still be alive for Zarita to further question and obtain just who else was given the bio agent."

"Agreed, Mr. President," the Commander replied, still showing no emotion whatsoever.

"So what am I to do with you? As soon as Zarita learns you were responsible for the assassination of her wife and the wife of Senator Ari, you are as good as dead, if she is indeed this Righteous Vigilante," President Lockley declared.

"I have arranged for my replacement. An encrypted communication line will be installed here in your office. You'll be briefed on all future top level missions before they are executed, as will my boss, the head of the IBI. However, I must warn you, if either of you ever leak this information, you'll be terminated. The Bops takes its mission very seriously. Brave, dedicated men and women spend their lives working behind the scenes to prevent such acts of terrorism as we can. You and the IBI head are potentially compromising leaks. So do be careful, if you value your life," the Commander replied sternly.

"Thank you. This is a wise move. No group can be allowed to wield ultimate power without any form of checks and balances on them," President Lockley declared.

"I take it that we are done here," the Commander stated emotionlessly.

"Except what I am to do about you and your failures," the president countered.

"I'm handling that. Goodbye," the Commander said. He bit down on a special tooth that released a powerful poison. His body jerked and was dead within seconds, before the president realized what had happened. He jumped up and summoned his staff, calling for a doctor and emergency personnel. Several came rushing into his office. One felt for the fallen man's pulse. He shook his head.

"Well, dispose of him please," President Lockley ordered, his face now quite white. Just then, a comm line buzzed. He returned to his desk and saw a new extension line was glowing. It had not been there yesterday! He picked up his communicator and pressed that button, "Yes?"

An emotionless female voice spoke. "President Humber, this is the new Commander. We are about to launch a Mission to take out those responsible for the biological attack on the Space Paradise. I'll call later with the outcome. That is all." She hung up.

Still rather stunned, President Lockley opened a secure channel to Emperor Kino. He had much to report to his emperor, whose theories had once again been validated. Emperor Kino advised, "Do what you have to do to stop these continuing biological attacks. They must cease, and all of these bio agent cylinders must be recovered. If we do not regain control of all the bio agent cylinders that are in the hands of terrorists, the very Imperium is doomed. Use any means necessary, but put an end to these attacks. That is your number one priority, President Lockley."

"It will be done, Emperor Kino," President Lockley replied.

Meanwhile, the new Commander of the Bops had to find a replacement for her post as the head of the Interrogation Department. Her first choice was Zarita, if she could somehow convince her to accept this post.
The End.

Other Books by Vic Broquard

Without Warning (fantasy)

The Trident Series: (fantasy)
  Volume 1 The Trident and the Book
  Volume 3 The Trident and the Scepter
  Volume3 The Trident and the Resurrection

The Adventures of Elizabeth Stanton Series: (science fiction)
  Volume 1 The Evolution of the Path
  Volume 2 The Great Messiah
  Volume 3 Of Kings and Queens and Troubadours
  Volume 4 Chaos in the Aftermath
  Volume 5 Power Plays
  Volume 6 Age of Exploration
  Volume 7 Abducted
  Volume 8 The Emperor and Empress
  Volume 9 A Job Worth Doing
  Volume 10 Degradation
  Volume 11 The Second Crusade
  Volume 12 When Worlds Collide
  Volume 13 Dark Ages

The Lindsey Barron Series: (fantasy)
  Volume 1 The Rod of the Apocalypse
  Volume 2 The Board of Governors
  Volume 3 The Crown of Moses
  Volume 4 Dominus for President
  Volume 5 The National Health Care Program
  Volume 6 States Justice
  Volume 7 Cross and Double-cross

Zoran Chronicles Series: (fantasy)
  Volume 1 A Dragon in Our Town
  Volume 2 Dragons, Power, Courts, and War

Planet of the Orange-red Sun Series: (science fiction)
    Volume 1 When Kingdoms Fall
    Volume 2 Dark Ages
    Volume 3 Age of the Towers
    Volume 4 Difficillis Exitus
    Volume 5 Age of the Lords
    Volume 6 The Renegade Tower
    Volume 7 Rebellions
    Volume 8 The Aliens Return
    Volume 9 Power Struggles
    Volume 10 Guilds, Genetics, and Gods
    Volume 11 Magi, Witches, Swords, and Superstitions
    Volume 12 The Voyage of the Eagle's Seed
    Volume 13 Justifications
    Volume 14 Responsibilities

The Return of the Wizards: Twelve Companions – The Making of Wizards (fantasy)